Scars *of* Sand *and* Soil

JEAN K. KRAVITZ

Helping talented writers publish exceptional books

Scars of Sand and Soil

Printed in the United States of America. For information, address
Acorn Publishing, LLC
3943 Irvine Blvd. Ste. 218, Irvine, CA 92602

www.acornpublishingllc.com

Interior design by Kat Ross
Cover design by Damonza

ISBN-13: 979-8-88528-114-0 (hardcover)
ISBN-13: 979-8-88528-113-3 (paperback)
Library of Congress Control Number: 2024919803

For my father, Joseph M. Kilcourse ~
Parting is such sweet sorrow

She knew she was dying, not by the clarion call of some guardian angel, but by the languor of her repose.

This must be, Simone figured, *what happens when you die a peaceful death.*

Outside, she heard the distant rumble of thunder. She had always loved thunder, how it cracked and rolled. Listening to it now, her thoughts wandered downstream over her life, folding around the pebbles of her memories. So many memories . . . *Remember*, she thought, *remember what? Who? Maman? Lucinda? Gabriel?*

Gabriel. She exhaled a shallow, fading breath. Everyone wants to lay claim to the beginning, but Gabriel had been at the center, and from the center both the beginning and the end had flowed.

OKEFENOKEE SWAMP 1864

God, it was hot. Too hot for February, but what difference did that make when you were already in Hell? Gabriel lay in his bunk, listening to the cockroaches as they scurried around him.

The guards banged on the walls of the chain gang's lean-tos.

"Get up, ya lazy son of a bitch," one of them growled at Gabriel.

He sat up, spitting after the guard. Another came by and cocked his rifle.

"C'mon," he snarled. "Swamp's waitin'."

Gabriel shuffled out, his leg irons rubbing. The guard watched him. "Mebbe one of them 'gators'll get ya t'day. I hears they likes to eat shit wrapped up in chains fer lunch."

Gabriel ignored him. He shuffled up to the other inmates, a motley crew of thieves and murderers, bonded together in misery.

The coffee was boiled water with wood chips. The

prisoners grumbled and a guard hissed, "Shet up! Ya shiftless pieces of horseshit's lucky to get this. Ya ain't gonna get no more . . . there's a war on. I jes' as soon send this to the front than waste it on y'all."

Gabriel filled his tin cup with the water. Seeing a tiger beetle on the ground, he picked it up and dropped it into his water. The heat of the liquid would soften its hard shell, and he'd snap off the head, ridding it of its pincers and poison sacs. Maybe later he'd find some giant water bugs or beetle larvae to munch on.

Gabriel didn't care that there was a war on, for he'd been in the camp for four years now. No matter what happened on the outside, it wasn't going to change his life here.

The prisoner next to Gabriel looked at the guards and muttered, "Wouldn't ya jes' like to take their old balls and feed 'em to the 'gators?"

"Yep."

"This heat's gonna poach our asses t'day, Cooper."

"Yep."

"'Course, goddamn skeeters might get us first."

Gabriel looked at his prison mate. A short pasty fellow, he must have once carried some bulk to his frame. Now he was just thin and scarred. "How long ya got, Mitchell?"

"Shit, Cooper, y'all as green as the day ya came. I got forever, man, and so do you."

Gabriel drained his cup and snapped off the beetle's head. He chewed on his bug with satisfaction.

Mitchell continued, "But I'm gonna get outta here; break fer freedom. You'll see."

Gabriel knew that Mitchell would go nowhere.

A bullwhip cracked and the day began.

Slash and dig. Gabriel worked silently amidst the hum of mosquitoes. He concentrated his rage on one man—the one responsible for his bondage. This was how he would get through another day.

He ignored the sweat dripping down his pale, semi-sallow skin. Grip and swing, grip and swing, a weakened cadence because of his shackles. *Bide yer time . . . 'cause it's a'comin' . . .*

Screams broke into his thoughts. An inmate had slipped into a bog, surprising an alligator. Gabriel turned in the direction of the man's cries. Good God, was that the crunch of bones he just heard? The guards made no move to help the prisoner. Instead, they cracked their whips. Everyone went back to work.

The convict's cries for help faded as Gabriel swung his machete harder. This was how swampland justice ruled.

He moved on, trying not to think about the poor dying bastard near him. Or was he a lucky bastard? Well, it didn't matter because it was no use worrying about others. Gabriel need only be concerned with his own plans.

EVENING OFFERS LITTLE SOLACE TO A TRAPPED MAN, whatever his prison may be. At least the darkness afforded some privacy, and there was no labor. Yet in that fleeting second between rest and sleep, despair lurked, and that was worse than any daytime struggle.

Gabriel ate his dinner of sodden swamp greens and

stale bread. He was chronically hungry, craving meat the most. At daybreak, he would listen to the birds and his mouth would water. What he wouldn't give to snag a turkey vulture, to roast it, dripping in its own juice . . .

"Son of a fucking bitch!" Gabriel jerked his head up. It was Mitchell. He had found a cooked cockroach in his greens.

"They put it here on purpose! Goddamn, *goddamn*!"

Two guards sauntered up as he threw his supper on the ground.

"Quit yer whinin' Mitchell," one said.

"Better watch where yer throwin' that food," warned the other, "or you'll be eatin' it off the ground."

Mitchell got up and staggered toward the guards, who shoved him back. He fell and one of the guards put his foot on his neck. He leaned in with his weight.

"I'm jes' sick an' tired of all yer cryin, Mitchell . . ."

The guard leaned in harder. Mitchell's face turned red and his eyes began to pop. Then, for the second time in one day, Gabriel heard the crunch of bone.

Mitchell lay prostrate while the guard gave him a final kick in the head. Looking around at everyone, he said, "Try to help him an' ya get the same."

"Jesus Christ," someone whispered, "I think they done kilt him."

The guards had moved out of earshot. Gabriel called Mitchell's name but heard no response.

"I'm tellin' ya, I think he's dead," another prisoner said, "I heard them bones a'snappin' in his neck."

Gabriel had heard enough. Exhausted, he rose and stumbled to his bunk. He flopped down and fell into an image-tainted sleep.

In his dreams, he thrust his head into the alligator's mouth. Just as the jaws snapped, he'd pull his head out. Such a treacherous game, and his laugh was a sleepy echo from faraway. Then in his dream's eye, he saw the guards stick their heads in the alligator's mouth, but they were not as quick. He saw their blood squirt, making him smile and breathe more easily.

COLONEL ROBERT TREMONT RUBBED HIS TIRED EYES. HE re-read the letter from his brother-in-law, Major Jerome Devereaux.

"This is not as far-fetched as it may seem as we prepare to meet the Federal forces. The Federals want Florida because she supplies so much for our troops — beef, salt, fruit, leather. We both know that if Florida is taken, we have no chance for survival. Therefore, we must build our strength with numbers, no matter the source. At least it affords us the opportunity to save our best soldiers for the final hour. These new ones can take the first fire, expending the enemy's energy. Then let our seasoned men surprise these naïve Yankees. They have never fought in raw swampland before.

I beseech of you, Robert, conscript the prison inmates!"

Did he want a company of murderers and thieves amongst his own men? Men who trusted him to write letters home for them. Men whose eyes he had closed for eternity.

Ironically, Tremont knew just where to look for a batch of criminals. His scouts had reported on a chain gang working the southeast edge of the Okefenokee Swamp. He recalled the conversation:

"They're an ugly bunch, sir."

"We're a pretty ugly bunch ourselves."

"No, sir, these men are different. Looks like they'd been burnt, cut. Almost like the Devil himself had made designs on their backs. But you shoulda seen them with those machetes. They were all shackled up and they swung those knives like they'd been doin' it all their lives."

I must be crazy to even consider this . . .

"All right, Jerome," he said out loud, "I'll conscript them. God help us all."

~

GABRIEL WAS AWAKE BEFORE DAWN. HEARING THE guards, he got up, his leg irons dragging. He looked outside to see two inmates carrying Mitchell's body away to the swamp, to disappear as if he had never lived.

Later, as they gathered in the early morning mist, Gabriel heard a commotion. He turned to see a trio of military men ride in. A White Confederate commander rode in first, the head guard trotting nervously in front of him.

As the prisoners were rounded up and brought before the commander, Gabriel

wondered what task was about to be pressed upon them.

Gabriel watched as Tremont's sharp eyes appraised them. Finally, he spoke, "I am Colonel Robert Alfred Tremont. On behalf of the Confederate States of America, I am here on a special request. The Confederacy is fighting for her life. She needs every man, no matter who he may be, to fight for her. There are no promises here, of who will live and who will die.

"But if you live, you will have paid your debt to society. And if you die, well, then you have paid your debt as well. You can choose to follow me to fight or you can continue your miserable existence here. We do not want cowards accompanying us to the front, only those of you who are still men at heart who are not afraid to fight for something greater than yourselves. All volunteers please step up."

Gabriel shoved men aside as he sprang forward. He stood before Tremont and stared at him, his light eyes blazing. With his dirt-streaked torso and ratty blond hair, he was the epitome of unsavory desperation.

Tremont's lip curled, and he chuckled grimly. "May your fervor stand you well, Soldier, when the blood that sprays your face is your own."

Gabriel felt a shiver of recognition as he watched Tremont turn to the head guard. "Release these volunteers from their shackles and leg irons. They are no longer prisoners." He paused. "And we'll take those shackles and leg irons, too."

"Oh, no, sir, this here ain't yer property—"

To Gabriel's delight, Tremont aimed his pistol at the guard. "These are now the property of the Department of South Carolina, Georgia, and Florida. Do you wish to challenge me?"

The guard took a step back, "No, sir."

"Then gather up these chains as my new soldiers are released. We will take it all with us."

The guard unshackled Gabriel first. Spitting inches

from Gabriel's bare feet, he growled, "You ain't gonna make it."

"Wanna bet?" Gabriel spit back and stepped away, rubbing his scabbed, blistered wrists.

Once every volunteer was unchained, the colonel surveyed them. "Fall in," he ordered.

The ex-convicts, all forty-four of them, milled about, confused. Tremont's men dismounted their horses and shoved them into rows. "When the colonel says to fall in, that means to get in formation to march!"

Once this was accomplished, Colonel Tremont wheeled his horse around, "Right Face! Forward! March!"

The column began to move. Gabriel did not look back, but as he was leaving a chatter of tweets and twitters rose above him. Gabriel peered up into the trees. It was as if the birds knew his good fortune and were now blessing him, offering him God-speed to a new life.

NEAR OLUSTEE, FLORIDA 1864

After about a mile, a prisoner spoke up. "Hey! When do we get there?"

One of the mounted soldiers laughed. "What's the hurry? Figger yer out on holiday?"

"Naw, I knowed it ain't no holiday."

"Damn right! Keep movin'!"

They passed farms and plantations, swampland and forest. People stared; young children waved. For Gabriel, it was like water to a dying man. No one, not even a child, had looked up to him in a long, long time.

Soon the first disciplinary action was taken when a prisoner tried to make a dash for freedom. A shot rang out. Gabriel turned to see the prisoner fall.

Everyone halted, and the colonel turned his horse around.

"Leave him where he is," he said to the soldier with the smoking rifle. He turned to the group. "That was a waste of good ammunition, and I'd hate to see it happen again. But if any of you choose to run like a dog, you will be shot like one and left to rot where you drop."

Then he turned back around and they continued southeast, the afternoon sun at their backs.

PUS, MAGGOTS, AND MILDEW. GABRIEL PUT HIS HAND over his nose as the men around him complained. The veteran soldiers smiled.

First the smell, then the sounds. They approached a field hospital, most likely treating members of the Cow Cavalry, militiamen who protected inland Florida from Union foraging parties who raided ranches and captured cattle.

They passed a pile of black and green limbs. A doctor, wearing a blood-soaked butcher's apron, came outside the surgical tent and stretched, the saw still in his hand. One of the wounded men, lying on a pallet outside, waved at the passing group. "See y'all here tomorrow, boys!"

The rear-flanking soldiers watched Gabriel flash a smile and wave back. They looked at one another. "That son of a bitch is crazy," one commented.

Gabriel heard him, but he didn't care. The image of Mitchell, squashed and defenseless, still haunted him. He vowed that he, Gabriel Sutherland Cooper, would never let himself die under another man's boot.

IN THE DISTANCE ROSE THE SMOKE OF MANY FIRES. As they hobbled into their new camp, all eyes turned in their direction.

"Jesus Christ," Gabriel heard someone say.

The colonel ordered two soldiers forward. "Help get these men situated; they need food. And for God's sake," he looked at Gabriel, noting his keloid-scarred back, "try and get some shirts for the worst of them."

The larger of the two, a burly man with a fair, ruddy complexion, came over to Gabriel, shaking his head in disgust. "What a goddamned day it is when we gotta get us murderers and thieves to help us fight."

"You may find yerself sorry you said that."

The soldier paused, snarling at Gabriel, but was interrupted by the colonel, "Coleman! I gave you an order!"

Coleman stepped off to follow Colonel Tremont's orders.

Gabriel laughed softly and called after him, "Don't play with fire 'cause it maybe come straight from Hell."

Coleman turned and looked at Gabriel more closely, seeing for the first time his rutted scars and discolored phosphate burns. He turned to the whole group.

"All of you follow me," he said in a less aggressive tone.

They followed Coleman to an open space. The other soldier began to pass out blankets. "Y'all's only get one; ain't barely enough fer us real soldiers as it is."

Gabriel silently took the blanket. *I'll show you, shit-cracker, who's the real soldier here.*

Coleman came up behind him and Gabriel whirled around, his fists up. Coleman snorted, handing him a shirt. "Here, prison boy, put this on. Yer a damned mess if I ever saw one."

Gabriel took the rough-hewn garment and pulled it over his head.

Coleman left, complaining about finding food for a bunch of good-for-nothing convicts. Gabriel sat down, then lay back on the sweet grass, looking at the sky above him. It reminded him of days long gone, when he was a boy and would catch a lazy afternoon for himself. Those were the good days all right; too bad he'd been too young to appreciate them. Well, a man could appreciate the memory though, couldn't he? Feeling himself relax, Gabriel drifted off to sleep. This time, there were no nightmares to plague him.

A PALE, GRAY-EYED SOLDIER NUDGED HIM AWAKE. "GET up. The colonel wants to talk to y'all."

Gabriel's stomach growled as he sat up. He saw a grasshopper perched on a nearby blade of grass, and he grabbed it, biting into its head and thorax.

The other soldier stared as he reached out to help Gabriel to his feet. Gabriel swatted his hand away.

"It's mine," he snapped in a menacing tone.

"I don't want yer fuckin' bug! Jesus Christ, we all's shoulda gotten us some low-down n------ers for all the good you prison boys are gonna do us." He walked back to Private Coleman's campsite.

"Crazy bastard's eatin' bugs," Gabriel heard him say. Then he picked up his harmonica, filling the air with the doleful melody of *Old Folks at Home.*

Gabriel got to his feet as Coleman yelled at him, "For Chrissake, do ya need a goddamned mammy? The colonel's tent's over on the knoll." Coleman jerked his thumb in a northeast direction.

"Thanks."

"Only 'cause the colonel ordered me to look out for ya."

"I won't be needin' your help fer long."

Coleman opened his mouth to reply, but the gray-eyed soldier stopped him, tapping his temple. "He ain't right." *Old Folks at Home* filled the air once again.

Colonel Tremont was in a meeting, but dismissed his men when the sentry announced Gabriel's arrival.

Gabriel entered the tent. Lit by two kerosene lamps, it was hardly luxurious, with some crates that served as chairs and a cot strewn with papers.

Then something magnificent caught Gabriel's eye—a steel sword with a hilt of sterling silver and mother-of-pearl inlay. Gabriel went over to it. "Is this yer weapon?"

"No, it isn't."

"Then why's it here?"

"It's a family heirloom."

"Ya brought a keepsake from home?"

"My mother wanted me to have it for good luck."

"Well, ain't that a woman's fool notion."

"Yes, but I didn't bring you here to discuss my mother's fool notions. Sit, soldier." He handed Gabriel a plate of salt pork and hard tack. "I know you missed supper."

Gabriel devoured the food, acting more like a wild beast than a soldier in the company of his commanding officer.

"What's your name?" Tremont asked as Gabriel licked his fingers.

"Who wants to know?"

"I do!" snapped Tremont. "And while we're at it, let's get one thing straight. You always answer when I speak to you and you finish it with 'sir.'"

Gabriel was silent.

"Otherwise, I'll send you back to where you came from."

"My name is Gabriel Sutherland Cooper . . . sir."

"You seem lighthearted about going to war."

"Well, I at least got me a chance fer freedom. More'n I can say 'bout where I was afore."

"How long were you there?"

"Four years, seven months, and fourteen days."

"And how much more before you finished your sentence?"

It took Gabriel a while to count this on his fingers. "Sixteen years, four months, and twenty-eight days."

"What was your crime?"

Gabriel looked almost sheepish. "They says I was a thief. Warn't true. Then they said I tried to free a slave. Warn't true. But then they accused me of attempted murder. That was true."

Tremont paled at the casual confession, but his voice remained calm. "Well, Mr. Cooper, then perhaps you'll enjoy this job. I need you to sit guard over the rest of the company you came in with today."

Gabriel frowned. "I ain't no guard dog, sir."

"Did I say you were?"

"Well, no, sir, not right out, ya didn't—"

"Of course, I didn't! Now you listen to me. I have a

hunch that you were good with a machete and that you're also good with a rifle-musket. I also have the feeling that you are unafraid to use either one. Am I correct?"

"Yes, sir!"

"Well, I need you to sit guard tonight over those men you came in with. Some are going to try to sneak off in the night, and I can't afford that. Can you stop them?"

A smile spread over Gabriel's face. "Yes, sir."

Tremont scowled, picking up on Gabriel's enthusiasm. "Don't harm them unless absolutely necessary."

"Yes, sir."

He stared at Gabriel as if he were made of blast powder.

"You go on duty effective immediately, and you go off duty at dawn. I'll give you sleep time then. Tomorrow we are going to try and teach your company some drill and see how they can shoot. Anything you miss, I'll have Private Coleman teach you. You can guard with one of the machetes I took from the chain gang."

Tremont stood up. He called for the sentry to fetch one of the machetes. When he returned, Tremont handed it to Gabriel. "Keep it close, Cooper."

"It'll be a pleasure, sir."

"Yes, that's what I'm afraid of."

ON THE WAY BACK TO HIS CAMPSITE, GABRIEL PICKED UP a smooth, medium-sized stone. He returned to find Coleman waiting for him.

"'Bout time, prison boy; some of us got real work tomorrow and want some shut-eye."

Smiling, Gabriel walked up to him. Coleman held his ground, but Gabriel noticed him nervously shifting his feet. He flashed the machete and tapped its point to Coleman's chest. Staring into the other man's eyes, he whispered, "I wouldn't keep callin' me that if'n I was you, 'cause yer tongue might find itself hangin' off this here blade."

Beads of sweat laced Coleman's upper lip. "Y'all's crazy."

"Y'all just keep thinkin' that and," Gabriel's lips curled back as he spit the words, "keep the hell away from me."

Coleman retreated, not daring to turn his back as he did so.

"G'night!" Gabriel called softly. "Sleep tight!" He turned back and looked at his charge of ex-convicts who had watched the exchange.

Gabriel sat down and took out the stone he had found. He began to rub the stone against the flat edge of the blade. As he was doing so, he said soothingly, "Now y'all's get to sleep. An' no yeller-bellied runnin' off in the night, hear me? 'Cause if you do, I'll test how sharp I'm a makin' this knife by usin' it on *you*."

One by one, the men fell asleep. Gabriel sat there, whistling tunelessly, sharpening his machete late into the night.

Reveille sounded at dawn. Coleman came by and told him from a safe distance that he was off-duty. Gabriel took his blanket to a clump of pine trees and lay down.

Back at his tent, Colonel Tremont sipped a cup of ground acorns in hot water, cursing the Federal blockades for the absence of coffee. He watched Coleman approach. He saluted and Tremont indicated the overturned crate for Coleman to sit on.

"What brings you here, Private?" he asked, surveying the distance. He watched as General Beauregard's latest arrival of troops brought in their provisions.

"Well, sir, it's about that convict you asked me to watch."

"Soldier, Coleman, he's a soldier now."

"Yes, sir. And I been watchin' him, but, Colonel, somethin' ain't right with him. He's a little . . . touched in the head, if ya know what I mean."

Tremont smiled grimly. *So, I'm not the only one who has noticed.* "I think he could be brilliant in battle."

"Yes, sir, maybe so. But we all's gotta live with him until then."

"Did he do something, Private?"

"No, sir. But he talks."

"A lot of men talk, Private."

"No, sir, I mean, he talks crazy talk. And I get the feelin' that he's gonna do what he talks about."

Goddamn it. Tremont's voice was soft, but firm, "Don't go starting trouble where there is none. We're going into battle very soon. Concentrate on that."

"Yes, sir."

"You should get back to your company, Private. Go get some food before the day starts."

"Yes, sir," Coleman saluted Tremont. As he turned to go, Tremont added, "And you're relieved of your duties with the new soldier, Coleman. I'll take care of matters from now on."

Coleman's whole posture sagged with relief. "Thank you, sir." He drew himself up and again saluted. Then he turned about face and headed down the knoll in a half-skip, half-run.

Tremont sat motionless a few minutes more. He drained his sad cup of coffee and stood up. He thought of Gabriel. *He's blast powder, all right. Shit. I just need him to go off in the right place at the right time.*

THE NOISE AND MIDDAY SUN WOKE GABRIEL. HE SAT UP, watching horses pull caissons of ammunition and cannons attached to limbers. He called out to a soldier nearby, "What y'all doin'?"

The soldier, a lanky teenager with a scraggly beard and bandaged arm, turned around. "Movin' closer in to Olustee; Yankee troops are comin' in near Lake City. We're gonna stop 'em!"

"Where's the group of ex-cons that come in yesterday?"

The boy jerked his head to the west. "They all's back yonder. Colonel's lookin' 'em over."

Gabriel stood up, grabbing his machete and blanket. "Much appreciate yer information."

They were easy to find as they were the only unit not

participating in drills or digging bulwarks in the pine-barrens. Gabriel fell into formation, laying his blanket and his machete at his feet.

Colonel Tremont approached. "Good morning, soldier; I trust you slept well?"

"Yes, sir."

"A job well done, soldier. Everyone is here today."

"Thank you, sir."

Tremont moved to the front of the group. "How many of you can shoot? Raise your hand."

All hands went up. The colonel sighed. "Alright, how many of you can shoot straight?" Again, all hands were raised.

"Jesus Christ," muttered Tremont as his aides smirked. "Who has had to shoot something to save his life?"

Fewer hands went up this time. Colonel Tremont pointed to the man nearest him. "You, what did you do?"

"I shot me a 'gator, chargin' me. Right 'tween the eyes."

Tremont rolled his eyes. "Do you think I am asking you this for pleasure? I need to know if you can shoot well enough to save your own skin tomorrow. So once again you fool, what did you do?"

"Shot into the air and scared the 'gator away." Laughter followed his reply.

Colonel Tremont pointed to the next man who had raised his hand. "You, tell me what you did . . ."

And on it went, until Tremont's gaze fell upon Gabriel. "You, Cooper, how's your aim?"

"Good enough fer huntin'."

"Hunting what?"

"Possum, 'gators, snakes, men if I had to."

"Did you ever shoot a man?"

"Yes, sir."

"How?"

"The bastard tried to run off with one o' our pigs. Got him first in the leg an' finished him off in the head." The casualness of his statement made several men turn and stare. To break the tension, Tremont cleared his throat and addressed the entire unit.

"All of you will receive a rifle-musket and a cartridge-box with some extra bullets."

As the guns were passed out, Tremont cautioned, "We don't have a lot of ammunition, boys, so don't waste it. Aim at them as they come at you. Shoot them before they shoot you. Lay low, take aim, and fire. And if one of your comrades falls, well," he paused, "take his ammunition and keep fighting.

"You are now Company S of the 14th Florida. Sergeant McDougall is now in charge of you." Tremont turned to a weathered Irishman with a lazy eye whose Celtic skin looked as if it were going to blister under the punishing sun.

"Sergeant, they are all yours." Then he muttered under his breath, "And watch the one we talked about."

"Yes, sir," said the sergeant, glancing over at Gabriel.

Tremont left then, to oversee the artillery transport and the trees being cleared near the Olustee Railroad Station. This bunch of unredeemed ex-convicts was now the problem of someone else. Even the one named Gabriel Sutherland Cooper.

~

THE CONFISCATED PRISON CHAINS AND LEG IRONS WERE going to be shoved into the cannons and blasted at the enemy. Anything was fair weaponry at this point in the war; if it could be shoved down a cannon's bore it was used, including glass, rocks, and railroad irons.

All the infantrymen were now hunkered down in the woods. Evening campfires were extinguished early.

The youngest of the ex-cons in Company S spoke softly into the darkness. "Ain't anyone scared?"

"What y'all gettin so yeller fer, McRae?" another ex-convict hissed. "If ya think yer all gonna really fight, y'all's stupider than ya look. First goddamn chance I get I'm a'runnin'. Ain't no matter what that stupid-assed, pea-brained colonel said afore. They cain't watch us all out there. So, keep it to yerself, McRae. It don't matter if ya's sceered shitless or ya ain't."

Gabriel's derision cut the darkness. "Jesus Christ, Jasper. Y'all's sounds more scairt than he is. Right outta yer sorry britches."

"I oughtta break yer shit-livin' neck fer that, Cooper."

"We'll see tomorrow whose shit-livin' neck gets broke. An' it won't be mine."

"Save your breath for some prayers," came Sergeant McDougall's stern voice. "If you need to talk, talk to God. He's the only One who's really gonna listen to ya lads. Or care about what ya have to say, He Is."

Gabriel could hear McRae stir next to him. "Thanks for stickin' up fer me, Cooper," McRae whispered.

"Twarn't nothin'."

"Cooper? Do ya really think yer gonna make it tomorrow?"

"Yep."

"Think I'll make it, too?"

"That's up to you, kid."

"Think the Sergeant's right? Think God will care if I ask Him?"

"God stopped carin' 'bout us a long time ago, McRae. No point in tryin' to change His mind now."

"I don't wanna die tomorrow."

"Then don't."

"Easy fer you to say. Y'all ain't afraid o' nothin'."

Gabriel wondered if that could be true because he certainly was not nervous. "Shet up, McRae. Get some sleep. It's better for you than all this blabbin'."

McRae did not reply and Gabriel began to relax. Then he heard in the softest of whispers, "Our Father, Who Art in Heaven . . ."

❧ 3 ❧

OLUSTEE, FLORIDA 1864

Gabriel awoke to the chatter of kingfishers and other birds, feeling a misty breeze as it passed through the woods. Wasn't there supposed to be a battle? Instead of bullets he saw men sitting up, playing cards, or eating their hardtack.

McRae noticed that Gabriel was awake. "Y'all kin sure sleep through a lotta noise."

"What noise?"

"All these Rebs actin' like it's a big party out here."

Gabriel stood up and went to find a place to relieve himself. When he returned, McRae was still sitting there. "Ain't ya never gonna move?"

"Keep thinkin' if I move, they'll start shootin', and I'll be kilt."

"Are ya just gonna sit here when the shootin' does start?"

McRae turned apprehensive eyes upon him. Gabriel changed the subject. "Hey, I don't even know yer first name."

"Eli."

"An' where's ya from?"

"Same place as you."

"Naw, that ain't what I'm talkin' about."

"Donaldsonville. Not too far from N'Awlins."

"Y'all's a long way from home."

"Yeah, don't I know it." Eli began to doodle in the dirt with a twig. "How long was y'all in prison, Cooper?"

"'Bout four years. You?"

"Almost two years. What was ya in fer?"

"Attempted murder an' other things. You?"

"Horse thievin'." Eli started a game of tic-tac-toe in the dirt. "Did your mama, you know? Did your mama ever write to ya when y'all's was in there?"

"No."

"How come?"

"She cain't write. And she ain't alive."

"Oh." Eli threw the twig aside. "My mama cain't write neither, but my brother can. I thought mebbe she'd send a letter to me through him."

"Never did, huh?"

"Naw."

"Could ya have read it if she did send one?"

Eli nodded. "I can read simple-like. Enough ta get through a letter. I've read some o' the Bible."

Gabriel spit. "Bet that was a mighty comfort to y'all these past couple o' years."

"Ain't y'all never read the Bible?"

"Nope, cain't read."

Their conversation was cut short by Sergeant McDougall. "Ya lads hungry?"

Eli nodded. "A little."

"Then ya better get yourselves something to eat. Dog Robber's got somethin' cookin', though God knows what 'tis." He looked at Gabriel and Eli. "Ya don't want to see the elephant on an empty stomach, laddies."

Gabriel and Eli stood up.

"*Yessir*," said Eli, although Gabriel remained silent.

It was not lost on McDougall. "God help ya, man," he said as he walked away, shaking his head.

THE GUNFIRE BEGAN IN THE EARLY AFTERNOON, AND Gabriel was catapulted into his first battle.

Sargeant McDougall was yelling, "Into position! They're comin' at us, boy-os!"

Minié Bullets and canisters flew at the men. Gabriel cursed as he hurried to load his rifle-musket in what was a slow, cumbersome process.

"Don't fire 'til ya see 'em! Keep your finger off the trigger until you're ready for the kill shot!"

Gabriel itched to pull the trigger. He felt like a sitting duck and well, that wasn't what he had come this far for. He crawled over the bulwarks while McDougall cursed and screamed for him to stay in position. He could see men in blue uniforms quickly advancing and slithered on his belly to shelter behind the nearest tree. He didn't realize that he had been followed until he heard Eli's voice.

"Cooper! Where we goin'?"

Gabriel looked back at Eli. "What the hell ya doin', McRae?"

"I'm followin' you!"

"Ah, shit, go back!"

"Naw, I'm followin' you!"

"Shit," Gabriel turned away to concentrate on what was in front of him.

Maybe it was the spillage of other men's blood, or maybe it was the screams, but something finally cleared his mind and made him take aim. He crept forward, whistling, "Blue, blue, blue, ya better shoo, shoo, shoo, 'cause I'm a comin' for you!"

He was close now to the incoming Union infantry. He inched forward, careful to keep low. A blue uniform suddenly appeared, and Gabriel rose up on his knees and fired. The Union soldier, a tall Black man, buckled before him. Blood spattered Gabriel's face and shirt.

"Shoo, shoo, shoo! Off to Hell with you!" He was surprised to hear himself laughing.

Jesus Christ Almighty, they were charging! He scrambled into the undergrowth and loaded up his musket-rifle. He fired again and another one fell. Then Gabriel saw a dark movement out of the corner of his eye. He rolled away just in time to miss the soldier's bayonet. Hopping to his feet, he swung the butt of his rifle at the man's head. The soldier fell to the ground, dazed. Gabriel grabbed the man's bayonet and thrust it into the fallen soldier's chest.

He found a Colt .44 pistol on the dead man along with a cartridge-box full of bullets. Now he could fight like a real soldier and not an ex-con with an old nag of a weapon.

As the battle intensified, Gabriel slithered into the marshy wetness that led to the nearby shores of Ocean Pond.

A Union commander was trying to rally his troops. Gabriel took careful aim with his new pistol. The bullet tore half the commander's face off. He fell off his horse, flinging his repeating carbine in a wide arc that landed in the grasses nearby.

Gabriel had never seen a gun like that before. He was gonna take it back with him and learn how it worked. In the meantime, his Colt .44 would suit him just fine.

It was just all so easy! Gabriel picked off soldier after soldier as they ran by. This little hand-held beauty shot off several rounds before he had to reload, which was simply putting new bullets into the chambers. Two men had fallen dead on top of each other right in front of him. He now had his own little bulwark to continue his pick and shoot, pick and shoot.

Gabriel began to run low on bullets. He'd have to go back to the musket-rifle. Grabbing a blood and gristle-spattered knapsack off the bodies in front of him, he shoved ammunition and his pistol into it. Dragging along the repeating carbine and musket-rifle, he crawled toward a felled tree. He crawled into a hollowed-out portion of the trunk and stayed there.

Now in his own little sniper's nest, Gabriel loaded, aimed, and shot the poor devils in the back. He became methodical, mesmerized by the steady kickback of the rifle. For the first time in years, he felt as if he was where he was meant to be.

The shooting continued until dark when Brigadier General Seymour's troops began to retreat. Gabriel stayed quiet, watching the Union soldiers fall back in a receding blue tide.

Only when the gun smoke hung undisturbed by

whizzing bullets did Gabriel emerge from his hiding place. His eyes stinging and his throat scratchy, he retraced his steps back toward camp. As he came to a clearing littered with dead and dying men, Gabriel stood up and sloshed through mud mixed with blood. He shook off one or two desperate hands that grabbed his pant leg. He wanted to get back and show the colonel and that doomsday bastard McDougall that not only had he survived, but he had *thrived*. And he had new weapons to show off, too.

Everywhere, men lay where they had fallen. Some were contorted and grotesque; others cried out, begging for water. Gabriel picked his way around them all. He picked his way around them, that is, until he came upon Eli McRae.

The teenager lay on a bed of ferns, his entrails spilling from his open abdomen. His breath came in shallow gasps as he stared wide-eyed at the tree branches overhead. Gabriel knelt beside him.

"Jesus, Eli . . ."

Blood trickled from McRae's nose and mouth. He fixed his glassy eyes on Gabriel. "I prayed I wouldn't die," he gasped.

"Naw, an' ya ain't gonna." Gabriel reassured him, "'cause I'm gonna get y'all to the hospital."

"Naw, not that place we saw, with that stink?" McRae's nose spurted more blood. Gabriel wiped it with the edge of his shirt.

Gabriel moved to lift him, but when he slid his hand under his shoulders, McRae vomited up blood and esophageal tissue. Gabriel recoiled, drawing his hand away.

McRae lay there, ashen. He focused a fading stare on Gabriel. "Will ya . . . do somethin' fer me?"

Gabriel nodded, unable to speak.

"Will ya . . . find my parents? Tell 'em . . . I died a soldier?"

"Yep, sure I will."

McRae smiled a beautiful, innocent smile that reflected the sweet boy that still lived within him. "That'll make 'em proud."

He spewed out more blood and exhaled his final breath.

Aw, Eli . . . Gabriel sat and stared at the dead youth, a seesaw of pain gnawing at his insides. Losing this new friend brought back all that old, familiar grief that he struggled to repress. Finally, he closed the young man's eyes.

"They'll be right proud, Eli."

Gabriel stood up. He had to move on. And remember that God never answered prayers, no matter how fervently they were said.

Soon he came upon his own company. Exhausted and bleeding soldiers worked by the light of lanterns and campfires, lifting wounded men onto makeshift stretchers and then horse-drawn ambulances. The dead would be placed into graves being dug by yet another team of soldiers.

Gabriel approached one of these men as he dragged the body of a middle-aged man toward a grave.

"Where's the colonel?" he asked.

"Dunno. Gimme a hand here, will ya? This poor bastard's head's gonna come off if someone don't hold it while I move 'im."

Gabriel took hold of the man's head and held it in place as the other man inched the body closer to the deep hole. He looked at Gabriel and grinned as he wiped the blood trickling down his tanned face, his rotting front teeth protruding slightly. "If'n I hadn'ta slipped in the fuckin' mud, the bastard woulda gotten me clean through. Then you'da been rollin' my sorry ass into this here ground."

Gabriel grinned back. "Glad the goddamned mud's good fer somethin'."

The other man held out his hand. "Name's Johnnie."

Gabriel gripped Johnnie's hand. "Much obliged. Name's Cooper, Gabriel Cooper."

"Well, Gabe, let's get this poor bastard into this here grave. Mebbe he can rest in peace then."

They worked together to get the body over the lip of the hole. But as it fell, the remaining intact tendons of the neck tore and the head and body separated.

"Well, shit," Johnnie muttered.

A couple of other men with shovels came up behind them and began to throw dirt into the grave. Johnny moved on to another body and motioned for Gabriel to follow him.

Gabriel stopped and watched as the ambulances jolted toward that very same field hospital that they had passed the other day. Johnnie's voice broke into his thoughts.

"Hey, Gabe, are y'all's gonna help me or not?"

Gabriel turned and grabbed another dead man's legs as Johnnie lifted him under the armpits.

"Is them doctorin' carts comin' back?" Gabriel asked Johnnie as they lifted the shrapnel-torn corpse.

" 'Course they're acomin' back. Sometimes it takes days to find 'em all and clear 'em outta here. 'Course by then most o' the boys left're dead already." Johnnie sighed. "Manassas and Antietam—remember that?"

"Naw, twarn't there."

"So many boys tore up, jest couldn't get to 'em all. It was a damn shame." Johnnie wiped more trickling blood off his cheek.

"Mebbe ya should get to a doctor yerself."

"I'll doctor it myself when we're done here. It bleeds a lot, but it's jest a flesh wound. Now let's keep movin' 'cause I don't wanna come back tomorrow and finish this. These bodies'll be stinkin' worse than an unwashed whore come sun-up. An' besides, we're makin' a good team out here, you an' me."

IT WASN'T LONG BEFORE COLONEL TREMONT SPOTTED Gabriel. He was riding his horse up and down the lines, surveying the damage. They had chased the enemy down the road back to Jacksonville. Still, it was hard for Tremont to watch the loading of the ambulances, to view the dead. Every corpse reminded him of . . . *stop!* He sighed, thinking victory was never sweet.

He was surprised to see Gabriel chatting with Johnnie Primrose. He looked more closely, realizing that Cooper looked like he was enjoying himself! Could it be that he had found a friend? *Hmm, maybe he does possess a heart. Who would've thought it possible?*

As if he felt eyes upon him, Gabriel turned around and saw the colonel. He said something to Primrose and walked over to Tremont.

"Evenin' . . . sir."

"Good evening, Cooper. I see you came through this fight unscathed."

"Yes, sir. And lookie here!" As the colonel dismounted, Gabriel jogged over to some thick brush and took out a concealed knapsack.

"It's a real Yankee issue revolver, and I killed me a bunch o' Yanks with it," Gabriel offered.

"You got yourself one of Mr. Lincoln's guns," said the colonel, examining the carbine, noting the triumph in Gabriel's voice.

"Come ag'in?"

Tremont saw his confusion. Gabriel's prison years must have left him with large gaps of knowledge.

"This is a Spencer Repeating Carbine," explained the colonel, looking down the barrel of the rifle. "It's also known as Mr. Lincoln's gun because President Lincoln himself is very taken with it. Did you get ammunition for it?"

"Naw, warn't able to get close enough for that."

"Well, there are thousands of them out there, especially among the Union cavalry."

Gabriel chuckled. "Well, I'll just have ta shoot me some more o' them fancy cavalry boys."

Colonel Tremont studied the man opposite him. *He did have that element of blast powder, but it seemed to be working in a way that benefitted them all. Thank God.* "I'll have to see if I can't get you some more bullets for the Colt .44."

"Hell, ya mean that, Colonel? That's right nice of ya! Ain't had somethin' nice done like that fer me fer . . ." His voice trailed off.

Tremont handed the carbine back to Gabriel. "Looks like war suits you well, Cooper."

"Well, it sure beats prison, sir."

"And how's working out here after the battle?"

"Rather be doin' this than bein' one o' them poor bastards goin' off to get chopped up."

"I can't argue with that. I see you're working with Corporal Primrose."

"Johnnie?"

"Yes. He knows his way around a battlefield. Been with me for a couple of years now." Suddenly, Colonel Tremont called out, "Corporal Primrose!"

Johnnie made his way over to Gabriel and Tremont. "Yes, sir!"

Tremont frowned. "Corporal, you're bleeding."

"Yes, sir. It ain't nothin' sir."

"Make sure you get it taken care of."

"Yes, sir! I'll take care of it myself."

"Good enough." Tremont gestured to Gabriel. "Has Private Cooper been of good service to you?"

Johnnie grinned. "Oh, yes, sir! He's a right good guy!"

"Keep up the good work."

Relieved and feeling he knew Cooper just a tiny bit better, Tremont remounted his horse and saluted them both.

"Gentlemen, carry on. I wish you both Godspeed in your task."

Johnnie saluted Tremont and nudged Gabriel to do the same.

After Tremont had left, Gabriel and Johnnie went back to work.

"Hey, Johnnie," Gabriel said. "Thanks fer sayin' that."

"Sayin' what?"

"About me bein' a right good guy."

"Yer all right, Gabe. I'm honored to work with ya."

A flicker of hope sparked in Gabriel. Maybe, just maybe, things were looking up. He welcomed the new and unfamiliar feeling.

IT WAS WELL PAST MIDNIGHT WHEN THEY PLACED THEIR last body into a grave. Johnnie looked peaked. "I'd better set to doctorin' this here flesh wound. What d'ya say we help put some dirt on these graves tomorrow?" He paused. "Don't know where ya been sleepin' afore, but y'all's welcome to come back to our campsite fer the night. I'm sure there's gonna be unclaimed sleepin' gear."

"Thanks," said Gabriel, "but I gotta do somethin' first. A kid I know was kilt out in the forest and I dunno if they found him . . ."

Johnnie went over to a pile of shovels. He came back with one and a lantern in the other hand. "Pay it no mind, Gabe," he said, handing the lantern and shovel to him. "Give him the proper burial he deserves. I'll see ya here tomorrow?"

"Yep."

"Thanks fer yer help t'day, Gabe."

"Twarn't nothin'. And Johnnie"—he grinned—"bandage that thing afore ya bleed to death. I don't wanna have to be diggin' a grave fer yer sorry ass tomorrow."

Johnnie laughed. "Yep, will do, Gabe, will do. G'night now."

Gabriel returned to the forest. He held the lantern in front of him, as everything looked different at night. He finally found the tree that McRae was under. Eli was still there, although he had become carrion for wild animals because parts of him were now missing. Amidst the cries and whimpers of the wounded still out there, Gabriel set the lantern down and began to clear the undergrowth.

A few hours later, Gabriel scooped up McRae's half-eaten remains and gently dropped them into the square hole. He shoveled the soft earth back on top of the body.

It was daybreak when he finished. He marked the grave with two twigs tied into a cross and stuck it on top of the burial mound.

"Only 'cause ya said yer prayers, Eli McRae, even if they wasn't answered. Rest in peace." Then he picked up the shovel and lantern and headed back.

NONE OF GABRIEL'S PRISON MATES HAD SURVIVED THE battle. Word that he was the sole survivor traveled fast, but Gabriel didn't know anything about this until he met up with Johnnie the next day.

Johnnie's head was bandaged with a filthy rag, and he flashed his rotting teeth in a grin. "There ya are; get yer chore done?"

"Yeah." Gabriel noticed that several men had stopped working and were staring at him. Finally, one of them spoke.

"Y'all's from the chain-gang that come in a few days ago?"

"Yeah, what of it?"

To his amazement, the soldier held out his hand. "Well, I been hearin' all sorts o' things 'bout ya. Heard y'all's the only one who come out alive. Also heard that ya kilt dozens o' Yanks."

Gabriel shook the man's hand. "Found me a place where I could watch all them damn fools an' I jest shot the hell outta them. It was jest so easy, I coulda—" He stopped himself upon seeing the men's faces. "I jest did what I was s'posed to do."

Johnnie spoke up. "An' not only that. He come back here an' help me like no other. Then he done gone and stayed up all night buryin' his friend that got kilt out in the forest. An' sure enough, here he is agin, comin' to help us."

All the other men stepped up and held out their hands. Gabriel shook each one of them. Never had anything felt so good. Not even killing the enemy.

THE CONFEDERATE VICTORY AT OLUSTEE SECURED Florida's interior. No longer was there concern that the

Yankees could establish a state government loyal to the Union and Lincoln Administration.

There were no major land battles in early 1864 until Thursday, May 5, when Union and Rebel armies clashed on the Orange Turnpike in Virginia. Full combat ensued until evening, when both armies entrenched themselves east of Germanna Plank Road and waited to continue what would historically be known as the Battle of the Wilderness.

It was a two-day battle that segued into another collection of battles known as the Battle of Spotsylvania Court House.

By the time both campaigns were over, thirty-three thousand Union soldiers lay dead. It was unknown how many Confederates had died, but now a new threat arose —the war of attrition. While the North could replace its soldiers, the South could not. And although this was how Gabriel came to be enlisted as a Confederate soldier, Grant now used the war of attrition to the Union's benefit in a number of maneuvers: the attack on Richmond, occupying the Shenandoah Valley, Sherman's march to Savannah, taking over the railroad lines of West Virginia, and capturing Mobile, Alabama.

In response, Gabriel's regiment was deployed to help block Sherman's march to Atlanta.

Gabriel didn't think of the vast armies that awaited him. Rather, he looked forward to using weaponry far more efficient than the musket-rifle he was first issued. Colonel Tremont had even kept his promise to acquire extra ammunition for his revolver. Gabriel could hardly wait to use those bullets.

THEY TRAVELED NORTH, FOLLOWING THE MACON AND Western Railroad, passing through small towns like Jonesboro and way stations like Rough and Ready. They pushed past Atlanta and on into Cherokee Georgia.

Gabriel watched the refugees fleeing south, families strung along the roads with their supplies and livestock. This was a colossal expansion of his world, but while he took it in with childlike wonder, there was still a grown man's search of the new faces he encountered—not for someone he loved but for someone he hated. It was a face he'd make it his life's work to find. Or die trying.

At April's end they arrived at Rocky Face Ridge, a mountain of granite and stone just past Dalton. They were going to fight alongside "Old Joe" Johnston, becoming part of an amassed army of sixty-five thousand men, supported by 187 cannons. What they didn't know was that they would be facing a hundred thousand Union soldiers who had brought with them 254 pieces of artillery.

By this time, Gabriel was part of Johnnie Primrose's company and regiment, the 12th Florida Infantry. Though not a native of Jacksonville, he was a native Floridian and that was good enough. Finally, he belonged. It had been a long time since he'd felt anything like that.

He treasured his friendship with Johnnie Primrose, holding sacred Johnnie's trust in him. Johnnie's ready smile lightened his heart, making him less defensive.

Within hours of arriving, Gabriel's regiment got its order to relieve the pickets for the evening. Throughout the night the men would stand watch, listening, keeping an eye out for the charge of Union fighters.

Gabriel had never been a picket before, but he didn't complain. His willingness to help with anything had quelled the rumors that he was a crazy, bloodthirsty man.

All of this was also not lost on Colonel Tremont, who continued to keep an eye on him throughout the campaigns. While deep down he still harbored unease at the man, he had to admit that Gabriel was one of the best fighters he had ever seen.

THE AFTERNOON HEAT SHIMMERED OFF THE CRAGGY rocks of the ridge. Gabriel crouched alongside Johnnie on picket duty.

Johnnie sighed. "This is gonna be a long night, Gabe."

"How so?" Gabriel looked over the barrel of his gun, his eyes scouring the landscape.

Another soldier spoke up. "He don't like the fightin' like y'all do, Gabe."

"Who says I like the fightin'?"

The other soldier chuckled. "Shit, Gabe, ain't never seen no one get so happy like y'all do when thar's a fight comin' on."

There was a rustling in the pine thicket opposite them. Gabriel aimed and shot into the forest. A voice taunted him from the undergrowth.

"C'mon, ya damned rebs, shoot like you mean it."

Gabriel swore under his breath and fired another shot.

"Is that how you crackers use a weapon? No wonder we're winnin' this war."

"Come agin," Gabriel retorted. "Sure that ain't some ugly Yank woman talkin' to us? I hear's the Yankee women folk fight better'n the men. I hear's them're uglier'n skinny sows—"

He was cut off by a volley of shots. Gabriel laughed. "Now we're talkin'." He fired back.

The other soldiers alongside him joined in the shooting. Gabriel yelled again, "C'mon, ya ugly old women! Hitch up them petticoats and fight like ya mean it. Or go back to the whorehouses y'all came from."

Furious gunfire was the reply. He turned to Johnnie and grinned.

"Cover me. I'm gonna go see if'n I can slit me a nice Yankee throat."

"Aw hell, Gabe, stay put! Yer gonna get yerself kilt out there."

But Gabriel had already begun to slither away. He edged himself farther into the thick undergrowth, crawling on his belly, a dagger in his mouth. He had learned how to hunt alligators in the swamp like this, but Yankees were so much easier.

Gabriel used the waning light to his advantage. He was getting close enough to hear voices.

A couple of white Yankees farther down the picket line were ignoring the gunfire and playing cards. Gabriel could hear the rattle of the dice from still other games nearby.

"What're they shootin' at down yonder?" one of the soldiers asked.

"I dunno. Some reb got under their skin. Gonna show 'em what real shootin's like, I guess."

"Secesh bastards! They holler and scream in battle like a bunch of banshees. It'll be damn nice to see Atlanta burn and see these bastards sent off to the Hell they came from."

One of the men stood up. "I gotta take a pee. Think it's safe to go to that patch of trees?"

"Over the line here? Reynolds, why you wanna go over the breastwork? Some damned Reb might see you and take a shot."

"'Cause the trees are right there. And besides, Owens, how many times do I have to tell you? Them Rebs can't shoot for nothin'. That's why we're winnin' this war. 'Cause they got no teeth, no brains, and no eye for shootin'. None of 'em's round here, anyway. They wouldn't have the balls to get this close to real soldiers."

In a few minutes, Gabriel saw the blue-clad form slip over the breastworks, coming close to the thicket he was laying in. He watched as the soldier came within feet of him and stopped. As he heard the splash of urine hit the tree trunk, Gabriel sprang up and in one swift movement he bared the man's throat, dragging his knife across his jugular. Gasping, the soldier toppled over. He held his hands to his throat, the blood gushing through his fingers. Gabriel smiled down at him.

"Should be more careful 'bout what ya say," Gabriel whispered to the dying man. "An' by the way, yer gonna get ta Hell way afore I do!" He cut a swath of hair from the man's beard and shoved it in his pocket. He pilfered the man's pockets. Then he dropped down and slithered away in the underbrush. As he passed the soldiers still playing cards, he heard one of them ask, "My God, how long does it take for Reynolds to take a piss?"

Johnnie Primrose was stunned when Gabriel told him what he'd done. "Jesus and Jehosophat, Gabe, what'd y'all do that fer?"

"Them's talkin' down on us like that; I set 'em straight."

Johnnie and several of the other men still stared at him. "Hell, Gabe . . ."

"Here's a piece of the Yank's beard," offered Gabriel, "jes' so ya know I ain't tellin' no tall tale."

Johnnie looked at Gabriel with sudden insight. "We all know where ya came from, Gabe. Ain't no man can survive the swamps on a chain gang without havin' some kind o' grit. Ain't that right, boys?"

There were gestures and comments of affirmation, and one of the men grinned at Gabriel. "But it's a helluva story."

There was a round of laughter as everyone left to take up their positions again.

"Good work," one of them said, clapping Gabriel on the back.

"I hate to be the blue-coated bastard that comes up against you," said another.

Gabriel turned to Johnnie. "Y'all thinks I'm crazy, don't ya?

Johnnie shook his head. "Naw. I just ain't much fer killin', Gabe. Y'all are better suited to this part o' the war than me."

"What other part o' war is there, Johnnie?"

"There's all sorts o' parts, but it's the doctorin' fer me. If'n I coulda done the doctorin' I woulda been happy as a pig in mud."

The whiz of a bullet suddenly passed between them. Johnnie grinned. "Here we go—show those Yanks that Gabe Cooper's out to get 'em an' they all's better pray that it's his bullets that reach 'em afore he does!"

By the time the sun bared its seething face the next morning, outrage swelled that some "goddamned murderous Reb" had killed a man when he was at his most vulnerable.

Outnumbered and outgunned, the Rebels repelled the Union soldiers with wits as well as bullets. At Dug Gap, they rolled boulders onto the advancing Yanks who outnumbered them ten to one.

However, Sherman's advance and flank campaigning forced the Confederate army to new positions, pushing them farther and farther south toward Atlanta.

Gabriel and Johnnie fought side by side from Rocky Face Ridge to Dalton to Resaca, and finally to Kennesaw Mountain. For many who would survive this fight, they would be absorbed into a campaign for Tennessee, but for Johnny and Gabriel, the fighting would stop. For Johnnie, his personal ceasefire was a blessing, but for Gabriel, it was an unknown outcome, one that he would not fully appreciate until years later.

KENNESAW MOUNTAIN WAS ONE OF THE LAST CHANCES TO stop Sherman before his armies crossed the Chattahoochee River. Once he did, Atlanta would be within reach. Rumors flew among the ranks as tensions ran high and tempers short. Surgeons sharpened their saws as orders to inspect cartridge boxes travelled down the lines.

Legendary generals were seen riding together, looking over the designated battlefield, while men watched Union and Confederate generals share whiskey as they conversed with each other.

One advantage of Kennesaw was that Gabriel could now bathe in the Chattahoochee River. With the temporary ceasefires, men could safely clean themselves. As they washed their lice-ridden clothes, Johnnie joked, "At least if'n we get kilt on the mountain we'll get to the Pearly Gates clean 'stead o' smellin' like we jest fought a war."

On the evening of June 26, men slept with an ear open for battle and sure enough, a cannon shot was fired the next morning.

Grapeshot and canister, Minié Balls and musket shells that exploded inside the flesh they hit. Concussive volleys were thrown back and forth in ear-splitting waves.

Gabriel waited behind the breastworks, trying to quell his impatience. His carbine was at the ready and he carried on his person the same heavy-gauge, Union-issued knife that he had used on that poor pissing Yankee.

It was a magnificent site, he thought, watching the masses of deep blue surge forward beneath colorful banners. Too bad the assault would soon dissolve into hand-to-hand combat, ruining the fine formation.

Rounds of Confederate artillery blew apart rows of Union soldiers. Unable to wait anymore, Gabriel moved amidst a shower of blood and bone, leaping over the breastworks with a Rebel yell.

He swung his dagger, eviscerating any Yankee he encountered. Gunfire sparks and the cannons' flashes triggered small brush fires everywhere. Men, felled by both bullet and bayonet, were consumed alive by the flames, screaming as they turned into grotesque, oily char.

Gabriel, staying low, worked his way sideways to a dense thicket. He faded into the blackening smoke, looking for a place to snipe at the enemy. He crawled over the wounded who cried and cursed until, suddenly, he was stopped in his tracks.

Was this serendipity or destiny? Was this chance or the whimsy of a cruel God? Whatever it was, he stopped and looked at the wounded Rebel in his path. And Gabriel knew it was him.

Pinned beneath his gaze was the man who had taken his life away as he had known it, sending him to prison and destroying his family. Gabriel's nostrils flared as his heart threatened to burst from his chest. He dropped down beside the fallen soldier.

"Well now, I'll bet y'all didn't think this day was gonna come." The rage in his voice burned his throat.

Mason Hugo, suffering from two broken legs and a broken arm, stared at Gabriel as if he were an apparition. He struggled to get away. Gabriel leaned on his legs. Mason yelped as Gabriel laughed. "Did y'all think I'd rot in that hell hole y'all sent me to?"

"Please, have mercy on a dying man."

"Ya always were a whiny bastard, nothin' but a lyin', snivellin' excuse of a man." He put more pressure on Mason's legs and watched tears of pain fill his eyes. "Naw, ya ain't dyin' lest I kill ya. Which I'm tempted to do."

Mason shoved weakly at Gabriel with his good arm, and Gabriel responded by twisting his broken one. Mason screamed, "Oh Christ, have mercy!"

"Mercy? There ain't no such thing when it comes to me and you."

Gabriel twisted his arm again, and Mason cried piteously, "Then kill me! Kill me and get it over with."

Gabriel recalled Mason's words from long ago. *And here you are, ready to go to the chain gang to live out your life, wishing you were dead . . .*

"That would be the charitable thing to do, wouldn't it, Hugo? Remember them days when I was in the jail an' y'all was so sure I was goin' away fer life? An' y'all would come on by an' sit outside my cell with yer fancy food and fine wine, drinkin' an' carryin' on, so sure that y'all had ruined me? Remember what ya said back then, Hugo? Remember? Y'all said I'd go to the chain gang and live my life wishin' I was dead . . . an' ya just loved callin' me yer doomed friend . . . remember? Well, guess what, my doomed friend, guess what? Now yer gonna live out yer life wishin' *you* was dead!"

Nearby brush was on fire, so Gabriel pulled out his dagger and crawled over to the flames. He held it in the flames until it glowed. Then, crawling back to Mason, he pressed the flat of the blade across his lips.

Mason writhed, his mouth foaming. The skin blackened and his lips tore away.

"That'll teach ya t' tell lies, ya stinkin', shitty wretch. Next time ya feel like settin' another man up with yer yeller-bellied lies, jest take a good look at yerself."

Mason's head rolled to one side as he passed out. Gabriel grabbed him under the armpits and dragged him back toward the breastworks.

"Hey," he yelled at a messenger who was scurrying toward the rear of the fighting. "Where's the medics?"

"Don't know and can't say as I care right now. I gotta get this message over to General Cheatham."

"Well, I got a wounded man here."

"And what of it?"

"Well, I want to get him to the rear. I got more fightin' to do, otherwise I'd take him myself."

The messenger peered at Mason. "Jesus, look at him!"

"Burnin' tree branch fell across his face. It'll heal."

"Not too prettily, it won't. Is he hurt otherwise?"

"Some broken bones."

"Then leave him here. He'll get picked up by n' by." He glanced again at Mason. "With a face like that, he might be better off dead."

Gabriel grinned. "Ya think?"

The messenger stared at him. "Funny what war makes men smile over. Leave him here, and he'll be one o' the lucky ones. Some of those boys out there're gettin' burned alive."

Gabriel laid Mason on the ground as the messenger left. "Don't know if'n I'd call ya one o' the lucky ones. 'Cause ya got me now. An' that ain't so lucky."

~

HE SLID DOWN A ONCE VERDANT HILL, NOW SLIMY WITH the offal of human agony. Bloated bodies littered the decline, rotting in the heat and humidity. Gabriel cut back into the forest, knowing he was at a safe distance from any of the actual fighting. Suddenly, he stopped. He swore he had heard the word, "Mama," so he stopped and listened for it again.

There it was, unmistakable this time. Gabriel parted the bushes, his bayonet drawn, and peered into the face of a terrified young white boy. Tears and mud streaking his face, he shrunk away. "Please don't kill me."

Gabriel felt a pinch in his heart as he noticed the boy wore the same wide-eyed wonderment that Eli McRae had. "You Yanks must be hurtin' real bad if y'all are bringing young uns such as yerself to the fight."

"I ain't no kid."

"Hell, yes you are! I heard yer cryin' an' carryin' on. What happened to y'all?"

The boy touched the bloodied rip in his pant leg. "I got shot." Fresh tears welled up in his eyes. "I never even used my gun. It got knocked outta my hand, and then I got shot. It hurts real bad, mister."

"Don't look like it's gonna kill ya. Y'all better come with me."

"But you're a Reb!"

"So what if I am? Y'all needs a doctor ta look at that leg o' yours."

"Aren't you supposed to kill me?"

"Y'all can be my first prisoner o' war instead."

"Oh God, a prisoner!"

"Shet up now, I'm only funnin' ya. Truth is, y'all needs a doctor and then y'all needs ta git home to yer mama. She's wantin' y'all home as bad as y'all wants to be thar."

"I can't go home. My mama'll skin me alive."

"I doubt that."

Gabriel slipped one arm under the boy's legs and coaxed him to put an arm around his neck. As he lifted him, he said, "Y'all's lucky ya didn't git yer head blown off. Didn't no one tell ya y'all was too young fer these goin's on?"

"I lied about my age."

"Now, that's a kid for ya. An' all them bastards runnin' this war, none of 'em figgered y'all was fibbin'?"

The boy shook his head. "Isn't like anyone knew me to say differently."

"Well, y'all looks like a kid to me an' it ain't like I needs anyone ta tell me differently neither."

"I can hold my own out there. Bet I coulda killed a couple of Rebs if I'd gotten the chance."

Gabriel grinned. "I ain't sayin' y'all couldn't, boy. An' a lot o' Rebs wouldn't a'cared that y'all's barely old enough to piss behind a tree. They'd a killed ya, too."

They were skirting the battlefield, listening to the distant thuds of the artillery and crack of gunfire.

They broke behind Confederate lines, heading for the field hospital. Suddenly another soldier jumped in his path. Seeing the boy's uniform, the wild-eyed veteran snapped, "No pris'ners! Ain't takin' no pris'ners t'day!"

"Says who?" Gabriel growled.

"Says me!"

"An' who the hell are you?"

The veteran spit. "Ain't no matter who I am."

"Y'all's better git over now an' let me through." Gabriel took a step, but the other man blocked his way.

"He's a blue-bellied son-of-a-bitch, an' should get his just desserts like all the rest o' the Yanks we whupped t'day. Drop him!"

And Gabriel did just that. He dropped the boy and shoved the other soldier backward. The man fell, spread-eagled. In an instant, Gabriel was on him with a feral snarl, his dagger with bits of Mason's charred skin still on it pointed at his upper lip. "I don't care no more'n for y'all as I do t'other side. It's all the same ta me. So if'n anyone's gonna die, it's gonna be you. I'll jes' take this here handy knife an' shove it through yer head till it comes out the back side an' yer brains become animal food."

Gabriel moved the point of the dagger slightly so that it rested under the other man's nose. He flicked the point of the dagger upward, slicing the man's nostril.

The soldier scrambled away as blood trickled over his lips. "Y'all's fuckin' crazy!"

Their standoff had caught the attention of several nearby Rebel soldiers. Waving the dagger at all of them Gabriel hissed, "Yeah, big fuckin' crazy!" He laughed outright then, picked up the boy and moved past. As they headed on their way, the boy stared, awestruck. Gabriel looked at him. "Now y'all's got somethin' to tell yer mama about."

IF THE KID HAD BEEN SCARED BEFORE, HE PANICKED WHEN they reached the hospital. Blood-soaked soldiers lay in lines, the moans of pain mingled with the stink of putre-faction. The boy gagged as they passed a pile of amputated limbs. Gabriel hitched him up closer. "It ain't no summer picnic, is it?"

They entered at the front and Gabriel knew carrying a boy in Union dress would draw attention. Luckily it came from an army chaplain.

"What do we have here?" he asked as he approached them.

"I found this young 'un out in the bushes," Gabriel explained, "looks like he's been hit in the leg. Thought mebbe he could use some doctorin'.'"

"It was very Christian of you, soldier, to turn the other cheek and bring him in. How old are you, son?"

"I'll be fourteen next week, sir."

"You're a bit young for this sort of business."

"Yes, sir."

"Did you run away to join the army?"

"Yes, sir."

"God was with you, son."

"Yes, sir."

"Now, tell me your name."

"David Nathaniel Tremont, sir."

Gabriel recognized the last name immediately. The chaplain continued, "We have a Colonel Tremont leading a number of our brigades; very noble soldier."

David offered, "I have an Uncle Robert who's a Reb officer."

The chaplain's eyes met Gabriel's. He sighed, "A family divided. Not the only one here. Let's see if I can get a doctor for you."

Horse and deer flies swarmed above the wounded as they passed by.

Gabriel mused, "Not real sure where I can leave ya so as y'all will get some attention."

"Please, please don't leave me here!"

Just then a surgeon approached. Being Colonel Tremont's nephew had its advantages.

The surgeon's face and apron were streaked with blood. "What's the problem here?"

"He's shot in the leg."

"Well, he's got to be on the ground where I can examine the wound."

Gabriel laid David down between two mortally wounded soldiers. As the doctor knelt down the boy tried to stand. "He's gonna cut off my leg!"

Gabriel clamped a hand over David's mouth. "Shet up!"

This subdued David while the doctor examined the wound. "The bullet's gonna have to come out. Wait here; I'll go get a clean instrument."

Hearing this, David bit Gabriel's hand, clawing to get away. Gabriel dragged David to his feet. He drew back his fist, punching him in the face. As David's legs buckled, he heard the surgeon chuckle. "Works better than chloroform."

There were no open operating tables, so the surgeon extracted the bullet there on the ground. He finished quickly. "No bone hit. Your little bluecoat's lucky." He handed the bullet to Gabriel. "He can keep it as a souvenir." He paused. "But he'll die in Andersonville, you know."

Gabriel had heard about Andersonville. Rife with

disease and starvation, thirty thousand Union POWs lived in a space meant for ten thousand.

"He ain't goin' to no prison."

The doctor sighed. "You'd better watch out for your fool kid, then."

Gabriel scooped the limp David into his arms. He moved him outside just as Colonel Tremont strode up. He peered into David's face. "My God. Follow me."

They moved to the far rear of the camp. The colonel approached his tent, waving his aides away. He moved the flap aside. "Lay him on my cot."

Gabriel laid the unconscious boy down. "He's out cold."

"Why's that?"

"Shot in the leg. He was a'carryin on an' such, doc couldn't get close. So, I punched him. He was done fer then."

Colonel Tremont stared at the boy. "He's a spitting image of his father; I'd have known him anywhere. How did you find him?"

"Hidin' in a bush and afeard I was gonna kill him."

"And why didn't you?"

"I ain't no baby killer, Colonel. I likes my fight, but I ain't no baby killer."

"Hmm, even when the baby's the enemy?"

"Ain't no enemy here, just a fool young 'un."

Tremont shook his head, bewildered. "I appreciate your moral compass, Cooper, although, I have to admit, you are a puzzle."

"I didn't know he was yer nephew 'til he done told the rev'rnd . . . Sir."

David stirred. Colonel Tremont knelt beside him.

"David, I am your Uncle Robert. You are safe here with me."

David mumbled, "I've heard my pa talk about you, but it wasn't good stuff."

Colonel Tremont smiled sadly. "No, I'm sure not. However, your father and I were very close growing up. And I'm going to try and get word to him that you are all right."

"He doesn't know I'm in the army. I ran away so I could fight, just like him, but I didn't tell my mother I was going."

"Then they both should know as soon as possible. You have a man's courage, David, but you are still a boy. This is no place for you."

"I know," David motioned toward Gabriel. "He kinda said all that before."

"Did he?" Colonel Tremont looked at Gabriel. "You surprise me over and over, Cooper. But I am grateful."

Gabriel nodded. "I best be leavin', sir. Get back to the fightin'."

"When did you last eat?"

"Afore the battle started."

"Then you must join us for dinner, Cooper."

"Sir, I was figurin' on gettin' back to the fightin'."

For a man who had eaten insects to stave off hunger, dinner was a feast.

"There will be plenty of fighting tomorrow, Cooper. Tonight, you will have a proper meal and that's an order."

~

FOR A MAN WHO HAD EATEN INSECTS TO STAVE OFF hunger, dinner was a feast. As the colonel watched Gabriel inhale his food, he asked, "What've you been eating in the field?"

"Whatever I can get my hands on."

Colonel Tremont shook his head. "We are in such short supply of everything. Is there nothing at all at the front?"

"We eat whatever we can find."

"I hear the foraging parties have brought in food, but there isn't much in these parts. We got a lot on our march up here. You must've eaten well then."

"Some of the dead Yanks got some eats on 'em." As David stared at him, he continued, "I allus search fer eats an' bullets."

Colonel Tremont smiled grimly as he turned to his nephew. "This is the reality of war, David. And if it weren't for Private Cooper, you might've been one of the ones getting picked over."

"I know."

"Everyone thinks war is exciting, but when you've seen as much of it as I have, you think differently."

David shoulders sagged.

"Are you tired?" asked the colonel.

"Yes, sir. My leg hurts. And my jaw does, too." He shot a look at Gabriel.

As the boy hobbled over to his uncle's cot, the colonel motioned Gabriel to accompany him outside. Once out of earshot, Colonel Tremont said, "He is technically a prisoner of war, but I'm not sending him to Andersonville."

"No, sir."

"I don't want him involved with this war anymore," continued the colonel, "but I can't leave him unguarded, either. My boys won't tolerate the enemy in their midst, no matter how young he is." The colonel paused. "He's going to need someone to watch over him, someone I can trust, which is why I'm assigning you as his bodyguard for the duration of this war."

"Aw, Jesus, Colonel, don't say that!"

"This is an order, Cooper. He trusts you. And"—he took a deep breath—"I trust you. I'm sure you would defend him to anyone who tried to do him harm."

"But my place ain't here, sir! Y'all know where I belong, y'all's said it yerself!"

"It may be where you want to be, but it doesn't make a damn bit of difference if you're there anymore, Cooper. We're holding Kennesaw, but we're gonna lose Atlanta. Once Atlanta goes, the South will be split in two, and we're finished. Whether you're up at the front or back here, the outcome will be the same. My nephew, however, could have a very different outcome if left back here alone."

"Aw Hell," Gabriel choked out the words. "Yes, sir."

"Good. Then you will sleep outside my tent beginning tonight. Come daybreak, you'll be left alone. You are to keep David as far away from the other soldiers as possible. I don't want my troops' morale damaged, thinking we are giving special privileges to a prisoner of war. Is that clear?"

Gabriel did not respond immediately, so Colonel Tremont said, "I will take that as a 'Yes, sir.' Your duty begins now."

As the colonel turned to leave, Gabriel found his

voice. "Colonel," Tremont stopped. "Sir, I'm a'wonderin' if'n y'all could do one thing in exchange fer me watchin' yer nephew."

"What the hell, Cooper?"

"It ain't fer me, sir. It's fer Corporal Primrose. He'd rather be back here helpin' with the doctorin' than bein' at the front. Not that he ain't got grit, but he rather be tendin' to the wounded. He ain't like me, Colonel." Gabriel added, "He don't like the killin'."

Colonel Tremont nodded. "Corporal Primrose does have a knack for patching up wounds and the surgeons need all the assistance they can get. I'll assign Corporal Primrose herewith to this corps' field hospital."

Gabriel smiled a rare, heartfelt smile. "Thank you, Colonel, that's right nice of you."

The colonel signaled for his horse. "Stay vigilant, Cooper."

GABRIEL WATCHED THE COLONEL HEAD OFF TOWARD THE artillery fire, wishing he was going with him.

He went back into the tent. Since David was fast asleep, he allowed himself to nod off. But even as he dozed, he kept an ear open for the ambulances. On one of them was the man he intended for his own ragged dagger of terror. *"Live out your life wishing you were dead . . ."* Now it was Mason's turn to reap what he had sown. Gabriel smiled. May the harvest be bountiful.

ALTHOUGH HE WAS DEFEATED AT KENNESAW MOUNTAIN, Sherman continued inching toward Atlanta. As the fighting became even more desperate, Gabriel found himself propelled toward a different battle.

Mason Hugo was picked up and transported to the field hospital just as Gabriel had planned. Now he was one of many, waiting for his bones to be set and something, if anything, to be done for his face.

In order to check on Mason, Gabriel insisted that David be taken back to the field hospital for a follow-up.

David grumbled as he limped alongside Gabriel. "Don't see why I gotta go back there. I feel fine."

"'Ya got a wound and it needs checkin'. Now quit complainin'."

"How come the doctor can't come to my uncle's tent?"

"'Cause they got enough to do without havin' ta chase all over tarnation to see to a bullet wound."

"But my uncle's a colonel. They should come to his tent."

Gabriel stopped. "Are my ears hearin' right? Are y'all sayin' that 'cause yer uncle's a colonel that y'all should get special treatment?"

"Well—"

"Well, nothin'! Remember yer the enemy, boy, and that ya could've been some vulture's dinner. Now walk on like the man ya want everyone to think ya are."

As they approached the hospital, David rubbed his chin. "I think you broke my jaw."

"All the more reason y'all should be here."

Gabriel spotted Johnnie Primrose kneeling near a wounded soldier. "Johnnie!"

Johnnie turned, his tired face breaking into a messy, gap-toothed smile. "Ya wily son of a bitch! Ain't I glad to see y'all's okay! Where the hell ya been?"

Gabriel grinned. "Got myself in a pre-dicament," he replied and gestured to David. "This here's David Tremont. He's the colonel's nephew."

Johnnie stared at the boy's uniform. "What the hell?"

"Found this fella wounded on the mountain. Turns out he ran off to be in the army like his pa. When colonel found out I'd fetched him from the field, he assigned me to watch over him."

"I can watch over myself," interjected David, but Gabriel silenced him with a look.

"As I was sayin', Colonel knows he's a Yank, but he warn't fer sendin' him to Andersonville, so he ordered me to watch over the kid 'til we can git him back to his own pa." Then, "Got business at the hospital?"

"Gabe, ya ain't never gonna believe this. Colonel calls fer me a few days ago and says they're real short o' surgical assistants in the hospital. Wants me to help there and says we got enough soldiers willin' to fight, but not all of 'em gots the stomach fer doctorin'. It's like he knew all about how I prefer the doctorin'." Suddenly his eyes narrowed. "Wait a minute. You been spendin' all this time with the colonel?"

Gabriel grin grew wider, "Hell, Johnnie, I wanted to get somethin' fer my troubles of leavin' the front. I figgered one of us should be happy with where we're put."

"Ya wily son of a bitch," Johnnie said again, but his eyes shone.

"I told the colonel ya had grit with the best of 'em,

but that y'all had a knack fer doctorin' wounds. Ain't like y'all's got a patsy's job helpin' out here."

"Ain't that the truth. I must've helped with a dozen amputations these last couple o' days."

"Yep, speakin' o' which," Gabriel glanced at David, "I need t' see if a doctor can spare a moment to look at this kid's leg. Can ya sit with him while I git someone to check on him?"

"I can tell ya now, Gabe, them doctors been workin' night n' day. They're most likely all in surgery."

"I'll jes' take a peek."

"See what y'all kin find. And Gabe," Johnnie held out his hand. "Thanks. I owe ya one."

Gabriel shook Johnny's hand and grinned. Then he entered the hospital.

Up and down the rows he went until he saw him with his left arm in a sling and both legs in makeshift splints. Mason's face was bandaged and his eyes were closed.

A soldier laying in the next cot asked, "He kin to ya?"

"Naw, jes' an ol' friend. Thought mebbe I'd git him awake."

"Naw, they give him opium to make him sleep. He's a damn misery if he's awake. They had to take a lot o' the flesh away an' part of his tongue, too. Said it was startin' ta rot. He's gonna be one ugly cuss when it's over." He sighed. "Helluva thing, bein' burned on the mouth like that. Helluva thing. There somethin' ya want me t' tell him when he wakes up?"

"Jes' tell him an ol' friend stopped by. An' that I'll be back."

"Ya got a name?"

"No need. He'll know who yer talkin' about." Then Gabriel turned and left.

Outside, he approached Johnnie and David. "Y'all's were right, they're all busy."

"Yep, they're a cuttin' an' sawin' 'round the clock. Well, I best be goin' back in. Keep yerself outta trouble, ya hear?"

"I'll try."

"Yeah, like hell ya will." Johnnie chuckled as he walked off.

David looked relieved at not having to see a doctor. "What're we gonna do now?"

"Hell if I know, boy. Ain't never had extra time fer doin' nothin' afore."

But as the day wore on and David rested in the tent, Gabriel took time to reflect on Mason's sorry state. He congratulated himself, for he liked the harvest he was starting to reap.

DAVID SPENT THE NEXT FEW DAYS RECUPERATING. Gabriel dozed off one lazy afternoon and awakened to see David sitting up and reading.

"What y'all got there?" Gabriel asked, stretching.

"My uncle's journal."

"Journal?"

"It's really interesting. Want a look?"

"Naw. It ain't no use to me, an' it don't sound like somethin' y'all oughtta be readin' neither. Sounds like a man's business with hisself."

"It is. But I was bored. My uncle left it under the pillow here."

"Y'all must be feelin' better."

"Except for my jaw. Why'd ya hit me so hard?"

"'Cause ya was catterwallin'. How else was the doctor gonna get that bullet outta yer leg?"

David reddened. "I guess I'm a pretty lousy soldier."

"Naw, y'ain't. Hell, I seen bigger men cry fer less."

"Really?"

"Ain't no tellin' how a man'll act when he's faced with seein' th'elephant. Some o'yer biggest talkers'll be the biggest cowards y'all ever did see. An' others take to it better'n their mama's cookin'."

"How could anyone like this?"

"Depends on where y'all's been afore."

"You must like it."

"It ain't the worst place I been in."

"Well, you're sure good at it. I don't know what would've happened if those crazy Rebs we ran into woulda found me."

"Same as if some of them boys returnin' from battle t'day would see ya." Gabriel stood up. "If'n yer well enough to go readin' what ain't yer business, then we'd better find us a cooler place to stay outta trouble. It's hotter'n hell in here."

David moved his leg and winced.

Gabriel nodded. "Y'all better move it or it's gonna stiffen up like a wooden peg." He grinned. "Peg-leg Davie'll be yer new moniker."

David struggled to rise. "I don't want any wooden leg!"

Gabriel laughed and helped David to his feet. They

emerged into the airless humidity and headed for the nearby trees.

As they settled onto the cool forest floor, Gabriel reached into his pocket. "Here," he said, handing a bullet to Davie. "Doc pulled this outta yer leg. Y'all's can show ever'body how it was taken outta ya when ya was a prisoner o'war. An' ya kin even say they didn't use nothin' neither to take away the pain."

David's eyes lit up. "I'm gonna keep it with me always." He paused. "You'd rather be out fighting, wouldn't you?"

"Yep. I gotta taste fer the fight."

"That's for sure. The way you went at that Reb when you found me, I thought you were gonna kill him."

"I would've if'n he didn't let us pass."

"Where'd you learn to fight like that?"

"A long time ago in another life."

"Do you think maybe you could teach me?"

"To fight?"

"Well, yes, as soon as I'm better, of course. What else are we going to do all day?"

"Ain't y'all know how ta fight?"

"Not like that. I have mostly sisters. And nobody else was around after the war started."

"I 'spose y'all could learn a few things from me. But I ain't doin' it fer free. Y'all's gotta give me somethin' in return."

"I don't have anything to give."

"Y'all knows how ta read, don't ya? An' I'll bet yer real good at cipherin' numbers. How's about I teach y'all how to fight, an' y'all teach me to figger with my numbers an' letters?"

"I didn't know you couldn't read."

"Ain't never learned, but I'm a thinkin' it's somethin' I oughtta know."

"My dad says everyone should know how to read, even the slaves. Especially since President Lincoln set them free. Don't you think so?"

"Cain't speak fer no slaves. But I un's from the swamps, an' ain't nobody can read thar. But I ain't goin' back to the swamps."

"I can teach you, it's easy."

"Then we gots us a deal?"

"We oughtta shake on this, like gentlemen."

Gabriel laughed and held out his hand. "Ain't never thought o'myself as a gentleman, but we gots us a deal, boy. An' yer right. What the hell else are we gonna do all day?"

4

FULTON COUNTY, GEORGIA 1864

While the battles of Ezra Church and Marietta raged, David taught Gabriel his alphabet, phonetics, and arithmetic. The colonel's diary became Gabriel's primer.

Atlanta burned and fell while Gabriel sweated over his new skills. As they deployed to other battles, Gabriel strung sentences together and ciphered numbers. As David gritted his teeth during the long marches, Gabriel would grit his teeth over spelling and grammar.

They marched into Tennessee and Gabriel finally found himself reading with greater ease. Now it was David's turn to feel the clumsy beginner as Gabriel taught him how to maintain his balance, duck his blows, and center his punch.

Franklin and Nashville. These two battles decimated the Army of Tennessee, repelling it back to Mississippi. The reinstated Joseph E. Johnston marched his withered army back to the Carolinas. After some weak fighting to stave off the advancing Sherman, the army finally withdrew to Greensboro.

Safe from battle, Gabriel and David created a world of their own. Gabriel bonded to David as if he were a younger brother, a salve for the aching loss of his own family. In turn, Gabriel became the big brother David never had.

April 9, 1865 ended life as they knew it. At the Appomattox Courthouse, Lee surrendered to Grant. Johnston soon followed suit, surrendering to Sherman. On that day, Gabriel, along with thousands of others, became a prisoner of war.

This was a technicality, however, for all Gabriel had to do was sign a paper stating that he would never again take up arms against the United States.

He pondered this out loud to David. "Ya know, good thing I know how to sign my name now that we're gonna have ta do it ta go home."

"Do you think with the assassination of President Lincoln the war's gonna start up again? I heard secesh rebs just talking about it."

"Ya cain't fight a war if there ain't nothin' ta fight with. We're bare bones, Davie. Ya cain't fight a war on that."

"I heard that Sherman is giving rations to everyone to get them on their way."

"That's only right of him considerin' the mess he made of these here parts."

"Gabriel, where are you gonna go from here?"

"I don't rightly know, Davie."

"What about your family?"

"Don't have no family to go to."

"None?"

"Nope."

"Why not?"

"Them all was lost to me a long time ago."

"How come?"

Gabriel cuffed David on the shoulder. "Y'all sure do ask a lot o' questions." He stared off into the distance. "I made a promise once to a friend who asked me with his dyin' breath to pay a visit to his folks. Guess I'll start with that."

"Where do his folks live?"

"Outside o' New Orleans."

"Don't suppose you'd come to Maryland, would you?"

"Maryland! Now why would I—" David's expression stopped Gabriel. His voice softened, "Davie, y'all's gotta life ta go back to an' it don't have no place fer the likes o' me."

"Sure it does, Gabe. You could work for my dad. I could teach you what I learn in school, I could—"

"Now wait a minute. How d'ya know I want that?"

David was silent.

Gabriel continued, "I's got my own road to travel."

"But you don't know where you're going or what you're gonna do."

"But that don't mean it's any less my journey. Now we both seen the elephant and lived ta tell about it. That's a good start for the rest of our lives, but it don't mean our lives are goin' down the same road. We both gotta find our own way."

"So, we'll never see each other again?"

"Now didn't y'all jes' teach me how ta read an' write?

Soon as I can, I'll write ya. Tell ya how I'm keepin' up an'such."

David brightened. "And maybe I can find someone to fight with."

Gabriel laughed. "Now don't y'all go gettin' yerself in trouble."

"So, we'll keep in touch? Maybe see one another again?"

The faces of Gabriel's three younger brothers flashed before him. He swallowed hard. "Davie, we'll allus be friends."

COLONEL TREMONT CALLED FOR GABRIEL TO STOP BY HIS tent.

Gabriel made his way over there and stepped into the tent. He saluted. He was so different now from the skinny, desperate man who had first joined up to fight. He smiled at David, who was sitting inside with the colonel.

"Getting your things in order, Cooper?" asked the colonel.

"Yes sir; jes' signed my name for the first time, thanks to yer nephew here."

The colonel turned to David. "You know, David, I could hardly believe my eyes when Cooper brought you to our camp. But your being here never let me forget that there were families on both sides who prayed every day that their sons would come home to them. So, thank God it's over because now we can all move on. I've sent word to your father, who will be arriving soon to bring you home."

"Thank you, Uncle Robert, for everything."

The colonel smiled and turned to Gabriel. "You did well, Cooper. You fulfilled your duty as a soldier and now you are free to go." He paused. "I am forever indebted to you."

"Thank you, sir."

"Where are you going to from here?"

"Well, I promised a friend who died back in Ocean Pond that I'd call on his kin over in Louisiana."

"Would you consider sticking around here for a few days to meet my brother when he comes for David? You deserve his thanks."

Seeing the look on David's face, Gabriel nodded. "That would be right nice, sir."

"Good. Now, if you'll excuse me, I have some matters to attend to. It's almost as much work finishing up a war as it is starting one." He stepped outside, leaving Gabriel and David to talk with each other.

Gabriel clapped David on the back. "So, yer daddy's on his way. Bet he'll be surprised to see how y'all's changed."

"I guess I have grown taller."

"More'n that. Y'all's done more'n grown taller, Davie, y'all's grown into a man."

JOHNNIE PRIMROSE CAME OVER TO SAY GOOD-BYE. HE found Gabriel and David playing cards.

"Come join us," said Gabriel. "I'm gettin' whupped by this upstart here."

"Naw, guys, I'm a-leavin' t'day. Gonna go home, find my little sweetheart and see if she'll marry her soldier come home."

"Travelin' by yerself?"

"Naw, gotta a couple o' boys goin' with me at least to Georgia. After that I'll prob'ly be by my lonesome. How 'bout y'all?"

"Soon as my dad comes for me," answered David. "I'm goin' home to Maryland. Gabe's goin' to Louisiana."

Johnny looked at Gabriel. "Well, if ya ever find yer way down ta Marion County, Florida, come on by."

"Will do, Johnnie."

The sound of pounding hooves made them turn their heads. David sprang to his feet, recognizing the Union cavalcade.

"Let yer uncle see him first," Gabriel commanded quietly. "Remember, yer a soldier now. Ya wait yer turn."

Brigadier General Edward Tremont, Jr., rode forward to meet Colonel Robert Tremont. He dismounted, handing the reins to one of his aides.

Both men saluted each other.

Colonel Tremont spoke first. "It's a pity for two brothers to have to meet this way after so long."

"I have come for my son."

Gabriel whispered to David, "Walk like the man you are. Salute yer father when y'all approach him."

Men parted the way for David to approach his father. He saluted him.

Edward returned the salute. There was a smattering of applause as father and son embraced. Gabriel stepped forward and saluted.

Colonel Tremont said, "This is Private Gabriel Cooper. He rescued David after he had been wounded and has watched over him ever since."

Edward held out his hand. "My deepest gratitude to you, Mr. Cooper."

"Your son proved hisself a man, General. He behaved like a soldier at all times and did ya proud."

Edward turned to David. "Well, David, you ran off like a boy and now you come home a man. You do know you will receive a man's consequences for running off like that?"

David nodded. "Yes, sir. I can take it, sir, whatever you see fit as a punishment for me."

The general laughed. "Oh, it won't be me, David, it'll be your mother. And she's a far harder taskmaster than I am."

There was a ripple of laughter and then Robert said to his brother, "I have something for you, General."

He turned to an aide who handed him the beautiful sword Gabriel had seen on that first meeting in the colonel's tent.

Robert offered the sword to Edward. "It's Charlie's."

Edward looked at the sword sadly. "You were there."

"Yes."

"Did you kill him?"

"Good God, no. Do you really think I could kill our own brother? He wanted me to have it, but now I give it to you. For our mother."

"Our mother's dead. She passed six months ago from pneumonia."

As Robert digested this news, Edward continued, "This would have been no comfort to her, anyway. She barely survived Charles's death. First you and then Charles; she was never the same after that."

Edward turned to Gabriel. "Mr. Cooper, you should have this. My brother, Charles, commanded with this sword, fighting to protect and save the Union, just as you did for David. It would be fitting for you to have it."

Astounded, Gabriel took the sword. "I am honored, sir."

"Keep it as a symbol of your bravery and compassion. My brother would have liked that."

David mounted a large bay mare as Gabriel said, "I'm gonna write to ya, Davie, an' when ya write back tell me 'bout all the pretty girls who wanna kiss ya now that yer a soldier back from the war."

David blushed and Gabriel smiled. "Y'all stay outta trouble now, ya hear?"

Johnnie and Gabriel stood together, watching the cavalcade leave. The colonel had retreated into his tent.

"Poor ol' Colonel," mused Johnnie. "Sure got a gutful o' bitter medicine t'day with his one brother actin' like he kilt t'other. Hell, he was beside hisself when his brother got shot."

"You were there?"

"Hell yes. Was the second Battle o' Manassas. I look up an' I see the colonel starin' down yonder at this Yankee commander who'd just given the damned order for his column to charge. An' all of a sudden, this Yank falls outta his saddle an' next thing I know Colonel's gallopin' over there, so I go a runnin' after him. Cain't believe I didn't get kilt. Anyway, he bends down over the officer an' then I heard someone say, 'Well I'll be goddamned, they're brothers.' Next thing I knowed, the colonel stands up, gets back on his horse, but he's got a look on his face that I ain't never seen afore . . . an' I ain't never seen since. An' he had that sword with him."

By now they had reached the place where they had left their card game. Johnnie sighed. "Well, Gabe, I best be movin' on. When y'all headin' out?"

"T'morrow after I get my rations."

"Well, friend, y'all keep yerself outta trouble down in Louisiana. An' like I said, if'n yer ever in Jacksonville, y'all's jest come on by."

The two men hugged. Johnny flashed Gabriel one of his smiles, beautiful despite his rotting teeth, and then headed off, leaving Gabriel to his own journey.

COLONEL TREMONT WAS SIGNING OFF PAPERS FOR THE quartermaster when Gabriel approached him. "Good morning, Cooper."

"Good morning, sir. I came to say g'bye."

The colonel straightened up and smiled. "May your new life bring you much success."

"Thank you, sir."

Tremont's eyes rested on the sword that hung in its sheath from Gabriel's belt. "Take good care of that sword, Cooper, for it belonged to a great man."

"Yes, sir. It'll always remind me of you, sir."

"I appreciate that, Cooper."

"Thank you fer all ya did fer me. Y'all saved my life."

The colonel shook Gabriel's hand. "You saved your own life, Cooper. Nobody's responsible for that but you."

Colonel Tremont watched Gabriel's retreating figure and the sword, his taunting reminder of a wound that might never heal, clanking by his side . . .

Charles lay there, a gaping wound in his chest. Robert put pressure on it, trying to stem the flow of blood. Charles placed a cooling hand on Robert's own.

"No use now, Bobby."

"Please hang on, Charlie—we can't end this way!"

A tear trickled from the corner of Charles's eye, "We don't have a choice, Bobby, Take my sword—you won fair and square. Didn't know you had so many boys here."

Before Robert could reply, Charles sighed his last words, "I've missed you."

Robert's heart cracked with grief as Charles slipped away. A sob caught in his throat and one of Charles's soldiers knelt beside him. "You best be gettin' outta here, sir; we'll take care of your brother, but we can't take care of you." As Robert mounted his horse, the soldier gave him Charles's sword. Even though he hadn't fired that shot, Robert would always feel as if he had killed his own brother. The sword would remind him of that.

Robert's family felt betrayed by him for living in the South, for marrying into a pro-slavery family, and for fighting for the Confederacy.

And now he had just lost the one keepsake linking him to his past. Ah, maybe it was just as well. To use Charlie's words, Gabriel had won fair and square. Surely

it was worth the length of steel that had been given
to him.

"Good luck, Cooper," he said as Gabriel diminished
in the distance. "May your courage stand you well . . .
and may the blood that sprays your face *never* be your
own."

5

DONALDSONVILLE, LOUISIANA 1865

G abriel walked from Greensboro through Winston-Salem, turning south and crossing the Blue Ridge Mountains. He travelled eastward along the Tennessee/Mississippi border to Memphis, where he then picked up the Mississippi. Bolivar and Tallula; Vicksburg and Natchez. He crossed the ankle bend of Louisiana, heading for Donaldsonville.

Gabriel hunted, foraged, and slept under the stars. Widowed women would take him in for a few days. He would mend their fences, patch their walls, or help them till their fields. Many wanted him to stay on and mend their hearts. Gabriel would oblige temporarily, but it was New Orleans that he had settled his future upon.

Donaldsonville sat on the Mississippi River between Baton Rouge and New Orleans. An unfortunate location in wartime, it had been caught in the crossfire between the Partisan Rangers and Union Navy gunboats. Its plantations and buildings had been torched, as had all places of habitation nine miles north and six miles south of the town.

Gabriel entered Donaldsonville, walking into what should have been a general store.

One of the men there asked, "Y'all need somethin'?"

"The McRae Farm."

"Y'all's gone too far. Double back 'bout three miles then head east. Go 'bout a mile or so till ya come to the first set o' fields, or what's left o'them. Follow 'em on back 'til ya gets to the farmhouse. Cain't say fer sure it's still standin'."

"Thanks."

Gabriel reached the McRae fields in late afternoon. The man at the general store was right about the fields being gone. He followed a dirt road rutted from heavy artillery and horses' hooves. As he approached a large, dilapidated clapboard house, a door creaked open and a double-barreled shotgun poked through, pointed at him.

"What y'all want?" a voice called from the inside.

"I knew Eli McRae," he called back.

"So?"

"I was with him in the war."

"He warn't in the war."

"Well, no, not at first he wasn't. Was in prison with me. Then the army came an' released some of us pris'ners so's we's could fight in the war. An' Eli was a'fightin' next to me."

A slip of an old white woman emerged, still aiming the shotgun. "An' so?"

"Well, ma'am, I'm a'comin' to pay my respects."

"What d'ya mean, respects?"

"Are y'all his mama, ma'am?"

"I am. What d'ya mean, respects?" She did not lower the gun.

"Well, ma'am, I fought next to him an' he was a good soldier, but, ma'am, I'm sorry to say that he was kilt a while back. An' I'm a'comin' to pay my respects to his family. He was a fine soldier, Mrs. McRae, one of the best an' bravest I ever saw."

The old woman lowered the shotgun. Her voice wavered, "Why don't ya come in?"

Gabriel stepped up onto the porch and into the house. An old man sat in a cane rocking chair, an overcoat covering his legs despite the hot, sticky weather. His sallow face resembled Eli's.

"Fella's come with news of Eli, Pa," said the woman. She turned to Gabriel. "Y'all tell him. I cain't."

Eli's father bowed his head when he heard Gabriel's news.

The old woman sighed. "Where's he buried?"

"Just outside Olustee, Florida."

"Y'all say he died a brave man?"

"Yes, ma'am."

"Be right nice if ya stayed fer supper. We don't have much, but we're willin' t' share."

"Thank ya, ma'am, I'd be happy to."

"Well, sit yerself down by Pa here, an' I'll put some food on the table."

Gabriel sat quietly with the old man as the old woman prepared dinner.

Finally, she said, "Come on to the table. I killed me a rabbit this mornin' so ya get some roasted meat with yer corn. Got a little corn coffee, too."

"Thank ya kindly, ma'am."

They ate in silence. Afterward, the old woman put the old man to bed. She joined Gabriel who was sitting on the porch steps.

She looked up at the stars. "We got us four sons an' Eli was our youngest. The other three were kilt early on, and we was hopin' that Eli, bein' in prison an' all, would get hisself home to us safe." She brushed a tear off her parched, withered cheek. "I knowed it was a selfish thing fer me ta want him ta stay outta this war. But I'm a mother, ain't I? Ain't it only natural that I'm loyal ta my family first before I'm loyal ta the Cause?

"He was our last hope. But now I see that God didn't see fit to spare none of our children. I guess He wanted 'em all to Hisself."

"I don't think God had nothin' to do with this, ma'am."

"God has everythin' to do with everythin'. Ya gotta a place to stay?"

"No, ma'am."

"You're welcome to stay the night, comin' out here an' all. Ya can sleep in the boys' room. The wind whistles through 'cause we got lots of work to do on this here house. I was waitin' fer Eli to come home an' help us." She stood up then and walked into the house, leaving Gabriel alone to digest her pain.

AFTER THE OLD COUPLE HAD LOST THEIR CROPS TO General Butler's fires, they could only plant some corn and vegetables near the house. Their barn and smokehouse had been razed and all the livestock taken. The house had been spared because the commanding officer had taken pity on them for their old age.

Gabriel stayed with the couple for several weeks. He hunted and fished for them, building a small smokehouse so that they could hang their meats and have something to eat in the winter. He chopped wood, repaired the house, and slowly the couple came to look at him as a son, even if they knew they would not have him forever.

Gabriel knew it was time to leave when Betsy began to pressure him to go to church with them.

She had been disappointed when Gabriel told her he was going to travel to New Orleans. "It's a place of sin and infamy," she scoffed, her voice laden with judgement.

"That may be, but I gotta hankerin' to see what it's all about."

"Well, nothin' good never came from there. Don't be surprised if ya find yerself caught up in the work of the Devil himself."

"I'll take my chances."

"Ya know yer always welcome here, Gabriel."

"Thank ya kindly, ma'am, and thank ya fer makin' me feel like family."

"Well, don't forget us altogether. The worst is when ya think yer forgotten."

Gabriel picked up his knapsack with his sword hidden inside. He glanced at the old, shabby house one last time. Then he turned and headed for the river, never looking back again.

6

NEW ORLEANS 1865

Gabriel had just entered *Faubourg Sainte Marie*, having just left *Le Vieux Carre*, viewing an array of humanity like he had never seen before. Still, New Orleans was only a skeleton of its former splendor. Built by the French on a crescent-shaped stretch of levee in the early 1700s, it had been a bejeweled prima donna, reigning over trade and commerce upon the Mississippi. But since General Butler's occupation, New Orleans had been starved and vandalized, many of its occupants fleeing. Others had succumbed to malaria, smallpox, and other diseases of the back swamp, a cypress wetland that stretched from behind the city to Lake Pontchartrain.

He meandered down the street, paying no attention to anything in particular, when he saw her. She was sitting on the front steps of a general store whose display window had been shattered. She held her hand which was wrapped in a rag, and Gabriel could see the blood beginning to seep through the bandaging.

As he stared at this girl, Gabriel heard Betsy's voice: *a*

place of sin and infamy . . . This girl did not look like she came from such iniquity.

With a mass of dark brown hair pulled back and captured in a snood, she sat there as if she were made of porcelain. Her cheeks were ruddy in her round alabaster face and her cherubic, pouting lips were set in a determined line. But it was her eyes that took his breath away. Blue with green flecks, they were the color of what men drowned in. Ringed by long, dark eyelashes, those raging eyes did not flutter coquettishly, but stared back at him with a strange, piercing gaze.

"We are closed for business today," she said.

"I reckoned that."

"You don't look like a carpetbagger."

"Do I sound like a carpetbagger to y'all?"

"*Touche, Monsieur*! Is there something I can help you with?" Her voice had an upturned curl to it.

"I'm a' lookin' fer work."

"There is no money to pay you."

"I can work fer a meal an' a place to stay."

"I don't suppose you could wield a bullwhip, could you? What we really need is someone to guard this place at night."

"I could do that, ma'am."

"Snap a whip?"

"Yes, ma'am, I have more experience with that than y'all can imagine."

"Were you an overseer?"

"No, ma'am."

"Good. Overseers are despicable."

"Do you always offer such opinions on a first meetin'?"

The young woman ignored his question. "Well, *Monsieur*, I would like to be the one to hire you, but you must speak to my father. He makes all the important decisions in our family." Her sarcasm was palpable. She continued, "Perhaps you can help me set the store straight. There are some things I just can't lift."

She rose, and he followed her, noticing the soft curvature to her figure. "Come see this mess. I don't even know where to begin."

"Well, y'all can start by findin' a better bandage fer yer finger."

As the young woman hesitated, Gabriel asked, "May I?" He reached for her hand, but she drew back. He stopped. "I meant no disrespect. It's just that I saw enough wounds in the war an' thought—"

"I'm aware of what you thought, but I can take care of myself, thank you."

"I ain't properly introduced myself. Name's Gabriel Cooper."

"Simone Livingston."

"It's my pleasure, ma'am." Then, he turned from her and lifted a small barrel. "Where would you like me to put this?"

Simone worked alongside Gabriel until her father appeared. His skin was so white as to appear spectral, and his breath was labored. His eyes settled on Gabriel with the same gaze as his daughter's.

Simone spoke softly, "Papa, meet Mr. Gabriel Cooper. Says he'll work for room and board. He also said he's good with a bullwhip."

"So, you hired him without asking me first?" The accent was British.

"No. I let him help me with some of the heavier things."

Simone's father appraised Gabriel. "You're looking for a job, are you?"

"Yes, sir, I am."

"You live in these parts, do you?"

"No, sir. I'm from Florida. Not too far from Alabama."

"Mobile?"

"I reckon a fer piece from Mobile."

"You talk like a cracker."

"Reckon I am a cracker, sir."

"But you can use a bullwhip?"

"Yes, sir."

"You know we have no money to pay you."

"That is what your daughter said."

"Did she tell you anything else?"

"Well, yes, sir, she was kind enough ta say that y'all might be able to give me room an' board as payment."

"Did my daughter extend you the courtesy of supper as well?"

Gabriel watched the hatred pass over Simone's face as her father turned his back upon her.

"No, sir, I cain't say she did."

"Well, that's not surprising since my daughter always forgets her place. She should've invited you to supper and left the talk of hiring to me. Would you care to join us? We can talk about your employment then."

"It would be right nice to join y'all fer supper,"

"We live at 82 Gironde Street, and we eat at six p.m."

"Mr. Livingston, may I suggest something?"

"Yes?"

"If it's no difference to you, I'd like to stay here until such time as I leave fer yer home an' make sure no one tries any more thievin'. I also thought maybe I could board up this here front window. I noticed some old wood y'all had in the back storeroom that might work right nice fer the job."

Mr. Livingston smiled coolly. "Such an eager young man, but by all means, if you think it will help to keep the hooligans and carpetbaggers out."

He left and Simone followed. She flashed one last look at Gabriel, who felt as if a bolt of electricity had shot through him. There was something churning behind those eyes. How long would it take before he found out what it was?

IT WAS A SHORT WALK TO THE SMALL, TWO-STORY STUCCO that Simone and her father called home. With only a couple of steps leading to the front door, it was uncharacteristic of the Spanish architecture that left its mark on the nearby *Vieux Carre*. Gabriel noticed the tall side gate, blocking the view into the back. The front windows were shuttered and unwelcoming.

So, this is where she lives . . . He had thought about her all afternoon.

Simone answered his knock on the front door. "Welcome."

Gabriel stepped inside, looking around. Functional would be a charitable term for the décor. The table and chairs in the dining room were stark, and the walls, covered in a bland damask, were bare except for a simple wooden cross.

"May I take your coat?" Simone asked. "My father is in the parlor. Supper will be served soon."

She seemed so wooden, so mechanical; was this the same spirited girl he had met this afternoon?

The parlor was also functional with a couple of stiff-backed chairs that sat around a small table adorned with nothing but the Holy Bible and a kerosene lamp.

Mr. Livingston stood up shakily and extended his hand. "Mr. Cooper, welcome to our humble home."

As they both sat down, it dawned on Gabriel that the only other place less welcoming than this had been the lean-tos from his chain gang days. "Thank you for havin' me."

Mr. Livingston shrugged. "Taste the food first, and then see if you want to thank me. My daughter is not always consistent in her culinary accomplishments." He switched the topic. "Are you a God-fearing man, Mr. Cooper?"

"I reckon so, sir."

"Are you a Christian?"

"Yes, sir, I was raised a Christian."

"There's a difference between being a Christian and being raised a Christian. Being raised a Christian you are a child and have no choice. But to *be* a Christian well, that's a choice you have to make for yourself. You choose to know Jesus Christ as your Lord and Savior, and to abide by His rules."

Well, if he wanted a Christian, he'd get a Christian…

"Sir, I'm an honest man, so's I'm gonna to tell ya the truth. I ain't been to church in a long time, but that don't mean that when I was on them battlefields I didn't pray to Almighty God fer deliverance an' it don't mean that I didn't thank Him an' His Son Jesus fer savin' my sorry soul. I believe it was nothin' short of a miracle that I was able to fight fer the Cause an' it's nothin' short of a miracle that I'm a'sittin afore y'all here today."

Mr. Livingston nodded. "I appreciate your honesty, Mr. Cooper. I am a sick man who is short of breath, and I have chest pains occasionally. I need more than a night guard. I need someone to help me at the store in the daytime. Then at night, I need for you to sleep in the store." He paused for breath. "Are you a light sleeper?"

I'll be a peg-legged pirate if ya want me to be. "Yes, sir, I am."

"Can you crack a whip well enough to keep desperate thieves at bay?"

Gabriel smiled. "I'm a tellin' ya the truth, sir, when I say I know how to make a man think twice afore he crosses me."

Mr. Livingston wheezed. "You won't be encountering soldiers in combat, Mr. Cooper, merely hungry people. That kind of force won't be necessary here."

"All's I'm a sayin' is y'all can rest easy at night if I'm in there."

"I have no money to pay you, but I can offer you modest room and board. You can make part of the back storeroom your place to live and you can have meals at the house. I will keep a tab of wages as I'm sure somehow the Lord will provide. Just don't expect anything soon.

"The store opens at nine and closes at five Monday through Saturday. You can have all day Sunday off. You stay on the premises *every night* beginning right after supper until the next morning, regardless of whether you've had the day off. It leaves you with no real time to go out in the evening, but then again, a man is tempted to keep company with thieves and drunkards if he allows himself to be out in the night hours." Mr. Livingston held out his hand. "You can start working tonight."

Gabriel shook the older man's hand. "Thank you, sir."

Just then the parlor door opened and Simone stood in the doorway. "Supper is ready."

Mr. Livingston gestured toward Gabriel. "We have a new handyman and night guard, Simone."

Simone looked at Gabriel and, in her eyes, he saw the blue-green depths of an angry sea.

"Congratulations, Mr. Cooper. Welcome to our happy family."

❧ 7 ☙

NEW ORLEANS 1865

Gabriel worked hard at his new life. Peter Livingston was humorless and controlling, but he put up with it to gain his trust.

Gaining his daughter's trust was another story. Pleasant enough, Simone held Gabriel at arm's length. Occasionally, Gabriel would catch her staring into space with a sad expression, and he often wondered at the cause.

He decided to stop by the house one day to see if he could borrow a Bible. It was early afternoon and he decided to go around the back. What he saw there took him by surprise.

There was a porch canopied by honeysuckle while dormant lilac bushes caressed the railings and tickled the porch steps. A magnolia tree sat to the side, flanked by camellia bushes, blooms like little ruffled petticoats. Gayfeather promised a midsummer riot of pink and purple, and climbing roses clung to trellises in cascades of yellow and white.

He had discovered how the lovely Miss Livingston spent her time.

The kitchen door was ajar and he could see Simone inside, kneading dough. She appeared to be lost in thought.

Gabriel called out to her, "Hello . . ."

Simone whirled around. "*Mon Dieu!* You scared me."

"I'm sorry." Gabriel couldn't take his eyes off her.

"Is there something you need, *Monsieur*?"

"Well, yes, ma'am. I was a-wonderin' if'n y'all had a spare Bible around."

"Are you joking?"

"No, ma'am, I'm not. Is something wrong with that?"

"Oh no, of course not. Your question surprised me, that's all. Let me clean my hands, and I'll give you my copy."

"Don't look the Bible-readin' type, do I?"

Simone blushed. "I meant nothing by that. I'll give you my copy."

"The evenin' gets long, and I need somethin' ta pass the time."

She stopped and stared. "This is for your reading pleasure only?"

"I'd read somethin' else if there's was anythin' else ta be had."

"What do you like to read?"

Now it was Gabriel's turn to blush. He looked down, turning his hat in his hands. "Ta tell ya the truth, Miss Livingston, I only jest learned to read durin' the war. I'm still a-practicin'."

The ice in Simone seemed to melt a little. "Why don't

you come in, Mr. Cooper and sit down? I'll be right back."

She came back to the kitchen holding a translation of Voltaire's *Candide*. She handed it to him.

"It's a small volume, but very witty. This was my mother's copy." She hesitated. "But I will trust you with it."

Gabriel took the book, "I'm honored." He paused. "I didn't know y'all had books in here."

"I have books. I keep them hidden." She caught herself before she said any more.

Gabriel understood. "We all have secrets."

"He really would not approve if he knew."

"He won't know." Gabriel stood up. "Thank ya kindly, Miss Livingston. I'll take good care of this and get it back to ya right quick."

"Good afternoon, *Monsieur*."

As soon as he left, Simone rushed to the front window. Peeking through the shutter's slats she watched him cross the street. Her insides were churning. Without realizing, Gabriel had reached out and touched the person she was, instead of the person she always pretended to be. And that was terrifying.

GABRIEL RETURNED *CANDIDE* A FEW DAYS LATER. AS HE came around the back, Simone saw him and Gabriel thought he saw her smile.

He ascended the back steps, taking off his cap. "I brought your book back."

"Would you like to come in for a moment?"

Gabriel obliged, sitting down at the table where she was peeling vegetables.

"Would you like a glass of water?" she asked.

"Yes, ma'am, I would."

She poured him a glass from a pitcher on the sideboard. Sitting down opposite him, she did not resume her chore, but sat and watched him. Gabriel noticed her eyes were calm.

"That was a right funny book," he said.

"What did you find so funny?"

"I never heard 'bout adventures such as these fellers had. An awful lot of runnin' in circles and it got me laughin' at some o' their troubles. But after all that runnin' round, all them fellas jest wanted ta sit an' argue if their troubles were fer the best." He chuckled. "Sounded like a fool notion t' me."

"Sometimes it helps to feel that your suffering is worth something."

"Who's got time after a hard day's work fer such notions?"

"Don't you ever wonder if all you've gone through will amount to some good?"

"Ain't no use thinkin' on it."

"Well, they do come to that conclusion at the end of the book, you know."

"I'd a left that fool notion a long time afore they did, afore I'd gotten myself into as much trouble as that poor cuss did."

"Perhaps you would have stayed in Eldorado."

Gabriel stared out the window with a faraway look. "Sounds like that fella, Candide, had business ta finish."

"But why bother? He was in a wonderful place. He could've stayed there his whole life and been happy."

"Not if'n he had business that was eatin' at him."

"Well, I always thought it so silly that Candide did not stay in Eldorado."

"He wanted to brag about his riches and ta rescue his true love."

"I believe the first part of your statement more than the second part."

"Are ya sayin', Ms. Livingston, that y'all don't believe in true love?"

"Yes, I suppose I am."

"Well, well . . ."

"*Alors,* you did not expect that answer, did you?"

"No ma'am, cain't say as I did. Most of the ladies I've met have themselves set on findin' true love."

"Well, *Monsieur Cooper,* I'm not most ladies. And," she leaned forward, "are you going to tell me that you'd leave paradise to find a woman who may not even be able to be rescued? Just because you thought you loved her?"

Gabriel leaned in and whispered, "It depends on the woman, Miss Livingston."

They stared into each other's eyes for a moment and then Gabriel stood up. "I best be gettin' back. I thank ya kindly again for the book."

After he left, Simone sat and pondered what he'd said. *It depends on the woman.* She thought back to a time when she thought she was going to be rescued. She had been young and in love, but she hadn't been that woman. It was as simple and as brutal as that.

Simone picked up her knife and began to peel vegetables once more.

~

SHE CONTINUED TO LEND GABRIEL BOOKS. THE MONTHS passed as they discussed Homer, Hawthorne, and Kipling. Simone noticed Gabriel's language was changing and his vocabulary was increasing with appropriate grammar and pronunciations. She found herself looking forward to their times together, to seeing his boyish grin when he gently teased her, or the way he grew so animated when sharing what he had learned from his reading.

Gabriel came by one day to find Simone sitting under the magnolia tree.

"You sure make a lovely garden," he commented as he looked at the darkening clouds overhead. She seemed somber as he sat down on the garden bench beside her.

"Thank you. I enjoy gardening."

"You don't enjoy much else, do you?"

"No."

"This warn't—wasn't—the life you wanted, was it?"

"No."

"But the flowers make you happy."

A horrifying tear had seeped out of Simone's eye. Before she could move, Gabriel lifted his hand and gently wiped it away. Color crept up her neck and flushed her face.

"I'm sorry if I made you uncomfortable," Gabriel apologized.

"It's all right. It's only that . . . well, these were the flowers my mother loved. My father hates that I tend this garden, but he is too sick to stop me, so I just do as I please with it."

"Why would he hate such a thing?"

"Because my father hates me, can't you tell?"

"Ain't —pardon me—*isn't* hate a strong word?"

Simone's eyes were the color of the benthic deep. "I'm dirt to him." She looked away. "And now I suppose you think I'm crazy."

"I would never think that."

Thunder cracked overhead as heavy raindrops began to fall.

Gabriel and Simone hurried inside where Simone busied herself kindling the fire. "Would you like some tea? It's made from the beebalm. You know we can't afford real tea."

"Whatever you have I'm grateful for."

"Don't be so sure of that."

"I am sure of that, but I have a question."

"You want to know why I said what I did."

"You are one smart little lady."

Simone sat down at the table. "It might take a while."

"Well, I got time. There wasn't much doin' at the store when I left."

"Doing. there wasn't much *doing* at the store when you left."

"Now you're stalling."

"Perhaps. Listen well, then, for I will only tell it once and I don't want any questions when I'm done."

"It's a deal." And Gabriel sat back to hear her story.

SIMONE'S MOTHER WAS JOSEPHINE DAUPHINE CHEVALIER. Parisian and much younger than her husband, Josephine was delighted when she discovered she was pregnant. Peter had wanted a son, but Josephine could not have been happier when a daughter arrived.

Introduced into Creole Society by the great Monsieur Valcour Aime, Josephine and Simone were invited to balls and parties. Working to start his business, Peter hardly ever accompanied them, but this was forgiven amongst Josephine's newfound friends.

Simi, as she was affectionately called, was the center of Josephine's life. She went to day school at *L'Acadamie des Jeune Filles Catholique* near their home in *Le Vieux Carre.*

Instead of teaching the drudgework of women, Josephine tutored Simone in the classics. They had a Black freedwoman, Delcine, who helped with housework and cooking. *Maman* found slavery to be barbaric, so she insisted on paid help only.

According to *maman*, marrying well and having an education were not mutually exclusive, so Simi was to achieve both. That is, until the unthinkable happened.

Simone had just turned eleven when Josephine again became pregnant. It was a difficult pregnancy, but the labor and delivery killed Josephine, along with the baby she was giving birth to. It had been a boy.

Peter was devastated. He could not find consolation in anything, least of all his daughter. After her mother's death, Peter withdrew Simone from the girls' academy, fired Delcine, and moved to the *Faubourg Sainte Marie.* Josephine's friends came to call, but they were turned away and soon the calling cards began to dwindle. Peter was not interested in Creole traditions. The memories were too much, Simone heard him say.

Simone was lonely and terrified of her new life.

When they moved, she took clippings of her mother's flowers to plant at the new house. Those were the only living connections she had as all the friends and acquaintances had been banished. Even her nickname, *Simi,* was dropped.

Peter, to teach Simone the chores of womanhood, hired the stern Mrs. Patrick. A white, no-nonsense Revivalist, she carried her message of Jesus's Salvation into their home and to the ears of Peter Livingston.

Peter embraced Revivalism. At these meetings, he met a girl named Cora, a timid thing of sixteen years. She and Simone could have been sisters rather than prospective stepmother and stepdaughter.

When Peter married Cora right after her seventeenth birthday, Simone was no closer to his bride than when he first brought her home to Sunday dinner. Disjointed and lost, she rejected Cora.

To ease the tension in his home, Peter decided to send Simone away to live with her Uncle Everett and Aunt Eliza.

Simone had been distraught. "But why, *Papa,*" she cried. "Why?"

"Cora is the lady of the house now. She is my wife."

"She may be your wife, but she is nothing to me!"

Peter's eyes never left hers. Her eyes were his eyes, and they mirrored each other's hostility.

"Pack your bags, Simone. We leave tomorrow."

"I'm in the way, aren't I, *Papa?*"

"Simone, I am warning you."

Overflowing with resentment, she blurted, "Tell me, *Papa,* what have I ever done to you?"

Peter clenched his teeth. "Simone, if you continue with this—"

But there was no going back. "What is it, *Papa*? What was the great sin that I committed for you to despise me so except that I was born a girl?"

THERE WAS NO RAILROAD TO TAKE HER OUT TO Calcasieu Parish on the Texas-Louisiana border. Travel was by horse and then flatboat. It was a backwater place, and Peter had to pay Everett to come out and meet them halfway. Simone learned that he had paid her uncle seventy-five dollars to take her in. She had gone for far less than the price of a cheap slave.

Simone stood by as her father loaded the rented wagon with her trunks of clothing and shoes. Cora approached her. "I'm sure you'll have a lovely time."

Simone bent her head, sweating under her summer bonnet. She didn't want this woman-child to speak to her.

Cora tried again. "I went to a farm once. My great uncle's. I loved the cows . . . and the horses . . . " She realized that Simone was listening.

Simone said softly. "I like animals."

Encouraged, Cora continued. "I watched the cows being milked, once. *Squirt, squirt, squirt,* into those old buckets. It was the funniest sight to me. And all them cows, mooin' and complainin', as if the nigras weren't goin' fast enough."

"What do they sound like?"

"The cows? Well, kind of . . . low-voiced and maybe a bit growly . . ."

"Like how?"

"Well . . ."

"How do they sound?"

"Oh, my word," said Cora, but this was the closest Simone had ever let her get, so she tried to mimic the lowing of a cow.

Simone broke into giggles. Peter slammed the back of the wagon shut and turned to them.

Cora, thrilled to have broken the ice with Simone, squeezed Simone's hand.

"I hope you have a wonderful time, Simone," she said breathlessly, and, then with a glance at her husband, she continued, "When you get back, we can all be a happy family. You, me, your daddy . . . and the new baby that's on the way."

First confusion and then comprehension, and finally, betrayal upon betrayal. Simone's smile slid away, her cold stare saying what she could not. Cora put her hand to her mouth, trying to re-capture the words that had destroyed the final chance for a friendship.

Peter spoke. "It's time we get on the road." He turned to his wife and kissed her goodbye. "I'll be back soon."

Tears welled up in Cora's eyes. "I'll miss you."

Simone stood watching this exchange of affection. How she hated them both!

As she climbed onto the wagon's seat, she did not take her gaze off Cora. As they pulled away, she continued to stare. And she knew she would never live with Cora or her father again.

~

Eliza Hampstead Livingston was a tall, sparse woman whose length of limb was matched only by the length of her facial features. She and her husband, Everett, had two sons and owned a small farm. They had one slave, a woman whom her husband would never let go of, no matter how much Eliza begged him.

Eliza had always wanted a daughter of her own, for she longed for that feminine connection. So, when her brother-in-law had written, asking if young Simone could come and live with them, she jumped at the chance. After all, thirteen years old was still young enough to make a daughter out of her.

All these things ran through Eliza's mind as she stood at the trading post on the bend of the Sabine River. Her two sons stood there as well, though not nearly as eagerly as their mother. Sammy was fourteen and Everett Jr. was fifteen, and both were willful, independent teenagers. Their father, on the other hand, kept all musings to himself even as he kept most of his actions to himself. His wife was aware of only his most obvious behaviors, knowing when he planted and when he harvested, when he came in for meals, and when he crept into bed at night.

Eliza detected the outline of the flatboat down the waterway, bringing not only supplies for the trading post, but also her husband and niece.

As the boat docked, she spotted who she presumed to be her niece. She watched Simone come down the short gangplank, her wide-eyed stare at its fullest.

Eliza approached the lost-looking girl. "Simone?"

Simone looked at her, unblinking, but said nothing.

"Is your name Simone, honey?"

Simone nodded as Eliza began to chafe under the child's stare. She smiled to break the tension. "I'm your Aunt Eliza. Sugar, you must be so, so tired and hungry! Have you eaten?"

Simone looked beyond Eliza to see her cousins approaching. Eliza turned and acknowledged them. "Simone, these here are your cousins, Everett, Jr., and Samuel. We call him Sammy."

Everett and the boys loaded her trunks onto the buckboard as Eliza continued to fuss over Simone. She insisted that she sit in the front between her and Everett. As Simone sweltered in her travel outfit, Eliza kept a running monologue all the way home. Simone tried to listen as Eliza pointed out the berry bushes, commenting on how she could pick berries for fresh homemade cobbler.

"You've probably never done that, bein' in the city an' all," she rambled. She pointed out the small log church that they attended. "There ain't no school in these parts, but that don't matter for y'all, havin' been to such a fancy school in the city since ya was a little thing. I s'pose ya know everything there is 'bout such book-learnin' subjects. But church, well, that's where a young lady such as yerrself is goin' to make a life's worth of friends, so ya mustn't ever miss church . . ."

On and on she went until they turned up a dirt road that would lead them to home.

To their right were cotton fields and to their left, peach orchards yielding the last of their late summer fruit. Eliza proudly told Simone that it was all Livingston land, and how she consistently made award-winning peach pies. She leaned in conspiratorially.

"I'll show y'all how to make the best pie in all of Louisiana and Texas combined. It's been my secret recipe, but I'll share it with y'all." She squeezed Simone's hand.

Suddenly, the conversation ended, followed by a silence as cool as the breeze Simone yearned for. And it was then that Simone saw her.

She was standing by the roadside, balancing a bucket of peaches on her hip. Dark-skinned and doe-eyed, she stood with a certain jauntiness that could almost be taken for defiance.

Eliza hissed at her as they drew near, "You're just now gatherin' the peaches?"

"I been in the kitchen, Miss 'Liza, an' roastin' the chickens an' in the washhouse. This here been the only time I been able ta gets out." Her voice was strong and clear, sharper than Simone would have expected.

"I told you I wanted fresh peach pie for dessert."

"Miss 'Liza, y'all will have fresh peach pie. By the time meal's cooked an' served, the peach pie will be ready."

"I want dinner served early. This child is tired and hungry and doesn't need to hear your excuses."

The slave's gaze shifted to Simone. Simone looked back at her with her disarming feline stare. Their eyes locked briefly, and then the slave turned back to Eliza. "I'll gets yo peach pie ready, Miss 'Liza." She turned and began to walk up the road, her hips swaying languidly under her flimsy skirt.

Simone noticed that Eliza was staring at her husband as his eyes were locked on those slow, swaying hips.

Eliza clucked her tongue, breaking her husband's reverie. He flapped the reins and the horses moved faster. As they passed the slave, Eliza said to her husband, "That girl needs a whippin'."

"She doesn't need any whipping," Everett replied, keeping his eyes on the road. His clipped British accent was just like Simone's father's.

"She's a smart-mouthed nigra and needs to know her place."

"You always think she's a smart-mouthed Negro, Eliza, no matter what the girl does you think she's a smart-mouthed Negro."

"Uppity. Someone needs to take that outta her. I suppose it'll have to be me."

They pulled up to the pine log farmhouse and Everett turned to her. "You will leave her alone, do you hear me?" His eyes bored through his wife.

"Yer always protectin' her. Will there never be an end to my humiliation?"

Everett got down off the wagon and the boys, who had been having a spitting contest off the back, jumped out. Everett came around to Eliza's side to help her and Simone down.

Simone turned to see the slave woman come up the road. Eliza had shooed her boys inside, following them into the house.

Simone and Everett watched the woman enter the front courtyard and head for the back of the house. Everett broke into her thoughts.

"You better go on in, Missie. Stop staring at the help."

Embarrassed, Simone hurried into the house. Whatever shortcomings Eliza had it was not in the way of housekeeping. Simone took in the white, tatted lace curtains and buttercup chintz-covered chairs. She wanted to touch the paisley papered walls.

All that charm dissipated as Simone listened to Eliza berate the slave woman in the kitchen. She busied herself looking at family daguerreotypes. There was one in particular: a group of people at the base of a large magnolia tree, one of the couples sitting on a low branch. She recognized her Aunt Eliza, although she didn't look as horsey as she did now. And that was Uncle Everett next to her and then . . . she gasped. There was her father, *smiling* and sitting next to him was her mother. She looked as Simone wished to remember her, before her second, nauseating pregnancy, before she took the small, premature boy and Simone's happy childhood with her into eternity.

Tears welled up in Simone's eyes. She did not hear Eliza come up behind her. "Come with me, honey. I'll show y'all your room."

Simone ascended a wide staircase, and walked down a long hallway, wallpapered in floral crimson. A high window at the end cast dark, bloodstained shadows on the wall.

Eliza opened the last door at the end. "Here we are." She strode across the room and opened a window. Then she gestured toward a small featherbed. "This was mine when I was a little girl. Now it's yours."

Simone said nothing, but Eliza felt the weight of her

gaze. "I know it's been a long day, honey. How 'bout I get you some water to freshen yourself with and y'all take a little rest until supper?"

After she was gone, Simone gazed out the window. Everett Jr. and Sammy were helping their father water down the horses. She looked at some chickens scratching the dirt in the hen yard. Was the slave woman around?

There was a soft knock on the door and there she was. "Mind if'n I come in, young Mistress?"

Simone watched her as she brought in the pitcher with a bowl and towels. Her back still turned, she asked, "Do ya allus stare at every folk that pass yo way?"

"What's your name?"

"Lucinda," she replied. Then she left.

Lucinda, Latin for light.

Simone now tore off her bonnet, unbuttoned her blouse, and unlaced her shoes. She poured some of the cool water into the bowl, splashing it onto her face, rubbing it over her neck and down her non-existent cleavage.

She knew she couldn't rest. She peeked out her door, listening. Hearing nothing, she crept down the hall, peering into the rooms as she went. There was her cousins' room, with two twin beds and riding tack on the walls above them. Another room had bolts of calico cloth with an abundance of notions strewn on a central table.

The next door was closed. She turned the knob slowly and looked in.

A double featherbed with a pine headboard sat against one wall. A full-length mirror stood in one corner, a chair in the other with a pair of men's trousers draped over it.

She'd never stood before a full-length mirror. Simone crossed the room, holding her breath. She exhaled when she heard Eliza and Lucinda outside.

What was she expecting to see when she turned and faced herself? Something better, surely, than the flat, curveless image before her. The image stared back at her and she noticed the eyes. God forbid, they were her father's eyes. Ugh!

Disappointed, Simone slipped out of the bedroom. She wanted to go downstairs and see her mother again.

She crept down to the first floor. She could hear Lucinda in the kitchen. She approached the wall of daguerreotypes, but the picture had been removed. Defeated, Simone returned upstairs. She went to her bedroom and lay down on the bed.

Suppertime came. Simone sat at the table, staring at her food. Talk centered around a cow with an infected udder.

Finally, Sammy addressed her. "How come you don't talk?"

"Sammy!" clucked Eliza. "Leave the child be."

"But she don't talk."

"Sammy, eat your dinner. Simone will speak to y'all when she's a mind to."

"Maybe she can't talk, maybe she can't understand us. Maybe she's a dummy!"

"Samuel!"

Sammy went back to eating, but as soon as his mother looked away, he kicked Simone under the table and mouthed the word "Dummy!" at her.

In a wan voice, she asked, "May I be excused?"

Eliza smiled. "Honey, you go on upstairs and rest, and I'll have Lucinda bring you some fresh peach pie."

Keeping her eyes down, Simone folded her napkin beside her plate and left the table. She heard Everett Jr. say, "See, she can talk, ya lunkhead!"

Simone sat on the edge of her bed watching the dusk slowly succumb to darkness.

She heard the door open, but only turned when she heard Lucinda's voice. "I know's da feelin', ta look into da darkness like it a blanket over ma achin' heart."

"What does your heart ache for?"

"I s'pose I'd want ta be back wif my mama."

"Me, too."

"Yo mama's wif God, chile. Y'all's got some livin' ta do afore's ya gets ta see her agin."

"Where's your mama?"

"Last I saw her she was in Alabama. Mebbe she wif God now, too. I sure hope so."

Simone understood. They were two unwilling transplants, misfits tied together by a thread of misfortune. "Is that where you were born? Alabama?"

"Don' rightly know. I's born on da beach somewheres 'tween Florida an' Alabama. Dat's what da odder granny slave told me afore she died."

"So you don't know where you're from?"

"'Spose not, chile, 'spose not."

"I don't want to be here."

Lucinda set down a plate of pie on the bureau. "I knows dat feelin', too. Eat da pie, chile. I bakes a heavn'ly pie, so don' set it ta waste."

"Thank you."

"Y'all's come down ta the kitchen tomorrow mornin'.

I'll give ya some o' my biscuits fresh from da oven an' milk fresh from da cows." Then she retreated, the darkness folding in behind her.

Simone took a bite of the pie. It was indeed heavenly. Outside, the moon rose farther into the night sky. Maybe things would get better; maybe she'd even like the farm. She had to admit she was curious about it. And she wanted to know what an infected udder was.

SIMONE AWOKE TO THE ROOSTER CROWING. SHE SAT UP and looked around, wondering where her clothes were. She had barely managed to open her trunks last night before exhaustion overtook her. Even the chamber pot that she had used was empty.

The door opened and Eliza entered. "Good morning!"

"Good morning. Where are all my clothes?"

"Oh, honey, I put them all away last night after y'all fell asleep. The room was so unkempt."

"What happened to the chamber pot?"

"What happened to it?"

"It was full. I was going to empty it this morning."

"Lucinda emptied it."

"But shouldn't I empty it?"

"That's what we have a nigra for." Eliza went to the armoire and pulled open the doors. "I was looking at your wardrobe last night and honey, y'all need some dresses that are more useful than these fancy city outfits. We'll have to get started right away. Thank goodness I thought ahead and ordered some sensible calico for y'all.

Let's see here," she pulled out a dress. "This pink cotton one will do for today."

Before Simone could say anything, Eliza turned to her. "I think it would be best, dear, if you tried to become part of the family. That would start by rising when we do." She laughed. "You're not in the city anymore. Out here in the country, we all get up *before* the rooster crows."

After she left, Simone swung out of bed and went to the armoire. She pulled out a blue dress instead. There was a soft knock on the door. She looked up as Lucinda stepped in, carrying water for her pitcher and bowl.

"Mornin', Miss Simone."

"Good morning."

Lucinda poured the water into the pitcher. Then she motioned to the dress, the collar and sleeves trimmed in English lace. "Dat's a pretty frock but it be too fancy fo mornin' chores."

"My aunt wants me to wear the pink one. But I'm wearing this one instead."

Lucinda clucked her tongue. "You best wears the pink one. Miss 'Liza want ever one to do as she say."

"I've been dressing myself for years. I want to wear the blue dress."

Lucinda shrugged. "I only be tellin' ya, that's all."

"Well, which one do you like?"

Lucinda inspected the clothing. "Da blue one."

"Then it's settled."

Lucinda raised her eyebrows. "I wants ta see der Missus' face when ya comes in wif somepin on different from what she say."

"Will she be mad?"

"She won't be smilin'."

"I'll be down soon."

"I's gots da feelin' dat we's gonna see some fiery times 'round here."

Lucinda made sure she was in the dining room when Simone entered. Everett and the boys were deep in a conversation about Louisiana and Mississippi seceding.

Eliza frowned. "Simone, was something wrong with the pink dress?"

"No." Simone took her seat and placed her napkin on her lap. She met Eliza's gaze. "I wanted to wear the blue one instead."

"I see," Eliza replied coolly. "Simone, the pink was perfectly suited for what we were going to do today." She looked up at Lucinda, who was pouring her coffee in a slow dribble.

"Do ya think y'all could do something other than dawdle in here?"

Lucinda filled the coffee cup, but as she turned away, Simone saw the tiniest of smiles.

Simone repeated, "I wanted to wear the blue dress."

Eliza's eyes narrowed to slits. "All right dear, this time we can let it go, but when I ask you to wear a particular dress, then y'all ought to wear it."

Simone looked at the food in front of her and for the first time in days, ate a full meal.

Simone could see Eliza was simmering, but she did not care. She hoped to get a moment alone with Lucinda, so they could share a laugh.

As TIME WENT BY, SIMONE REALIZED THAT HER EASY friendship with Lucinda stoked Eliza's temper.

One morning, as she bantered with Lucinda, Eliza pulled her aside. "Y'all might want to keep your distance from that Lucifer woman."

"But we were simply feeding the——"

"I don't care!" Eliza's fingers tightened around Simone's wrist, "Now listen to me well, missy, 'cause I ain't in the mood for repeatin' myself. That there's a n----
--er and a slave. Y'all ain't sisters, ya hear me? There's to be no chit-chattin', no gigglin' an' if I hear any more, well"—she put her face close to Simone's—"I'll take it outta Lucifer's hide over there. Everett or no Everett, that n-------er ain't gettin' a hold of my daughter, too. Now git yerself upstairs. Y'all need ta be fitted for some new clothes. No more of this fancy city finery!" She gave Simone a shove toward the house.

Her daughter? Simone looked back suddenly to see the triumphant look that Eliza shot Lucinda and how Lucinda's shoulders sagged as she fed the chickens.

Simone tried to show affection toward Eliza, but she could not put distance between herself and Lucinda. She sought her out as often as she could.

Eliza, however, continued to abuse Lucinda. She slapped and shoved her, and Simone even saw her dump a pail of pig slops on her.

It was the worst, however, when Everett called Lucinda to help in the fields. That was when Eliza really smoldered, and Lucinda retreated into herself.

Such was a day in early April, when the wild strawberries were ripe and Simone was rolling dough in the kitchen. They were going to make strawberry tarts for the church picnic.

Simone rolled the dough silently as Eliza moved about the kitchen, muttering. Finally, she burst out, "That Lucifer woman! She didn't pick enough berries!"

She snatched the rolling pin out of Simone's hands. "I could kill her!" she screamed.

Alarmed, Simone backed away. "Maybe I should go get some more."

Tears filled Eliza's eyes as she crumpled into a kitchen chair. "Yes, I suppose you should . . ."

Simone bolted out the door as Eliza began to sob. She didn't understand any of this. Lucinda obviously didn't want to go to the fields to help Everett. Simone noticed how she was always so quiet when she returned and avoided eye contact with everyone.

When she was far enough away, Simone took off her shoes and stockings. She could see the ridge of birch, ash, and acacia trees bordering the riverbank ahead.

She entered their shade and began looking for strawberries. Humming, she pulled the plump fruit from their stems and dropped them into the bucket.

The river, rushing toward the Gulf of Mexico, beckoned to her. Setting the pail down, she hitched up her skirts and waded in. The water frothed around her knees and she bent over to splash some on her face. Suddenly she detected movement, and what she saw made her scramble back into the undergrowth.

Lucinda stood upstream, undressing at the water's edge. Naked, she waded into the water.

Simone crouched, fascinated, as Lucinda immersed

herself. How could she get this far from the fields without someone coming after her?

Lucinda washed herself wearily, and Simone realized that she'd better get home. As she crept away, she wondered how Lucinda could get away for such fun. She'd have to ask her so it would be their secret to share from now on.

BUT LUCINDA DID MIND. SHE TURNED ON THE SHOCKED girl. "Ain't nobody ever tell ya dat it's bad, bad, *bad*! Ta peeps on odder folk in dar private moments?"

"I-I'm sorry, Lucinda, it just looked like such fun . . . I'd never tell anyone . . ."

"Y'all's best be mindin' yer own business!"

"Lucinda . . . I didn't mean to spy on you. It was such a hot day and I was happy to see you could get away to the river . . ."

"I tells ya, Miss Simone, it ain't what it looked lak, and ya best be mindin' yer own business!"

"I just didn't know how you managed to get away from my Uncle Everett, that's all."

"Der ain't no sech thing as gettin' away fer me!" Lucinda hissed. "Y'all's see somethin' an ya gets it in yer head dat I'm havin' a play time. Well, y'all's don' know nothin' an' ya best keep yer mouth shut about it! Ferget ya ever saw me dar at the river!"

"I'm sorry."

Simone stung from Lucinda's anger for several days. Finally, it was Lucinda who spoke, restoring her confidence in their relationship.

"Y'all's been mighty quiet," she said one day when Simone wandered into the barn where she was raking dung.

"I thought you hated me."

"Chile, that's a fool notion."

"Well, you were so mad at me for seeing you at the river."

"It ain't nice to peeps on odder folks, even if'n ya thinks it's in fun. I knows y'all meant no harm, but ya gots ta know dat my time at da river ain't a happy time."

"I told you, I was only looking for strawberries. And well, I wanted to jump in myself . . ."

"An' why din't ya?"

"I didn't think it would be proper . . ."

Lucinda looked up from her raking. "Proper stopped ya dis time, but Lawd knows it ain't gonna stop ya fer long."

"I was afraid you weren't my friend anymore."

"Ya got lots ta learn, chile. But y'all's keep yo heart as clean as it is t'day, an' I always be yo friend."

Simone heard the backdoor creak. "I'd better go. I've got a fitting for another new dress. Ugh!"

"Get da hay an' muck off yer shoes. Be a tongue-lashin' fer dat."

Simone scraped her shoes on the ground as she headed for the house. Eliza was in the sewing room, absorbed in another ugly calico creation.

Simone thought of Lucinda's rags and wondered if anyone found it shameful how she was dressed.

She knocked softly on the sewing room door and stepped inside. Her feelings had grown steadily colder for her aunt. She hated her cruelty, and then there was that awful notion that Eliza kept bringing up about Simone being "her new daughter."

"Get undressed to your petticoat." Eliza barely looked up from where she was stitching a seam. "The bodice is complete and today we fit the skirt."

Simone undressed. The calico was printed with clusters of tiny reddish-brown flowers on a creamy background. Simone hated all the dresses Eliza had made, but the woman never stopped. Perhaps she thought if she changed enough dresses, she would change Simone as well?

Eliza draped the skirt around her waist. She pulled it tight and added, "I should take in another half inch on each side, to account for the corset."

"Does the corset have to be so tight?"

"Why of course it does! Do you think a lady gets a tiny waist naturally? We are goin' to make your waist tiny *and* the envy of all the girls your age."

Yes, make me tiny, Aunt Eliza. Bind me so tight that I can't speak. Because if I do, you may not be so inclined to want me as a daughter!

After the fitting Simone hurried back to the barn, but Lucinda was gone. A sweet bay mare whinnied at her and Simone approached.

"I don't have any carrots for you," she said. The horse nuzzled her soft lips in Simone's hair, and she sadly laid her head on the mare's neck.

SIMONE LEARNED THE ROUTINES OF FARM LIFE. SHE

pickled vegetables and churned butter; she slopped pigs and milked cows alongside Lucinda.

Simone never did reconcile herself to Eliza, and her Uncle Everett remained an enigma, until one day when she discovered something that changed everything.

Simone never questioned Lucinda again about that afternoon by the river. So, when Eliza requested that she find Lucinda, she cringed inwardly, as she had last seen Lucinda head to the orchards with Uncle Everett.

It was a spring-scented, dappled afternoon. Simone went down the dirt road, jumping between the shadows of sunlight. As she entered the orchard, Simone craned her neck, looking up and down the rows of trees.

Suddenly she heard an odd, guttural sound and what she saw she'd never forget. Lucinda was on the ground with Everett on top of her, pushing between her thighs. His face was contorted in an expression of . . . of what? Lucinda, her skirt pushed up around her waist, lay motionless with her legs apart, staring at the branches above her. Sensing someone, she turned her head and rested her eyes on Simone, who could not stop staring.

Her uncle's thrusting came faster and faster until he yelped and then collapsed on top of Lucinda. Slowly, he followed Lucinda's gaze and Simone bounded off, finally stumbling back onto the dirt road. Now she knew why Lucinda went to the river . . .

She crossed the orchard, trying to make her feet pound harder and faster than her heart. She headed for the trees on the riverbank, plunging into their shrouded protection. She could never tell her Aunt Eliza what she had just seen, but Eliza knew, didn't she? That was why she hated Lucinda so! But it wasn't Lucinda's fault, was it?

She came to the river's edge, stripped off her shoes and stockings and let the water swirl about her ankles. She splashed water on her face, trying to collect herself.

She knew she had to return to the house, but she feared that no matter what she said, Eliza would know she was lying.

As she turned to go, she looked up and down the river one last time. And there, in the distance, she saw a figure disrobe and move toward the water. She disappeared into the trees and left Lucinda to her privacy.

When she got to the house, her uncle was already there. Eliza clucked merrily at Simone as she entered through the back door.

"Honey, looks like I sent you on a wild goose chase! Uncle Everett here sent Lucinda over to the Hansen's farm to borrow some pruning tools. You must have run all over the place!"

Simone managed a weak smile and slipped past them. She retreated to her bedroom, where she sat on the edge of her bed like she did the day she arrived, feeling even more miserable than she had back then.

After dinner, Simone went out to the stable. She found Lucinda there, feeding a few stolen carrots to the horses.

"What were you doing out there?" Simone's voice trembled.

Lucinda remained silent, continuing to feed the horses.

"It was evil, wasn't it?"

Finally, Lucinda turned to her, her voice low with melancholy. "Listen! You may be white like da sand I was born on, an' ah might be Black like da soil y'all plants in, but we bof"—she pointed a prophetic finger at her—"we bof be dirt undah da Mastah's feet."

And with that she swept past Simone, leaving her in the twilight's shadows.

The next morning, Eliza approached Simone, her eyes swollen from crying. "You have to go. I feel like I'm losing a daughter, but he said he never wanted a daughter. You have to go."

There was a schooner that had recently arrived and it was on this vessel that Simone would travel back to New Orleans, this time alone.

So, there she was once again, waiting to be shunted back to where she came from, her only sin being that she had witnessed a rape.

She had wanted to say goodbye to Lucinda, but Eliza made sure that was out of the question. Yet Simone would never forget her, and she knew she at least had control over that.

As her trunks were once again carried on board, Simone felt a satisfaction that they contained none of the new dresses that Eliza had made. Eliza had wanted her to take those with her as well, but Simone had refused.

"I hate them," she had said to the distraught woman as she packed everything else. This time her aunt stood by silently and let her do what she wanted.

Simone boarded the schooner and stood at the port

side staring down at Eliza. As the schooner pushed away, Simone found her voice and yelled, "I would have never been your daughter, never!"

The schooner pushed away into deeper water and Simone's voice rose to a scream. "And you'll never be my mother! Never, never. *Never*!"

She left her aunt standing there, stunned, as the current carried Simone back to a place she did not even know if she could call home.

IT SEEMED A SHORTER VOYAGE TO FRANKLIN THAN THE first time. The schooner docked and Simone, with the help of the captain, descended the gangplank. Her eyes scanned the crowd of dockworkers, sugar merchants, and slaves for her father. Finally, she spotted him; he looked exhausted and somehow defeated.

He watched her approach, saying nothing.

"Are you well, Papa?"

It was then that she learned, only six days prior, that Cora had gone into labor. She had hemorrhaged and died, much as her mother had done, and she, too, took the baby with her. And once again, it had been a boy.

SIMONE SAT BACK AND STARED AT GABRIEL. "EVERETT sent a refund to my father. Money changed hands not once but twice to get rid of me. Like I was a piece of human garbage."

"You are not garbage. I have known human garbage,

and you, Miss Livingston, are about as far from garbage as one can be."

Simone's smiled sadly. "Aren't you sweet, *Monsieur.* But you don't know everything about me."

"No, but I know nothing would change my opinion of you."

Simone stared at her dry, cracked hands. "He's not a well man and . . . I just wish he would go. How different things would be . . ."

Just then they heard the front door slam. Startled, Simone watched her father enter the kitchen, dripping wet.

He looked at them and then said to Gabriel, "You're fired."

"No, *Papa*!"

Peter turned. "You have nothing to say in this. You've invited him in, shamelessly, and once again tempted a man with your wiles. You've done your damage, and now he must go."

Gabriel stood up. "Please don't insult the lady."

"Lady? Is that what you think she is?" He looked at Simone. "Is that what you fooled him into thinking you are?"

Simone crossed the floor and in a froth of rage, slapped her father. "You are a pig."

"You are ungrateful, an insolent—"

But before Peter could finish, he bent over, clutching his chest. He slumped to the floor.

Simone stared, wide-eyed. "We must get the doctor!"

Gabriel knew it was too late. "He's gone."

"I did this," Simone breathed.

"No, he did it to himself."

"But I slapped him, I upset him, I—"

"You gave him what was coming to him. If you hadn't done something, I would have."

"Oh, good Lord."

"Miss Livingston, who should I call for?"

"Dr. Louis, *s'il vous plait*. He will most likely be at Charity Hospital."

"You'll be all right while I'm gone?"

Simone nodded. "Of course; oh, I hate for you to go out. The weather is frightful!"

Gabriel leaned over and kissed the top of Simone's head. She looked up, startled.

Gabriel was contrite. "My apologies, Miss Livingston. That was very forward of me."

"*Non*, don't apologize." She hesitated and then said, "And, *Monsieur*, you may call me Simone."

THE HOUSE BECAME A WHIRLWIND OF ACTIVITY. EVEN THE dreaded Mrs. Patrick offered her help. Simone would have refused, but she was repulsed at the prospect of washing her father's body, so she let Mrs. Patrick step in to make all the arrangements.

Simone insisted that the funeral be simple, a small procession to the tomb where Peter would be interred alongside her mother. While her mother had a lovely marble statue to mark her resting place, Simone had only a small iron cross erected to honor her father. There was barely enough money for the living in these times, let alone the dead.

"Keep us, O Lord, and help us to remember that it is

by your Divine Will that you Giveth and You Taketh Away . . ."

Simone stood in the Catholic section of Saint Louis Number 1 Cemetery, hidden beneath her black veil and delaine shawl. She stared at her mother's tomb, making a mental note to scrub the slate and pull out the weeds before All Saints' Day. Her thoughts wandered. She fingered the telegram still in her hands. It was a response from her Uncle Everett that they could not come to New Orleans for the funeral. As if she really cared.

"For thine is the Kingdom and the Power and the Glory forever! Amen!"

A flower was pressed into her hand by Mrs. Patrick. "Place the flower on his coffin. For your father, God bless his soul."

Simone looked at this woman who had been the cause of so much misery. "This is the last order you will ever give me, do you understand?"

Mrs. Patrick ignored her, handing Peter's Bible to Simone. "I know that's your grief talking. Take his Bible and read from it so it does your insolent spirit some good."

Simone took the few steps to the vault and peered at her father's coffin. She let the flower drop where she stood and instead, she opened the Bible and stuck the telegram in it. Then she pitched the holy book into the vault. It hit the casket with a thud.

Saying nothing and looking at no one, she turned and walked away.

Amongst gasps and whispers of, "She's lost herself to the grief," Gabriel watched her go. He knew this wasn't grief and he stood, the newcomer, feeling a familiarity with her that was stronger than anybody else who knew her far longer could lay claim to.

8

NEW ORLEANS 1866

October 18, 1866

D*EAR DAVIE,*
How are you? I told you I would write to you when I got settled and so here I am, in New Orleans. I got a job as a handyman for a nice lady here. I also watch the store at night because there are so many looters and thieves that there is always a danger the store will get broken into. Lots of freed slaves wander around here day and night, thinking they can take whatever they want because they feel equal to all white men now. Why, not too long ago, a freedman even tried to kidnap a young lady right off the street, claiming he was going to marry her because he was as good as a white man now!

Of course, you must have heard of the riot that occurred here in late July. There was to be a reconvened meeting of the state convention at the Mechanics' Institute here in the city. Fighting broke out and rioting spilled into the streets. Hundreds were killed and it reminded me of war time all over again.

It's hard to make a living here. There's no real money because the Confederate dollar is no good now and there's no real Union money to be had. I work for room and board and it will do for now. Besides, I like the company I keep.

As you can tell, I am keeping up with my reading and writing. The lady who owns the store helps me a lot with spelling and pronunciation. She also lends me good books to read and we often discuss them after supper. The reading also helps me pass the time at night.

How are things in Baltimore? Write to me as I am anxious to hear how you are doing.

Yours truly,
Gabriel Cooper

November 18, 1866

DEAR GABRIEL,

I'm back in school again, studying hard and trying to make amends for my absence during the war. My mother was very sore at me for running away and joining the army. She's had a rough time of it with the loss of my Uncle Charlie and my Uncle Robert not really a part of our family anymore. She often weeps inconsolably and tells people she lost two brothers in the war.

Of course, we all heard about the New Orleans riots. I was home on summer break when the news reached us. My family had many discussions of it as it has swung the tide of dissent toward President Johnson. Sentiments favoring leniency with the South has all but disappeared among the people we know here in Baltimore and in Washington, DC.

I don't suppose life in New Orleans will get much easier for you *anytime soon. Reconstruction is only going to get tougher with most of the Union feeling the South has reverted to its old ways.*

I look forward to hearing from you again soon. Keep up all the good work with the reading and writing.

Your Good Friend Always,

David, aka "Davie"

P.S.

I engaged in a sparring session with one of my roommates, but I almost broke his jaw. The headmaster said if I ever tried that again I'd be expelled. That would really upset my mother! I admit, though, it left quite a bruise on my opponent's jaw. I'm sure you would've been proud of it if you could've seen it.

AFTER HER FATHER WAS LAID TO REST, SIMONE STARTED her new life with alacrity. The day after the funeral, she came over to the store early.

She stood there looking ethereal, her black dress outlined by the sun's rays as Gabriel opened the store's front door. She lifted her veil and smiled. "Good morning, Mr. Cooper. We need to talk."

"And a good day to you, Miss Livingston. How are you?"

"I thought I told you that you could call me Simone."

"Only if you call me Gabriel."

"Very well, Gabriel. I would like a word with you. Why don't you come to the house now for some breakfast?"

"I'll get my coat."

As they left, he said, "You know, it isn't safe for you to

be wandering these streets by yourself early in the morning."

"Probably not, but I wanted to speak to you before anyone spotted me."

"Without seeming too forward, I think you should allow me to call on you before the store is to open. I can be your escort until such time as it's safe for a lady to be out by herself."

They turned onto Gironde Street, and Simone allowed Gabriel to open her front door for her. Once inside, she hung up her veiled bonnet and cloak. "I'm going to leave the store closed for the rest of the week. I need to decide how I want the business to go. Besides, the good citizens of our community would be appalled to see me doing business so soon after my father's death. Of course," she smirked, "after my behavior at graveside, they may not be appalled at anything I do."

Gabriel chuckled. "Letting people think you've lost your mind has its advantages."

"Yes, and I intend to let them keep thinking that."

She cranked open the kitchen window. "My father never liked me to open the windows downstairs. But now I'm going to have them open from the moment I wake until the moment I sleep. And he always wanted to sit down to three meals a day. I'm no longer cooking three meals a day. You don't mind a cold lunch, do you?"

"Does this mean I'm staying on?"

"*Oui, Monsieur*, if you are willing to try new ideas."

"Sounds like you've already started making decisions."

"I have. My father only sold to his church community. He wouldn't sell to any of the carpetbaggers, but they're the ones with the real money."

"He was very particular who he did business with."

"Pride isn't going to put food on the table. I'm going to open business to them. At a higher price, but I'm going to offer them deals and hospitality. The Northern wives seem desperate for friends, and they didn't ask to come down here. So why not show them some kindness? *Alors,* I'll have business booming and turning a profit in no time."

"Your regular customers may not be so kindly to y'all at church on Sundays."

"Then I'll not go to church." She filled up two cups of bergamot tea. "I just can't accept things the way they are right now."

"The way they are right now?"

"*Oui.* I'm no longer going to be . . . dirt under the Master's feet."

"That's an interesting turn of phrase."

"It was the best words of wisdom I ever received."

"From that slave you knew on your uncle's farm, right?"

Simone stopped and stared at Gabriel. "I'm impressed that you remember."

"I remember most things. Whether I want to or not."

"I am the same."

Then we shall either love or hate each other. "So, Simone, what does this all mean for you? What do you want?"

"I want to be who I want to be, not someone I'm told to be."

Just then there was a knock on the back door, but

before Simone could answer it, Mrs. Patrick stepped into the kitchen.

Simone's face became a mask of ice. Ignoring Mrs. Patrick's look of disapproval at Gabriel, she asked, "Yes? May I help you, Mrs. Patrick?"

"I was simply coming by to see how you are getting on."

"Very well, thank you. You do know Mr. Cooper, don't you?"

Mrs. Patrick barely nodded to Gabriel before continuing, "We were all a bit concerned for you after the funeral."

Simone went over and held the back door open. "*Mais non*, Mrs. Patrick, there is no need for concern. Thank you for stopping by."

"Are you sure there is no need for anything?"

"No."

"We will see you at church on Sunday?"

"Likely not, Mrs. Patrick."

"But we were all expecting—"

"Of course, but I plan to go back to the church of my childhood."

"The Catholic Church? But, you have been gone so many years—"

"That was my father's choice, not mine."

Mrs. Patrick grew agitated as Simone continued to hold the door open. "You've always been such a proud, willful young thing. And you know what the Lord says, 'Pride goeth before a fall.'"

"I'll take my chances. And I would say it was a pleasure to have you stop by, but then you would have to add dishonesty to my already copious list of sins. Good day, Mrs. Patrick."

Simone shut the back door in the woman's face. She turned around, smiling at Gabriel. "Now, where were we? *Mais oui,* we were discussing business . . ."

ONE OF THE FIRST THINGS SIMONE DID WAS POST A SIGN outside her store: *Under New Ownership*. Then she shortened the lines of credit to her father's old customers while opening business to carpetbaggers and their wives. Treating them all warmly and fairly, they rewarded her with a booming business. And bona fide Union cash.

She went around the countryside, shopping at foreclosures and estate sales, picking up everything from fine china to European tapestries for a fraction of their value. Then she turned around and sold the goods at full European market price to her new customers. What she couldn't acquire locally, Simone turned to her father's overseas contacts, reaching out to European textile mills and factories. And wherever she went she brought Gabriel with her, earning herself a sound business reputation.

Peter's old customers were outraged. Simone reminded them that they should not judge the person they were in debt to. She learned to never let friendship get in the way of business. She liked having more business acquaintances than friends.

At home, Simone brought all her books out of hiding. She adorned the windows with Chantilly lace, while art and curios from *Le Vieux Carré* began to brighten her surroundings. And there were always fresh flowers brought in from her garden.

As Christmas of 1866 neared, Simone planned her first soiree. She made a small guest list and put Gabriel at the top.

As he sat in the kitchen sipping coffee one morning, Simone said, "I have something for you." Then she added, "Actually, two things."

"And it's not even Christmas," he teased.

She reached into the pocket of her apron and withdrew a brown envelope. Her eyes were bright with green flecks standing out in their sea of blue. Gabriel opened the envelope to find $50.

"You've worked hard, *Monsieur*, you deserve a wage. This is for the month of November. It will be my pleasure to continue a monthly wage of $50 for you, providing business keeps on the way it has been."

This was the first paycheck Gabriel had ever collected. As he stared at the money, Simone asked, "Is something wrong?"

"No, I've never had a wage before."

"Never? How can that be?"

"It's just been that way." How could he explain this?

Simone saw his discomfort. "*Alors*, I have something else for you."

She reached again into her apron pocket and brought forth a white envelope. It had Gabriel's name scrawled on the front of it and was closed in sealing wax that bore her initials.

"This is fancy," he said, breaking the seal. Now Gabriel stared at the first formal invitation he had ever received for her soiree on New Year's Eve, complete with dinner and a short musical program.

Gabriel looked up at Simone and she flushed crimson. "It would be an honor if you would attend, *Monsieur.*"

"Are you sure you want me there?"

"Why would I not?"

"Simone, I'm a simple man. I've never—"

Simone cut him off. "Perhaps I have been too forward. Please forgive me."

She began to clear the dishes. Gabriel came up behind her. "Please try to understand."

"What was I thinking?" she reflected, "I know so little about you, and what's worse, I know so little about myself."

His hands ran the curve of her corset. "Perhaps," he said, softly kissing the top of her head, "we should try to learn together."

She turned and faced him. "I don't know—"But he silenced her with a finger to her lips.

"I know this much about me," he murmured, "and I know this much about you." And he tilted her chin up, kissing her softly on the lips.

The world slid away for a fleeting moment. Afterward, Gabriel cupped her face in his hands. "You don't know how long I've waited to do that," he whispered.

"*Mon Dieu . . .*"

"Perhaps I've been too forward; but I don't think so."

She closed her eyes. "No, you haven't, but what now?"

"What now?" he echoed. "Well, I don't have a crystal ball, Simone. But I can say that I would be most pleased to attend your party."

December 9, 1866

DEAR DAVIE,

I read your letter and it gave me a chuckle. A bad bruise for your roommate, eh? Good for you!

I've had a successful time of it since we last corresponded. Business, at least in the store I work in, has picked up a good deal. Not only is Miss Livingston, the lady I work for, a nice and sensible woman, but she is also real smart. She has a knack for knowing what her customers want. She has decided to satisfy the whims of the Northern travelers—carpetbaggers, if you will—who have come to make their fortunes in the Reconstruction. Consequently, she has become quite the expert on acquiring all the fancy things the Northern ladies crave to make a nice home here in New Orleans. They bring real Union money and this is what we need to survive down here. As a matter of fact, profit is so good that I've now started getting a real paycheck!

The festivities for Christmas and the New Year are many, despite the lingering hardship for most Southerners. The snap of firecrackers can be heard everywhere and Santa Clauses abound in the city.

There is much to see and do. I accompanied Miss Livingston the other afternoon on a stroll down Canal Street. We went to what is known as the Grand Bazaar, which houses all manner of retail. One of the merchants, B. Piffet, offered a fine array of items from all around the world; I've never seen such a display!

Miss Livingston is having a gathering at her home for the New Year. She has invited me, but I'm at a loss as to how to proceed. This is my debut as a "gentleman;" I have no capacity for small talk or for discussing the topics of the times. Perhaps I will use some of my paycheck to seek out an esteemed tailor to help me dress the part. I don't want to disappoint this lady nor be an embarrassment to her. As you may be able to tell, I am growing quite fond of her.

My wishes to you and your family for a Merry Christmas and Happy New Year.

Fondly,
Gabriel Cooper

GABRIEL SOUGHT OUT A SMALL TAILOR'S SHOP THAT boasted the purchase of a Singer sewing machine. By the time he was finished he had a fine black dress suit, a white waistcoat, and white necktie. He bought silk stockings and a pair of black opera pumps. To round out his outfit he bought himself a black top hat at a local haberdashery. He even had his hair trimmed and styled. Although he nearly spent his entire paycheck on all this, he also knew this was an investment in his future.

Christmas came and went and soon he found himself standing in the back storeroom, buttoning up his new evening coat for Simone's soiree. As he pulled on his white kid gloves, he reflected upon all the changes of the past two years. What would his family say if they could see him now?

The only person he knew who was still alive to gauge his success was Mason Hugo. Gabriel would have to call on Mason one day, but not yet. Not just yet . . .

Gabriel walked to Simone's house and knocked on the front door. Should he bow when she opened it? Tip his hat? He tried to think of something clever to say. *You look lovely, Miss Livingston . . . you are as beautiful as the flowers that bloom in your garden . . .*

"*Monseiur.*"

In his musings Gabriel had not heard the door open. They stared at each other, startled.

"*Monsieur,* welcome."

She was a vision of burgundy silk, her hair covered in a beaded snood. Yet he noticed that she did not wear the fashionable plunging neckline to her evening gown. The neckline was covered in an exquisite black embroidered lace, a pearl brooch at the base of her throat. He noticed the short cap sleeves and the lace fingerless mitts, all in vogue. Was the high neckline the last vestige of her forced Revivalist exile, obliging her to keep her lovely skin hidden? What other explanation could there be?

There were three other couples present, all white ambitious Northerners, and Simone introduced Gabriel to each of them: Arthur and Lillian Ashcroft; Veronica and Moses Del Cerro; the Martin Flannigans and their son, Stephen. Stephen was to be the violinist for the evening.

At dinner, Gabriel was seated next to Moses Del Cerro. "And where do you hail from, Mr. Cooper?" he asked amiably.

Ill at ease, Gabriel took a sip of Cabernet Sauvignon. "Florida."

"I was down in Florida for the Second Seminole War back in '42. Was just a young buck then, eager to make my mark in the military. I was there for the capture of old Chief Osceola." He chuckled. "If we hadn't captured that old bird, we'd still be fighting that war! Whereabouts you from?"

Gabriel took a second sip of wine. "I'm a swamp boy, Mr. Del Cerro. About seventy-five miles from Mobile."

Moses's eyes widened. "Really now! You sure don't talk like a swamp boy."

"I appreciate you saying that as I've been educating myself for some time now."

"I'm impressed. And how did you come to know our lovely Miss Livingston?"

The cravat Gabriel was wearing seemed to tighten. "I was passing through town right after the war. I applied for the position of night watchman at her store."

Gabriel could feel Moses's gaze intensify as he shifted in his chair. More questions would be coming. He headed them off with one of his own.

"Where do you come from, Mr. Del Cerro?"

Moses chuckled. "Enough about you, eh, Mr. Cooper? Well, fair enough. I'm a New Yorker by birth. Upstate, to be exact. But Mrs. Del Cerro and I moved to Manhattan after we married in '48."

"So, you decided not to make your mark in the military?"

"Keen observation, my man! No, I did not."

"And why not?"

Moses stroked his silver-streaked beard. "Let's just say better opportunities presented themselves."

Gabriel cut into the roast goose on his plate. He could not resist the brandied stuffing filled with raisins and chestnuts. He glanced at Simone and their eyes met.

The look was not lost on Moses. He leaned in and

whispered, "I wouldn't let that one slip by if I were you, Mr. Cooper."

"I don't intend to, Mr. Del Cerro."

"Call me Moses. I have a feeling we're going to be seeing quite a bit of one another in the coming months."

"I hope so, Moses. And please call me Gabriel."

Both men resumed their dinner and Gabriel relaxed. He felt as if he had passed some test, although he didn't know what the test was.

The evening continued with coffee and dessert, cognac and brandy for the gentlemen. But as Stephen finished the 2nd Movement from Spring of Vivaldi's Four Seasons, there was a heavy knock on the front door. Simone stood up. "*Encore*, Stephen! I will be right back."

She moved out of the parlor and into the hall. She did not realize that Gabriel had also slipped out of his seat and followed her, trailed even further by Moses.

Simone hurried down the hallway just as Delcine opened the front door. Simone stopped in her tracks. Outside stood Pastor Evans from Peter's old church. He raised his hat and looked past Delcine to Simone. "May I come in?"

Simone approached the door, unaware that Gabriel and Moses were watching the situation unfold.

"Good evening, Pastor," said Simone. "Such a late, unexpected call."

"I asked if I may come in?"

"I have company, Pastor. Is this urgent?"

"The retrieval of a lost soul is always urgent, Simone," the Pastor inched forward past Delcine.

Simone stepped between him and Delcine. "This is

not the time nor the place, Pastor Evans. Nor will it ever be, for that matter."

It was as if he had not heard her. "You are no stranger to the teachings of our Lord, Simone. There are clear duties for a man and for a woman. A man's duty is to provide for his family, to love them and protect them. A woman's duty is to serve her husband and to bear his children and nurture them." The pastor's voice was urgent. "And you are not fulfilling your Christian duties, Simone! Not only is it unbecoming, it is downright sinful. Now I know there are a number of suitors in our community who would court you and bring you to true happiness, if—"

"Stop!" Simone's voice was sharp and reactive. "Leave my home at once because you are not welcome here."

Pastor Evans stared at her. "You will learn your place one way or another, young lady!"

"I am not dirt under your feet anymore," Simone hissed. "Get out and don't come back!"

The pastor stepped back and Simone closed the door in his face. The sweet, whimsical melody of the 3rd Movement of Spring wafted down the hallway.

Gabriel watched this interlude with the calmest of expressions, the only sign of his white-knuckled rage being his clenched jaw. His concentration was on Simone and the danger he sensed. So great was his focus that he did not realize that he was being watched as well; in fact, Gabriel was being interviewed for a job. He just didn't know it yet.

~

SIMONE SAT, RUBBING HER TEMPLES. "I HAVE A TERRIBLE headache."

All the guests except Gabriel had left, none of them aware of what had transpired except for Moses Del Cerro, who had reassured Simone.

"No use stirring up controversy," he whispered to her as they left, but Simone was aggrieved. This evening had meant so much to her, and that wretched minister had nearly ruined everything. Delcine approached quietly.

"If it be all right with you, ma'am, I'd best be going. Sun will be coming up soon, and I'll have breakfast to make for my family."

Simone squeezed Delcine's hand. "Thank you, Delcine, for all your help." She handed her an envelope. "Happy New Year."

"Thank you, Miss Simone. I'm glad you're back."

"So am I."

"Good night y'all." She nodded to Gabriel.

Gabriel stood up. "Good night, ma'am." He opened the back door for her; a Black freedwoman always used the back door.

Gabriel sat down again facing Simone. "Are you going to be all right?"

"Yes, I just need some rest."

"Well, I'd better be going then." He reached for her hand across the table. "Stop worrying yourself!"

"He goes by Pastor, but that man is a white devil! He could hurt the business."

Gabriel gave her hand a squeeze. "Nothing that you can't overcome, Simone."

The touch of his hand made her tingle. "Perhaps it will be all right."

"That's my girl," said Gabriel. He stood up and drew Simone to her feet. "You were beautiful tonight." He kissed her tenderly. She breathed in his scent of cognac and fine cigar.

Would he have kissed her again in that private moment? Would his hands have cupped her face, moved to her shoulders, finally caressing the small of her back? Perhaps, except that they were interrupted by the frantic pounding on her front door.

It was Delcine. Above the clanging church bells she cried, "The store! The store is on fire!"

Gabriel bolted forward into the night as Simone grabbed her cloak and followed Delcine. The smell of smoke permeated the air.

She hurried down the street and around the corner. Men were shouting and she saw a crowd gathering. Delcine tried to keep her from getting too close.

"Miss Simone, it's not safe! Let the men put it out first!"

Simone shook off Delcine's grip. "No, no, it's all going to burn! Oh, God, no!"

Volunteers from the Firemen's Charitable Association had arrived with their wagons, doing their best to douse the flames.

But it was not the flames that gave rise to Simone's scream. It was the sight of Gabriel disappearing into them. He had dropped his fine topcoat on the ground and had plunged through the front door.

Simone sank to her knees. Delcine wrapped her arms around her as they huddled together.

Gabriel did not have time to explain to Simone that he had things in that store that needed to be saved. Nor could he articulate that he understood danger in ways most men didn't; that it was far more perilous for him to sacrifice those things to the inferno, for they were sacred to him.

He dropped to his hands and knees, knowing he had only minutes to get what he could.

It was all stored underneath his cot. There was the sword, the box that held David's letters, and Simone's mother's copy of Homer's *Odyssey*. It was bookmarked with the last few dollars left of his first paycheck.

There was a window above his bed. Wrapping his hand in a rag that reeked suspiciously of kerosene, he slammed his fist through the glass. He grabbed what he had come for, tossing it all outside. Then as the flames gasped forward, Gabriel pulled himself up and through the opening. The broken glass of the window frame shredded his fine clothing, cutting him. Falling embers singed the back of his neck and hands. He plummeted forward then stood up shakily, retrieving the sword and *The Odyssey*. Davie's letters were strewn about, but the heat was too much and he would have to leave them. Someone pulled him away as the windows blew out and the store roof caved in.

Coughing and choking, concerned faces swam before him. But he ignored them as he searched the crowd looking for Simone.

There she was, crumpled beside Delcine, her face covered in her hands. He limped toward them. The firemen had brought in a second wagon and were now dousing the bakery and cobbler's shop next door.

Delcine saw him. "He's here, Miss Simone, don't despair! Thanks be to God!"

Gabriel laid his burned and bloody hand on Simone's head. Only then did she dare to look up, her face streaked with ash and tears.

Holding the sword in one blistered hand, Gabriel handed her the book with the other.

"I couldn't let this burn," he said simply.

"*Monsieur,*" she began, but her voice broke. "Oh, Gabriel, never do that again!" She allowed him to help her up. With desolate eyes she watched the raging flames.

One of the lead firefighters, a middle-aged man with a pot belly and long sideburns, approached Gabriel. "That was quite a feat of daring you took there, young man. This must be your business, I dare say."

"No sir, it's this here young lady's. I am merely her employee."

The fireman raised his eyebrows, but turned to Simone. "I am sorry for your loss of property, ma'am. Do you have any idea how this may have happened?"

"No."

The fireman sighed. "Sometimes there's just no explainin' these things. A random firecracker from last night's festivities could've been moldering about. A careless match thrown; so many people out and about, you know. Anything could have happened, I suppose." He surveyed the burning building. "Of course, ya never know who has evil on their mind, all these freedmen running about, you know, no one to supervise 'em anymore." He sighed again. "Well, like I said, I'm sorry for your losses here. And you sir." He chuckled grimly. "I'd shake your hand, but it's looking mighty painful."

Ya never know who has evil on their mind. . . evil in the form of self-righteousness? Gabriel looked at his blackened and blistered hand. "Thank you, kindly, sir, for your services."

"A Happy New Year to you. Ma'am." The fireman tipped his hat at Simone.

Simone said nothing as the fireman walked away. Others came up and offered their sympathies, but still Simone said nothing. Finally, she turned to Gabriel. "You have nowhere to sleep."

"I'll be all right," said Gabriel, his voice hoarse from the smoke.

"We have to get you to a doctor."

"I'm far more concerned for you." He turned to Delcine, who had been patiently standing nearby. How hard it must be, Gabriel wondered, to stand at the ready, knowing you were needed by your family, yet not allowing yourself to leave lest your white employer have a request for you . . .

Simone put her hand on Delcine's arm. "Go, Delcine, your family needs you. Happy New Year."

"Miss Simone, I'll be back tomorrow."

"Thank you, but take tomorrow off as well. Come the day after. Now go, for I've kept you too long as it is."

"Thank you," Delcine murmured.

After she had left, Gabriel took Simone's arm. "Come, let me take you home."

"I cannot leave all this."

Gabriel coughed, his mouth and throat filled with ash. "It isn't going anywhere."

He edged her along, but when she saw him wince in pain, she began to hurry. "You're hurt."

Gabriel was indeed feeling the throb of his burns. His

shirt and pants were bloodstained and his cough made his chest hurt.

Now it was Simone who guided him back to her house. She opened the door and led him into the kitchen.

"You need fresh air," she said, throwing open the back window.

Simone went outside and pumped some cold water into a bowl. Soon she was back inside, grabbing a half-used bottle of brandy.

She poured the liquor onto a clean cloth. "Your wounds must be cleaned, or they'll become infected. Hold still."

He gritted his teeth as she cleaned the burns. Simone paused at one point to warm the kettle over the fire. She filled another bowl with warm water, washing the soot away from his face and exposed arms.

"If you take off your shirt, *Monsieur*, I will wash the cuts you have on your torso."

Gabriel stiffened. "I will take care of those."

"But you are bleeding——"

"No!"

Color crept into Simone's cheeks. "As you wish." She left the room and returned with a bed sheet and scissors to create bandages.

Coughing and shaking, Gabriel touched her arm. "I meant no harshness, Simone."

"I was only trying to help."

"I know. It's just that——" Did he dare divulge that underneath the linen and fine cotton was a man branded by his past? "These are only scratches and you're exhausted already."

Simone bandaged both his hands and the back of his

neck. "It is a wonder you didn't burn alive," she observed, pinning the bandages into place. "You were so brave . . . and so silly."

"There are some things a man must do."

"I suppose, but it will be a cold day in Hades before a woman *ever* understands."

"Someday I will try and explain."

Simone looked deep into his cornflower blue eyes. "Would you please do that for me sometime? That would be so very . . . helpful."

"Go to sleep. I shall watch the house while you rest."

"You should rest, too, and you should do it here. You have no other place now."

"I don't think that would be proper."

"Proper is a vile word."

But Gabriel was adamant, sending her upstairs to sleep. He took a chair and placed it outside the front door, where he would sit guard. He didn't care if others wondered at his presence, for even the most unorthodox courtship had its boundaries, and he wanted everyone to know that he was a gentleman courting a lady.

9

NEW ORLEANS 1867

Moses Del Cerro liked to take long walks in the evening. Even after a late night out, he would often take a stroll. And so it was in the wee hours of New Year's morning, 1867, that Moses kissed his wife and said, "I am going out for some fresh air, my dear. I will be home soon."

He left his magnificent house, a two-story Italianate mansion in the 4th District. Moses had Gabriel on his mind and he headed back toward the area from which he had been earlier that evening.

He noticed an orange glow in the sky as he retraced the route to Simone's. He quickened his steps, realizing it was from Simone's neighborhood. He could hear the church bells tolling the emergency.

He arrived at the scene of the fire to see Gabriel talking with one of the firemen. He hung back in the shadows, watching. He saw Simone, crumpled against her housekeeper, and he surveyed the wreckage of the store. Something was afoot, but Moses was studying

Gabriel. He took in how Gabriel held himself, wary of his surroundings. And as if sensing he was being watched, Gabriel turned, looking in Moses's direction.

Moses was impressed with Gabriel's acuity. Now only a few more questions remained about Gabriel and he knew the answers would come in time. Moses was sure he would find a way to see if Gabriel was someone he could work with.

MOSES CALLED ON SIMONE LATER IN THE MORNING. HE approached Gabriel as he sat by the front door, staring into the distance.

"Gabriel, we meet again."

"Hello, Moses."

"It looks like you've been through some tribulations, my man. Are you sure the outside is the best place for you to be?"

"Simone is asleep upstairs. I don't want her disturbed."

"So you sit vigil outside. Frightful tragedy, the store burning like that. Do you know how it happened?"

"I've got some ideas."

"Really? Well, I've got a bit of time if you're in the mood to share your thoughts."

"We should probably talk in private."

"Well, that's perfect, because now you need a place to stay."

The hackles rose on Gabriel's neck. "I don't recall ever telling you that, Moses."

"That, my friend, is part of my job, but that is beside

the point. Veronica and I would be delighted to have you come and stay with us. And you can get those injuries tended to."

Gabriel looked at his bandaged hands. "They do smart, I have to admit."

"So, it's an acceptance?"

"Yes, thank you very much."

"Excellent! I'll send a carriage around at five. You can join us for dinner . . . unless of course, you want to dine with Simone."

"No, I think she needs her rest. I know she has some food left over from last night's meal."

"I'll have Veronica pack up a meal for Simone and have it brought over with the carriage."

"That would be right gentlemanly of you, sir," said Gabriel with a grin.

Moses grinned back, but he already knew that Gabriel was never going to be a friend. *One cannot mix business with pleasure.*

GABRIEL WATCHED THE CARRIAGE PULL UP LATER THAT day. An expensive, gleaming thing pulled by two gleaming horses. He noticed how it made people stop and stare. *Someday I will have a carriage just like this.*

The driver jumped down, then presented a large wicker basket.

"Dinner for the mistress of the house," he said quietly.

"Thank you," replied Gabriel as he opened the front door. "Please put it on the kitchen table."

Earlier, when Simone had awakened, he had told her of Moses's invitation.

She approved. "You must go and rest there. And stop worrying about me."

Gabriel boarded the carriage and it pulled forward, heading for St. Charles Avenue. He gazed with longing at the large, stately homes set back from the street. They pulled inside a gate, traversing a curved cobblestone lane that stopped in front of a large pale pink mansion. Gabriel took in the black filigreed iron adorning the double galleries and the marble colonnade that lined both the upper and lower porticos.

A Black footman emerged, opening the carriage door. "Welcome, sir." He stood politely by, ignoring Gabriel's grimy appearance as he alighted from the carriage and ascended the white marble steps. As the carriage pulled away, passing through the *porte cochere* on the side of the house, a Black butler opened the front door.

Gabriel stepped inside to see Moses waiting for him in the foyer, under a spacious cupola graced by an elegant winding staircase.

"You made it! You must be exhausted, old chap. Dinner's in an hour, so Frederick here will show you to your room. You can freshen up and ah, I hope you don't mind"—he met Gabriel's eyes-—"but I presumed you lost all your personal effects in the fire, so I had some new clothes brought over for you."

"Thank you."

"Still hoarse from the fire, eh? Well, maybe some good food paired with a nice merlot will help that old voice of yours. Show the gentleman to his room, Frederick."

Gabriel followed Frederick up the staircase and down a hall. The servant opened a door, stepping aside for Gabriel.

Gabriel had never seen such a room; tall, arched windows cast shadows on a mahogany writing desk with a set of glass French doors off to the side. His eyes rested on a double bed covered with a goose down comforter that faced a hearth in which a fire was crackling.

Frederick cleared his throat. "Sir, the water in the wash basin is warm and it would be best for your comfort to refresh yourself before it gets cold." Then he retreated, shutting the door quietly.

Gabriel stood there, alone amongst the luxury. An evening dinner suit was laid out. He approached the basin, where a washcloth and towel were folded next to it. A bar of scented French soap sat in a dish.

Carefully, Gabriel dipped the washcloth into the water. He breathed in the steam and the fragrance of fresh English terry cloth.

Slowly, Gabriel removed the grime of the last fourteen hours. Frederick knocked and entered several times, bringing fresh water and emptying the used soapy water, finally bringing ointment made of chalk and hogs' lard for his wounds. Slowly, Gabriel relaxed in his presence.

He was just putting on the white cotton shirt when Frederick entered for the last time. He brought some bandages for the back of his neck.

"Sir, these might help with the pain of a stiff collar as they are already treated with ointment."

Gabriel gritted his teeth as Frederick put the bandages in place, securing them with a sticking plaster made in the kitchen.

When he had finished, Gabriel turned up the collar and Frederick said to him, "The collar is slightly loose fitting as Mr. Del Cerro took extra care for your clothes not to increase the pressure on your wounds. I'm afraid, however, regardless of all the precautions we will abide by, you're going to have some scarring when the healing is done." He paused. "Dinner, sir, is in five minutes."

Gabriel looked at himself in the full-length mirror. Moses seemed to have an uncanny insight into all of Gabriel's habits and characteristics. Gabriel began to wonder who Moses Del Cerro really was.

He turned to the side. The bandages thickened his neck, but that was temporary. Just the scars would remain.

Well, no matter. He was familiar with scars. Besides, it was time for dinner and he was starving.

He slept the sleep of the dead that night, in a bed he never knew could be so comfortable with sheets he never knew could be so soft. It was mid-morning when he awoke, and he lay there in the gloom of the drawn velvet drapes.

Like a creeping shadow, he recalled last night: the food brought on china platters; the sterling silver cutlery and the wine, a nice merlot just as Moses had promised.

Gabriel had sat across the table from Theresa, the Del Cerros' eleven-year-old daughter. She stared at him with her big brown eyes, smiling every time he looked at her. It reminded him of another lifetime, when his own younger sisters would grin at him as they sat around a simpler table, eating simpler food.

There was a soft knock on the door and Frederick entered.

"Good morning, sir," he said as he pulled back the drapes. "I trust you slept well?"

"Yes, thank you."

"I'll have fresh water brought up, and I also have fresh bandages and ointment when you are ready for your new dressings."

He left as quietly as he came. Gabriel rose out of bed and used the chamber pot. He was looking at the clothes in the armoire when there was another soft knock. A young Black houseboy entered with a bowl of steaming water. "Good morning, sir." He placed the bowl on the washstand, picked up the chamber pot and left.

Gabriel ached to own this luxury. But how could he ever pave his way to such opulence?

Frederick arrived with his wound dressings. "If you please, sir," he said, and waited for Gabriel to motion him forward.

He thinks I am a gentleman.

After Frederick changed his bandages, he said, "Your breakfast is waiting, sir," and helped Gabriel to put on his morning coat.

Moses was sitting in the family dining room, sipping coffee and reading the morning paper. He looked up as Gabriel entered. "I trust you slept well?"

"Very much so. Thank you."

A Black kitchen maid set a plate of ham and fried potatoes before him. As Gabriel carefully took up his fork and knife, he reminded himself to show restraint with the food. He was always going to have to restrain himself when he was around food.

As he ate, Moses chatted pleasantly about trivial things. He would arise from time to time to gaze out the dining room window and Gabriel got the distinct feeling that there were things on his mind.

Finally, Moses turned to him and said, "Why don't we finish our coffee in the library, old chap, where we can discuss a few matters of importance?"

There it was. Gabriel had gotten the feeling ever since Moses approached him yesterday that there was a motive behind his hospitality.

They left the dining room, crossed the foyer, and entered the library. Gabriel took in the expansive bookshelves, each with a ladder to reach any volume desired. On the south wall were two tall, arching windows, the green velvet drapes pulled back to let in the limpid winter light. A fire crackled in the fireplace.

Frederick arrived with a coffee service and pastry platter. He set it down on one of the credenzas and left.

"Good man, that Frederick," Moses mused. "Always knows what I need before I do."

"Has he been with you for long?"

"Only about eighteen months or so. I hired him right off the street outside the Freedmen's Bureau."

"How did you know he was the man for the job?"

Moses poured some coffee for Gabriel. "Sugar?"

"No. Black, thank you,"

"Black, straight, and with a bite." He smiled at Gabriel. "I would imagine nothing else. Now me, I'm a cream and sugar man. I like to soften the edges a little bit so it all goes down a little more smoothly." He gestured for Gabriel to have a seat.

"Truly, Moses, how did you know Frederick was the man for the job?"

"Ah, there is that persistence with which I've been so impressed. There's a lot to be told about a man just by the way he stands, the way he encounters a new situation. I noticed right away that Frederick was a man who held himself a little apart from the crowd. He did not jostle along in line, and he made no effort at small talk with anyone. Clearly, he had been a slave before, but he wasn't muscular, so I knew immediately he had been no field hand. His fingers, so long and finely tapered, why, those were the hands used to tending to the needs of a gentleman. So, I asked him a few questions about his background. I was spot-on, so I hired him right then and there."

Gabriel took a sip of coffee. Moses was studying him. "Not wanting any brandy in that coffee, are you?"

"No."

"Good. It's trouble if a man needs liquor to start his day."

"I hardly drink and never the hard stuff."

Moses was quiet for a moment and then leaned in conspiratorially. "So tell me, what are your thoughts on that dreadful fire?"

So, Moses wanted Gabriel to confide in him. Did Gabriel dare to do so?

"It was no accident."

"What makes you say that?"

"There was the smell of kerosene. And there was nothing there that could have sparked a fire. No firecrackers are tolerated in that vicinity. It's right by the hospital, and I've seen doctors scold passersby who were being too noisy."

"Who do you think did it?"

"I think it was that pastor who came by. He and his like have been grumbling about Simone's new way of doing business." Gabriel paused, then added, "I'm not a man who turns the other cheek, Moses. I don't even know if I believe in justice."

"What do you believe in?"

Gabriel gazed into the fire, watching the flaming embers float up the chimney. "Revenge."

Moses smiled. "Sometimes revenge is the only justice a man will get."

"Don't I know that."

Moses stood up and went to one of the bookshelves. He extricated a small, leather-bound manual.

"I don't loan this to just anybody," he said, handing it to Gabriel. "Only to those who I think will appreciate it. I also welcome additions to it."

"Additions?"

"Yes, you will understand when you've given it a thorough perusal."

He handed the book to Gabriel. There was a gold-leaf inscription: *The Avengers' Almanac*. "See if it isn't of some use to you but read it with discretion. Let me know if you find it of interest. Somehow, I think you will."

"I'll start on it now."

"Don't you first want to call on that lovely lady you have eyes for?"

Gabriel felt a shyness creep over him. Moses laughed. "Come now, Gabriel, it doesn't take brilliance to deduce she's the lady of your heart. And why shouldn't she be? She's refined, charming, and a fair maiden to look upon in these dreary times. She needs you now. She's been dreadfully insulted with the loss of her income and the spectacle it created. Go to her and set things right."

So much was veiled in what he said, but Gabriel understood. He needed to go to Simone, to reassure her and above all, to set things right.

"Vengeance is mine, and recompense, for the time when their foot shall slip; for the day of calamity is at hand, and their doom comes swiftly." ~Deuteronomy 32:35

GABRIEL HAD RETIRED TO HIS ROOM AFTER CALLING ON Simone. Delcine had been there when he arrived, as were Mrs. Ashcroft and Mrs. Flannigan whom he had met at Simone's *soiree*.

"How is she?" he asked Delcine when she answered the door.

Delcine shook her head. "Between you, me, and the good Lord, she puts on like she's strong, but this was a terrible blow to the young Miss. This laid an awful wound upon her heart." She glanced down the hallway. "Miss Livingston is in the parlor with her guests."

Delcine led him to the parlor and opened the door. Simone nodded cordially, "Good afternoon, Mr. Cooper, would you join us for tea?"

Gabriel immediately noticed the dark circles under Simone's eyes as the two other ladies smiled at him. He took a seat and Simone poured him some tea, offering him a plate.

"Our dear Lillian brought over some tea cakes. Would you care for one?"

"Now, how could I resist that?" Gabriel crooned and then, "Delicious! Why Mrs. Ashcroft, is this a secret family recipe?"

Lillian Ashcroft responded to the flattery, "How did you know, Mr. Cooper? It's been in my family for generations; brought over from Scotland."

"That is a treasure, I must say. I am honored to partake of your family's delightful confections."

Mrs. Ashcroft's eyes shone. "You speak so eloquently, Mr. Cooper. You must be a man of great learning. If you don't mind my asking, where did you acquire your schooling? You know, our Stephen will soon be of college age and I would dearly love for him to attend Amherst, which was my own father's alma mater. My dear husband tells me I should keep an open mind. Would it be too much to hope that you graduated from Amherst?"

Gabriel smiled, hiding his dismay. "Well, I'm sorry to say, Mrs. Ashcroft, but my schooling was interrupted with the war." He spoke warmly, bringing her into his fictitious memories. "I felt a need to avail myself to the Cause. So, I was taught by the firelight of a campfire, where Homer, Voltaire, and Aristotle were my professors. I'm so sorry to disappoint you."

"Oh no, no Mr. Cooper! Of course, you would feel the compunction to answer your call to battle, misguided as— Well, of course how silly of me to think otherwise. Please forgive my oversight."

This was a new danger. Gabriel realized that he

would always have to protect himself from his past if he wanted entry into these social circles.

He caught Simone gazing at him, her eyes softened to the teal of warm Caribbean waters. What was she thinking?

"WHILE THE GENTLEMAN'S DUEL IS CONDUCTED FOR THE restoration of honor, it hardly brings succor to the man whose wrongs reach deep within him, rooted in the obstruction of his livelihood or degradation of his possessions."

Gabriel read on. He knew the fire that had destroyed the store had been set, and he was positive he knew who did it. But did he really want to go to the police? The city was rife with racial tension and wild, unruly occupants. Who would bother to investigate a minister with an impeccable reputation? But even more than that, did he want the police to know who he was?

A gurgle of dread ran through him. Gabriel put down the book. No, it was up to him. The only justice he would seek would be from his own hand. And his guide would be *The Avengers' Almanac*.

HE BEGAN BY FINDING OUT WHERE THE GOOD MINISTER lived. This was easy, as Simone offered up the address without suspicion.

For several days Gabriel had accompanied her to the site of her burned store. It was as if she were returning to the grave of a dead child, beholden by her grief and horror.

They sat together one evening, as a cool drizzle saturated the ground outside. Simone gazed into the fire that crackled in the kitchen. "I don't know what to do."

"How so?"

"I don't have the money to rebuild."

"Would you consider a loan?"

"From a bank? That would be impossible in these times."

"From friends?"

Simone looked at him sadly. "Are they really my friends, *Monsieur?* Besides, I don't think taking their money would be wise. I don't want to be indebted to anyone. And who's to say that once I rebuild, it wouldn't burn again?"

Gabriel pressed a reassuring hand upon her arm. "I say, Simone."

"What do you mean?"

His eyes were steady upon her. "Never mind what I mean. I say, is all you need to know. I want to reassure you. It will never burn again because I say."

James Rory Evans saw the world in two ways: right and wrong. In his tidy home, all was right. For his church, his followers, all was right, at least for the most part. But occasionally one would stray. Of course, he tried to make it right for that sorry sinner, but what to do with the one, damn him or *her*, who insisted on flaunting his waywardness and thriving in it?

And so it was with Simone Livingston. She had strayed so far, so *brazenly*, surely her soul had been kidnapped by Satan. And what about that man, that strangely handsome, silent man who always seemed to be around her, with his icy blue eyes that surely hid a godless heart?

The pastor shuddered, but he had made it right. Burning the store was more than an act of admonishment. It was a purification.

He had tried to warn her, but she had spurned him, the wayward whore. *How dare she?*

He reflected upon this one evening as his housekeeper poked her head into his study.

"Goodnight, Pastor, I'll be leaving now."

"Goodnight, Mrs. Bell."

He heard the front door close quietly. He did not see the man in the shadows peer into his window.

GABRIEL SAT QUIETLY IN THE BUSHES BY THE PASTOR'S house for several hours, waiting and watching. Finally, the kerosene lamp was turned off. Gabriel followed the flickering light of one lone candle as it left the study and disappeared through an adjoining door.

Gabriel continued to bide his time. Hours went by, but finally he emerged, dressed in dark shabby clothes, a cap pulled low over his eyes. Making sure he left no footprints, he approached the house.

He had spent days watching the pastor's activity. To get inside the house, he posed as one more hungry rebel, calling when he knew the pastor was not home.

"Might there be somethin' in yer fine home that needs fixin'? I work fer food or money." He shifted his feet pathetically. "I got me an ailin' wife and four young uns at home."

Mrs. Bell, one of the pastor's white, long-time congregants, shook her head. "No, there's nothing here for you to do. But come in, and I'll see if I can't find something for you to take home to your wife."

"God's blessin' be upon ya, ma'am, fer yer Christian charity."

Mrs. Bell ushered him into the pastor's home and motioned him to sit on a bench in the hallway. She headed for the kitchen. Once Gabriel heard her in the back, he rose from the bench.

It was a small, one-story structure, simple in its layout. The pastor's study was the second door on Gabriel's right, diagonal from the parlor. Gabriel entered the study, noticing a closed door. It was to the left of the pastor's desk, whereas a window looking into the bushes was on the right. Gabriel went to the door and pushed it. There was a bed and nightstand against one wall and a bookshelf on the opposite wall. There were no windows.

Gabriel's gaze swept the room and he quickly retreated. He retraced his steps and sat down when Mrs. Bell reappeared with a parcel wrapped in brown paper.

"Here," she said, "some bread and molasses for your wife, and cookies for the children."

Gabriel stood up. "Thank ya kindly, ma'am."

"Your wife and family are in my prayers, sir," said Mrs. Bell as he left the house.

Gabriel relived that whole scenario as he eased open

the front door. A fog swirled around him, a dewy shield against any witnesses.

He felt his way carefully with a cane he had brought, as if he were a blind man. *Tap, tap, tap,* ever so softly, careful to detect any obstacles in his way. *Tap, tap, tap,* breach the doorway and round the corner. In his mind's eye Gabriel could see the layout he'd canvassed just days before.

He reached the pastor's bedroom. Guided by the man's soft snoring, Gabriel crept in. He had strapped a pillow under his baggy shirt; it doubled as disguise and weapon.

Pastor Evans lay on his back, slack-jawed. He was no match for the man who stuffed the pillow so hard, so swiftly onto his face that he barely struggled. He certainly never uttered a sound.

Finally, Gabriel lifted the pillow and looked down. The man was dead, eyes wide open and mouth still agape. How unceremonious.

Gabriel lit the candle on the nightstand and touched the flame to the pastor's coverlet. With a snap it sprang to fiery life.

Gabriel backed out of the room, closing the door as the flames engulfed the bed. He swiftly went to the study window, opened it, and climbed out. He then turned and closed the window; *leave everything as you found it.* Wiping his footprints from the dirt, he sidled to the front of the house and walked down the street. The neighbors were still asleep, oblivious to the inferno in their midst.

He headed over to Poydras Street, to the corner of St. Charles where he had hidden a knapsack in a clump of ferns behind a rusted fleur-de-lis gate. Gabriel stepped into the shadows and when he re-emerged, his appearance was transformed. Beneath his workaday costume he had been wearing an elegant linen shirt and pants of fine wool. He now donned a pair of fake spectacles, a top hat, and a nicely cut wool jacket.

He took his place on the street as a gentleman heading home. No questions would be asked of him. As he walked, his adrenaline began to level out and a growing satisfaction took its place. He had achieved justice for his beloved. He had made everything right.

THE NEXT MORNING, OVER HAM AND EGGS, MOSES AGAIN suggested that he and Gabriel take their coffee in the library. Once there, Moses picked up the daily edition of *The Picayune*. "You made the front page, my man," he commented, looking at the paper.

"Excuse me?"

"The front page, you made the front page. Congratulations!"

Gabriel took the paper from Moses, *"Dreadful fire engulfed the home and being of Pastor Rory Evans, originally of Baton Rouge, but long-standing respected citizen of New Orleans. Pastor Evans was the unfortunate victim of the reckless flame of a candle. He was burned in his bed at his residence on Liberty Street, situated not too far from the Protestant Cemetery."*

Gabriel looked for something that implicated him or raised suspicion. Finding nothing, he handed the paper back to Moses.

"This has no connection to me," Gabriel said, sipping his coffee.

"It has every connection to you."

Gabriel tensed and Moses continued, "I can see I've put you in a tenuous position, but you need not worry, Gabriel. How much do you think you know about me?"

"I know nothing about you."

"Well, then, what do you *think* you know about me?"

Gabriel's eyes narrowed. "Are you playing some kind of game?"

"No, but indulge me."

"Well, I think you're a businessman from up North, someone who has come to make money in the South—"

"A carpetbagger?"

"Well, yes."

"Vulgar term, but go on."

"Here to capitalize on the Reconstruction of the fallen Confederacy, although you're an astute businessman judging from the splendor and opulence you live in."

"What kind of business do you think I conduct?"

"I wouldn't venture to speculate, Moses."

Moses chuckled. "See, I knew from the moment I spoke to you that you were a very smart man. A smart man wouldn't entertain a speculation he had no evidence for. But you're more than smart, Gabriel. You're also cunning and, I might add, a little ruthless."

Gabriel shifted in his chair, feeling very uneasy.

"I deal in problem solving, Gabriel. A man, albeit a wealthy man, comes to me with a problem, and I solve it; sometimes the problem is straightforward, sometimes not so much. But the solution is *always* straightforward. Straightforward and just, because there is no solution without a problem and if a problem has been created by someone, then the solution put forth to eradicate the problem is just." He stopped and looked at Gabriel. "But for the solution to remain straightforward, the person who delivers it must be very, very good at what he does. Last night you delivered a solution to a problem created by the good Reverend. I saw the justice in you when the Reverend confronted Miss Livingston, the desire to eradicate the man who himself was the problem. I agree with you that he was the one who set fire to Miss Livingston's store.

"So, under the cloak of darkness and various disguises, you studied his habits. And you waited. You chose a night of no moon and the unexpected blessing of a dense fog. And then you solved the problem. Brilliantly, I might add. No show of bluster, no bravado. You killed him first I assume?"

Gabriel nodded. "I suffocated him with a pillow so no trace of assault was left behind."

Moses closed his eyes and shook his head blissfully. "Ah, *'Vengeance is mine, and recompense, for the time when their foot shall slip; for the day of calamity is at hand, and their doom comes swiftly.'*"

Gabriel would have thought he was in the presence of a lunatic, except he remembered the quote from that book Moses had given him to read.

Moses opened his eyes and continued. "You completed the solution with the appearance of an accidental fire. And no one was the wiser! Truly the work of a skilled craftsman." He grew suddenly somber. "But still,

Miss Livingston is out of an income and you are out of a job."

"Yes."

"Well, from a business perspective, Gabriel, you just proved yourself to be a solid investment. Most of the problems I am presented with need a solution such as the one you so masterfully delivered. But as you can see, it takes a certain man with a certain talent to keep the solution itself from turning into its own problem. Would you be interested in brokering such solutions for, let us say, less personal reasons?"

Moses's smile indicated that he knew the effect those carefully chosen words would have on Gabriel. "Do you want this, my friend?" He gestured to the expanse of the library. "Do you want to be able to take that lovely flame of your heart, wed her, bless her with a family, and take care of them all in a grand style?"

"You know I do."

"And what man wouldn't? But not everyone gets the opportunity. For every problem you solve, Gabriel, you will be paid handsomely. The bigger the problem, the bigger the pay. And what's more, I could help you invest some of that beautifully earned revenue so that it continues on paying you. You could invest in this country, in new industries just *beginning* to grab the land! Oh, there are so many opportunities . . ."

"This is a risky business, Moses."

"Ah, but that really depends on you, my man."

"What if something doesn't go as planned? What happens next?"

"You mean, what happens when you create a problem instead of a solution?"

"Yes."

Moses levelled a steady gaze at Gabriel. "Then you become the problem. And I would seek a solution."

Gabriel burst out laughing at the threat. "You underestimate me, Moses!"

Moses remained cool. "Every man who works for me must know the risks of his job."

"I know the risks all too well."

"Don't ever become a liability, Gabriel." Moses drew in a deep breath. "I would hate to have to treat you like one because I've come to like you."

"But it doesn't matter if you like me, does it?"

"No, it doesn't."

Moses reached into his trouser pocket and took out his money clip. "Let's end this on a more cheerful note." He handed some bills to Gabriel. "Consider that a reward for a job well done," he said, "and think about my offer to you. Either way, the money's yours."

As Moses got up to leave the library, he paused. "You know, maybe if John Wilkes Booth used a little of your method, he might still be alive today."

And with that he left. Gabriel counted out three hundred dollars in his hand. He'd never held so much money.

There was no need to think about this offer, for Gabriel knew this was his chance. Now he knew what talent he possessed that would give him the life he so yearned for. The only hitch was that it was a talent he had to keep to himself.

Moses Del Cerro was not the only person who read *The Picayune* that morning. Simone read the same article, but she reacted with a small, nagging thought that kept simmering in the back of her mind. *This is such an odd coincidence—or was this a coincidence?* She had sensed Gabriel's coolness when he had asked about where the pastor had lived, as if he was feigning a casual interest. *Was it a casual interest? Or was it hiding a pointed inquiry? How well did she really know this man who now kept so much of her company? Surely not . . . surely it was only a coincidence that the Pastor burned to death so soon following their confrontation, after her own store had burned down. Or wasn't it?*

They met again in the library after dinner, where Moses opened a bottle of brandy and then handed a snifter to Gabriel.

"I always like a nice brandy after a hard day." He raised his glass. "Cheers."

Gabriel let the smooth liquid warm his gullet. The two men sat down and Moses asked, "How was your day?"

"I called on Simone."

"All is well?"

"Yes, for now at least. She's in a quandary about her situation."

"I can only imagine. She has no one unless, of course, you step up to it."

"That's true."

"So, what are you going to do, my man?"

"I'm going to do exactly as you knew I would. I'm going to accept your offer."

"That is the best news I've had all day. Welcome aboard!"

They shook hands. Moses leaned back in his chair. "We have a lot of details to discuss."

"Yes."

"You must have a place where I can reach you. And you will travel a lot. I'll need to be able to reach you easily. It would be better if you settled in a place not . . . near here."

"What are you talking about?"

"Reconstruction is going to become very harsh. There's a proposal for the South to be re-sectioned into military governances. And you cannot be a part of that with the work you will be doing."

"Where shall I go?"

"Wherever I can get to you and where you can lose yourself in a crowd. A bustling city is my recommendation. Most of the jobs you have will be on the East Coast. Occasionally Chicago."

"What about travel expenses?"

"I cannot have a paper trail to me, so you pay for everything. Believe me, expenses will be a pittance compared to the commissions you will earn." Moses swirled the brandy around in his glass. "Obviously this won't be a career that you can discuss with anyone, not even your family. In fact, I'd recommend you come up with an alternative job description."

"Yes, I understand that."

"Nor will you ever be able to go out and share with your drinking buddies the, ah, stories of the hunt."

"I can keep things to myself."

"I have no doubt, but how about after a night of imbibing? You cannot take the chance. So, from here on out, you must live the life of a teetotaler."

"I rarely drink, Moses."

Moses continued, "You have an affinity for this type of work. And it's men like you who even the playing field. It's men like you who keep the peace, administer justice, and allow all those poor political bastards to go on thinking they really make a difference."

A smile twitched at Gabriel's lips. "I'll remember that, Moses, when I'm sitting in church on Sunday mornings."

Moses laughed. "I'm sure you will." He stood up and reached again into his pocket. He took out his money clip and peeled off some more bills. "Here's another hundred. Consider it a welcome to the family. Go buy something lovely for your sweetheart and let that beautiful girl know she's worth more than that sorry pile of ashes she used to make her living from."

Moses sat down and gazed at Gabriel. "Take her away from here, Gabriel. Make her yours. You'll need someone who warms your heart in the dead of night. And it might as well be someone you love."

SIMONE SAT OUTSIDE UNDER HER MAGNOLIA TREE. AN afternoon breeze had come up, whispering through her garden, but she paid little attention. Now that she was without income, her thoughts were occupied with staving off impending deprivation. She looked up to see Gabriel approaching. He sat down beside her.

She sighed. "I think the roses are going to bloom early this spring."

"Then why look so sad?"

"I think I shall have to let Delcine go because I can no longer afford her."

Tears began to roll down Simone's cheeks. Gabriel took out his handkerchief and offered it to her. She accepted it, silently dabbing her eyes and wiping her nose. "I was such a fool. I thought I could leave the past behind. How silly I was."

"Simone, look at me."

She turned to him, the green flecks in her eyes swallowed up in the oceans of her hurt.

"You can start again, you know."

"That's impossible."

His gaze swept the garden. "You know, I've read so many good books this past year because of you, and yet, can I find even one passage to assist me when I need it the most?" He paused. "I've been offered a job to work for Moses Del Cerro."

Simone smiled. "Oh, *Monsieur*, I am so happy for you!"

"But my happiness is not complete unless"—he stopped to compose himself—"unless you share it with me."

"*Monsieur* . . ."

Gabriel pressed on, "The work takes me out of the South. I have the chance to make a splendid living, but I don't want to do it without you." He knelt down on one knee and took both her hands in his. He kissed the back of each one as tears again pooled in her eyes. "Simone Margaret Livingston, will you marry me?"

She was being asked to take a step forward for which there was no turning back. And yet, could this be her opportunity? She didn't know Gabriel all that well, but truly, didn't he know her better than anyone else? She smiled. "*Oui, Monsieur,*" she whispered, "I will marry you."

10

NEW ORLEANS 1867

February 20, 1867

D*EAR DAVIE,*
     Since we last corresponded, the New Year has heralded opportunities I never believed possible for someone like me.

I have taken a job with a Northern-based company, working on special projects conducted in the government or in private industry. This country is changing, Davie, and I'm on the cusp of it! I get to be part of this new era of industry and invention.

Obviously, I no longer work for the fair Miss Livingston. It is, however, a moot point because her store was tragically destroyed in a fire on New Year's Eve. But more importantly, I've asked her to marry me, and she has accepted! Imagine me, a grown man who did not learn to read or write until I met you, now engaged to a beautiful young lady, educated, and refined! Can a more fanciful tale be conjured?

I regret the engagement will not be a proper length, as we will marry in June. I must start my job forthwith and need to relocate to the North, somewhere central to the hub of my activities. In the meantime, I have commissioned a lovely engagement ring for my betrothed: a pearl encircled by garnets in the shape of a flower. She does love her flowers! She tends to her garden as if the roses and camellias were her children.

Forgive me this rush of news before an inquiry as to your own wellbeing. I trust that all is well with you and your family? I trust also that you are keeping up with your studies and making your mama proud. As always, I look forward to your speedy reply.

Yours Truly,

Gabriel Cooper

March 6, 1867

Dear Gabriel,

Congratulations and best wishes! I can only surmise how happy you are. Clearly there are no lovely damsels here at school; just classes in philosophy and the dreaded Latin, and of course mathematics and the sciences. There is chapel service twice a week and I do enjoy horsemanship, but it's the games between the dormitory houses and student squadrons that I find most appealing. After that sparring session last fall, my friends put me up to start a boxing club, or "club of the pugilistic arts" so that it sounded more respectable when presented to the school board. Unbelievably, it was approved and I'm the star team member! The school board has even hired a coach so that we can receive formal training and begin competitions with other academies. And to think when I met you, I did not know a thing about fighting and now I'm learning to be a prize boxer!

My family is doing well, although my mother is not terribly happy about the boxing; however, my father has counselled her to keep still about the matter and let me acquire some skills in this area. I'm almost sixteen now and will soon be able to call myself a man; I should be able to fight like one. I truly desire to take my skills to the competitive arena statewide or even nationally.

Again, my congratulations on your upcoming wedding; I hope to hear from you again soon.

Your friend and best prize-fighter,
David Tremont

SIMONE AND GABRIEL WERE MARRIED ON JUNE 30, RIGHT after Simone's twentieth birthday. They were married in the gazebo of the Del Cerros' garden. It was a small, private affair, officiated by the Del Cerro family priest.

Simone wore a white silk gown fashioned after the latest trends in a new French industry known as *haute couture*. Her lace veil, taken from her late mother's trousseau, was cleaned and mended for the occasion, then attached to a coronet of orange blossoms and white roses from her own garden. The entire accessory wafted like gossamer over her silk bodice trimmed in lace and seed pearls.

Moses stood as Gabriel's groomsman and Delcine stood in as Simone's first and only bridesmaid.

She walked down the aisle by herself, a vision of silk and crinoline, her creamy complexion peeking through the veil in the dappled sunlight. Was she real, Gabriel thought to himself as he watched her approach him, was any of this real? But then he caught her tiny smile and he knew then that this was, indeed, his reality. He stepped forward to meet her and lifted her veil, barely able to breathe as he stared at her. He took one of her gloved hands, pressed it to his lips and together they stepped toward the priest.

IT WAS WELL INTO THE NIGHT. THEY HAD DINED ON HAM and pheasant with their small group of wedding guests, drank champagne, and strolled arm in arm around the beautiful garden that they had been married in. Now they had been brought back in a fabulous carriage to Simone's house where she stood, still in her wedding gown, waiting for Gabriel to open the front door. And open it he did, scooping her into his arms and carrying her, giggling, over the threshold.

They stood there, staring at each other in the candlelight. Gabriel took Simone's left hand and lifted it, studying the pale gold band that now rested against her engagement ring.

"Mrs. Cooper . . . I still can't believe it."

Simone smiled up at him, hardly the nervous bride. "You have your whole life to believe it, *Monsieur*."

He took her in his arms. He inhaled the smell of her hair, her skin. "Shall we go to bed?"

SHE HAD WAITED A LONG TIME FOR THIS, BUT STILL SHE felt a twinge of anxiety. She had come to the edge of such a threshold before, and she had paid dearly for it. Even though she had the reassurance of a wedding band, she couldn't help but fear that she would be orphaned in her desire.

She led Gabriel into her bedroom for the first time. She lit a couple of candles as he looked around.

"So this is where the lovely Mrs. Cooper spent her girlhood."

"*Oui,* although you make it sound far more charming than it really was." Simone motioned to the bed. "I bought a larger bed . . . for the occasion . . . ." Her voice trailed off awkwardly.

Gabriel laughed and pulled her to him. "God," he breathed, thinking he was going to devour her, "I love you!"

He pulled back and looked at her. He, too, had waited a long time for this, but he did not want to overwhelm her. She was, after all, his wife.

He kissed her gently, letting his hands wander over her like they never had before. He sought out the curves sequestered beneath her gown; her breasts, her hips, her buttocks. As she relaxed, her breath quickened and she let her kisses linger while she ran her fingers through his hair.

He reached behind her to unfasten the wedding gown with its column of silly buttons. His fingers wrestled with the little cloth-covered devils, nestled in their looped buttonholes, so much so that he finally turned her around so he could see better what he was doing. He didn't notice her stiffening every time he succeeded in undoing one.

But as he was about to slip the gown off her shoulders, Simone spoke up. To his amazement, she sounded tense. "Let me blow out these candles."

"No, I want to see you," and he kissed the back of her soft, ivory neck as his hands gently pushed the gown off her shoulders. He thought he heard her whimper, but assumed it was a virgin's anxiety and nothing more.

He pushed down the hoop skirt and the cotton pantaloons, running his hands over her full, firm thighs. He ran his hands up the front of her, caressing her pelvis. She stood there, frozen.

"Don't be so nervous," he murmured as he began to loosen her corset. But as he unsnapped the silk stockings, she tried to move past him to the candles. "No!" he said sharply, irritated. "I want to see you. I want to make love to you and see you."

He couldn't believe how anxious she had become, but as his eyes travelled down away from her terrified face, he suddenly knew why. A raspberry pink scar, furrowed in some places and raised in others, began just above her left collarbone, and traversed diagonally across her chest, ending in a nasty knot above the nipple of her right breast.

He cupped her breasts in his hands, kissing first the scar and then her cleavage. "This doesn't matter. Nothing matters because I love you."

He drew back the covers and pressed her upon the bed. As he laid her down, Simone undid her hair and shook it out, a torrent of dark tendrils and curls.

Gabriel stood above her staring, his mouth dry and his heart pounding. He undid his shirt and stripped it off, doing the same with his pants. Suddenly he stood there, naked before her, and he crawled onto the bed, stretching lengthwise beside her.

She looked down the length of him, and her eyes were drawn, predictably, to his penis. He took her hand, laying the flat of her palm on it. "Feel it."

He rubbed her hand up and down, watching her eyes widen and her pupils dilate. He knew she was ready. Then, fearing he was going to explode without ever getting inside her, he shoved her hand away. He got up on his knees and wedged himself between her legs, spreading them apart, exposing her entire womanhood before him. He ran his middle finger over all those delightful little parts, finding the tight little center that he would soon claim his spousal right to. She raised her pelvis responsively, crimson patches of arousal mottling her throat and breasts.

He slipped his finger inside of her. "Open your eyes. I want to see you. I want you to see me; see what I am doing."

She opened her eyes, looking at him through prisms of desire and excitement. She watched him as he withdrew his finger and said, "You've waited a long time, haven't you? Well, my darling, so have I, so have I . . ."

And with that he grabbed her ankles and pushed them up and back, hoisting up her knees. He placed himself at her opening and then, his blue eyes fixed upon her, he pierced her with a slow deliberate thrust. She yelped involuntarily as he broke her hymen, but he sank deep inside her, moving back and forth, back and forth. His hands sought her hands, and he kissed her deeply on the lips as he thrusted harder and faster, his breathing matching his movements. Simone arched her back, gasping for air, but it was Gabriel who climaxed first, clenching his teeth and then shouting, "You're mine, mine, *mine!*"

His words brought her crashing back to reality. But as she searched Gabriel's face in that instant, she saw nothing, nothing but a man in the throes of physical release. When he opened his eyes again, he smiled sweetly. Perhaps, she reassured herself, his claim was only one of passion.

Gabriel sank into her soft body, covering her damp face with kisses, not withdrawing from her. He felt warm and satisfied, but he had meant those words. He had claimed her as no religious ceremony could, in a primal act that created a basic, instinctive, and everlasting bond.

He rolled off her and cradled her in his arms. Wiping away the blood of her lost virginity with the edge of the sheet, he then began caressing her between her legs, kissing and sucking her breasts, bringing her to the orgasm she had not reached before. Then as she lay limp and relaxed, he traced that hideous scar of hers with his finger and asked, "How?"

He responded to her terrified silence with a whisper, "I know this is from a whip. I know it because you're not the only one." And he sat up so she could see the weals and knots of his past life.

Simone gasped and sat up beside him, touching his back. "Oh, my God. I always wondered why you never let me run my hands down your back."

"And I always wondered why you wore such high collars, especially when your skin was so lovely."

As they lay back down together, Gabriel murmured, "Tell me about it."

She could lie to him, say simply that it was an accident from a long time ago, but did she want to keep such a secret? Out of nowhere she heard Lucinda's voice, *We all be dirt under the Master's feet.* No, she must tell; secrets like this turned you into dirt.

Gabriel watched the emotions play over her face. "You must always remember that I love you. And I know more than you think."

She looked at him, alarmed. "What are you talking about?"

He raised himself up on one elbow, his finger tracing the fullness of her mouth. "These lips, I can tell they've been kissed before. I knew there had been someone before me, more than just a bumbling boy of your childhood. Someone more serious, older, who had taught you things. I even wondered if you were a virgin. Who was it, Simone? Who took you only so far in love and then left you with only . . . a scar?"

Simone stared at him, wondering how it could all be so obvious.

It was as if he could read her mind. "Nobody knows these things but me. All others think they know you. But there is more. You are more . . . and that is why I love you so. This scar"—again, he touched it--—"tells of a tale I must know. We cannot have such secrets between us."

Finally, Simone found her voice. "All right; I suppose you, if anyone, should know this."

And with that she began to recount a memory that was as deep and permanent as any mark a whip could make.

WHILE HER MOTHER HAD DELIGHTED IN HER precociousness, Simone's father found her troublesome. After his second wife died, Peter forced Simone to do what he considered proper women's work. He was done with female relationships.

As soon as Simone returned, Peter laid down the rules. Never was she to be unchaperoned. Her duties were strictly bound to church and home.

Feeling trapped, Simone succumbed to the oppression and slowly, she began to suffocate.

But occasionally there were opportunities to see the world. Market day was when Simone accompanied their neighbor, the elderly widow Hartford, to the French Market in *Le Vieux Carre*. The widow was kind and generous and would often buy Simone extra groceries. The trip always ended with them at a café, having beignets and chicory coffee.

Simone loved going to the French Market. The sights and smells reminded her of her childhood, although Mrs. Hartford was very protective of her while they were out. They were, after all, in a Yankee-occupied city.

Simone was fifteen on that spring market day. She remembered it to be lovely, filled with dogwood and blooming lilacs. But she knew something was wrong when she saw the widow's Black slave, Otis, show up on foot. He smiled apologetically.

"Mornin', Miss Simone. I's was ordered by Missus to come by and tell y'all that Missus won't be goin' ta mahket t'day. She be ailin' dis mornin' an' not up to da trip."

Simone's heart sank. "What's wrong with her?"

"Aw, it's da cough an' ya know Miz Hartford. She a' worryin' she gonna get da fever. Ma wife's made her some fine tea with them herbs from da garden an' she be right in no time. But she ain't fit ta be goin' ta mahket, ya understan', Miss Simone, ma'am."

The hell I do, thought Simone, but she smiled sympathetically. "Of course, Otis. Your Frannie makes wonderful medicines. Wish Mrs. Hartford well for me."

"Thank ya kindly, Miss Simone." He stood there, waiting for Simone to excuse him.

"Please tell Mrs. Hartford I'll call when she's feeling better."

"Yes'm, thank ya, ma'am." He lifted his hat and turned on his heel.

Simone watched him leave. She could not make herself go back in the house. Suddenly, she felt uncontrollable defiance. *I'm going anyway.*

She would take a different route through the city, so no one would know her. She didn't think about Yankee soldiers or any of the dangers of the Occupation. She was too excited about her few hours of unchaperoned freedom.

Quietly, her head down, she stepped onto the street, blending into the ebb and flow of pedestrians. When she had been in Mrs. Hartford's carriage with the curtains drawn, she never knew how she got to different places outside her neighborhood. It wasn't long before she found herself in an unsavory area near the port of New Orleans.

For a moment she was filled with panic, but soon fascination prevailed. She saw saloons, brothels and women sitting in windows, provocatively dressed. Were these the "bad girls" that Mrs. Patrick insisted she would become if she did not attend church and mind her place in her father's house?

What did the bad girls do? Where did they live? She crossed to the other side of the street and approached one of the buildings where she saw girls peering out from the floors above. The temptation to peek was too strong. Was this how Eve felt when she had tasted the apple?

Men's voices mingled with girls' laughter and there was music from a piano. One of the windows was cracked open and Simone moved to peer inside. She could hardly believe her eyes as she watched men drinking, smoking, and fondling these girls in ways that made her blush. She watched in rapt fascination as these girls worked the room, pushing their flesh at the men, familiar in a way that Simone found both compelling and contemptible. She remembered Lucinda and her uncle, but this somehow wasn't like that. This seemed enjoyable...

She stood, as if her shoes were nailed there, oblivious to the tall, white Union soldier, dressed in an officer's naval uniform, who came up and stood beside her.

Finally, he spoke. "Are you looking for someone?"

Simone whirled around her eyes wide with alarm. "Excuse me," she stammered.

When she tried to move past him, he blocked her way. "Don't tell me you were going to inquire within about a job?" His brown eyes twinkled.

"Please let me by. I seem to have taken the wrong turn."

"Really? You seem to be exactly where you want to be."

"No, you misunderstand! I am on my way to market." Suddenly she noticed that he was chuckling, and anger began to replace her fear. "Let me by! Don't you have better things to do here?"

He laughed outright. "I like your wit, Miss . . .?"

Simone tried again to move past him and again he blocked her way. "Ma'am, this is not a safe place for a young lady. I'll escort you to where you are going."

"Oh, please don't! It's the first time I've been out alone in—" She stopped herself before she divulged her entire secret. "You need not escort me anywhere."

She could tell that this soldier was maybe fifteen years her senior and used to getting what he wanted. He bowed formally. "Captain Malcolm Beaumont, ma'am, of the United States Navy. And I *will* escort you to where you are going."

Simone rolled her eyes. She began to walk but he kept stride with her, steering her away from the lascivious stares of drunken men.

As they reached the end of the street Simone said, "I'll be going now. You need not come along, really."

He ignored her request. "I've never seen a lady— much less such a young one—out by herself in this town. How is it that you came to be unescorted?"

"I was on my way to market. The lady I usually go with was sick, so I decided to go by myself. Please, Captain, please let me go."

"You do know there are laws which forbid your protest against my company, don't you? Unless of course, you wish to be treated as one of the girls you were so avidly spying upon."

Simone had heard of this law from both Mrs. Patrick and Mrs. Hartford, that any woman who treated a Union soldier with contempt would be treated as a "bad girl," avoiding the proper word of "prostitute."

"Oh God," Simone muttered, "just take me to the edge of my neighborhood. I can't be seen with you."

"As you wish, my dear mademoiselle, but only under one condition."

"And what would that be?"

"Tell me your name."

Simone was silent.

"Tell me your name or I will escort you right to your door."

"Simone."

"And your last name?"

"Livingston."

"It is a pleasure to make your acquaintance, Miss Livingston. I am at your service. And I will only take you to the edge of your neighborhood."

She began to walk away. He caught up with ease. "So, you were going to market, but you have nothing to show for your troubles today."

Simone pursed her lips. "I have you to show for my troubles."

Captain Beaumont chuckled. "True. But I meant, you have nothing in your basket."

"Nor should I have anything. Otherwise, I'd have to explain to my father how I got food when I wasn't supposed to have even left the house."

"But you have to eat."

"You Yankees seem to have taken all the food for yourselves."

He laughed then and said, "You aren't a bit afraid of me, are you?"

Simone did not answer him and they walked on, leaving the riverfront and the port, turning up Canal

Street. Amidst the bobtail streetcars and activity, Simone turned to him. "I'm close to home now. You can leave me here."

"It was a great pleasure to meet you, Miss Livingston."

"I really must go." With that Simone stepped off the sidewalk and lost herself in the throngs of horses, wagons, and people.

~

SIMONE MADE IT HOME BEFORE HER FATHER AND PUT THE day behind her. It was only the next morning that a catastrophe threatened.

As the sun rose, Simone entered the kitchen and opened the back window. She loved these few quiet moments before she was harnessed to her chores. As she opened the back door, she found a sack at her feet. She picked it up and a small slip of paper fell out.

Miss Livingston,
So you might have something to show
For your troubles yesterday.
Most Sincerely,
Captain Beaumont

"*Mon Dieu!*" Simone glanced around, making sure that she was indeed alone. Then she peeked inside the sack to find a small slab of ham, half a dozen eggs, an onion and potatoes, butter, and two tea cakes wrapped in cheese cloth.

Where had he gotten all of this and, good God, how

did he know where she lived? Simone crossed the kitchen and threw open the door to their tiny raised cellar. There in the cramped space she searched for a hiding place.

She could store the butter, eggs, potatoes and onion safely as they would not be so out of place. But the ham and tea cakes? *Well, the hell with him*, Simone thought as her father came to mind. She'd store the tea cakes in her room and eat them herself. But the ham? She'd at least eat some of it and she'd keep it down here for now. She knew her father would likely not venture here, for food was women's work. After he left for the store, she'd fetch it and have a slice of it with a tea cake. She smiled. What a lovely surprise, even if it was from a Yankee who knew where she lived.

A Yankee who knew where she lived. She thought of the tall, handsome soldier who almost turned her day into a disaster. Well, if she ever saw him again—which, of course, she wouldn't—she'd have to thank him.

Simone stuffed the food under the basement steps. As she set the water to boil, she thought of different ways to dispose of the ham when she'd had her fill of it. She couldn't keep it for too long, it was too risky. She couldn't give it away, for people would ask questions. She couldn't bury it, for what if an animal dug it up? No, she'd have to dispose of it in the back swamp.

Later that day, when she had set the dinner vegetables to cooking and her father had returned to the store, Simone drew the curtains and sat down with the newfound food. As her teeth sunk into the smoked meat she shivered. How long had it been since she'd had something like this? As she ate, an idea struck her. What if she sliced the ham, hid it in her room and then just discarded the bone? Rotting ham would smell, so she could only keep what she could eat in forty-eight hours. The rest would have to go tonight, after her father went to bed.

Lost in her own thoughts, she allowed the pot over the fire to boil over. Now the boiled turnips and potatoes would be like slop and she had just ruined good food by scheming on how to get rid of even better. Well, she could thank that Yankee Captain for that as well.

First, she saw the flashes of lightning, then she heard the thunder. *Mon Dieu*, there was going to be a storm. If the storm broke soon, she wouldn't be able to go to the back swamp.

She had spent the afternoon figuring out how to make her way to that place, filled with creatures and insects and scourges such as Yellow Fever. She'd found an old map her mother had once used in her geography lessons. Thankfully she wasn't afraid of the dark or thunderstorms.

When her father left for his church meeting, she cut up what she thought she could eat of the ham. She stored it upstairs in her closet and put the remainder in the sack from which it had come. She stuffed herself with the second teacake, brushing the telltale crumbs off the table. Now all she had to do was wait.

Later, she heard her father open the front door. "Simone!" he called from the front entryway.

Simone emerged from the kitchen. "What is it?"

"Did you not hear me enter? Here, take my coat and hat."

Simone helped her father. "Would you like a cup of tea?"

"What, that swill you brew from the garden?"

"The price of tea is very high, *Papa*. It's the best I can do with the allowance you give me."

"Well, it isn't going to get better anytime soon. That beast Butler has the city in a stranglehold. He probably keeps the best tea for himself." He wiped his forehead with a handkerchief. "I'm feeling poorly."

Simone watched her father ascend the narrow stairs. As soon as she heard his bedroom door close, she went to the parlor to glance at the small grandfather clock hanging on the wall. It was half past nine. Outside the wind was blowing furiously, but still no rain.

Simone went upstairs. Better to go to her room and sit in her mother's rocking chair where she could watch the lightning that was travelling in from the Gulf.

SHE MUST HAVE DOZED OFF, FOR SUDDENLY SHE HEARD the clock strike ten. Had she not just sat down? The thunder followed the lightning closely now. Simone wrapped her shawl tightly around her and shut her window. She picked up the sack and snuck down the stairs. With shaking fingers, she unlatched the back door feeling, as the storm rumbled and flashed, a tiny, quivering thrill.

She slipped around the side of the house and quickly crossed the street. The night breeze was cool, drying the sweat that beaded her forehead and soaked her bodice.

There was no rain yet, but it wouldn't be long now before there'd be a deluge.

Down, down the narrow side streets she went, smelling the fermentation and algae of the bayou waters. Soon she was in mud. She stopped and removed her shoes and stockings. Mud and swamp grass curled up between her toes as the first heavy droplets of rain began to fall. Lightning flashed, lighting up the swamp. When she could go no further, she heaved the entire sack into the darkness. It landed with a gulping splash.

Lightning flashed again, and suddenly, as Simone turned to go, a man stepped in front of her. Simone shrieked and almost sank into the mud. The stranger lifted his kerosene lamp to his face and Simone saw it was Captain Beaumont.

"*Mon Dieu!*" she cried, looking up at him. "You again! What in God's name are you doing here?"

The captain stared back at her. "I should ask you the same thing!"

"You nearly scared me to death!"

"And nothing else about this does? C'mon," he said grabbing her arm, as the rain pelted down, "let's get to shelter."

He propelled her forward with a heavy hand. As they got to the first neighborhood, he pulled her beneath the eaves of a storefront. Around them the rain poured.

Simone narrowed her eyes at him. "Were you following me?"

"As a matter of fact, I was. And what in God's name, were you doing out there? You do know that your city is under martial law and if you were caught doing whatever you were doing, you could find yourself arrested and sent off to Ship Island?"

Simone thought of the infamous Confederate P.O.W. prison. A frightened tear rolled down her cheek. "Certainly, *Capitaine*, if you can find it in your heart to give me food, you must also have it in your heart to show me mercy."

"I have no intention of sending you to Ship Island, Miss Livingston. I am merely cautioning you on the peril of your actions."

She squeezed her trembling hands together. "Thank you, *mon Capitaine.*" *Mon Capitaine . . .?* Somehow the possessive fit.

"But you still have not answered my question."

Simone tried to smile. "You must understand. I could not keep all your ham. It would raise suspicions and my father is a very strict man. How could I explain such a wonderful specimen of meat? You must realize, *mon Capitaine*, we are not rich citizens; we barely get by."

"And the rest of the food?"

"Ah, well, I have kept everything else. And as for the teacakes, I ate them both, thank you very much."

His expression softened. "I apologize for putting you in such a compromising position."

Simone forgot herself and put her hand on his arm. "Compromising? *Mais non!* It was an adventure! Really, I should thank you."

As the storm abated, he offered her his arm. "May I escort you home?"

She took his arm in a soft, ladylike grip. "You may escort me nearly home. I cannot take the chance of being seen with you, especially at this hour."

As they made their way back, he asked, "Weren't you afraid at all?"

"No, in fact, I can't understand why I've never done this before!"

"You are an amazing young lady. If you were a man, I'd want you commanding at my side in battle."

"Such an odd compliment, but I'll accept it."

"Please do. Your courage is remarkable."

"But I could never command at your side, *mon Capitaine*. I would be on wrong side of the war, sir. Remember, I belong to the Confederacy."

"With all due respect, ma'am, there will be no Confederacy at the end of this. You and I are of the same nation, and yes, we would fight on the same side."

"Why were you following me?"

"I have been following you since I first laid eyes upon you."

"I should be dismayed to hear this, and yet I am not. What do you want from me?"

"I want you to have dinner with me."

Simone stopped and looked up at him, troubled at his forwardness. "That would be highly improper, even dangerous for me."

"Somehow, I don't think you care about what is proper or improper. And as for danger, what do you call sneaking out past curfew in a city that is occupied by the enemy?" He pressed on, "You must have dinner with me. You must, or I will call for you at your doorstep."

Oh God, where was this going to end? "I told you my father is a very strict man."

"But not a very discerning one, Miss Livingston. How did you get out tonight without him knowing?"

"I had to wait until he was asleep. Are you saying you would wait until midnight to have dinner with me?"

"Yes, that is exactly what I am saying."

Thoughts of a secret rendezvous, eating forbidden food with this handsome stranger captivated her imagination. How could she resist this? "When would you want to have dinner with me?"

"Tomorrow night."

Simone felt the hot rush of blood to her cheeks and she said, "It would have to be late. After eleven."

"Of course."

"Where would I meet you?"

"At the edge of the swamp where I found you tonight. We will go where no one will recognize or question you."

"I must come home straight away after dining with you."

Of course, what kind of gentleman would I be to keep a lady out to all hours of the night?"

"Then after tomorrow night will you leave me alone?"

"Don't hasten our parting, Miss Livingston. You may even enjoy my company and want to see me again."

"This is an absurdity."

"We live in an absurd time."

"You are the enemy."

"I am not the enemy. The walls we build between each other are."

"You fancy yourself clever."

"And you fancy yourself a young lady who thinks independently. I like that. Is that so wrong?"

They were nearing their point of departure. He affirmed, "I shall see you tomorrow night then."

Simone hesitated. *Have I gone mad?*

It was as if he read her thoughts. "Do not consider disappointing me, Miss Livingston. Remember, I will come knocking at your door if you do not show up tomorrow night."

She knew there was no way out. "Of course, I will be there. But do me one favor."

"And what is that?"

"Never consider yourself *not* the enemy!" Wrapping her shawl tightly around her, she crossed the street and hurried into a blanket of darkness.

Still barefoot, Simone tiptoed into her house. All was quiet. By the rain's steady cadence she undressed, wiping her feet and legs clean.

After she crawled into bed, she lay awake, listening to the rain.

Did tonight really happen? She closed her eyes and her breathing deepened. Only time would tell.

THE NEXT DAY, SIMONE REPEATED TO HERSELF, *AFTER tonight there will be no more contact* . . . but somehow, she knew this was not true.

Why, why did her insides, particularly her insides *down there*, feel as if they were turning into a wet puddle of . . . what? Whenever she thought of him her body responded in ways she had never experienced before. What was happening?

As the sun set and the hour neared, she grew so tense

she thought she'd burst. Finally, her father put down his bible and stretched.

"Good night."

"Good night."

Simone went back to the embroidery she was working on. She pricked her finger and drew blood as she listened to his receding footsteps. The grandfather clock ticked maddeningly on the wall. Finally, she could stand it no longer. She went upstairs.

Tonight, there were no thunderstorms, nothing to cover any sounds she might make leaving the house. But surely no creaking floors or hinges could be louder than her pounding heart.

Muffled but vigorous snoring came through her father's door. In her room, she pulled back the bedcovers, placing her pillows where her body should be.

It was ten fifteen. She took her shoes in one hand and wrapped her shawl around her. Holding her breath, she tiptoed out her bedroom and back down the stairs.

Once outside, Simone put on her shoes, opened the back gate, and crossed the street.

She hurried away from her house, wondering again at the madness she had gotten herself into. But then again, had she not been forced into this?

She neared her destination, glancing around furtively. He could be anywhere between here and that hideous mud pit she had waded into last night.

To her relief, Malcolm Beaumont stepped out from the shadows. A smile played on his lips. "You made it, my brave little soldier."

"Did I have a choice?" She was afraid to show how happy she was to see him.

He offered her his arm and she took it with confidence. "Where are we going?"

"Someplace private and safe."

His carriage was waiting in a grove. The driver, a young soldier, kept his eyes averted.

Malcolm opened the door and helped her inside. She settled herself back in the plush interior as the carriage began to move. As he settled in next to her, she asked, "And from what good home did you steal this?"

Malcolm chuckled. "Do you consider me a thief?"

"Surely your army doesn't hand out such finery."

"It is called commandeering, my dear Miss Livingston. It is my right to commandeer all equipment that might be needed by the Union forces in this campaign."

"So now I am part of your 'campaign?'"

This time he laughed outright. "Hardly, Miss Livingston, hardly. Enjoy this! How many opportunities will you ever have like this again? This is something you can tell your grandchildren about one day."

"I doubt that. I think I'll be too ashamed to ever admit to anything like this."

"Ah, yes, once again you chastise me with declarations of shame and impropriety. You do not fool me, for you are not ashamed of this, no matter how much you tell me differently."

He was right, although she would never admit it to him. She sent a silent prayer to a God she barely believed in, that He would deliver her from calamity if this Captain's intentions were less than honorable.

The carriage wended its way through town, finally pulling to a stop. Malcolm offered her his hand and she was glad for her summer gloves, as her hands were cold and clammy.

She alighted upon the ground and immediately turned to Malcolm, appalled. She was back at that brothel where they had first met. Malcolm smiled courteously and offered her his arm.

Simone recoiled. "Take me home! How dare you bring me to this place?"

Malcolm looked at her patiently. "You are curious, are you not? Remember, it is only for dinner and nothing more. And some of the best food in New Orleans is served in this establishment." He gestured to the soldier to take the carriage away. "I told you I would take you to a place where nobody would recognize you. The owner of this place has arranged for us to dine privately so your anonymity is assured. That is, if you get out of the street."

Those words sent Simone flying up the steps and into the brothel, where the madam was waiting for them. Miss B, nicknamed The Professor, appraised the young girl with a professional eye. She squinted into her monocle and tapped the glass jar that held her pet cockroach, Jimmy.

"Well, Captain Beaumont," she gurgled in a drawl dulled with smoke and opium vapors, "who do we have here?"

Malcolm bowed. "May I introduce Miss Simone Livingston; Simone, this is Miss B, the owner of this fine establishment who has made all of this possible tonight."

Simone stared at Miss B who observed, "Such a look of distaste. Are your manners too good to be used in a house of gentlemanly recreation?"

Her forthrightness prompted a response from Simone. "*Mais non, Madame.* I'm just dismayed that my name is bandied about so freely."

Miss B laughed, her crown of red hair bobbing in the candlelight. A dimple crept into her aging, ivory cheeks. "The girl fancies herself important. Well, don't worry; the safekeeping of secrets is the butter to my bread." Miss B got up from the chaise lounge on which she had settled her overflowing frame. She handed the jar with the cockroach to a young houseboy. "Feed Jimmy something."

Miss B opened a side door. "Down the hall on the left. Enjoy your evenin'." She began to ascend the stairs, but stopped and turned. "I serve the best, the brightest and the bravest here, Miss Livingston. A little French thing like y'all would do nicely working for me."

Hot, prickling color inflamed Simone's cheeks. Before she could say anything, Malcolm steered her through the side door and down the hallway. As they walked, Simone heard laughter and a wanton cry that inflamed her cheeks even more. Malcolm opened a door to reveal a private parlor with a table set for two inside, complete with a white tablecloth and gleaming dishes. To Simone's surprise, the room was tasteful.

Another slave wheeled in a serving cart. His gaze lowered, he uncovered each dish; roasted leg of lamb, potatoes, chutney, and carrots glazed in brown sugar and pecans.

Simone stared. "No wonder no one else has anything to eat. It's all here!"

Malcolm smiled and picked up a huge carving knife. He set to slicing the meat.

Simone watched, ill at ease. Malcolm seemed to notice her discomfort. "Relax and enjoy. You have spent far too many hours looking after others, which is a pity. If you were my lady, I would never let you lift a finger in drudgery."

Simone was suddenly aware of her own roughened hands as she folded them in her lap. "You are used to this kind of thing, aren't you?"

"What kind of thing?"

"This, the best life has to offer."

"Is that so terrible?"

"No, just unfamiliar."

He sat down opposite her. "Guilty as charged. I am used to the finer things in life. I come from a New York shipping family. I expect one day I will carry on that tradition."

"You must have had it all: boarding school, college…"

Malcolm peered at her. "Why, you're jealous! Would you want the same?"

"Of course, who wouldn't?"

"Not too many women, I dare say." He looked into her eyes. "Yet you speak so eloquently. You've obviously had opportunities for education."

"My mother oversaw my education. She was very well educated in France before she married my father."

"I see. She did a splendid job of it, and I should like to commend her."

"She died."

"I'm sorry to hear that, Miss Livingston."

"Thank you."

"So, it is just you and your father?"

"Yes."

"No siblings?"

"No."

"Your father is a lucky man to have such a lovely, dutiful daughter."

"May we speak of other things?"

Malcolm deftly switched the subject. "How is your dinner?"

"Exquisite!"

"So, you are glad you came then!"

"Well, don't be too pleased with yourself. I would have never dreamed coming to such a place and that woman who greeted us . . . such rudeness!"

"Ah, the Professor—how she hates to be called that–is a shrewd businesswoman. She saw a beautiful, accomplished young lady who would be a prize in her repertoire of girls. There was nothing personal about it."

"Why do you call her The Professor?"

Malcolm chuckled, "She has a preponderance to lecture, especially if she has imbibed of the spirits. She fancies herself an expert on many topics."

"Is she a learned woman?"

Malcolm shrugged. "To be honest with you, I've never really listened."

"Well, she is most repulsive if you ask me. Really, do you think so little of me that you would bring me to such a place?"

Malcolm took a sip of wine. "Why shouldn't a woman be allowed to see what only men are privy to? You obviously wanted to know. If nothing else, you would have the chance to eat like you haven't in years."

"Is it bad to be curious about something nobody will even talk about?"

"No. On the contrary it's what attracted me to you." He reached across the table, laying his hand atop hers. "I'm sorry if I offended you."

"You did not offend me."

"To be honest with someone is to give them the respect they deserve."

Simone looked away.

He took his hand off hers. "We play such silly games in this world. I've had all silliness stripped from me with this war. I hope you really do understand."

Her eyes met his. "Yes, I do understand."

The time flew by. She let him serve her and listened to him, offering her opinions.

Soon it was time to go home. The carriage was brought around and they moved swiftly through the still dark streets.

As they neared her drop-off point, he turned to her. "I want to see you again. Shall we meet once more?"

There was no hesitation this time. "Yes."

"The night after tomorrow?"

"Yes."

"Same time?"

"Yes."

"Same place?"

"Yes."

"You do not know what this means to me."

"Yes, I do. It means the same to me."

Malcolm reached out and took her hand. He lifted it to his lips and kissed it. "Until then."

"Until then." Simone stepped down onto the street and hurried off.

THE NEXT DAY WAS A BLUR, AND SIMONE WENT TO BED early that night, feigning a headache. She was awakened the next day to her father's knocking. "I'm sorry," she stammered. "I'll be right down."

She dressed and hurried downstairs. Peter was impatient. "Maybe you should get something from Dr. Irving for that headache."

"I am fine now."

"You can't sleep half the day away as a cure. Surely there is a more efficient remedy."

Simone set a plate of fried potatoes before Peter. She watched him eat the food she had gotten from Malcolm. If her father wasn't such a bloodless viper, she would've served him remnants of ham from her stash.

Peter ate quickly, irritated that he would be late opening the store. When he left, Simone turned her thoughts to tonight. *"If you were my lady, I would never let you lift a finger in drudgery . . ."*

Oh, Mon Dieu, please let him be the one! She thought as she beat the dust out of the rugs.

The hours crept until finally she sat after dinner with her father, doing embroidery. She kept her head bent, concentrating on the stitches. She was afraid if their eyes met, he would become suspicious.

Finally, Peter rose, "Good night."

"Good night."

She heard him ascend the stairs, then close his bedroom door. She put away her embroidery and tiptoed upstairs. He was snoring already, thank God!

She changed into a finer dress. For the first time she

was painfully conscious of how she looked. She combed out her hair and reset it in a chignon, covering it with a beaded snood. Then she gathered up her shawl and shoes and left the house.

Malcolm was again waiting and this time she almost ran to him. He pulled her close. "Come, let's hurry; I have thought of nothing besides you these last two days!"

He took her to the same carriage with the same driver. As they climbed inside, she asked, "Where are we going?"

"Somewhere new," he squeezed her hand. "Did you think I would take you to the same place as I did before?"

She let him hold her hand. She wasn't sure she should let him touch her, but she wanted to feel his skin on top of hers, his lips . . . *oh Dear God in Heaven . . .*

They sped along the levee and passed the city until they came to an old plantation house. It was deserted, but Simone asked no questions. She simply wanted to be with him.

She stepped into a foyer bathed in candlelight. The dining room table was set, but except for them, the house was empty. There was food once again with a bottle of wine nearby. As Malcolm pulled her chair out, he asked, "Would you care for some wine, my dear mademoiselle?"

"I've never had any."

"Would you like to try some tonight?"

"A little might be nice . . ."

As they ate together, he asked what she had done since the last he had seen her.

"Thought about you," she answered simply.

Malcolm reached for her hand. "Do you know how

hard it is to conduct the affairs of a war when your greatest battle lies within your heart?"

"So poetic, *mon Capitaine*." Simone squeezed his hand.

"As I said before, I have no time for games in this world, Miss Livingston. May I call you Simone? So, I say as I feel and what I feel for you is more than poetry. Truthfully, what I say is measured, for if I say too much too soon, I might frighten you away. And that would kill me faster than any Confederate bullet."

"You won't frighten me away. And yes, you may call me Simone."

"Please call me Malcolm."

"Malcolm . . . but you will always be *mon Capitaine.*"

They finished their dinner and he uncorked the wine. "It is a dessert wine sent to me by my family." He chuckled. "They would not want me to be without the finer things, even in war. That would be so uncivilized."

"Perhaps they would consider you courting a Confederate lady uncivilized as well."

His smile receded. "They are not allowed opinions regarding my choice of a lady. It is one thing to offer a wine, but it is another to tell me whom to love."

He poured her a small glass, and though she sipped it daintily, it didn't take long for the alcohol to relax her.

Malcolm stood up and took her hand. She followed him upstairs to a balcony set off the main suite. He opened the French doors and they stood, listening to the sounds of the bayou. Soon Malcolm said, "It seems as if I have loved you forever, Simone. I have looked for you in the faces of all the women that I have known and when I saw you, I knew it was you that I loved. Does that frighten you?"

It had been so long since she had felt love of any kind that she turned her face away from him, beginning to cry.

He gently turned her back to him. "Why are you crying?" His voice was dark with concern.

"I'm sorry . . ."

"You should never be sorry for what's in your heart."

Simone was mortified at her outburst. "Perhaps I should go."

Malcolm offered his handkerchief. "Now why would you say that?"

"I've made a spectacle of myself."

"Don't talk like that." He tilted her chin so that she was forced to meet his eyes, and then he kissed the salt of her tears.

Humiliation was soon replaced by passion as she felt his lips touch her cheeks and then seek her mouth. After it was over, he looked at her in the bedroom's candlelight. "This is the first time a man's lips have touched you?"

"Yes," she murmured, breathless.

"Ah," he smiled softly, "you are so sweet." And this time he drew her close and kissed her again, his lips pressing upon hers, willing hers to part in response. Almost by instinct she did so, and slowly his tongue sought hers in a kiss she had never even dreamed existed.

She was melting into this moment when there was a soft knock at the door. She jumped away and Malcolm reassured her, "It's my driver."

"Oh," she said, disappointed, for now she didn't want to go.

He caressed her cheek with the back of his hand.

"This is not the end, you know. It's only the beginning."
And he steered her toward the door.

They held hands as the carriage whisked them back
to their respective worlds. Simone wondered how she
would get through the next day and hoped that her
thoughts of him would sustain her. *It's only the beginning . . .*

He spoke into the darkness. "When shall we meet
again?"

Simone bit her lip. "I don't think I can manage seeing
you over the weekend, but oh, I wish it could be every
day!"

"Then let us plan for next week. How about Tuesday
night?"

"Yes."

"I love you."

"I . . . love you."

"You say it with such trepidation."

"I've never said such a thing before. It sounds very
bold."

"It's not bold, it's wonderful."

"But so impossible." She thought she was going to cry
again.

"Why?"

"How long can we do this?"

"Darling, always know that I love you. And I never let
go of what I love."

As the carriage pulled to a stop, and she rose to get
out, he grabbed her arm and pulled her back to him. He
kissed her once more and said vehemently, "I mean what
I say, Simone Livingston."

"Yes," she said, but she was preoccupied now with
getting home.

He released her then and she alighted from the carriage, returning once again to the chaos that people called a world.

She met him the following Tuesday and then again on Thursday. Simone loved their conversations, how he listened to her, held her, kissed her.

They returned repeatedly to the plantation house on the bayou. Simone had begun to think of it as their home, silently pretending that they were husband and wife. They were once again on the balcony. His arms had encircled her from behind and he breathed in the sweet smell of her hair. "You have such lovely hair. I wish I could take it down."

"Do as you wish."

With deft fingers he undid the pins that held the dark, luxurious mane in place. He ran his fingers through it and then moved it to one side so he could kiss the nape of her neck. Malcolm's tongue travelled over her neck and slowly, he turned her toward him, letting his tongue flick her jawline until he found her lips. Simone's arms encircled his neck, a growl in her throat. Her eyes were bright as if with fever, her cheeks flushed pink with desire.

"I want to touch you," he said softly. "I want to feel your bare skin, all of it."

"Oh," she breathed, "Malcolm . . . *oui* . . ."

He lifted her up in his arms and carried her inside to the huge four-poster bed. He laid her down and kissed her again. "You are like a rosebud, so perfect; so ready . . ."

She asked with blatant innocence, "Is this what . . . married people do?"

"Oh sweetheart," he murmured, unbuttoning her bodice, "This and so much more. If you were my wife, it would be so much more . . ."

Simone sank back into the pillows, the throbbing between her thighs making her squirm. Malcolm kissed her face and her neck, his lips travelling toward her cleavage. When he reached her corset, he brought her forward so he could begin unlacing it.

Simone whispered breathlessly, "Malcolm, this isn't proper . . ."

"No, darling, it isn't." He laid bare her breasts, her hard nipples pushing up at him. As he bent over her, he said tenderly, "It isn't proper at all, it's love." And with that he closed his mouth on her nipple.

Simone let out tiny, audible gasps. Oh God, how could she have known? How could she have gone so long without this?

Malcolm deftly removed his shirt, then pinned her with his powerful shoulders and chest. She gripped his back, wishing he would push her skirt down and touch her in that most secret of places.

There was a soft knock at the door. *Damn!* Malcolm froze immediately. "Yes," he called out in his commander's voice.

"It's time, isn't it?" Simone asked flatly, the ebbing waves of ecstasy leaving her in agony.

"Yes," he sighed. "I know, darling. I wish I could keep you here forever, but I can't."

Suddenly Simone was aware of her nakedness. She struggled off the bed, covering herself. Malcolm laced up her corset with harsh, angry movements, so much so that Simone looked at him questioningly as he helped her into her bodice. He met her gaze and asked a little harshly, "You have questions, don't you?"

"Yes." She turned her back to him.

"What are they?"

"I don't know."

He withdrew a brush from a vanity and began to brush her hair, his movements softening. "You know you can ask me anything."

"I know."

"You seem troubled."

"I'm . . . lost, Malcolm."

"I see." He wound her hair back and began to replace the pins.

She looked in the mirror he held before her. "Do all men know how to do a lady's hair?"

Malcolm chuckled. "All men with older sisters, I suppose."

He offered her his hand and said, "Come. Let's talk about your questions on the way home."

As they sat together in the swaying carriage, Simone finally asked, "You said you wished you could keep me forever, but you couldn't. What did you mean by that?"

"Are you asking me if you are just a fleeting moment in my life?"

"Well, yes."

"You are seared onto my heart forever, but we live in troubled times, my dear."

The carriage came to a stop. He drew her to him and kissed her with the same passion as in the bedroom.

As the door to the carriage opened and she rose to leave, Malcolm stopped her. "You must remember one thing, always," He was holding her hand tightly. "I do not lose what I love."

Simone alighted from the carriage and turned briefly, giving him a departing smile.

MALCOLM, AS ALWAYS, WATCHED HER GO. THE SMELL OF her clung to him, reminding him of his physical urges. He stuck his head out the carriage door and spoke softly to his driver.

The carriage headed for the riverfront. Though it was late, he knew Miss B would let him in.

Malcolm smiled, for it would be Simone's face that he would see underneath him, and it would be her body that he would feel, even though he would be paying to perform the act with someone else.

❧ II ❧
NEW ORLEANS 1862

Something was wrong; very, very wrong. Peter Livingston noticed it one night when he heard a surreptitious tiptoeing outside his door. Then he had heard the back door open with its familiar creak, and a diminishing echo as the familiar footfalls of his daughter receded away from the house. He tried to stay awake, but his weakening heart would not allow it and he fell asleep before she returned.

When he came downstairs the next morning, he did not see her so he went looking in the cellar, and that was where he had found that note under the stairwell: *"So you might have something for your troubles the other day. Captain Beaumont."* Who was Captain Beaumont? Was Simone, God Forbid, secretly meeting someone? That would explain why she was always humming. She had never sung to herself before.

He was determined to catch her in her guilt.

Simone was too elated with love to notice her father's stormy, stalking eyes. And when she snuck out again, she did not realize she was being followed. He kept a safe distance, following her far enough until she boarded the carriage and drove off.

He was desperate now. He wanted to catch her, humiliate her, to subdue her once and for all. He would follow her all the way to where she was going, even if it was into a man's bed . . .

LIKE A FRAYED THREAD IN A LOOSE WEAVE, SIMONE'S dream was unravelling. She did not realize the rendering of her fantasy until it almost killed her.

Malcolm and she had fallen into a wonderful, forbidden routine where he kissed her and caressed her until she arched her back and cried out, and then collapsed in his arms, weeping. Never once, however, did he penetrate her, not even with his finger. He wanted to save it, to pierce her when they both could no longer stand the tension. He found the stalling excited him, and when he later gave vent to his pressure at Miss B's, it was a virtual explosion that left both he and the whore he was with, limp. It was truly a grand finale to his evenings with Simone.

THE MOON WAS HIDDEN BEHIND A SHEATH OF CLOUDS AS Simone lay naked in Malcolm's arms. Malcolm, for his part, kept his pants on, but Simone could feel his bulging crotch up against her. She longed for him to unzip those pants and ply that bulge to her. She did not really understand what she was longing for, but she told Malcolm about it and he smiled.

"Do you think you're ready?" he asked, rubbing her crotch gently. She was hot and wet. "Maybe our time has arrived," he murmured as he pressed himself against her. Simone sank far back into the pillows, her hips moving involuntarily. Malcolm laid a hand on her belly.

"None of that now. You must save those luscious movements for me."

Simone blushed. "I'm sorry, I didn't mean to."

"Oh, but you did," said Malcolm as his lips encircled her breast. A kiss, a suckle, and then he brought his face close to hers. "It's the way it's supposed to be, darling, just save it for me; only for me."

Suddenly, the door burst open. Before Malcolm could reach his gun, a shot was fired. Simone burrowed into the bed, shaking in fear. She watched in disbelief as one man stood with a gun to Malcolm's head. "What do you want?" Malcolm asked in a steady, deadly voice.

"We be wantin' the deacon's daughter," was the reply. Another man approached Simone. She shrunk back when the man took her arm to pull her out of the bed. "Yer daddy be wantin' ya home."

"I'll take her home, leave her alone!" Malcolm's voice was filled with rage.

The man standing over Simone laughed. "No sir, we'll be takin' her home an' *you* leave her alone." As Simone struggled to hide her nakedness with the bed sheet, her father suddenly stepped into the room. He unfurled his bull whip and growled at the man next to Simone, "Step back."

Simone stared as her father looked her up and down.

"You're nothing but a whore, a whore, *a whore!*" And he cracked his whip at her. With a flick, a bloody swath was cut down Simone's chest to her breast. She heard Malcolm yell as the walls began to tilt and ripple. Somewhere faraway a gun went off, but all this faded as she descended into the kindly darkness of oblivion.

THROUGH A PAINFUL FOG SHE SAW OTIS AND HIS WIFE, Frannie, standing over her.

"She still got a fever," she heard Frannie say. Then she felt a cool, wet compress on her forehead. *Oh, Malcolm, you are so wonderful to me! I love you so! Please don't ever leave me . . .*

Otis shook his head as he stared at Simone. He knew now that he had betrayed her. Peter had approached him about his suspicions. Otis had then sought out the men who had tracked Simone and found her. If Simone died, it would be on him. He thought she had been in trouble.

Frannie laid a hand on his arm. "This warn't yo fault."

"Jes' take good care o' her." Otis left to tell Peter that she was too sick to move. But he would have lied to keep her with people who loved her. And God knows, that wasn't her father. Perhaps the one who loved her most had been taken from her. And it had been his fault.

THE WOUND, A BLOODY RIFT FROM NECK TO NIPPLE, WAS

infected. Simone's fever climbed. The gash seeped a green, stinking sepsis.

"Nothin' be helpin' no more," Frannie told Otis one evening. "She need a real doctor now."

"I'll tell her daddy." Otis headed for the door.

"It be nearly midnight, Otis!"

Otis turned. "If she be needin' a doctor, she gettin' a doctor." He shut the door, heading for Peter Livingston's home. It was about time Peter Livingston lost some sleep over his daughter.

PETER STUMBLED DOWN THE STAIRS AND OPENED THE door. His eyes widened to see Otis standing there.

Otis spoke first. "She be needin' a doctor, Mr. Livin's-ton, suh."

"I thought Frannie was taking good care of her."

"She be terrible sick now. Frannie ain't got no more medicine that can help."

"I want to see for myself."

"If Frannie say she cain't help no more, then it be bad, real bad."

Peter retreated into his house to dress himself. How was he going to explain all this to a doctor?

As he accompanied Otis to his little back house, he hoped that Otis was exaggerating. But when he saw Simone, Peter knew it was no exaggeration. Her mark of sin was infected and the infection was spreading.

"Get the doctor," he conceded. He looked down at Simone, who was twitching in her fevered sleep.

"Simone," he blurted out, although he wasn't sure

why. Was it to scold her for the trouble she was causing? To warn her that her mark of sin might turn into a mark of death? Whatever the reason, he did not expect for her to hear him, much less respond.

But she did hear him. Simone opened her eyes and they locked in that vivid stare father and daughter shared. Finally, Simone croaked, "I hate you; why don't you let me die?"

Peter stared, dumbfounded, as she closed her eyes again. And he realized that she was retreating from him and all he represented. Well, retreat if she must. Maybe she would be better off dead. Maybe he would be better off if she were dead, too.

DR. ANTON IRVING OBSERVED SIMONE AS SHE SHOOK with fever. That gash, if it ever healed, would scar. Pity, because she had such lovely skin. He looked at her father.

"How did this happen?"

Peter and the doctor stepped outside. "This mustn't go any further, doctor," Peter began in a low voice. "It was an accident. Last week, Otis was going to take Simone into town. The impatient girl did not wait for him to pick her up; she came over here instead. Well, Otis was trying to tame his spooked horse. To settle it, he grabbed the bullwhip and cracked it off to the side. Unbeknownst to him, Simone was in the way of the whip and it caught her flesh. I let her stay here because Frannie can tend to her better than I can and well, they felt so very bad. You know how these Negroes are. They took it upon themselves to fight an infection that was beyond their simple capabilities. Then, when she stood at death's door, they finally told me and well, I knew you had to be called. They meant no harm and they have both learned their lesson. They will keep me apprised from now on."

The doctor shook his head. "If her condition worsens, I want to know immediately."

"Certainly. Thank you, doctor."

Peter watched the doctor go. If Simone died, now at least he had an account he could tell people. And as for Otis and Frannie, well, who would believe a couple of old, broken-down slaves over him?

SLOWLY, SIMONE BEGAN TO REGAIN HER STRENGTH. Frannie sat on the edge of the bed, changing Simone's dressing. As she pulled the bandage away, skin came with it. Simone gritted her teeth. "Please don't let my father in here again."

"I'll try, honey." Frannie approached the wound with boiled water and iodine. Simone stared at Frannie, so intent on bringing her back to a world she now hated. "We really are, aren't we?"

Frannie stopped, holding the bloodied water and old dressings. "Really what?"

"Dirt under the Master's feet."

Frannie looked worried. "Now you be talkin' feverlike. You best rest an' catch yo strength."

Frannie turned and left Simone to her misery. The old woman was lucky she had other things to think about, but what did Simone have? Nothing but her feelings. And she would never let go of them. Not her anger nor her hatred. Never.

SHE KEPT THINKING HE WOULD COME BACK FOR HER. SHE spent her days wondering when he would arrive.

She didn't know how long she waited, but when the summer cooled, she began to fear that she was wrong.

Simone was moving about now, still clinging to the hope that Malcolm would come when Dr. Irving dropped by one day. He looked pleased at her progress, smiling at her. "Stay away from bullwhips the next time you're in a stable."

"Pardon me?"

"Your accident. Your father told me all about it. The next time you decide to surprise Otis, make sure he's not holding a bullwhip."

"Otis?"

The doctor took her pulse. "Your pulse is racing. Perhaps the recollection is too much for you."

"My father told you about this?"

"Yes, how you surprised Otis as he was cracking a whip to control a rearing horse. The tip of the whip accidentally caught you."

"Oh, Holy Mother of God."

"Not to worry, Miss Livingston. Your father bears no animosity toward Otis for this mishap. Truly, a Christian in his kindness." The doctor frowned. "You're very pale. You should save your strength for when you go home."

Holy Mother of God . . .

That evening, Simone approached Otis as he was

eating dinner, "Otis, please help me. Help me find my . . . friend. I need to know where he is."

The look on Otis' and Frannie's face spurned her on. "I can't go back to my father, he hates me. And I hate him. And my friend loved me. We loved each other. Otis, please." A sob escaped her. "You helped my father, now you have to help me!"

Otis pushed back his chair. "We be goin' after curfew; y'all need ta dress yoself as a boy. Frannie, ya got some o' widow's son's clothes from before he got grown?"

Frannie stared at him. "The two of you's is askin' fer more trouble." She turned to Simone. "Ain't y'all been through enough, Miss Simone? What you think yer gonna find out there in the dead o'night?"

"Maybe someone who loves me."

"Y'all's askin' fer a heap o' hurt. Yer almost at the marryin' age. Git yoself a 'spectable man. Then y'all's kin leave yer daddy the way ya's s'posed to, wif yer head held high an'—"

"And my throat cut. Frannie, I don't want anybody else. But he doesn't know where I am, so I have to find him!"

Otis spoke up. "Get her some clothes, Frannie. We be leavin' right after curfew. Make like we's comin' home from somewhere, so nobody be askin' anythin' of us." He turned to Simone. "Y'all's my young masta fer t'night."

Frannie hissed, "Otis, what in God's name y'all be thinkin'?"

"Shush, woman! The girl's gots ta see fer herself what is an' what ain't. I ain't standin' in the way o' that no more."

Frannie went outside to an old shed where she found

clothes that she thought would fit Simone. When she returned, she asked, "Don't y'all realize y'all need papers to move about dis city at night?"

Simone jumped in. "I can write a note of permission. Do you have pen and paper?"

"Sweet Lawd have mercy upon us all." Frannie turned and went to the big house.

Otis turned to Simone, "Y'all best be gettin' into dem clothes."

Frannie returned with stationary paper, a quill pen and ink jar. "Now see what we all's gotten ourself's into! Thank the Lawd the Widow was sleepin' 'cause I've broken one o' God's Commandments by stealin'."

Simone hung her head. "I'm sorry."

Otis interjected, "Let me look at ya, Miss Simone. Make sure that bandage be seen. Y'all cain't talk: cain't have no boy openin' his mouth and havin' a lady's voice spillin' out. Now tuck yo hair under dat hat."

Simone did as she was told. Otis continued, "I be talkin' fer ya t'night an' ya be ridin' the widow's horse an' I be walkin' by yo side. Keep yo head down an' keep that hat low. Now, we be needin' that note if'n y'all please, ma'am."

Simone wrote a note in her finest flourish, signing the Widow Hartford's name to it. She was now the widow's sick grandson being brought home.

Simone tucked the note in her waistcoat and Frannie hugged Simone, whispering, "Remember, chile, he be a man. He always was and always will be a man."

They turned down the street that Simone thought of as hers and Malcolm's street, just as she thought of their hideaway as hers and Malcolm's house. The curfew was in place and the taverns and brothels were quiet. She hunched down in her saddle, her hands slippery with sweat as they arrived at Miss B's whorehouse.

A pair of sailors watched Otis as he helped Simone down. Otis nodded at them. "Boy be needin' his mama."

The sailors laughed. "Well, you just tell that mama to drop what she's doin' and tend to her boy. She'll sure like that!"

"Please," Simone whispered to Otis, "it's not what you think."

"No, ma'am, I be prayin' it ain't."

A girl opened the door, and Otis said, "We be needin' Miss B."

The sailors laughed again. "The sow's got a piglet! Who'd a thought?"

The girl, wrapped in a thin dressing gown, stepped aside.

As they stood in the foyer, Simone couldn't help but notice how familiar the place smelled. Like Malcolm.

Miss B waddled in, a smoldering cheroot between her fingers. "It's a helluva time to be callin' on me. Couldn't y'all have waited until tomorrow?"

"No," said Simone as she pulled off her hat.

Miss B smiled. "Well, well. The French pretty has come back, dressed in disguise no less. Y'all be wantin' that job?" She took a puff off the cheroot and blew it in Simone's face. "Y'all know you can't fool the business that comes through here by pretendin' to be someone you're not. Those gentlemen pay for girls who look like girls. Y'all can't keep your virtue and make money, missy."

"I'm not here for a job, Miss B. I'm here for Captain Beaumont."

"Are you with child?"

"Of course not! I have to find him. You're the only one I know who might . . . know."

Miss B puffed again on her cheroot. "Did y'all really think he'd take ya with him? He's left town."

"No, you're wrong!" Simone choked back a sob.

Miss B waddled over to a spittoon and used it. "So, the little French girl thinks she knows men better than me. Listen, you stupid wench. The captain often came here, but after he met you, he became a regular. He would come every time he visited with you, and he'd wear out my best girls. But he hasn't been here for a while, which means he's either dead or he's moved on. And I'd have heard if he was dead. He's a naval man and if his ship sailed, so did he. And he'd have no room in his berth for a half-witted little Creole who fancied herself in love."

She flicked the burgeoning ashes into the spittoon. "Didn't your mama tell y'all never to set your hopes on a man?"

"My mother's dead."

"Well, that explains just about everythin'. Your precious captain isn't here an' I doubt he's comin' back. But I'll tell y'all one thing." Miss B looked into Simone's tearful eyes. "If y'all had signed on with me, I'd of taught ya, and I'd of taught ya well. Now, if y'all would excuse me, I would like to finish my smoke in peace. And don't be goin' out the front way ever again. Y'all can let your-selves out the back."

Simone stared after Miss B, knowing it was bad luck to come in one door and leave by another. So now the aging whore was wishing more calamity upon her. Simone put her hat on. The houseboy, holding the dirty spittoon, nodded his head toward the back door. Then he, too, left to empty the phlegm that had mixed with the ashes.

Simone and Otis went down the hallway she had been through before. On a sideboard she suddenly saw the cockroach, Jimmy. She picked up the jar and tucked it inside her coat.

They exited into a back alley and made their way over to their horse.

"Let's go, Otis," said Simone tiredly.

"Time to go home and let this go."

"No, let's go out to the house. You know, the place where it all . . . happened."

Otis looked at her. "If'n we be goin' out there, I ain't walkin'." He gathered the reins and mounted the horse. Then he pulled Simone up. "An' y'all better do somefin' with dat bug. What Frannie gone say if'n ya bring home a cockroach dat y'all stole from a whorehouse? I'd rather be caught out here afta curfew dan try to 'splain dat to her!"

"Let's just go, Otis."

"Okay," he said, "you da mastah." Then he softly kicked the horse's sides and they moved forward, an old slave and his young master, heading home from a visit to his mother, a wharf harlot.

MEN TALK JUST AS WOMEN DO, AND OTIS KNEW everything about that night. He knew where the plantation was and how the doomed couple had been found.

As they rode, Simone still clung to her hope. Perhaps Malcolm had left a clue for her at their house. But as they cleared the last clump of trees, Simone did not see a home welcoming back the wounded lover, but a mass of stark, charred ruins.

"Oh, my Lawd," breathed Otis. "This musta been terrible . . ."

"He did it."

"Who did it?"

"Malcolm did it. He set this fire." She laughed humorlessly. "Don't you see, Otis? He destroyed what we had. Miss B was right; he's gone and he's never coming back."

Simone slid off the saddle and stepped into the devastation. She took out the jar holding Jimmy and knelt down, unscrewing the lid. The cockroach skittered over the blackened wood and disappeared.

Otis spoke softly, "Miss Simone, we best be gettin' on home."

They remounted the horse and left. Each clop of the beast's hooves beat a new hopelessness into Simone's heart. As the moon faded and the sky lightenend, Simone decided that it was time to go home to her father. She hated him and the thought of living with him, but this was her fate. There was no point in postponing the inevitable.

~

Simone looked at Gabriel when she had finished her account. "Do you see, *Monsieur*, who you have married? I am nobody. I am betwixt and between, neither here nor there. By Malcolm I was loved, but never taken, by my father, I was useful, but never needed. I am not Creole, nor am I Cajun; I am not a Protestant, nor am I a Catholic. You might say I exist, but I do not live. I suppose, if you find me now too intolerable, we could have this marriage annulled." She smiled sadly. "And then I will have been wed, but never been a wife."

There was a tiny flicker in Gabriel's eyes. "Do you still love him?"

"He left me. How can I love someone who left me?"

"I love you. And you are somebody. You are my wife and you always will be. And you will be the mother of my children. And though you might not agree, you are a gift and I will be forever thankful for you."

Tears spilled down Simone's cheeks and Gabriel kissed them. "Only tears of happiness are allowed."

"That's what they are. Now, tell me about your scars."

Gabriel had forgotten that he, too, had a story to tell. Now it was his turn to be vulnerable.

As the first shafts of daylight sifted through the curtains, he began his story, one that he could never really leave behind, no matter how many books he read or how sophisticated he became. So, he reached back and began at a time in his life when nothing mattered but a good day of hunting alligator and being with his family.

GABRIEL WAS BORN IN THE SWAMPS SOMEWHERE BETWEEN Pensacola and Mobile. The eldest son, he was close to his mother, May Belle Harding Cooper, a sweet woman often abused by his alcoholic father. Fortunately, Elwood Cooper spent little time at home, leaving his wife and children to fend for themselves, relegating them all to the status known as white trash.

Gabriel learned how to hunt and shoot alligator at a young age by observing the Creek Indians. His mother, May Belle, would take the food he brought home and make a delicious alligator stew that she would sell to wealthy families around Pensacola, sometimes even as far away as Mobile. She also sold snake and alligator jerky, using a secret recipe that she shared with no one.

Gabriel's schooling were the lessons learned from an unforgiving world, although the education of a backwoods swamp did not prepare him for all encounters. Some vipers had legs and some alligators lived in very fine houses. And he knew nothing of dealing with creatures such as those.

AT SIXTEEN YEARS OLD, GABRIEL KNEW HOW TO MAKE HIS way through the murky swamp waters around his home, tendrils of Spanish Moss hanging above him. He navigated his canoe confidently, glancing at his newly purchased shotgun, a second-hand smoothbore musket that he was very proud of.

It was mid-morning when Gabriel heard the strangled sound of someone too scared to scream. Gabriel had heard his mother make that sound so he grounded his canoe and went to investigate. Peering into the brush, he discovered a young Black teenager, obviously a slave, backed up against a tree.

"Oh, Lawd, dey's gonna git me!"

Gabriel took aim with his musket as the boy was surrounded by snakes and was staring at a huge yellow anaconda that had been slithering toward him. Gabriel fired, blowing the snake's head off and scattering the other snakes into the underbrush.

With a shout a young white man burst through the bushes. He, too, was Gabriel's age. "What the hell are you doing?"

"Why, I heard a cry—"

"How dare you trifle with another man's property!"

"All I heard was a cry an' I was thinkin' mebbe—"

"You don't know how to think! I was trying to break this here piece of shit of his fear of snakes and now look what you've done! You've ruined the plan, and you've sent my snakes scattering into the swamp! And you've killed my prize anaconda, you white trash cracker!"

The slave let out another cry. "Dere's one, dere's one!"

A Burmese python, dark and patterned, was making its way toward the three boys. The young slaveowner's lips curled cruelly. "Pick him up, Eddie."

"Aw, mercy! Dat serpent don' know me! He's gwine bite!"

"Pick him up or it's fifty lashes for you!"

Trembling, Eddie bent down toward the snake. As it reared up, Eddie recoiled.

"Seventy lashes!"

Again, Eddie bent down, but as he did so, his master pushed him. "Be a man about it, you dog!"

No longer able to watch this, Gabriel grabbed the snake behind its jaws. He thrust it at his white counterpart, who flinched. Gabriel laughed. "Seems to me the white trash is you, makin' yer slave do somethin' you yerself's 'fraid of." He brought the snake closer. "Why don't *you* hold it, sissy boy?"

"Wait a minute." The white boy bent down and picked up a burlap sack. "Put it in here."

He held open the sack, but as soon as Gabriel dropped the snake into it, the white boy turned, swinging the sack at Gabriel. Gabriel ducked and hit him in the stomach with his rifle butt. The boy doubled over, and Gabriel pushed him down.

Gabriel picked up another snake and threw it on him as he tried to scramble away. Flinging the snake off, he struggled to his feet. "You're gonna regret this, Cracker!" He turned to Eddie. "Go get my horse, you spineless fuck! I'm gonna whip your worthless hide 'til it slides off your back and then you're gonna sleep with the snakes!"

Gabriel interjected, "What ya blamin' him fer? Yer the one who made the trouble."

"Don't say another word to me, Cracker! Do you know who you've crossed? I'm Mason Hugo. My father is Gordon Thackeray Hugo and we are from *Casa de la Riqueza*, the biggest plantation in these parts. And you just ruined his entire collection of snakes."

"Mebbe y'all shouldn't mess with stuff that ain't yourn."

"You meddled in the wrong man's business, Cracker!"

Gabriel laughed. "Whatever y'all call yerself, it shouldn't be a man. Y'all ain't nothin' but a soft, yeller-bellied babe, playin' nasty games on yer slave fer fun. An' now yer just mad 'cause I came an' showed y'all up for the coward y'all are."

"Shut up! I'm warning you, you're gonna regret this!"

"Naw, I don't think I am." He raised his gun and pointed it at Mason's face. The slave was bringing Mason's horse back, and Gabriel could see a beautiful half-stock hunting rifle tucked in his saddle. "Hand over that there gun."

"Why, you can't have that! It's my new hunting rifle."

"The hell I cain't. A baby like y'all ain't got no business playin' with a gun like that. Now hand it over."

When Mason still hesitated, Gabriel cocked his gun. "I mean what I say. I'll end this here squabble my way an' y'all won't be able to sleep in yer fine feather bed ever agin. How 'bout that, sissy boy? Got the stomach to take a bullet between the eyes?"

"Wait 'til I tell my father about you."

"Y'all's gonna run to yer daddy and tell him how ya got yer gun stolen from a backwoods boy who bested ya without even throwin' a punch? An' yer gonna tell him how ya took all his snakes out ta play nasty tricks with yer slave when y'all's afraid of 'em yerself? Can I come along an' watch?"

Mason stared red-faced as Gabriel continued, "Now ya'll best be gettin' outta here, afore I shoot the horse out from under ya. Ya wouldn't survive one night out in this here swamp."

Mason climbed into his saddle. "C'mon, Eddie, ya low-down, good-fer-nothin' bastard. It's all your fault!"

As Gabriel watched them leave, he realized that Mason had forgotten the snake in the burlap sack. Gabriel picked it up, grabbing the headless anaconda as well.

That night there was snake stew for dinner, but the skin of the anaconda was so lustrous that Gabriel took a portion of it to line his mother's favorite basket. For one bullet he had gotten two snakes and a new weapon; hunting had been good that day.

THEIR PATHS DID NOT CROSS FOR A COUPLE OF YEARS, BUT then there came a day when the two boys sealed their hatred for each other.

May Belle and her family had gone to Pensacola, bringing alligator stew and jerky for people to sample. A fine carriage pulled up and a woman stuck her head out. "What is it that you're selling, Missus?"

May Belle smiled, careful to hide the missing teeth her husband had knocked out. "Ma'am, this here's an alligator stew sure to please y'all. Might ya like to try a sample?"

Gabriel's little sister, Nadine, brought a bowl of stew to the carriage. The woman tasted it. "Why, my husband told me that he had tried an alligator stew from a woman in this area. It was the best he had ever tasted. Do you cook to order?"

"Yes, ma'am."

"I'm having a barbecue at my home in a fortnight. I

would love to surprise my husband with this dish. I will need enough for a hundred people. Could you do that?"

"Yes, ma'am, I sure can!"

"Lovely. I'm Mrs. Gordon Thackeray Hugo, of the Hugos in Santa Rosa County. Perhaps you know of our sugar plantation?"

May Belle nodded. "One of the finest families in all of Florida."

"Then I shall expect you two weeks from tomorrow. Be there at noon. And who might you be?"

"I'm Mrs. Elwood Cooper. These here are three of my children, Gabriel, Nadine, and Owen."

"In a fortnight, Mrs. Cooper, are we clear?"

"Yes, ma'am."

"I will expect you then."

"Thank you, ma'am."

Gabriel considered telling his mother of the exchange he'd had with Mason two years before. But then he thought the better of it. After all, why worry about an incident that was done and over with?

GABRIEL HUNTED FOR DAYS, BRINGING IN ENOUGH alligator to meet Mrs. Hugo's order. He skinned and gutted the giant creatures while Owen and Philip tenderized and cut them up, finally handing them over to May Belle for frying. The three youngest Coopers gathered wild onion and garlic to flavor the stew with.

It was Gabriel and May Belle who stayed up the entire night before the picnic, preparing the tubs of stew. They were finally finished by dawn.

They arrived at *Casa de la Riqueza* before noon. Gabriel and May Belle made their way to the back of the big house where a little slave girl opened the door.

"I have stew for Mistress Hugo's barbecue," May Belle said softly.

"Yes, ma'am. I'll fetch the cook, ma'am."

The cook came to the door, "Yes, ma'am, bring it on in. Mistress done tole me to be expectin' ya 'bout dis time."

Gabriel began unloading the heavy pots of stew. May Belle had also included several loaves of fresh bread, which he had put into the basket lined with the anaconda skin.

No sooner had he brought in the basket and the first tub when Mrs. Hugo entered the kitchen. Mrs. Hugo looked at the little slave girl. "Lizzie, why are you just standing around? Get to work before I shall slap you again!"

The child backed into the basket of bread and it tipped off the table, spilling the loaves everywhere.

Mrs. Hugo pounced upon Lizzie. "That's it! I'm gonna sell you, you no good little wretch! I've had it with you."

Lizzie darted past her to the cook, who stared at Mrs. Hugo. "She meant no harm, Mistress. Please don't sell my baby!"

"She's going, Adelia, and that's final."

Mrs. Hugo turned to May Belle and Gabriel. "Slaves! A necessary evil, I'm afraid. Now, let me see about paying you."

As soon as she left, Lizzie let out a wail as Adelia

stared into space, speaking to no one in particular, "Not again, dear God, not again . . ."

May Belle pulled out a chair. "Sit down, please, Adelia."

Adelia sat down, and Lizzie immediately crawled onto her lap.

Gabriel had now brought in the second pot of stew and set it on the floor. The kitchen door flew open and Mrs. Hugo entered, followed by Mason. He had grown in the last couple of years, and he and Gabriel were now the same height.

Mrs. Hugo barely contained herself looking at Adelia and her daughter. "What are you two doing now? Get up, both of you!"

May Belle spoke up. "Please understand, Mrs. Hugo. They were so upset . . ."

She was interrupted by Mason, whose face had turned ugly with recognition. "Mama, this here's the cracker that stole daddy's snakes, stole my rifle, and tried to set Eddie free!"

Mrs. Hugo turned on Gabriel. "So, you're the miscreant who came onto our property, stole my husband's prized viper collection and my son's gun!"

Gabriel could hardly believe his ears. "Why, that's a downright lie!"

Mason thrust May Belle's basket at his mother. "Look, this here's the skin of Daddy's anaconda! This piece o' white trash is using it in her basket!"

Gabriel growled, "Watch yer mouth!"

Mason's lip curled. "Why she's nothing but a white trash whore who probably conceived you in a——"

In the mist of Gabriel's rage, he saw his father, and it

was his father's jaw that he felt crack beneath his fist, his blood trickling between his fingers. He realized he was beating Mason only when he was pulled off him.

Mrs. Hugo was screaming, "Murdering thieves! Get out!"

Gabriel pulled his mother out of the kitchen and they scrambled onto the wagon. Gabriel urged the mule into a gallop and soon they were flying down the neatly raked lane that had led them to the Hugo mansion.

LATER THAT NIGHT THE SHERIFF SHOWED UP, STANDING there with his deputies as May Belle begged him not to arrest Gabriel.

But the sheriff was adamant. "Seems your son has ol' Elwood's temper, May Belle. Ain't no use in tryin' to hide it." He looked at Gabriel. "Be a man about it, boy. Don't add disgrace to the harm you've already done yer family."

What else could he do? Gabriel stepped forward, and he was led off into the night, his mother's cries ringing in his ears.

Gabriel sat in the Pensacola jail, waiting for the circuit judge to come to town. The rumors of Gabriel's savagery had spread throughout the region, re-hashed until Gabriel became the symbol of bad blood and Negro-loving whites.

Mason Hugo would bring Cuban cigars and Kentucky bourbon for the jailer, bribing his way in to see Gabriel. "How's that old mother of yours? I hear she's really struggling now that you put yourself in here and your no-good, drunken daddy never comes around. Crackers like you never rise above this, you know, Cooper. Didn't I tell you that you'd regret the day you crossed me? And here you are, ready to go live your life in a way that will make you wish you were dead. Not that you'd ever be more than just another swamp rat. Eventually you'd fornicate with some low-down girl like your mother, breed bastards like mosquitoes in a wet summer . . . we're all better off with you gone."

Gabriel bit the inside of his cheek making it bleed. Finally, Mason rose to leave.

"Oh, and it seems your daddy left y'all in a lot of debt, so my daddy bought your filthy hut. Your family's been turned out and your mama's on the road beggin' as we speak. 'Course she can always peddle your sisters. I guess they're kinda pretty in that easy, cracker sort of way."

Gabriel lunged at Mason, trying to reach him through the bars. "I'm gonna come back for y'all, ya filthy bastard! I ain't ever forgettin' this!"

"Say what you like, but the fact remains that I'm a free man and you're not. Probably never will be either."

Gabriel could hear Mason's laughter as he left the jailhouse, mounted his horse, and rode off. But Gabriel meant what he said. One day he would be back for Mason.

When the circuit judge arrived, there was an arraignment and a swift trial. The courtroom was packed, but Gabriel sat alone in his own private Golgotha.

He was found guilty of robbery and aggravated assault, and sentenced to thirty years. If he lived that long, Gabriel would be forty-eight years old when he was released from prison.

He was sent east to a labor camp near the Choctawhatchee River, where he began to earn the scars on his back. He then moved on to Tallahassee and nearby Gadsden County. Finally, his crew went further east yet to the Okefenokee Swamp, where Colonel Tremont found him.

He never saw his family again. One evening, as he ate a dinner of boiled apple snails, a guard approached with a letter from Mason Hugo. He sought out his friend, Mitchell, to read it.

May Belle Harding Cooper and her two sons, Jeremiah and Owen, had been found off the road to Camp Clinch, where they had succumbed to Yellow Fever. The half-eaten body of a little girl was found in the woods not far from the small family camp which turned out to be Penelope, his littlest sister. Nobody else was found.

Cruel as the news was, Gabriel now knew that by being found off the road to Camp Clinch, his family had been on their way to visit him. They had not abandoned him after all; they had been murdered. Now there was nothing and no one to live for, only a reason. A reason to get justice for them even if nothing else came of his life. And if he could do anything beyond that, well, that was just a gift of grace that he probably did not deserve.

～

SIMONE'S EYES WERE THE AQUA OF THE CARIBBEAN SEA. "My sweet *Monsieur*. You still want your revenge, don't you?"

"You know, all I wanted when I was on that convict gang was revenge. Revenge on the world, and particularly on Mason Hugo. Well, when I fought in the war I got my revenge on the world. I shot, I stabbed, I cut men in two. But then I saw Mason Hugo and I forgot about the world. We were on Kennesaw Mountain and there he was right at my feet." Gabriel propped himself on one elbow facing Simone. "But when I saw him, all I could think was, 'liar.' So, I heated my knife in a nearby fire and then pressed it to his lips. I tore them off. That was for him lying about me."

He looked to see Simone's reaction. There was none, so he continued, "Then I dragged him over to a place where the ambulances would find him."

"Why?"

"It wasn't an act of kindness, you know. I was glad to burn his lips for justice. The revenge was making sure he lived with what I'd done. I even went and saw him at the field hospital. By then he'd suffered an infection, and they'd had to take part of his tongue and cheek. He was asleep, and the fella next to him said he was in terrible pain." Gabriel smiled. "And that he'd be one ugly fella if and when he healed."

"I am so proud of you, *mon cheri*."

"I have to admit I don't want the revenge to stop there, Simone."

"And?"

"And I want him to see me now. A man who is his equal or better. And I want him to suffer over it."

"And you should make him suffer. His whole life, so he never ever forgets."

Gabriel was astonished that they, the ex-con and the deacon's daughter, were not so different after all.

He kissed her. She pulled him on top of her and as he made love to her again, he felt more than ever their connection. For the first time in his life, Gabriel marveled at serendipity. And a tiny part of him, tucked far away from the perils of conscious thought, wondered if there was a God who had finally decided to smile upon him and bless him with a love he craved, but felt he would never deserve.

August 14, 1867

D*EAR DAVIE,*
Imagine me, a happily married man! On June 30, I married Miss Simone Margaret Livingston of New Orleans. She has made me a very fine wife indeed, and she will make a very fine mother of my children.

As I wrote earlier, I took a job that requires me to re-locate. Hence, my new bride and I have moved to New York City! What better place to start a new life? The city is filled with theater and opera, fine retail establishments and boulevards you can stroll down for hours. It is a place of both bedlam and solitude—bedlam because of the crowds of people, the cabs, trains, and ships; solitude because you are at once lost in a sea of faces and never need to worry of who might recognize you.

We honeymooned at the Fifth Avenue Hotel and Simone delighted in their new vertical railway cars. Can you believe it, a private car that runs vertically inside the building and goes to every floor? We lived in the lap of luxury (we had a privy of our very own in our suite!) for a few short weeks, but have now rented a flat in uptown. From the looks of it, we will soon be a part of the great sprawl of this city, but for now we still have charming wooded lanes to walk down while still being close enough to all the stores and commerce. I plan to buy us a house as my beloved is very particular toward gardens, so I must find her a place where she can cultivate the flowers and shrubs she so dearly loves. Indeed, as a wedding gift, I have arranged for specimens from her former garden to be transported here via special freight.

I realize I must sound like a romantic old fool to you, but I tell you these things as I would a brother. I am a man happy with his current place in life and hopeful for an even brighter future, which, my dearest young friend, is all that I ever hope for you as well.

I remain Yours Truly,

Gabriel

As Gabriel left the post office and strode up Third Avenue, he reflected on how he was living in a fine apartment in one of the greatest cities in the world. And he had brought with him his bride, a woman whom he would have never thought he was worthy of. He only prayed that it wasn't a dream.

He turned and headed west on 19th Street. He knew Simone would be up and he wanted to go out before the day warmed.

She was sitting in the apartment's front room, waiting for him. "You were gone far too long, *Monsieur*," she teased.

"I was, was I? Well, we have the whole day ahead of us, my love. How about if we take a stroll to the Murray

Hill Reservoir? I hear the promenade on top has a most magnificent view."

"That sounds lovely."

"But then again, we could visit the Murray Hill Reservoir anytime, and you are more tempting than the Serpent's Apple . . ." He kissed her.

"Stop!" she chided him, laughing. "I took great pains to dress for the day. I will not un-do all my hard work! Let us go out and see the city!"

"All right, but only because I could never stand to disappoint you."

Simone took his arm. "May we never disappoint each other."

They lunched in a little café on 20th Street before they began their walk to the reservoir. As they approached, Simone gaped at the huge structure.

"There is a promenade on top?"

"Yes."

"But how do we get there?"

"Well, we certainly don't fly. We'll have to take the stairs."

"Why, it must be like climbing the pyramids of Egypt!"

Gabriel laughed. "Don't fret, my sweet, if it becomes too much, I shall carry you!"

Suddenly she stopped and stared, her expression a mixture of envy and longing. Gabriel followed her gaze. "Rutgers Female College . . . Mrs. Cooper, our afternoon awaits us."

Simone broke from her reverie. "Of course."

Gabriel steered her toward the stairway to the promenade. "I am told we can see for miles up there. As if we are on top of the world!"

Simone nodded and smiled. Her mind, however, was not on the promenade that awaited her, but on the Rutgers Female College she had just discovered.

ALTHOUGH THEIR FUTURE SEEMED SECURE, SIMONE received a monthly rent check from her home in New Orleans that she had rented to Delcine and her family. She insisted this money be stored away in her trousseau. Gabriel teased her, calling her the loveliest miser he had ever known.

"At least let me put the money in bonds for you so that it will accrue interest."

Simone had laughed. "I think not, *Monsieur*. I have seen how money fares in the government's hands. Have you forgotten the Confederacy?"

But Gabriel had a penchant for investing money. He could not forget Moses's words: *I could help you invest some of that beautifully earned revenue so that it continues on paying you …you could invest in this country, in groundbreaking industries…"* Moses had recently written Gabriel an introductory letter to the Ledbetter Bros., a brokerage firm on Wall Street. Gabriel kept the letter in his newly acquired safe. When he took the letter downtown, he decided to buy some bonds for Simone anyway. His new career required him to consider his own mortality. Simone had to be taken care of; his family would never be forsaken again. Buying bonds would help ensure that.

~

IT WAS MID-SEPTEMBER AND WHILE IT WAS STILL WARM, the breezes seemed especially cool to Gabriel and Simone.

Simone busied herself with their new apartment, spending her afternoons reading, doing embroidery or other fancy work. She now read *Godey's Lady's Book*, quoting it to Gabriel. Often, they would take afternoon walks, admiring the brilliance of an East Coast autumn.

They returned early one day as Simone felt faint.

"You do look peaked, my love," said Gabriel, guiding her to their front door.

"I don't know what has come over me," Simone replied, but she had an inkling with the nausea in the mornings, and her bloated waistline. She decided she would tell Gabriel tonight after dinner.

Gabriel unlaced her corset and helped her into a dressing gown. Once in bed, he kissed her softly, "Do not bother with dinner. I will get something for myself later."

No sooner had he done this than there was a knock on the front door. He opened it.

"Telegram for Mr. Gabriel Cooper," a young boy said, handing Gabriel an envelope.

"Thank you." Gabriel handed the boy a couple of pennies who tipped his cap and ran off.

The message was from Moses Del Cerro: *"Package en route via express attend to at once MDC"*

There it was, his first assignment. Now he had to wait for the dossier, but he must let Moses know he had received his telegram.

Gabriel grabbed his hat and headed out to the

Western Union Telegram office. On his way back he'd stop and get flowers for Simone. There was nothing like a sweet nosegay to tell her how much he cared.

He returned later to find Simone sitting up in bed. He went to her, holding out a nosegay of red chrysanthemums nestled in mullein leaves.

Simone squealed. "*Oh, Monsieur!* They speak so beautifully."

"They are meant to say, 'Get well, my love.'" Gabriel had read up on floriography, the current rage of Victorian society.

Simone beamed at him. Now was the time. "You must remember this arrangement well, *Monsieur* because you will be bringing it to me more frequently than not. I am with child."

Gabriel let out a whoop of joy, and Simone giggled as he bounced onto the bed, hugging her and smothering her face with kisses.

"When?"

"I'd like to confirm it with a doctor, but I think next May."

Gabriel hopped off the bed and began to pace. "We must get a housekeeper straightaway. You cannot be expected to keep a house in your condition. No, especially since—" He stopped suddenly.

"Especially since what?"

Gabriel's shoulders sagged a bit. "Especially since I am going away on business."

"For how long?"

"I don't know. I am awaiting the details of my assignment now."

"Oh."

"It is my job, Simone. I do it for all of us."

Simone felt the old clinch of abandonment. What if he liked being on the road more than being home? What if he left and never came back? What if, what if, what if…

She swallowed her anxiety. "Of course." She put his hand on her abdomen. "We will wait for you."

Gabriel enfolded her in his arms. "Well, you won't be lacking for friends while I'm away. I found two calling cards in our card receiver today."

"Really?"

Gabriel produced the cards from his frock coat. "Mrs. Dorian C. Holmstead and Mrs. Arthur P. Baumgartner." Both cards had the upper left corner folded, indicating that both ladies had left the cards themselves. "Soon you'll have so many friends you won't even miss me."

"I will always miss you. Where will you be going?"

"Ohio."

"So far away."

Gabriel did not avert his gaze from her, but he was appalled at the smoothness of his lie. Surely lying like this should never be so easy, should it?

Simone moved to get out of bed. "Shall I make you some tea?"

"No darling, you rest. I can make tea for myself."

"You are so good to me; so good and so true."

Gabriel kept his face inscrutable, but inside he was churning. So good and so true. Would she think other-wise if she knew the truth of his assignment? He vowed she should never discern more than the best of him, knowing that soon he would carry secrets that he dared not share with anyone, least of all with the woman he loved.

GABRIEL WAS TO REMOVE A LEAD CONTENDER FOR A boxing match between two Lower East Side men's clubs. Far from the gentlemen's clubs of Fifth Avenue, these were for the immigrant workingmen, supported by rival Irish gangs. The target was Paddy Duffy of the Galway Greens. He was to square off against Brian Donnally of the South Killarneys. Tommy Hogan, ambitious president of the Earl of Pearls, another rival club, was to step in for the fallen Duffy and "save the day," drawing the attention of certain Tammany Hall insiders. This was to be a quiet job so as not to raise the ire of the Galway Greens. Hence, it was a job given to Gabriel.

Gabriel put a plan in place. Paddy Duffy was a dock worker at South Street Seaport. His tavern was the Erin Go Bragh on Fletcher Street. If he wasn't working or training for the fight, he was at Erin's.

Gabriel needed a hiding place where he could develop a persona that no one could trace. He had to learn his character, get to know Paddy and to find that crack in his life that would allow for an accidental death. Death always flowed from life; you simply had to weaken the thin membrane that separated the two. Then, when the membrane gave way, no one was the wiser for it.

"YA WANT NO OTHER TENANTS, YA SAY?" THE WHITE Irishwoman eyed Gabriel suspiciously.

"No."

"Ten dollars a month then yous'll be payin'."

"That's robbery."

"Ach, go on with ya. We usually get four or five persons rentin' per shift down here fer one o' these rooms. They all pay their fair share, a dollar apiece, but if yer wantin' high fallutin' lodgins here in the Five Points"—she laughed, displaying her blackened gums—"well, Mr. Fancy Dandy, yer gonna have ta pay fer the other sots' space. Ten dollars it is, due on the first of the month and not a day later." She held out her hand. "It's the full ten dollars for the first rent, no matter when ya move in."

Gabriel reached into his pocket. No wonder the owners of these buildings lived in mansions.

The woman looked him up and down again. "What'd ya say yous call yerself?"

"Kevin. Kevin Kilcourse."

"Aye, that's right. Well, Mr. Kevin Kilcourse, welcome to the neighborhood."

After she had gone, Gabriel looked around. The place was windowless with a coal burning stove in the corner. He'd need a pot for cooking. There was a filthy mattress on the floor. Gabriel made a mental note to get a bucket and soap. This shanty was despicable, but he could disappear here. The only eyes that would witness his metamorphosis would be the rats and cockroaches that lived with him.

Gabriel set down his bag and pulled out the dossier. He slid it under the mattress. He would destroy the file tonight for he had memorized it already. But first he had to get supplies. The fetid smell of rot and waste was overpowering, but he'd better get used to it *because I'm one of them now.*

HE STAYED HIDDEN WHILE HE GREW A MOUSTACHE AND let his hair get scruffy. He also sent away for Hauel's Celebrated Vegetable Liquid Hair Dye to turn his hair and new moustache black. He studied how to be an Irishman and more importantly, how to be an Irishman who was familiar with Paddy Duffy.

He left Five Points early every morning, when all the men were going to work. He carried a lunch pail like they all did, keeping to himself but listening to their dialect, how they rolled their r's and swallowed syllables.

Gabriel made his way down to South Street Seaport to Pier 13 where Paddy Duffy worked. He watched for the young man every day. Then he would go over to the Erin after the evening work whistle blew, biding his time.

Gabriel was sitting at the bar, nursing a beer when Paddy and a group of his friends burst through the Erin Tavern door one evening.

"Hey-o, Jimmy, how 'bout the regular?" asked Paddy loudly. He was holding a bloody rag over his eye.

The bartender slid the beer over to him. "Cut yerself sparrin', did ya now, Paddy?"

Paddy grinned. "Aye. Ya shoulda seen the other lad. Ain't that right, boys?"

"He was a right bloody pulp he was," said one of them, clapping Paddy on the back.

"We'll have a helluva party here after ya win the fight, Paddy," the bartender grinned. Gabriel watched Paddy drain the Irish Stout and order another one. When the second glass came Paddy lifted it and called out, "Here's to November 2nd!"

"Aye, aye!" Everyone resounded. Another young man raised his glass. "Here's to kickin' Donnally's keester back to where he came from!"

"Aye, aye!"

Gabriel left. He had watched Paddy down three beers in succession and ideas were forming. Soon he would know just where the membrane around Paddy's life could be weakened.

PADDY DUFFY WAS YOUNG, BRASH, AND FULL OF confidence. He worked hard and he drank hard. He often left the bar drunk and sometimes he left alone, weaving his way home.

Gabriel frequented other taverns in the area, listening to the locals. He was thinking about how to get his hands on either chloroform or ether when the perfect opportunity presented itself.

He was at a place off Fulton Street called The Shamrock Sheila, watching a poker game. One of the players, a middle-aged white man, threw down his cards. One of the other players teased him, "Ya know, Doc, one o' these days yous goin' to need to be payin' up."

"Don't I bloody well know it! I'll get yous your money, Bobbie Sweeney, so's you can drink the bloody night away, that ya can."

Bobbie grinned. "Ach, doc, no need to be sore! I won fair and square, so I did."

"Aye, Bobbie, but it's a pain in me bloody arse to come up with the money. Lots o' ailin' patients an' sick weans, but no one with money."

"Yous'll make good for it, doc, sure as Ireland's in me heart." Bobbie stopped grinning. "And you'll make good for it soon, so I'm thinkin'."

The doctor turned to go and Gabriel followed him outside. "Pardon me, doctor, but might ya be willin' ta see another patient who's good for the payin'?"

"Aye, boyo, I'm always good for a payin' sot."

"I got me a pain in me back, somethin' bloody awful."

"Come by me office in the mornin' at eight."

"Righto, doc, righto."

"98 Water Street, just north of Pecks Slip. You'll see me shingle out front."

"Doc?"

"What now?"

"What d'ya call yourself?"

"O'Sullivan, Shandy O'Sullivan."

The next morning, Gabriel showed up at Dr. O'Sullivan's tiny office. The doctor looked at his watch. "Aye, right on time, so ya are. Come on in then, let's see what ails ya." He opened the door to the examining room.

"Actually, doc, I'm not here for me back."

"Well, then, what for?"

"I'm here for me da. Lost a leg in the War back in '63. Terrible pain, terrible. Gnaws at him like a bloody phantom, it does. The only way he can sleep is with the chloroform. I got money to buy a bottle off ya if yous can spare it."

The doctor stared at Gabriel. "What's your name again, boyo?"

"Kevin Kilcourse."

"Aye, well, Kevin, that's a right powerful medicine you're askin' of me. It can kill yous if not used properly."

"Me da's willin' ta take that chance, doc. He's been usin' the chloroform for years now, but the doc where we live upstate died, so I came down here lookin' to help him. Before I left, there was no relief, an' him writhin' an' cursin' to all the saints." He paused. "I got to thinkin' it'd be a help to yous as well, seein' how you owe a debt for your game last night an' Sweeney gettin' a wee bit impatient as he is."

"Och, Sweeney, that bloody buggar! Your da fought in the war, ya say?"

"Aye, 31st New York Infantry Brigade. We all fought together, me, me da, me two younger brothers." Gabriel bowed his head. "Me one brother, Owen, died on the field. Gettysburg. Same day as when me da was wounded."

"Ach, it was bad all around, Kevin, that it was. I was in the field hospital at Gettysburg. We sawed limbs off night and day on the poor lads. Well, I'm sorry for your da. But I'm tellin' ya now, I'll only do this the once, yous hear me? How much yous gonna be paying me?"

"I got me fifty dollars of hard-earned cash."

The doctor inhaled sharply. "Not many people have money the likes o' that lyin' around."

"I'm a workin' man with no family to support. I live cheap and I got a good streak o' luck with the cards. It adds up."

"Aye, so it does; wish I had me a streak o' luck. Well, let me get ya the bottle." He disappeared into the next room, returning quickly. "Now, don't be goin' tellin' the lads around here that I gave ya this. It's only because of your da an' me in the predicament I'm in that I'm doin' this."

Gabriel handed him the bills. "Aye, doc, as far as I'm concerned, we never spoke. An' yous won't ever be hearin' from the likes o' me again."

Gabriel tipped his cap to the doctor and left, curling his fingers around the bottle in his pocket.

THE BIG FIGHT WAS ONLY TWO WEEKS AWAY. GABRIEL watched and waited, hanging at the Erin. The time was coming when he would have to find a way to get Paddy to himself..

A thick, milky fog rolled in on Thursday, October 24. It had been a misty, overcast day that made men get a drink to warm up before they trekked home.

Gabriel now knew exactly where Paddy worked and what time he left. As the shipyard whistle blew at four thirty p.m., Gabriel watched Paddy lower his last load of cargo and run down the ship's gangplank.

Paddy's friends yelled at him. "Ach. Paddy, let's stop for a wee nip at Erin's."

Paddy laughed. "C'mon fellas, I got me trainin' to do."

"Ach, just a wee nip for good luck!"

Gabriel watched them head for the tavern. Something told him that this would be the night.

Gabriel entered the Erin later, when all the men were loosened up and jovial. He bought a round of Irish Stout for everyone. He went over to Paddy and clapped him on the back. "Aye, here's our lad, boys! Our Paddy's goin' to win the match against Donnally, so he is!" He winked at Paddy. "I got all me money on ya, Paddy, so I do." He motioned to the bartender. "A shot o' your finest Irish whiskey for all these lads!"

A cheer went up and Paddy turned to him, slurring his words, "Aye, thanks for that...ach, I can't recall your name . . ."

"Kevin."

"Aye, Kevin, thanks for that."

As Gabriel watched Paddy, he realized he'd have to use a lot of chloroform to knock the young man out. He watched as Paddy downed the whiskey.

Gabriel slipped outside, retiring into the shadows of a nearby alleyway. Paddy was on a binge and would outdrink his friends tonight. Then he'd leave by himself.

Just as he predicted, Paddy stumbled out long after his friends left. He belched, weaving his way down the street. Gabriel caught up to him. "Too much o' the whiskey, eh, Paddy?"

"Aye,"

"C'mon, boyo, I'll take ya home. Where d'ya live?"

"Nah, take me back to me ship . . ." He tried to focus his eyes. "Come again with yer name?"

"Kevin. An' what's yer ship, Paddy?"

"The Madrid . . . she's a lovely lass."

They walked on, searching, and Gabriel said, "Sure now, Paddy, that ya know which one she is?"

Paddy belched again. "Aye, as sure as me birthplace in Ireland." He waved his arm. "There she is, my lovely lady." He stumbled and Gabriel caught him. He tipped his cap at the night watchman who strolled by. Gabriel helped Paddy stumble up the gangplank as the watchman retreated into the fog.

Once on board, Paddy tripped on some rigging. He bumped up against the first mast and slid down. Soon he was snoring.

Gabriel reached into his pocket and withdrew the chloroform-soaked handkerchief, placing it firmly over Paddy's nose and mouth.

Paddy barely struggled as his breathing slowed to a stop. Seeing no witnesses, Gabriel dragged Paddy back to the stern of the ship and slipped him over the edge. The dead man fell into the frigid water with a splash.

Just as the night he murdered Pastor Evans, the fog let Gabriel leave as anonymously as he came. Gabriel breathed deeply, trying to push Paddy's trusting face out of his mind. *Shouldn't have drank so much, boyo.* Still, Paddy's image persisted. Gabriel had made him believe he was a friend. *Paddy shouldn't have been so trusting, right? Right?*

Agitated, Gabriel made his way back to his filthy room where he heated some leftover water in his bucket. He shaved his mustache, trimmed his hair and washed the dye out. By the time the sun rose over the eastern horizon, he looked blond and clean-shaven and certainly not like a man who belonged in the rat-infested tenements of Five Points. Maybe by changing back to his old self he could start anew; a cleansing of sorts and the unease of Paddy's murder would no longer haunt him.

Gabriel returned home expecting to see a rosy Simone being cared for by their new housekeeper. Instead, he walked in to see his wife by herself, somberly cutting a raw chicken, her mouth set grimly and dark circles under her eyes. She looked up to see him and a dry, lifeless smile cracked over her lips.

"Is everything all right?" he asked.

She didn't respond.

"Where is the housekeeper?"

"I fired her."

"But why?"

"I could not reach you, so I made the decision myself."

"But I hired her to be of help to you in your condition."

"There is no condition."

It took Gabriel a moment to comprehend what she was saying. "Oh, darling, I am so sorry. Are you all right?"

"I suppose so."

"Did you see a doctor?"

"Of course."

"When did this happen?"

"Three weeks ago, today."

"And you didn't want to keep the housekeeper?"

"No, I needed to keep myself busy, and if she did all the chores then I was left to think."

"I missed you."

"I missed you, too." Her tone was lackluster.

"I'm sorry I was not here."

Simone turned from him. "You must excuse me. I have work to do."

Her words were an echo of the trapped, miserable girl he first knew. No, never again! He would have to find a way to help her. The only problem was that he had no idea how.

~

THE NEXT MORNING GABRIEL WALKED DOWN TO THE corner of Nineteenth and Park Avenue, where he bought a copy of the *New York Herald* and the *New York Sun*. He then headed home.

When he entered the apartment, he went to the dining room and opened the papers in earnest. On the second page of the *Sun* he saw it: *"Boxing Hopeful Found Dead in the East River. . . Paddy Duffy of the Galway Greens was found floating face down in the water off of Pier 13 in the East River. Known to imbibe in the alcoholic spirits that plague so many Irishmen of these parts, his death seems to be the tragic result of an unsteady gait too close to the water. . . ."*

Simone entered with coffee and eggs, sitting down opposite him. She studied him.

"You have such an odd expression on your face. What are you reading?"

Gabriel snapped the paper shut and looked at her. "I'm just . . . reading."

"It looked as if you were searching for something in particular."

They finished their breakfast wordlessly. As Simone cleared the dishes, Gabriel stood up. "I will be back at noontime."

As he stepped out into the sunshine, Gabriel seized upon an idea. He would telegram Delcine and express-ship clippings from Simone's old garden. She needed them now, not when they had a new house.

He walked to the Telegram Office and sent one to Delcine and then one to Moses. He then headed over to the post office where he mailed Moses the newspaper article.

On his way back, Gabriel stopped and bought another nosegay for Simone. This time it would say, "Cheer up, for my heart is true and my love will always sustain you."

Tommy Hogan replaced Paddy Duffy in the notorious "Fight for Ireland." Tommy won the match after going bare-fisted for five rounds with Brian Donnally. He was photographed with William S. Tweed, Grand Sachem of Tammany Hall. Gabriel clipped out the newspaper article and sent it to Moses. He did not send the adjoining article about Paddy Duffy, how he had been the main supporter of his widowed mother and his nine younger siblings. Gabriel also did not clip out Paddy's mother's statement that she would never stop grieving for her poor, lost boy. Instead, he stored that article in his safe, wondering why he felt compelled to do so.

Gabriel went on another assignment in December, but Simone now had friends to call on. That is, when she wasn't tending to her new indoor garden. The next generation of her old garden arrived before Thanksgiving, and Gabriel was right about it lifting Simone's spirits. She turned one of the spare bedrooms with an Eastern exposure into her "garden room," stripping the windows of their curtains to let the light stream over her lovely "children." In this room Simone healed, coaxing herself out of the inner grief of her miscarriage.

Soon hope replaced the terror. As Christmas came and went, Simone again noticed the symptoms of pregnancy. Since Gabriel was about to leave on business again, she kept the news to herself. She would tell him her happy secret when he returned.

She wanted for nothing. Gabriel invested their money, studying the *New York Times* and the tombstone ads every day. What's more, he also listened to his wife. He listened to her comments about soap, dishware, even fashion trends. Based upon innocent daily prattle, he bought shares in companies that reflected the routine of life. With intuition and Moses's voice in his ear, *"It takes money to make money,"* he made his way down to the Ledbetter brokerage house often, wads of cash stuffed on his person.

Gabriel came home from his assignment in mid-February and a radiant Simone strode toward him. She kissed him and smiled. "Welcome home, *Monsieur.* You smell like . . . a journey."

"It has been a journey," breathed Gabriel, pushing the face of his latest victim out of his mind's eye. According to the obituary, the man had died of a brain hemorrhage, but Gabriel knew better.

"Come, I want to hear all about your trip."

Gabriel hung up his coat and hat and removed his

gloves. He went to the dining room and sat down. It felt so good to be home.

Simone entered the dining room, holding a cup of tea. "Or would you prefer coffee?"

"No. Just sit here for a moment so I can look at you."

"How was your trip?"

The image of Herbert Eldred flooded back, the sleeping form of the fat old Welsh banker, snoring as Gabriel sat in the dark, waiting for him to turn on his side. He sat there, listening to his wife snoring just as shamelessly in the bedroom next door. Finally, he tickled Herbert's exposed foot, prompting Herbert to stir and turn, facing the window. Then, lighting a small candle and setting it down on the bed stand, he held a handkerchief soaked in chloroform to the old man's nose. With stealth and precision, Gabriel deftly inserted the ice pick and tapped it with a small hammer. Not too much pressure, for the outer ear could not be damaged. Gabriel blew out the candle, shoved everything he'd brought into his knapsack, and climbed out the window.

He thought he'd be less bothered about ending the life of an old rich man who had lived well and cheated many, but still his defenseless dead form permeated Gabriel's dreams. Gabriel would then lie awake, waiting for the dawn as he reassured himself that all he was doing was balancing the scales of justice and providing for the future of his family.

He broke from his reverie to see Simone still waiting expectantly.

"Oh . . . I'm sorry, darling, I am so very tired. It has been a long trip."

"Did you have to travel far?"

"Texas," he lied.

"Was the weather warm?"

"I am not in the mood to talk about this, darling."

"You never tell me of your adventures. Why is that? We used to discuss everything."

Gabriel ignored her. "Tell me instead about what you have been doing. Have you been able to get out despite the weather?"

Reluctantly, Simone stood up and left the dining room. She returned with a pair of ladies' boots in hand.

"Marie Holmstead and I had a day out. It was a beautiful day! *Godey's Ladies' Book* advertised a sale at Lord &Taylor's. Marie and I made a day of it, and I bought a pair of beaver felt boots at Hershel Shoes. They have the most wonderful fine leather foxing. I hoped you wouldn't mind because my feet freeze in this weather."

Gabriel listened to his wife, glad that she had stopped asking about where he'd been.

That night they lay in each others' arms, listening to the wind clatter outside.

"You smell so good," Gabriel murmured. "You always smell so good."

"Do I smell like motherhood?"

"Should you?"

"Yes!"

He encircled his arms around her, pressing her down in the pillows. "I love you so!"

She returned his kisses and he croaked, "Get on your knees." She looked at him questioningly and he said, "It's from behind."

Simone got up on her hands and knees and Gabriel shoved several pillows under her abdomen. Then he hitched up her hips and glided into her. He thrust with some force, causing them both to orgasm quickly.

Gabriel pulled her to him once more. He kissed her in the crook of her neck, his hand cupping her right breast, fingering the erect nipple and the darkened areola.

It was a serene moment. Gabriel lay still, feeling reassured. Maybe his loss of long ago would now have a counterbalance, for now he was finally going to have a family of his own.

And yet, somehow the counterbalance did not feel complete. Mason Hugo was still out there somewhere. Gabriel would have to check on him sometime. After the baby was born, he decided. When the time was right.

For wanderers seeking succor, self-delusion is often taken for premonition. Gabriel awoke to Simone's cries of pain. He lit the kerosene lamp.

"What is wrong?"

"Oh God, I'm bleeding—get the doctor!"

"What doctor?"

"*Mon Dieu,* Dr. Rory on 14th Street! Hurry!"

Gabriel jammed on his shoes, grabbing his overcoat on the way out. Skittering on the icy sidewalk, he headed southward. There were no cabs available at three a.m.

He reached 14th Street, but which way to go? He yelled the doctor's name.

"Dr. Rory, I need Dr. Rory! Someone help, help, help!"

Soon a window was flung open. "Good God, man, people are trying to sleep!"

"I need Dr. Rory!"

"Head west."

Gabriel pressed on, yelling Dr. Rory's name. Finally, someone yelled, "He's four doors down on the other side."

Gabriel followed the directions, leaping up the steps and pounding on the door.

An older gentleman opened the door, already dressed for travel.

Gabriel tried to quiet his heaving self. "You knew I was coming?"

"The whole city knew you were coming. Now where am I going and why?"

"My wife, Simone Cooper; we live on 19th Avenue—"

Gabriel leaped from the steps, sprinting as he tried to outpace disaster.

He reached his building alongside the doctor who pulled his mare up to a hitching rail. "Please see to it that my horse gets some water."

Gabriel found a scrub bucket and brought the horse cold, clean water. He watched her put her nose in the bucket. "I'll bet you've seen a bunch of us miserable husbands in the middle of the night, haven't you?"

The horse raised her head and gazed at Gabriel. He patted her neck. "Yep, this is old news to you—same call, different house. But do you know how it turns out?"

As if in response, she turned her head away, and Gabriel left the bucket there. He ascended the steps, feeling helpless. He may know how to murder men and face down bullets, but help the woman he loved as she lay suffering? He had not a clue in the world.

Dawn broke, and still the doctor did not emerge from the bedroom. Gabriel heard Simone cry out so he knew she wasn't dead.

Finally, the door to their bedroom opened and the doctor motioned to Gabriel.

Simone was asleep as Dr. Rory explained, "I had to scrape her out, and she's lost a lot of blood."

Gabriel eyed the blood-soaked sheets and the porcelain basin filled with bloody gauze, bits of membrane and tissue stuck to the weave. The doctor handed the basin to Gabriel.

"Take this out and burn the contents; it's the slough and bad lining that was left over."

"And the sheets?"

"Burn those, too, if you can afford it. That much blood will never come out."

"And my wife?"

"It was a bad miscarriage. Watch her for the next twenty-four hours. If she develops a fever, call for me immediately. Childbed fever is her greatest risk. Oh, and —" He shook his head. "She'll never be able to carry a child to term. Another miscarriage like this could kill her. I suggest you send away for some gentlemanly prophylactics for her own good."

For her own good. Gabriel watched the doctor pack up his instruments.

"My fee is four dollars for this visit."

"Four dollars?"

"Yes. You can pay me in installments if you wish. Two dollars today and two dollars next month if that is more agreeable to you."

"No, no. I will pay now." Gabriel left the bedroom and went into his office to his safe.

He met the doctor in the hallway, who pocketed his payment. "She's had some chloroform and should sleep into the afternoon. She'll need rest and nourishment, followed by regular exercise in a couple of weeks."

Gabriel nodded. "And check for fever . . ."

"Yes, especially in the next twenty-four hours."

After the doctor left, Gabriel took a box of matches, bundled the sheets, and tucked them under his arm. Refusing to look at the contents in the basin, he picked it up and went outside.

Gabriel went to the far end of an open field across the street and cleared a spot in the snow. He dropped the sheets down and ignited them. But as he tipped the basin forward, he noticed a tiny lump swiftly slide on its clotted bed into the fire. Gabriel realized that this bluish black lump was his baby. He grabbed at it just as a flame licked at the oversized, presumptive head.

He was too late. The fetus curled in on itself and for a brief, terrible moment, Gabriel thought he smelled burning flesh. This wasn't vengeance on someone he hated, this was happenstance upon someone he loved.

Gabriel threw snow on the fire. Then, with trembling fingers, he searched through the embers until he found the charred little lump, the perfect, infinitesimal body fused into the fetal head. He could not tell if it was a boy or a girl; it was just a tiny, precious human being. He laid the smoking child in the palm of his hand. Then he turned his head and vomited.

Gabriel tossed the basin into the nearby woods. Still carrying his child in his hand, he went back inside to where Simone lay sleeping. He opened his dresser drawer and pulled out a fine linen handkerchief in which he tenderly enfolded the fetus. Then he went to his safe and opened it. Well, there would never be any birth certificates stored in here, but there would be a child. He closed the safe door. He would buy the most beautiful snuff box he could find to put the fetus in, a part of their family as much in death as it would have been in life.

SIMONE AWOKE TO FIND GABRIEL LYING BY HER SIDE. HE was facing her, dozing, and when she stirred, his eyes popped open.

Her eyes filled with tears. "*Monsieur . . .*"

He choked back his own. "Don't cry, my love; it couldn't be helped."

"I am a failure."

"No, no, you are not."

"Did the doctor say anything?"

Gabriel tried to find words that would not devastate her. He stroked her hair. "Yes, he did . . . This almost killed you, do you know that?"

She did not respond, but simply waited for a thin thread of reassurance of some kind. That is not what she received.

"The doctor feels it is too dangerous for you to try

another pregnancy. He does not feel you can carry a baby to term."

"I have no purpose."

Gabriel kissed her tears. "Don't say that!"

"I have failed as a wife."

"Simone, you loved me when no one else would. You accepted my scars, the ones on the outside and the ones on the inside. You taught me how to be a civilized man, to remember what it felt like to be somebody. You could never fail me!"

"You are so kind. I love you with all my heart."

He took her hand and held it to his cheek. "We have both overcome so much. We will overcome this. Together."

"I would have died had I been here without you."

"That is too terrible to consider. I would be nowhere without you."

"Please don't go away again for a long time, Gabriel, please."

"I will stay here for as long as you need me."

He heard a knock at the front door. "Perhaps that is Dr. Rory again."

He went to the front door in his bare feet, fully expecting to see the grizzled doctor. Instead, it was a young boy, holding an envelope in his hands.

"Telegram for Mr. Gabriel Cooper."

Gabriel's heart sank. He took the telegram, giving the boy a dime for his troubles on such a cold day.

Gabriel opened the envelope, knowing he had another assignment. And this one was urgent. Gabriel would have to take this, and he needed to set out without delay.

~

GABRIEL STUDIED THE DOSSIER, SITTING IN HIS PRIVATE train car, headed for Chicago. There was strife among the meat packers and someone had requested an untimely death. Gabriel studied a map of Chicago's Union Stock Yards, but his concentration was weak. Finally, he put away his papers.

His thoughts were really on his wife. She had lain there just two days ago, her eyes revealing all that she was not saying to him. He had gotten her the best nurse he could find, paying the woman two months' salary in advance.

"Even if she insists she does not need you," he had instructed her, "you stay on. I don't want her left alone."

He knew Simone felt betrayed. She had begged him not to go, to wire Moses that there was a family emergency. "Surely there is someone who can go in your place?"

"There is not. I am the one with . . . the expertise."

She had turned away from him. "Then get out now."

So he had left, picking up his bag and nodding to the nurse on his way out.

Gabriel closed his eyes, trying to gather his thoughts. They would find their happiness again. But he had to succeed at this job. Otherwise, they may never know life in the way he imagined it. He could be killed or worse...

There, that gave him focus. He picked up the map of the stockyards again. He would deal with their miseries when he returned. Now there was business to do, for he had a problem to solve.

HANS HARTMANN, AN AFFLUENT MEATPACKER, WAS TO BE caught in a stampede. Mr. Hartmann liked to show his business associates the fatted cattle of the stockyards every weekday at approximately eleven am. On the appointed morning, Gabriel had spotted the pot-bellied German, yelling at workers not to splatter cow dung on his good pants. He was followed by two other men to a crowded pen where he would stay for a while.

Gabriel slipped into a nearby pen. While Mr. Hartmann chatted and chuckled, Gabriel entered the cattle's flight zone, flapping his arms and lunging at the beasts. The animals panicked and crashed through the loosened gate, charging the astounded Mr. Hartmann, who slipped on the frozen ground to escape them; he and his associates had been mowed down. Gabriel had taken off the other way screaming, "Stampede!" to all who were in earshot.

As he took a cab home from the train station a few days later, Gabriel re-read the article from the *Chicago Times*. Authorities were looking for the *"unskilled workman who caused the beasts to rampage, killing Mr. Hartmann and his associates."* They were looking for a tall fellow with broad shoulders, brown hair, and a prominent scar across his left cheek. This fellow was new to the yards, but of course, Gabriel had washed the brown hair dye out of his hair and wiped off the scar so painstakingly applied. The authorities would never find their unskilled perp. *Pity about the associates—will you stop already? They were probably no better than Hartmann and deserved to die.*

The cab pulled to a stop in front of his home and

Gabriel alighted. He ascended the steps, hesitating as he laid his hand on the doorknob. It had been over a month since he and Simone had seen each other. The only thing he could offer her was the husband he wanted to be, for she could never see him for what he had become. The partial was always going to have to suffice for the whole. This conclusion pained Gabriel with an unexplained sadness as he turned the knob and stepped into the foyer.

As March sleet turned into April rain, he and Simone came to an understanding. He would come and go as needed. She would do whatever it was that women without children did.

At first, Simone stayed inside. She stopped reading the classics and began to read the daily papers, beginning with the *New York Times*. After that, she progressed to the *New York Herald,* and then on to the penny papers. For some reason, she was enthralled with the penny papers' police reports of crime and tragedy in the Lower East Side. Friendships were beginning to wane with the arrival of children and soon she would be completely out of these circles.

As spring arrived, she found herself wanting to explore Manhattan. An ad in *Godey's Lady's Book* calling for enrollment in Rutgers Female College had caught her eye. Would she perhaps qualify?

Simone left her home on a spring day amid the screams of childbirth from next door. The laboring woman's cries pushed her to hurry over to Fifth Avenue. Her thoughts drifted. *We both be dirt under the Master's feet...*

She wished she knew what had happened to Lucinda. The law had abolished slavery, but did that mean it was gone? Not if you were a woman. Well, she wanted to change that for herself and maybe for the Lucindas in the world.

As Simone approached 41st Street, she could see the college with its gables, faux battlements, and cathedral windows. She took a deep breath and opened the door.

Two young ladies watched her enter. "May I help you?" one asked.

"I'd like to inquire about your enrollment for the fall."

"Please, have a seat while I summon Mr. Farthing for you."

Simone looked around. Her eyes settled on the girl at the other desk, who smiled at her. "This is a very nice college. Where are you from?"

"Pardon me?"

"Forgive me; we get so many visitors and you don't speak as if—"

"I am from New Orleans."

"Oh, you are from the Secesh- er, the South."

"Now I live here. My husband and I moved here last year."

"You are married."

"Yes."

"Married women don't usually apply."

Just then the door opened and the other young lady emerged. "Mr. Farthing will see you now."

Simone stood up and walked into a heavily paneled room. A man stood behind a large, walnut desk. Bowing slightly, he held out his hand. Balding and bespectacled, he said, "I am Gregory Farthing, Headmaster of Enrollment and Student Affairs."

Simone took his pale, bony hand, feeling how cold it was through her gloves' scalloped silk. "Simone Cooper, sir."

"Have a seat, my dear."

Simone sat down opposite Mr. Farthing. He clasped his hands and studied her. "So, Miss Rittenhauer tells me that you wish to enroll in the fall?"

"Yes."

"We have a fine class of ladies assembling for September. Usually, their first visit here is arranged by a letter from their father and then they visit, chaperoned, of course. You seem to have just dropped in," he smiled, "as if from the sky. You say your last name is Cooper?"

"Yes."

"It is not a familiar name. Are you from New York?"

"My husband and I just moved here from New Orleans."

"Your husband?"

"Yes."

Mr. Farthing cleared his throat. "This seems most . . . irregular. We do not have any married ladies at the school." He rubbed his chin and stared at the papers on his desk. "Why do you wish to enroll in college if you are already wedded?"

Simone sat very straight and still, not taking her eyes from Mr. Farthing's face. "To get an education."

"Yes, but to what end?"

"The end is in itself, sir."

"What does your husband have to say about this, Mrs. Cooper?"

"My husband is quite willing to support my endeavor."

Mr. Farthing raised an eyebrow. "An indulgent man to be sure. But surely, he will not tolerate such whimsy when children come along. I assume you have no children yet?"

Simone stood up. "I am sorry to have wasted your time, Mr. Farthing."

Mr. Farthing stood up, seemingly relieved. "I am sorry we could not be of assistance to you, Mrs. Cooper."

He came around the desk and opened the door. "Good luck now," he murmured as she passed by.

Simone could feel all eyes on her as she opened the door and emerged into the sunshine. She walked briskly down Fifth Avenue. When she reached her apartment, she was accosted by the wail of a newborn baby. She hurried inside, slamming the door. She went from room to room, drawing all the drapes. Then she ran to her bedroom. With great, gulping sobs, she undressed and donned her nightgown, pulled back the covers, and crawled into bed.

How long can one languish, hidden from the world? Simone sealed herself away, ignoring the calls of friends. Despite her protests, Gabriel hired a housekeeper. "You are not yourself, Simone, and besides, one day there will be a whole staff of servants. You might as well adjust to it now."

She had shrunk from him in response, just as she had

when he had approached her romantically and she saw he was wearing a condom.

"What is that!"

"It is a prophylactic, my dear . . ."

"No! As if I am some prostitute!" She pushed him away.

"Simone, the doctor prescribed this—"

"*Non*, it is only for whores!"

"Listen to me," he had roared, "you cannot have another failed pregnancy and this is your only protection!"

"*Non, Monsieur,* not tonight. Not any night if you insist on . . . those things."

He had left her alone then. The silence between them lengthened, so much so that when he received his next assignment, he was happy to leave. What's more, he took the box of condoms with him. Perhaps they would be of use to him while he was away.

SIMONE WANDERED THROUGH THE APARTMENT AFTER Gabriel left, barely speaking to the new housekeeper, who was a Black woman of Caribbean descent named Elizabeth.

It was the smell of autumn that finally tempted her to open her front door. Perhaps the cool chill would settle her, assuaging the fever of loss that smoldered constantly.

Simone was entranced with the leaves, loving the carpet of colors that she walked upon. Soon she was venturing out farther every day now that she had no one to really come home to.

One afternoon, Simone headed south on Fifth Avenue. She felt like she was once again fifteen, sneaking away on a forbidden journey. She still heard the same warnings about going out alone, only now it was the dangerous neighborhoods filled with immigrants, their dirty, disease-ridden children running through streets begging and thieving. If you must, send your housekeeper or cook to the Lower East Side; better they track through the muck than you.

Simone felt pulled toward those very neighborhoods. As the sun crept toward the western horizon, she walked on.

Then she spotted a small child. Not just any child, but a wan, snot-nosed little girl whose terrified look reminded Simone of what she had felt for so many years. One eye red-rimmed and leaky, the little girl stood in her stained pinafore and looked around. She couldn't be more than five or six years old.

Simone approached the child. "No need to be scared," she coaxed. "Are you lost?"

The child started to cry. "I've lost me brother."

"*Cherie*, do you know where you live?"

The child shook her head. "Where's Joe?" she asked as tears and bits of green oozed onto her cheek.

"Is Joe your brother?"

The child nodded.

"Well, which way did you come from?"

The child pointed southward. Simone took a handkerchief out of her reticule. "Here, wipe your eyes and nose with this."

The little girl held the handkerchief to her nose. "It smells lovely."

"You may keep it."

"Oh, thank you, ma'am."

"You can't be out here after dark. We should try to get you home."

Simone held out her hand and the little girl took it as they walked to the corner of Broadway and 23rd. As they waited for a horse tram, Simone asked her, "What is your name?"

"Pegeen."

"Pegeen what?"

"Pegeen O'Connelly. What is your name?"

"I am Mrs. Cooper."

"Aye, 'tis a pleasure to meet ya." Pegeen let go of Simone's hand and curtsied.

"Why, *Cherie*, such a lovely curtsy!"

"Me mum says ya must always curtsy to the gentry. She made me practice before we came here, she did."

"And where did you come from?"

"County Cork."

The tram pulled up, crowded with people. Simone pressed a nickel into Pegeen's hand, "Give this to the driver when we board."

The conductor, seeing Simone's finely stitched tarlatan basque with matching hat and gloves, tipped his hat to her, but could not help staring at the child.

Simone smiled, "Could you, kind sir, please tell us how to get to the Lower East Side?"

"It's no place for a lady such as yourself, ma'am, especially with the sun setting in an hour . . . ."

Simone took Pegeen's nickel from her hand and pressed it into the conductor's, "The child must get home, and I will not send her into the darkness by herself."

"Well, if you insist, ma'am, you take this here tram back up to Union Square West. Then wait for the next tram going East on 14th Street. You'll want to take that to 1st Street. Disembark there and head south. Cross Houston Street and you'll be right in the neighborhood between the Lower East Side and the Bowery. Don't go west past the Bowery, whatever you do. That will take you to Five Points, and that is no place for any decent human being during night or day."

"Thank you, kind sir."

The conductor cleared his throat. "There's a thousand waifs like her, lookin' for home. A nice genteel lady such as yourself could be doing this every day if you're not careful."

"Then every day of my life would have a purpose."

Simone and Pegeen finally crossed Houston Street long after dark. Pegeen's teeth were chattering and Simone took off her soft woolen shawl, wrapping it around her.

The little girl fingered the shawl. "It's made by the angels 'tis."

A policeman, walking his beat, approached them. He tipped his cap. "Evening, ma'am."

"Good evening, sir."

"It is a cold evening to be out and about without a coat."

"Indeed. I am trying to take this child home as I found her by Fifth Avenue this afternoon. She seems not to know where she lives, but I surmised that it must be in this area."

The officer looked at Pegeen. "What's your name, child?"

The little girl started to shake. "Pegeen O'Connelly, sir."

"No need to be frightened, little miss, I don't bite. Are you any relation to Joseph O'Connelly?"

"He's me brother."

"Pity for you. The family lives on Norfolk Street, just off Delancey. I can take her from here."

"No, thank you. I wish to take her."

"Come then, I'll escort you. This is no time of night for a lady such as yourself to be wandering these streets."

The streets were still teeming. The saloons were booming, and wagons filled with all sorts of goods passed by. Simone stood out, inviting curious stares.

Frying onions and potatoes, pork and bacon mixed with stagnant slop, piss and shit. People watched the fine lady with the dirty child and policeman. Some called out questions to which the officer answered, "Mind your own matters." Simone glanced in through a few opened tenement doors. Soot-stained walls, women bent over fires or a wash tub; children were everywhere.

Suddenly Pegeen cried, "Mama!"

A woman ran up, "Oh, sweet Jesus, my love, where have ya been?" The woman hugged Pegeen and then looked at her. "What have ya about ya, love? Ach, you're dressed like a queen!"

The woman stood up. She was haggard and looked from the officer to her daughter. "Where's Joe? He was supposed to take ya with him today."

"He took me to the fancy part of town and told me

to wait for him there. When he didn't come back, this nice lady found me."

Simone held out her gloved hand. "I am Mrs. Gabriel Cooper, *Madame*."

The woman kept her hand to herself. "Me hands aren't fit to touch a lady."

"You are as much a lady as I am."

Onlookers snickered, but the woman extended her rough-nailed, calloused hand. Simone grasped it and for an instant their gaze crossed both class and culture.

"I can't thank ya enough, ma'am, for your kindness in helpin' me child," said Pegeen's mother.

The officer cleared his throat. "Mrs. O'Connelly, take your daughter home and give the good lady her shawl back. She's walked long enough in the chill to keep your daughter warm."

The woman quickly handed the shawl to Simone. "I can't thank ya enough."

"It was my pleasure, and she behaved herself very well today."

The woman blushed. "God Bless ya for all you've done."

"And what is your name?"

"Me? I'm Mrs. Francis O'Connelly."

One of the neighbors hooted. "Ach, Sheila, as if ya were a Duchess!"

Simone looked up and stared at the neighbor who quickly retreated inside.

Simone took a couple of silver dollars out of her reticule. She handed them to Mrs. O'Connelly.

"Here, purchase some medicine for Pegeen's eye."

"Aye, ma'am, thank ya kindly."

"I hope we meet again, Mrs. O'Connelly."

Mrs. O'Connelly smiled grimly. "That would mean one o' me lambs has gone missin' again, so if it's all right by yous, I'll pass on that hope."

And with that she left, dragging Pegeen behind her.

The officer sighed. "Well, ma'am, that was very Christian of you, it was. Now let's get you home."

He escorted Simone to a livery stable on Rivington. The livery boy, a Black Cuban, took one look at Simone and hitched the best horse to his only second-hand Hansom cab. He said to the officer, "No footmen here so I'll drive her myself."

The policeman tipped his hat at Simone. "Have a good evening now, ma'am."

"Thank you for your assistance, sir."

The officer nodded to the driver. "Her safety is in your hands, boy, so don't let any hooligans near this cab, or it'll be you I'll come lookin' for."

Simone was oblivious to this exchange, preoccupied with all that she'd seen and heard tonight. Was this how all these people lived, with no hope of anything better?

Why doesn't somebody do something? Why don't I do something? Maybe this is my calling . . .

Simone did not realize the cab had pulled up in front of her apartment. Nor, after she alighted from the carriage, did she notice the wail of the Holmsteads' little son or Gabriel's silhouette in their parlor window.

She opened her front door to see her husband, and for the first time in months, she broke into a wide, happy smile. *"Monsieur!"*

Gabriel, relieved, enfolded her in his arms. "I was about to send out the cavalry for you."

She stood back then and unpinned her hat, letting her shawl fall to the floor. "Oh, Gabriel, today was an answer to my prayers!"

He picked up her shawl and hung it up. "Do you realize it is almost ten? Tell me about your adventure, my prodigal wife."

"There are so many women and children, Gabriel, who need me."

"Really? And who might they be?"

Simone proceeded to tell him about her afternoon and evening. She grew increasingly animated as she described the poverty of the Lower East Side. "It's the immigrant mothers who need the education the most. Once a woman is married with children her fate is sealed. This is true for all women, but for these poor women who have travelled halfway around the world? They live like caged animals in rooms with no air and hardly a window. I could hardly stand to see it."

"Most people don't see it unless they live there themselves."

"It's deplorable! But what if these women could learn to read, to keep a ledger, to understand information for themselves? I would have to start small, but something has to be done—"

Gabriel leaned over and kissed her.

"*Monsieur,* now is not the time."

"No, it is not, but I am just so happy."

"About what?"

"To see you so happy after so many months of sadness. I wondered if I would ever see you smile again."

"My happiness cannot be like that of most other women, but perhaps it lies elsewhere." Her eyes searched his. "By being a woman, I possess a fatal flaw in the eyes of society. You must stand in kindred spirit with me for me to succeed."

Suddenly he felt needed, and this time he had the power to help. "Of course, darling, you know I can never refuse you."

Simone threw her arms around him. "Thank you, *Monsieur*, you will not regret this."

He smiled. "Welcome back my dearest—I've missed you so very, very much!"

MANHATTAN 1877

June 19, 1877

DEAR GABRIEL,
I welcomed your letter with enthusiasm, as news from you always puts me in good cheer. My days are long and the labor of the common man is bleak. I know you have risen above such tribulations. The turbulence of the financial climate always astounds me and yet you sail through it as if it is a sea of glass.

I do appreciate your rehabilitation of broken businesses and foreclosed farms. Indeed, it is the septic carnage wrought by a handful of greedy men from the Panic of 1873. Your keeping former owners working for you with a fair wage is praiseworthy.

As an attorney, I have cast my lot with the thousands who toil from sunrise to sunset for mere pennies on the dollar. I have fought for them in our courts of so-called justice. The robber barons and titans of industry have an iron-fisted grip on our laws and legislation and I would wager that they have a grip on most judges as well.

And so, I turn my energies elsewhere, to more desperate and dangerous pursuits. I will not divulge details, but recent cuts to the workers' wages on the Baltimore and Ohio Railroad has prompted a quiet outrage that may soon explode.

As such, I go forth into battle as I could not a dozen years ago. I have strategized as a general would and now it is time for me to ready my men for the fight. The hour has not yet come. That, I'm afraid, is dependent upon the Capitalists and their insatiable desire to cut off the very hands that feed them.

I remain truly yours,
Davie

~

August 25, 1877

Dear Davie,

If it were not for you and your care to teach me to read, I would have never risen above my inauspicious beginnings.

A man must do what makes his existence more than mere survival. For me it is to keep my wife in comfort in our home on Fifth Avenue even as she toils to educate the foreign masses that flock to our city. Ironically, we live our lives as if on parallel train tracks, those tracks so painstakingly laid by the men whose employers you oppose.

You are correct that I have found success in my business investments. And yet, I live in obscurity for I am gone often and tarry for no one. While my lovely Simone attends elegant dinners and the opera with her prominent benefactors, I must accept that she has grown accustomed to my absences at such events. My business casts my travels far and wide and my commitments are to strangers she's never even heard of. Hence, we live as if on two sides of a divide with a yawning chasm between us. We wave to each other and pantomime our most significant news, but gone are the days of inti-mate whispers or the meaningful glances that tell us that our hearts are still in tandem.

A melancholy note, to be sure, but this is the mediocrity of daily living. Thus, I turn to Capitalism to rise above mere survival even as you seek meaning through the rally of the working man. As such, I can only applaud you, for every man must seek his own path.

Always your Greatest Ally in all you Believe,
Gabriel

AH, WHERE DOES ONE GO FROM HERE, PONDERED GABRIEL as he posted his letter to Davie Tremont. His dear friend was like Simone, driven to do something greater than himself. But what about his own soul? He was a wealthy man, but did anyone know he existed? He lived a life partitioned by shadows, for nobody knew his true profession. And in his true profession, only one man knew his real name. Not even his lovely, purposeful wife knew who he really was or what he did.

Gabriel had told Simone a few years ago that he had quit working for Moses, but that, too, was a lie. He was inexorably tied to Moses, especially since the country still suffered from a deep depression. His pay had grown with the importance of the assignments. It was easier, however, to say he was self-employed with his investments as it explained their lifestyle of a brownstone on lower Fifth Avenue with servants and an attached greenhouse for Simone's beloved blooms. They could've moved farther up Fifth Avenue, but Simone had refused. She wanted to be near her work, a philanthropy that was meant to assuage a life with no direction, but now seemed to have become her life.

She had started with Mrs. O'Connelly, whose child she had escorted home back in '68. Simone had discovered that Mrs. O'Connelly did not even know how to write her own name.

Simone had started visiting Mrs. O'Connelly to teach her how to read. They worked together in the mornings until one day Mrs. O'Connelly muttered, "I don't know how I'm gonna keep this up after the wee un's born."

"Are you with child?"

"Yes, ma'am. I can't help it."

"What does your husband say?"

"Ach, he'd rather it not be, he would, but what can we do? We's husband and wife so we are."

Simone was quiet and then said, "Mrs. O'Connelly, I'm a Catholic, too. I know the church's teachings, but sometimes I believe God has mercy upon us women."

"Mercy?"

"Hear me out, Mrs. O'Connelly, because I know the Church does not share our burdens."

"It's no burden, it's me duty."

"Is it not also your duty to make sure that the children you already have are clothed and fed? When they get sick how do you pay for the doctor? Your husband's pay won't stretch if children keep arriving."

Mrs. O'Connelly's eyes narrowed. "Surely you're not sayin' what I'm thinkin'—"

Simone shook her head. "Oh, no, I would never suggest such a thing! You should have your baby and count it as the blessing it will be. But I'm thinking . . . to prevent another baby after that."

"That's against the Church."

"But is it against God? What if one of your wee ones fell sick and you had no money for the doctor because of all the mouths you had to feed, and God forbid, the wee one dies? What do priests know of sick children and not enough money to care for them? What do they know of a mother's heart? What do they really know?"

Mrs. O'Connelly sighed. "I've listened to the Church all me life. I've tried to be a good Catholic. But as God above is me witness, sometimes I lay awake at night and wonder to meself, 'How much more can I take?'"

"I understand."

"Ach, listen to me runnin' on."

Simone pressed Mrs. O'Connelly's hand. "A wise friend once told me that it doesn't matter who we are or where we come from. As women we are all dirt—" She corrected herself. "We are all the same in the eyes of men and society. And we must help each other. I could help you with . . . supplies . . . for you and your husband . . . for the good of your family."

From there it went from simple charitable work to Simone's raging, singular focus. Through Gabriel, she sent away for condoms and quietly handed them out to women who needed them. Her set of students grew and she took on tutors. Wages were now needed so she began to fundraise. She was charming and endeared herself to many, particularly those who lived farther up Fifth Avenue. She was their darling pet project, so articulate and fashionable with the heart of an angel. Who could resist inviting her to their social gatherings? Donations rolled in, although no one knew about the condoms.

Pity, Gabriel thought, that he could never partake in

any of this. How could he ever break from his past if he was not received into society? And yet, he could never risk recognition. So, he remained anonymous. He sighed, contemplating this as he walked home from the post office.

He ascended the steps of his house and unlocked the front door. He opened it to find Mrs. Sweeney, the main housekeeper, coming down the hall. "Good day, Mr. Cooper. Lunch will be ready in half an hour."

"Would you bring me the morning papers, Mrs. Sweeney? I would like to catch up on them before the evening editions come in."

"Yes, of course, sir. Do you wish for them in the library?"

"Yes, thank you. Any callers while I was away?"

"No sir."

"Has the mail arrived?"

"No sir, not yet, and no special telegrams."

Telegrams from Moses were still sent to the house, but they were delivered to the servants' entrance where someone was always around to receive them.

Gabriel retired to the library. As he sat down in an overstuffed chair, Mrs. Sweeney brought in some lemonade on a tray. "Such a warm day out, sir."

"I suppose we should be like our neighbors and leave for Newport in the summer."

Mrs. Sweeney handed him a glass with a linen napkin. "It is what most of the gentry do, but I doubt Mrs. Cooper would find it suitable. She has so much important work to do here in the city."

The comment irritated Gabriel. "Leave the papers here on the table."

Mrs. Sweeney complied, surprised by his terse tone. After she left, Gabriel grabbed the first paper, where the society page caught his eye: *Costume Ball at the George Cornelius Harrington Summer Residence Heralds the Closing of the Season in Newport.*

He scanned the article and saw Moses's name on the guest list. Moses and Veronica were in Newport?

Why did this man, who demanded Gabriel travel to the 15th ward of Algiers just to meet with him and discuss business amidst river rats and water beetles, not stop on his way to Newport to call on him? Why, thought Gabriel, he probably transferred trains here in New York City before catching the steamer to Newport. He probably even stayed here a few days to give his wife a chance to shop. Was he not worth a social call?

Furious, Gabriel swept his arm across the mahogany table, sending the papers and lemonade flying. He hurled the pitcher at the fireplace, where it smashed and splintered, sending shards onto the fine parquet floor.

Mrs. Sweeney hurried in and stared at the wet, slivered mess before her.

Gabriel turned to her. "What is it now?"

"Lunch, sir, is served."

He told the household staff that he was not to be disturbed for the rest of the day and to let his wife know accordingly. He sat in his office and brooded.

Slowly, a course of action formed. So many years, so many milestones. And yet, where was the reconciliation with the past? Was there any balm for his troubled heart? Gabriel decided he needed to go back to where it all began. He had to show someone, somewhere who he was and how far he had come. And he knew exactly who that person should be.

GABRIEL SOMETIMES VISITED PENSACOLA. HE'D GO BY the Hugo plantation. Someone still lived there, but the place was dilapidated. He'd inquire about it from time to time.

The answer was always the same: some old soldier who was burned badly in some battle lived there. The family had been important before the war, but not so much now.

Gabriel would then go back to his life, biding his time.

Now the time had come. Gabriel ferried across to Brooklyn to his document maker. Within the day he had obtained his Doctor of Divinity Degree and crossed back to Manhattan as the Reverend Martin Benton. He packed a worn portmanteau with old clothes, darkened spectacles, a cane, hair color, a soap and water mixture for his eyes, and a bible. He left word with the staff that he would be gone for several weeks.

Gabriel stayed down in Five Points for a few days. Nobody ever asked questions in Five Points.

He sequestered himself, coloring his hair silver and working a tack into his shoe that would irritate the ball of his left foot. He experimented with the soap solution to achieve the effect of watering, red rimmed eyes. He grew and colored a beard.

Gabriel then took a train bound for Philadelphia. He disembarked there, checking into a boardinghouse where he could perfect his new persona.

The good Reverend walked with a stoop and a distinct limp. He wore dark glasses because of an eye condition he had developed. He was not a well man and he wanted to settle in Mobile. "To live near my son," he had confided to the head of the boardinghouse, "since the Good Lord called my wife Home, why, I feel the need to spend my days near family."

The olive-skinned woman had smiled indulgently, feeling perhaps she could charm the good widower into staying longer. Maybe he didn't need his family if a sensible, loyal woman was around.

The good reverend did not seem interested in her, however, and he was content to eat his meals in affable silence. Afterward, he'd excuse himself, "For a little meditation on God's Word." Then Gabriel would retire to his room to memorize biblical quotes.

The next morning, Reverend Benton would come to breakfast, eat quietly, and leave. He would spend the day limping about town, perfecting his gait and his painful squint. He also grew out some sideburns which he also colored silver.

Two weeks later, he was southbound for Mobile. Once there, Gabriel began the complicated journey to Pensacola. He took the 10:35 p.m. eastbound Mobile and Montgomery to just outside Pollard where he picked up the 1:36 a.m. Pensacola and Louisville, arriving in Pensacola at 5:15 a.m. It was still dark when he approached a new hotel on Palafox Street. The night clerk rushed to Gabriel's aid as he struggled with his portmanteau. "Comin' in from Mobile, sir?"

Gabriel rested on his cane. The tack in his shoe was doing its job. "It's a devilish journey."

The clerk handed Gabriel a key. "Room 110, suh. Here, I'll show y'all to yer room."

"God bless you, son."

"No trouble at all."

They walked slowly to the room and the clerk opened the door. "Is there anything else I can get you, Mr. . . . .?"

"Reverend. Reverend Martin Benton."

"Of course, Reverend, my apologies."

"No need to apologize, young man, but is there a place where an ailing man can get a sarsaparilla later on?"

"Why, yes sir, they serve a fine array o' fountain drinks over at Oswald's General Store. Fact is, Mr. Oswald just put in a new counter fer ice cream sodas an' the like. Fer the folks stayin' fer the winter. Y'all can get a mighty fine Mint Julep there, too. And fer yer dinin' convenience, the dinin' room here opens at seven a.m."

"Sounds like Heaven to an old, time-worn traveler." Gabriel took off his glasses, dabbing at the bloodshot, tearing eyes. "Thank you for your kind help, son."

After the clerk left, Gabriel took off his glasses and his shoes. He laid down on the bed to rest his eyes. Before he knew it, he was sound asleep.

It was late morning when Gabriel arose. He dressed

quickly and went to the hotel dining room for an early lunch.

He sat at the back, observing as he ate. Pensacola had grown due to a winter season of Northern visitors. Maybe he, too, would be a Northern visitor; that is, if all went well.

He paid for his meal and left, walking slowly out into the thick heat. As he wiped his forehead with his handkerchief, he was convinced he knew one or two passersby. They, of course, did not recognize him, for he had been a skinny, barefoot teenager the last time anyone saw him. Besides, most would think him dead by now.

Gabriel made his way over to Oswald's. He hobbled into the store, taking a seat at the soda fountain. The owner, a middle-aged white man named Chuncey Oswald, approached him. "Howdy, sir. What can I get for y'all?"

"A sarsaparilla, please."

Chuncey pulled out a glass from under the counter and then disappeared into the back. He returned with a bottle of dark brown liquid and poured it into a glass.

"Two cents," he said with a smile. "Visitin'?"

"Just arrived here this morning."

"Came in from Pollard, did ya? Lotta pussyfootin' jes' to go forty-five miles, but that's the railroad for ya. Got business this way?"

"Well, I'm hoping to retire here. Looking for some good property. Any good bargains you know of?"

"Well, the only one I know of right off an' it's 'cause I got kinfolk out that way is the ole Hugo plantation. Seems the ol' family's still there, but their place is fallin' down around 'em. The son's a wounded veteran an' ain't been out this way in years, but when he did show up, they had to put a cloth over his face. Anyway, seems they're like squatters out there. Word is they're livin' on the good graces of the bank—won't turn 'em out bein' that they fought for the Cause an' all. Maybe for the right price they might give up an' move on."

Gabriel quivered with excitement. He put his two cents on the counter and struggled to his feet. "Thank you kindly, sir, for your hospitality and conversation."

Chuncey wiped the counter. "Once y'all get settled y'all come back to Oswald's. We'll treat ya like the family y'are."

Gabriel tipped his hat and hobbled away. He looked at his pocket watch. Half past noon. There was still time to go out and see the Hugo property. And if he was lucky, maybe he could get back in time to visit the bank.

GABRIEL WALKED OVER TO THE LIVERY STABLE ON Intendentia Street. He passed the old jailhouse, now boarded up. Criminals were taken to the new jailhouse on Jefferson and Main, an idyllic facility compared to the filthy hovel he had been in. Passing the jailhouse, he fought the temptation to pull himself up to his full height. *Not now, but one day soon . . .*

Gabriel entered the livery stable quietly, where a skinny boy with red hair and freckles approached him.

"May ah help y'all?"

"Yes, I'd like to rent a horse for the afternoon."

The boy looked him up and down. "Meanin' no disrespect sir, but y'all kin ride?"

"Yes, son, I can. I may not be able to run, but I most surely can ride." He smiled. "But do bring me a gentle nag, one that can find its way home even if I can't."

The boy left and returned with a middle-aged chestnut mare. "She's slow but steady. And she knows how to get home for dinner."

"Bless her equine heart." Gabriel handed the boy a quarter and gave him his cane to hold as he hitched himself into the saddle. He drew in a sharp breath at the tack in his shoe.

"Y'all okay, mister?"

"Yes, son, I am. Thank you for asking." He wheeled the horse around and exited.

If he truly were a Reverend, Gabriel would be enjoying God's scenery around him. He would appreciate the cicadas' buzzing and the wildflowers growing amongst the trees and tall grasses. Instead, he ignored it all, recalling that one letter he had received from Mason so long ago. Now it resided in his office safe, buried under deeds of contract, and next to the bejeweled snuff box that held his miscarried child of yesteryear. Gabriel remembered every word of that letter:

"I find a perverse joy in writing to you, pathetic convict Cooper, to inform you that you have lost everything. May you rot in Hell alongside your family. May they be the victims of an unending feast of maggots and may you all suffer together in that eternal inferno…"

Gabriel turned his horse down an old familiar road, the one that was once the stuff of nightmares. The lane was now rock-strewn and pitted; the weeping willows trapped in unholy matrimony with native crossvine. Gabriel rode as if in a trance, his eyes fixed on the big house ahead of him, on the now sagging porch and shaggy front lawn choked with prickly poppy and salt bush.

Two figures were working in the distance. The women wore straw hats, while one was bent over with a basket and the other had a hoe. He stayed there for a few minutes until one of them saw him. Gabriel turned his horse around. No need for any conversation now.

As he rode back down the lane, a troubling thought festered within him. He had not seen Mason Hugo. Was he too late? Had he died? He kicked the sides of his horse, and she broke into a trot. Now he had to get back to town and find out if the best part of his plan had been ruined.

GABRIEL RETURNED HIS HORSE BY LATE AFTERNOON. HE left the livery, hobbled down the street and rounded the corner to the bank.

He approached the teller, a bespectacled man with a dark mole on his right cheek. "I am inquiring about a specific property in the surrounding countryside."

"Yes of course, Mr . . .?"

"The Reverend Marvin Benton."

"This is under the bank president's purview, Reverend. You must speak with him." The teller opened the gate that separated the bank personnel from the customers. "His name is Mr. Espinoza, but he will see you now."

The teller opened a polished pine wood door for

Gabriel. A man of Hispanic heritage and in his early forties came around his desk. He held out his hand.

"Good day! I am Cedro Espinoza, bank president. How may I help you on this fine afternoon?"

"May I sit down?" Gabriel asked. "My legs aren't what they used to be."

"Yes, of course! May I get you a glass of water?"

"No, no thank you."

Cedro sat down behind his desk. "What can I do for you?"

Gabriel waxed nostalgic. "You know, Mr. Espinoza, I grew up on a farm in New Jersey. I loved it there, but I loved God's Word more, so I became a Man of the Cloth; had a church in Brooklyn for twenty-five years. But now I can't take the cold weather, yet I want to have land again. I've heard it's beautiful here in Florida—the land of flowers or so they say. I've heard there's an old plantation in these here parts, owned by the Hugos . . .?"

A glimmer of hope flickered in Cedro Espinoza's eyes. "We are in possession of that plantation, Reverend."

"I was told I should make . . . inquiries. Are inquiries in order, Mr. Espinoza?"

"That would depend, Reverend. Are you qualified to do so?"

"I can have fifteen thousand dollars to you by tomorrow afternoon. But I would like to know more about the family that owns the place."

Cedro stared at Gabriel. "I am a God-fearing, church-going man, Reverend, but this is the first time I think I've truly had a prayer answered. That property has been a thorn in my side ever since I took my job here a year ago. I took over from the old bank president who was friends with the Hugo family. While I certainly value loyalty, there must be some sort of separation when it comes to business. My predecessor had been carrying the Hugo debt for over a decade when he retired. Seems old Thackeray Hugo got himself killed back in 1863 and then the son, Mason, was severely wounded. He has to walk with two canes and is a fright to look at. Any income to be brought in falls on the sister and mother. They take in washing, sell vegetables, and have relied on my predecessor's loyalty to forgive them their debt. I've wanted to call in the debt ever since I came to this office, but"—Mr. Espinoza spread out his hands—"you understand. This must be handled with discretion. If you wish to buy the property, I am happy to consider your proposal."

"What will happen to them?"

"Well, their debt will be paid and they will have to leave. The war was hard on everyone, but nobody else I know of has ridden out their debt for as long as these folks have. It's time to solve the problem."

Yes, it was time to solve the problem. Gabriel stood up and put his hat back on. He shook Cedro's hand. "I'll have the money wired tomorrow."

"Excellent, Reverend. Welcome to Pensacola."

"What the wicked dreads will come upon him, but the desire of the righteous will be granted."

"Pardon me?"

"Proverbs 10, Verse 24. Forgive a tired man his ramblings, Mr. Espinoza. God works in mysterious ways."

"Yes, He does," rejoined Cedro as he escorted the

Reverend out of his office. Finally, God had heard his prayers to take that infernal property off his hands. And it couldn't come from a more upstanding man.

GABRIEL ARRANGED FOR THE WIRE TRANSFER TO THE Bank of Pensacola. He limped in, his eyes watering pathetically.

"Good afternoon, Reverend," said Cedro, pulling out a chair.

"Good afternoon, Mr. Espinoza."

Cedro sat down opposite him. "I am both honored and pleased to present you with the bill of sale and deed of property which, as soon as you sign, is all yours."

Gabriel picked up the fountain pen. He had waited so long for this. His hand was shaking as he pressed the pen to the paper and signed his falsified name.

Cedro brought over a tray of cookies and drinks. "This calls for a celebration!" He poured the sarsaparilla into two glasses. "Here's to the new owner of *Casa de la Riqueza*! May it bring you the wealth it once boasted and the contentment you are now seeking."

Gabriel sipped the frothy libation. "Mr. Espinoza, I have much to settle before I take up permanent residence here. Let the original owners live in peace for now. When I come down again, I will pay them a visit."

"As you wish, Reverend, but the property was lost to them a decade ago. I owe them no notice of impending eviction. However, if you want to tell them yourself, so be it."

"Let's keep this sale in confidence until then, yes?"

"Yes, of course."

Gabriel put down his glass. "Thank you, Mr. Espinoza."

Cedro saw Gabriel to the door. "Until the next time, sir. Safe travels back to New York."

"God keep you until we meet again." Gabriel left, the deed of ownership in his hand. Now to get to back to New York, where his last will and testament would be drafted, for the Reverend did not have long to live.

THE REVEREND MARTIN BENSON SENT A COPY OF HIS last will and testament to Cedro Espinoza, thinking it prudent to have his affairs in order. In his will he had bequeathed *Casa de la Riqueza* and all its surrounding properties to Gabriel Sutherland Cooper, *"who has been like a son to me in these last painful, lonely years . . . and in the event of Mr. Cooper's demise, then the property should be deeded to his wife, Mrs. Simone Livingston Cooper."*

Gabriel let time go by. One evening, as he was reading the Society page in the library, he saw that Simone and his name was on several guest lists. He realized that he had never met any of these people. Was he that invisible?

Simone entered the room with a soft whoosh of skirts. "*Monsieur,*" she crooned, "the season is almost upon us."

Gabriel put down his paper. "My dear, the season is almost upon *you*. I see my name here, but who are these people?"

Simone smiled patiently. "I do not travel as you do,

Gabriel; I am bound by the East River and the Hudson for all my alliances. Unlike you, who lays claim to the entire nation as your business enterprise, I must tend to my small circle here in the city." She cocked her head to one side. "Would you accompany me to the Van de Haas ball?"

"Etta Van de Haas? Is that the homely one?"

"*Monsieur!* If it weren't for her, I would never have met the patrons who are now funding the new school I have plans for."

"You mean, if it weren't for her relation to an obscure British Baroness and that rich old man she is married to. It's her faint British bloodline and his ancient money that allows her to be in the company of *the* Mrs. Astor, even if it was just once last summer in Newport."

"Will you accompany me or not?"

"No, I will not."

"Will you at least come with me to the opening of the opera in a fortnight? We have been invited to sit in the Tidwells' box."

"Let us at least be forthright with each other, Simone. *We* have not been invited, *you* have been invited. I do not even know the Tidwells. I think they would feel imposed upon if you suddenly presented your prodigal husband at such an important affair. That is, if they are even aware that you have a husband."

"Oh, for goodness' sake!" Simone stood up and headed for the door. "You know, Gabriel, it wouldn't harm you to come with me as my husband for once!"

Gabriel's voice was smooth. "Appreciate the fact that I make it a point to be home for Thanksgiving and Christmas, but I certainly don't want to see your pretentious friends more than I have to. It's enough to give a self-respecting man digestive aggravation."

"Save your vulgar opinions for your own friends," snapped Simone as she slammed the door behind her.

Gabriel stared into the fire. *What friends would those be?* he wondered. He didn't have any, nor would anyone care if he did develop digestive aggravation. He had no voice and no presence, so what did he have? Only death. He could call it a counterbalance for justice or retribution, but in the end, it was death. That was his legacy, his silent, pathetic footprint that no one would understand even if they knew.

He decided to go back to Pensacola as soon as possible.

THIS TIME, GABRIEL TOOK A STEAMSHIP FROM MOBILE TO Pensacola. In his new portmanteau that befitted a man of status instead of a disheveled reverend, he carried the papers to take over the Hugo plantation.

He stood at the railway of the small steamer as it rounded into Pensacola Bay. He took off his hat because now he didn't care if anyone recognized him. He was coming as the man he had always wanted to be.

WHILE MUCH OF THE NATION WAS IN THE GRIP OF A WINTER chill, Gabriel sat in his sporty phaeton as the driver breezed toward *Casa de la Riqueza.* He held onto his gray bowler hat, which matched his grey broadcloth suit. He looked at one of his ruby cufflinks, admiring the gem's vermilion depths. Would the red of the Hell he hoped to send Mason Hugo into have such rich prisms as these jewels he now wore?

The driver turned down the plantation's rutted lane. Gabriel fingered his popular Peacemaker, a Colt .45 inscribed in mother-of- pearl with his initials.

They pulled up to the big house. Gabriel alighted from the carriage and handed a dollar to the driver.

"This will likely take all day, so you might as well relax. I'll make sure the fine ladies of the house give you some lunch."

The driver pulled his phaeton into the shade and unhitched his horse. He pulled out his harmonica and began playing *What a Friend We Have in Jesus,* as Gabriel knocked on the front door.

Mason's sister opened the door, and Gabriel tipped his hat. "Miss Suzanna Hugo, I am Gabriel Sutherland Cooper, coming to avenge my past and collect on debts long overdue. I begin with an order of eviction for you from this property."

Suzanna's eyes widened, which made Gabriel smile. "Come now, ma'am, did you really think you all could get away with murder?"

Suzanna turned on her heel, yelling for her mother. Gabriel stepped inside, relishing his entrance into the big house through the front door.

Georgina Hugo came down the hallway, hardly the commanding figure she had once been. Time had passed and the seasons had etched themselves upon her face. Gone was the pampered white complexion he remembered, replaced by sun damage and furrows. She was a crone, and Gabriel swelled with satisfaction.

She stopped a few feet from him. "I only know one Gabriel Cooper, and he is long gone. Tell me who y'all really are!"

Gabriel took a step toward her. "I *am* Gabriel Sutherland Cooper, and I'm collecting on debts long overdue."

"That is not possible." Her voice shook.

"Look at me, Georgina Hugo. Do you not still see the boy you once tried to destroy? Look at my eyes. Surely you cannot forget them. Look at the hair. It's the same color that it was the day you falsely accused me. I was incapable of committing such crimes back then, but I am very capable of committing them now."

There was a yelp at the end of the hallway. Mason Hugo hobbled toward them on two canes, spittle dribbling down his chin.

Gabriel watched him and announced, "I can do to you what I did to him."

He took in Mason's torn face, which had suffered repeated infections where his lips and tongue had once been. The flesh around his jaw was gone, blackened bicuspids and molars peeking through. A nostril had been partly removed.

Mason began to yell unintelligibly, and Gabriel took out a linen handkerchief.

"This is a handkerchief made of the finest English linen. It's imported, cleaned, and pressed by my own housekeeping staff. I would give it to you, but I don't throw pearls to swine. So, shut up and listen to me. It's my turn now.

"This is my property, my house, my fields, my land.

And you must vacate it today." Gabriel pulled out his pistol. He pointed it first at Georgina who curled away from him, and then at Mason's sister.

"Shall I discard your family as easily as you discarded mine? I have the deeds, the money, and the power. And I will use it on you just like you used it on me. An eye for an eye, or more appropriately for you, a lie for a lie. You have eight hours to leave this place."

Suzanna broke from the huddle. Georgina hissed, "Where are you going?"

"I'm getting the cart and wagon ready."

"Have you lost your mind? Get the sheriff!"

Suzanna turned on her mother. "Look at our Mason! Look at him! This isn't a war wound, mother!" She pointed at Gabriel. "*He* did that! Do you want to tempt a monster who is capable of that?"

Gabriel raised his eyebrows. "Perhaps if your dear Suzanna had been born a son you might still be the house of wealth you were always so vulgar to boast about. Mason would certainly have made a better daughter and your Suzanna would have undoubtedly made a better son. Your children, I'm afraid, are freaks of nature."

Georgina went to Mason, wiping the drool from his chin. Then with a final, stricken glance at Gabriel, she escorted Mason away.

Gabriel watched the Hugo women load two wagons, one to be pulled by a donkey and the other by a mule. Gabriel recalled the sleek palominos they once had. They scurried around, whimpering that they needed more time.

"I never got more time. My mother, May Belle Harding, never got more time. How *dare* you ask for more time."

Finally, Georgina climbed into the first wagon and took the reins of the mule. She stared at Gabriel and spat.

Gabriel shrugged. "The vexation of a fool is known at once, but the prudent man ignores an insult. Proverbs 12:16. You always were a nasty woman. I would expect nothing less of you now that justice has come for you."

"You're a thief, that's what you are!"

"All of this was purchased legally, whereas you, you lawless bitch, your husband of rotting memory and that stinking coward you call your son, you three stole my family's home out from under us. You turned my family out to die in the swamp while you told shameless lies that put me away. You may think me a thief, *Madame*, but I know you are a murderer."

"*No!* It's you who's turning out a sick man and his family. We lost everything in the war and now you are stealing the walls that protect us from the elements."

"No, Mrs. Hugo, I am simply reaping what you have sown."

Gabriel sauntered up to the second wagon. Suzanna was already in the driver's seat, reins at the ready. She stared straight ahead, avoiding Gabriel's gaze. Gabriel came around and stared at Mason, who was in a wheelchair in the back.

"It's so fitting that your tongue was cut away. And keep this in mind as you continue on to the Hell you had once wished upon me: *'He who guards his mouth preserves his life; he who opens wide his lips comes to ruin.'* Now get off my property. May your bones sink into the swamp as did my own family's. You all deserve nothing more than what you did to those less fortunate than you."

The wagons began to move. Mason began to yell. Gabriel watched him go, the roaring in his ears and gut settling like the hiss of sea foam left by a crashing wave. He felt he could loosen his grip and just enjoy this moment when he had finally achieved justice for all he had lost and would never get back. He sat there until Mason's cries faded away and all Gabriel heard was the rustle of palmettos swaying playfully in the warm Gulf breeze.

GABRIEL TELEGRAMMED SIMONE SAYING HE WOULD BE home for Christmas, but not before. She was having tea with Etta Van de Haas when she read the telegram.

"Well, it seems my husband won't be able to make it to your Christmas ball after all. He sends his regrets."

"My dearest friend, I am sorry for your disappointment. But I do have cousins who are travelling from Philadelphia to attend, and you may certainly be accompanied by one of them if you'd like."

Simone set her cup down. "Thank you, Etta, but I daresay your cousins should accompany someone far more clever and charming than old, dreary me."

Etta laughed. "You are positively droll; you'll probably be the life of the party!"

"Now who is being droll?"

Etta stood up. "I must be getting on if I want to stop by the Franklin Tobins. Old Aunt Jane hasn't been well."

"That is a shame; please give her my regards."

"I will."

Mr. Sweeney stood in the grand foyer, holding Etta's wrap and muff. Simone waved and watched as her friend's footman opened the carriage door and she climbed in. Mr. Sweeney turned to Simone. "Is there anything else I can do for you, Madame?"

"No, thank you, Mr. Sweeney, I shall be in my office until dinner." On her way there, she stopped in the drawing room to read Gabriel's telegram again. Then, with a flick of her wrist, she tossed it into the fire that crackled in the grate.

A WINTER BALL ALWAYS CALLS FOR A NEW DRESS. SIMONE had her seamstress come to her home for a final fitting.

Her seamstress, unknown to her circle of Fifth Avenue patrons, was one of the reasons that Simone was such a social success. Karen Lynn, a young Scandinavian immigrant, was selling handmade lace on Broadway when Simone had discovered her.

That was seven years ago. Now she was an established dressmaker, with a shop uptown and house nearby.

Victorian evening wear still presented challenges. While the skirts were now more fitted with cascade bustles at the back and cuirass bodices fitted over the waistline and hips, they still featured plunging necklines that, for Simone, offered up that damnable scar. She feared its fleshy revelation would be a topic of conjecture, so Karen made sure to stitch in a sheer Swiss voile at the neckline of her gowns; sheer enough to appear fashionable, yet opaque enough to mask the cosmetics over the scar.

Now Simone stood in front of her mirror. The gown, a deep royal blue, reflected a ring of that same color around her irises. The voile at the base of her neck was stitched with tiny seed pearls matching the pearl and sapphire earrings that she would wear to the event.

"You are an artist and a genius, Karen!"

"Thank you, Mrs. Cooper. I am very pleased with the fit."

Simone went to her boudoir and opened her formal glove box. "I picked these up from the glover yesterday. Let's see how they go with the gown."

She pulled out a pair of ice blue, sixteen-button Mousquetaire kid opera gloves. As she pulled them up over her elbows, they took on the dress's sheen. Simone picked up a comb adorned with seed pearls and sapphires and stuck it in her upswept hair. "What do you think?"

"You will be the belle of the ball!"

"I am married and far too old to be a belle."

"You will be the admiration of all the gentlemen present and the envy of all the ladies."

"It is too bad Mr. Cooper cannot accompany me and see this for himself."

"He must be proud, nevertheless, to have you represent him."

Simone did not smile at the compliment. She did not think that this sentiment ever crossed Gabriel's mind.

THERE WAS A SMALL CROWD GATHERED AROUND ETTA Van de Haas's home when Simone's carriage pulled up. She alighted to comments and stares. She walked up the red carpet, her eyes cast down and her gloved hands tucked into a mink muff. The beveled doors swung open before her as if on cue.

As a liveryman took her mink cape and muff, Simone joined the line to greet Etta and her husband. As she stood before them, Etta kissed Simone on the cheek and grabbed her hands.

"It's going to be a fabulous evening and there are so many people you must meet!"

Simone smiled and moved away into the drawing room where the guests were gathering while an immense Christmas tree twinkled in the candlelight. Etta approached her and took her hand.

"Come, my dear, there is someone you must simply meet! He and his wife are philanthropists of the highest sort."

She did not see him at first, only the woman he was conversing with, a tall blond in an evergreen velvet gown.

Etta chirped, "Mr. Malcolm Beaumont, may I present to you Mrs. Gabriel Sutherland Cooper? This is the lady whose charitable works I mentioned to you earlier."

Simone's chest constricted. She offered her gloved hand, her blue-ringed eyes meeting his. Above her ringing ears she heard his familiar voice, "It is my honor, Mrs. Cooper, how do you do?"

Speechless, Simone nodded graciously. She felt heat prickle her chest and neck, flushing a bloom of pink upon her cheeks. Anyone who noticed would think she was radiant.

Etta prattled on about Simone's work as Simone and Malcolm stared at each other in a privately shared horror.

Dinner was announced. Lightheaded, Simone realized that she was seated next to Malcolm.

"Such a fortuitous calamity," Malcolm murmured with that smile she knew so well. Then, as baked oysters were served, he observed softly, "So, you are married."

"As are you."

"Do you have children, Mrs. Cooper?"

"Do you?"

"Ah, still so reluctant to answer my queries! Some things never change."

Enough. Simone smiled coyly at him, "I gave you all my answers once, and where did it get me?"

She noticed the creases deepen around his eyes, those rich brown eyes that had once caressed and claimed her as much as his hands. "A bad business that we must surely not speak of here."

"Yes, trickery and betrayal are hardly the conversation for this elegant affair. However, I do remember you priding yourself on saying whatever passed your fancy if it was to your advantage. Things have changed very much, Mr. Beaumont, especially in my opinion of you."

His smile remained fixed. "Please, Mrs. Cooper, not here."

"Ah, Mr. Beaumont, so many years have passed, we really do not know each other now do we? Tell me, do you have children?"

"Four sons."

"You must be so very happy."

"Hardly."

"Such a dubious answer from such a blessed man."

Before anything more could be said, a cream of turkey soup was served. Simone dipped her spoon into the opaque broth. She heard the woman on the other side of Malcolm ask, "Oh, Mr. Beaumont, and how is our dear Evelyn?"

"Thank you kindly for asking, Mrs. Nielson. She is resting comfortably tonight. I was hesitant to leave her bedside, but she insisted that I come and represent us, and give my regards to all our good friends."

"Of course. And please give her our regards. If her health permits, I will call on her next week."

Simone turned her attention to others around her and the dinnertime passed amicably. Afterward, they moved into the ballroom where a string ensemble was playing.

Malcolm caught up with her and bowed. "May I have this next dance, madame?"

Simone fluttered her fan before her face and looked up at him with her brilliant eyes. "You may not." Then she added, "Kindly remove yourself from my presence, Mr. Beaumont. I wish to enjoy at least a portion of my evening."

Malcolm smiled. "As you wish, Mrs. Cooper." And with that he turned and lost himself in the multitude of guests.

It was after midnight when Simone fetched her cape and muff. As she stood waiting for her carriage, she realized Malcolm was once again beside her.

"You were as if an answer to prayer, tonight, Mrs. Cooper. I hope I will see you again."

Simone inhaled the warm smell of cigar and cognac on him. "May that *never* come to pass!"

She climbed into her waiting carriage and glanced at him. He stood so tall and broad, and yet, he looked so forlorn. Still, she hoped she never saw him again.

Or did she? Simone fought her physical arousal. Malcolm had abandoned her and yet she had moved on. Now, she had so much more and she wasn't dirt under *anyone's* feet.

The carriage stopped in front of her house. The liveryman helped Simone down and she ascended the steps unaccompanied.

Before she could open it, the door swung open. There stood Gabriel in his shirtsleeves, his face tanned from his time in Florida.

"Oh!" she cried stepping into the grand foyer. "You're home!"

Gabriel, still euphoric from his vengeance, smiled down at her. "Did you miss me?"

"Oh, *Monsieur*!" she cried, throwing her arms around him. "You have no idea! You simply have no idea whatsoever!"

And with that he scooped her into his arms and carried her upstairs, leaving a trail of mink and kid as they headed for the bedroom like newlyweds.

March 6, 1878

D*EAR DAVIE,*

With the anticipation of spring comes hope for better things in our country. This damnable depression that began in 1873 drags on. Yet, as I look for signs of recovery, I see a few bright spots, although ever so fragile. I, too, feel the pinch of revenue's draught and like a man parched of water, am eager to again take my fill of success.

As I read the newspapers, I can only imagine your dismay at the demise of justice for the freed slaves of the South. The repeal of Reconstruction has brought a renewed suppression of the Black man, sending reverberations northward. Perhaps you are tempted to take on his plight in addition to the railroad man's? Remember that your life is as a scale of weights: while one side may have an accrual of allies, make sure that the other side does not tip by the weight of your enemies.

As for myself, these last three months have seen the scales of my life held in blissful balance with a chance to spend time with my lovely wife. Indeed, we have rekindled an amiable companionship that allows us to sit by the fire most evenings, reading the latest novels and literary works. I have enjoyed the warmth of hearth and home this winter season—it is a balm upon my restless soul.

I do not engage the fantasy that all this will continue indefinitely, but I hope the feeling remains that all is well, provided I always return safely home.

I remain your brother in heart,
Gabriel

May 9, 1878

DEAR GABRIEL,

I rejoice in your happiness. And yet, your success magnifies the two worlds I straddle. On the one hand, when I visit my parents, I enjoy the comforts of their fine home in Baltimore. We are well-fed and clothed, and attend the opera and theater. Then, because my conscience allows me no respite, I return to the dark alleys of poverty and industrial bondage where men, women and children are fed to the beast of greed and profit.

I played a hand in the Railroad Strike of 1877. And, as your last letter so eloquently warned, the scales tipped with the accrual of many enemies. As a result, I left the battlefield of the spike and rail, travelling to the northeast. Perhaps if I had travelled southward to Alabama or Mississippi, I would have been tempted to fight for the Black man. Instead, I observed a funeral for a breaker boy in Lackawanna County, who was crushed to death by falling in a coal chute as he tried to separate slag from coal with his bleeding fingers. I don't know which part of the tragedy I deem more heartbreaking: the fact that he was eleven years old or that no one stopped any of the coal processing when the accident occurred. His body was simply fetched at the end of the day, and arrangements made by his people who seem to be deadened to the horrors of the life they lead.

Now, I know as any educated man who is a realist, that the progress of this country was once gleaned from the sweat of slaves. And now that this cesspool of misery and bondage has dried up, the greedy demand satiation from elsewhere, and where is that? The working man is the next best fuel to stoke the fires of industry and capitalism. I have thus cast my lot with the miners. For the dead boy's sake and all those who will occupy future coffins if all of us continue to stand idly by.

With Affection and Hope for your Continued Happiness,
Davie

DAVIE'S LETTER ARRIVED WHEN GABRIEL WAS ONCE AGAIN traveling. Simone still endured long silences when he was away, wondering why she never received so much as a telegram when he was gone. And the peculiar way he studied the newspapers, as if he was always searching for something . . . did all husbands read the papers as if their lives depended on it?

She finally rented space off Rutgers and the trolley line due to her time spent in the Bowery, Five Points, and the Lower East Side. From here she now ran her charity, and in quiet moments, watched the neighborhood from her second story window.

It was on such a day, as Simone sat listening to the summer rain, that she read the society page:

Funeral for Mrs. Malcolm Xavier Beaumont III

So, Malcolm's wife had died. All of Manhattan's elite had journeyed back from Newport to attend the service. Simone had read about her, the Brahmin princess of Philadelphia's finest, a spectacular union of two titanic families. Slender and delicate, she was everything a Society husband could hope for. Except for healthy. Plagued by migraines, she bore Malcolm four sons in quick succession before collapsing with rheumatic fever two years ago. She had been an invalid ever since.

Simone could not help but compare the woman whom Malcolm had finally picked for a wife to herself who, at the age of fifteen, had loved him so completely. She still mourned that young girl's pain.

There was a knock at the door. Thinking it was one of her tutors, she got up and opened it, but it was not a tutor. It was Malcolm.

He stood with his hat in his hands. Gone was the pleasant aloofness that he wore like an overcoat, replaced instead by the forlornness that she had noticed when she left Etta's party.

"May I come in?"

She opened the door wider. Malcolm entered, sitting on one of the two chairs in front of the office's grate.

"Would you like a cup of tea?" Simone asked as she closed the door.

"No, thank you."

"My condolences on the loss of your wife."

"Thank you. She is at peace now, God rest her soul." He turned the rim of his hat in his hands. "Must we keep the formalities?"

Simone took his hat. "Here, let me hang this up for

you. Somehow, I think you are going to be staying a while."

"I know what you're thinking."

"Do you?"

"You're thinking it is highly inappropriate of me to call on you so soon after my wife has passed away."

"Does that concern you?"

"No. Of all the things I've imagined you thinking of me, inappropriate would be the least of my worries." He rubbed a shaking hand across his eyes. "God forgive me, Simone, but when I saw you in December, I thought a ghost was before me. I thought you were dead."

"Dead!"

"Yes, dead. Remember that terrible night so long ago, that had promised to be so divine? It ended with me shot and wounded. It took time for me to recover and come looking for you. I went to your home and confronted your father." He paused, shaking his head. "I can't imagine the life you lived with that man. He told me you were somewhere else, dying. I went crazy, grabbing him so he would tell me where you were. The old rat fainted instead. I thought I had killed him, so I left. I was frantic, trying to think of where you might be. I searched in vain for several days and then I got orders to move up to Baton Rouge."

"You burned down our house."

"How did you know that?"

"You were not the only one who went out looking for answers. I did nearly die and I bear the physical scars."

"Oh, dear God, Simone—"

"Malcolm, do me the courtesy of hearing what I have to say." She levelled her teal blue gaze at him. "How kindly it would end for the both of us if I said there were no scars. But there are. I bear the scars of a whip that cut into my skin and festered, leaving a weal of flesh that has never faded with time. But more painful than that, you cut into my heart. I have thought all these years that you had abandoned me after I had fallen so hopelessly in love with you. It has been a cruel recollection that has lain dormant until I saw you in December."

"It was never my intention to hurt you, Simone. I loved you."

"But not enough to return to find my grave, or to see if my despicable father was telling the truth. I waited for you. I went back to Miss B's brothel, thinking she would know where you were. But that old *cochon*, that pig, told me nothing. So, I went out to what I thought of as our home, but when I saw it burned to the ground, I knew you had left forever."

He looked as though he might cry. "But I never really left, Simone. I never stopped loving you."

Simone's lips curled into a cold smile. "Oh, please, Malcolm, don't fancy me an idiot."

"No, you must hear me out! I came back to New York after the war and worked in my family's shipping company. I married the girl I was supposed to."

"Evelyn?"

"Yes, Evelyn. She was very sweet, very proper. She gave me no trouble, but she gave me no joy, either, except for the children she bore me. I knew that my real joy— my passion—had gone with you. And then I laid eyes upon you at the Van de Haas affair, and the joy came back, but it rode in on the Hounds of Hell. Here I was, tethered to a declining wife and sons who still rely upon me, and you were spoken for, married to another man who wakes up to your lovely face every day, your sweet voice, to feel the silkiness of your creamy skin—"

"Enough!" Simone's cheeks colored. "Don't you dare come to *my* office, interrupt *my* afternoon, and throw yourself upon *my* mercy, hoping to somehow seduce me with your words! There is no place in my heart for it, Malcolm, not anymore."

Was that guilt that she detected creeping into those heavily lashed eyes? Was it shame that seemed to make the lines deepen about his mouth?

"I know we stand an ocean apart, Simone, but—" his voice dropped to a desperate whisper, "*I had to come and speak to you!*"

"What is it that you really want?"

"I can't be sure."

"Be honest with me."

"Your husband travels a great deal, does he not?"

"How do you come to that assumption?"

"Why, Henrietta Van de Haas, of course. She answered many questions about you."

"And why would she do that?"

Malcolm smiled, his suave composure surfacing for the first time that day. "Well, if I am to make a sizable donation to your very worthy cause . . . what is it? Yes, your schooling of the masses in this godforsaken part of town, then I should be informed of the charity and the proprietor of that charity."

"Don't make fun of it, it is very worthwhile."

"He is away a great deal, is he not, Simone?"

"Yes, but what concern is that of yours?"

"The evenings are going to be long and quiet for me,

dear lovely Simone. I thought perhaps we might share some hours together, to reconcile our past. I don't want to go to my grave feeling as if you hate me."

Surely, he could not mean a rekindling of their love?

"I'm sure you are familiar with the quote of Heraclitus of Ephesus?" she asked calmly.

"Vaguely, but I am sure you can re-educate me."

"'No man ever steps in the same river twice.' Surely, I don't need to educate you on the meaning of the quote?"

When Malcolm did not reply, she continued. "Besides the fact that I have a love for and a fidelity to the man I am married to, there is no repeating of our youth, Malcolm. We have both simply moved on, and it can never be the same."

"I am not asking for it to be the same. I am simply asking for a rekindling of a friendship. A chat over dinner or a stroll in Central Park in the spring. Or we could visit Washington Square where the Ailanthus trees offer such a cooling shade in summertime. I am not asking to re-visit that foregone part of our lives, I am only asking to give it a softer, more deserving ending."

"I am a very busy woman, Malcolm. I rarely stroll in Central Park or Washington Square. Many times, my dinner is taken right here in my office."

"I am only asking to be friends, Simone. I will stroll with you in the slums if it's what you prefer or bring you dinner right to your very desk. Frankly, I find dinner uptown to be insufferable."

"And I suppose you find Central Park tiresome as well?"

"It depends on whom I'm with."

"Are you always so dreadfully honest with every person you call on?"

"How I have missed you! But you know as well as I that we live in a society that cannot face honesty. Most of the ladies and gentlemen I call on would swoon if they heard me talk the way I talk to you."

"So, you speak to them with gentility, but I am only good for hearing your crudeness that you disguise as 'honesty?'"

She saw terror flash in Malcolm's eyes. "Simone, I speak to you from the heart. I trust you with my innermost thoughts. Do you not understand how sacred you are to me?"

Simone stood up. "You should leave now, Malcolm."

"Have I offended you?"

"No, but you should properly mourn your wife. Consider her and the handsome family she gave you. Then, if you wish to call on me, send me a proper calling card. But please do not think you can just barge in on me again. I don't sneak to swamps, nor do I dine in whorehouses any longer."

Malcolm stood up. He reached to kiss her hand, but she pulled away.

"Goodbye, Malcolm."

"Goodbye, my good friend."

Before he crossed the threshold, Malcolm looked at her one last time. "You were the one who got away." Then he left.

Simone watched him from her window. She was in turmoil, but deep down she hoped he would never return. She had come to enjoy the comfortable routine of a life largely unfettered by men.

$\mathcal{H}$ I 5 $\mathcal{H}$

GATLINBURG, TENNESSEE 1878

Someone wanted Horace Omni dead. Was it his speculative interests in logging? The saltpeter mines he owned? Or was it his growing involvement in the state's Democratic Party? Gabriel didn't know. All he knew was that Mr. Omni used prison inmates to work his mines because he'd once said they were the most expendable for such filthy, dangerous work. Ironic that Mr. Omni's final reckoning would come from a man who had once been so "expendable."

Throughout September Gabriel sat in the woods overlooking the Omni estate. Accessible only by a narrow mountain road from Gatlinburg, Gabriel watched the fat, aging white man come and go regularly, visiting his mistress in town. Every Friday in the late afternoon, Mr. Omni left his home and had his driver take him down the mountainside to the charming Miss Cornelia Goodwin. To Gabriel's amusement, he always took a phaeton, sitting shamelessly in the open carriage. Then, he was back on Sunday mornings in time to pick up his wife for church. They'd turn around and head back to Gatlinburg in a more sedate brougham, in keeping with the family's image.

Gabriel knew that by two p.m. on Friday the big house was quiet, and the stable boys typically took the afternoon off, heading out to go fishing or ride horses. There were a couple of hounds on the premises and no one paid any attention to their indiscriminate barking. To get on the property, Gabriel planned to feed them squirrel meat laced with a sedative. That would be tricky, for the dogs had to appear lazy, but not drugged.

To disguise a pattern of activity, Gabriel travelled around acquiring supplies for this assignment. He went to Knoxville for a monkey wrench, a couple of box wrenches and screwdrivers in several sizes. To sedate the dogs, he travelled to Nashville and purchased a bottle of potassium bromide from a local doctor, complaining of insomnia over his time in the war. To figure the right dose of sedative, he travelled far and wide, trying varying amounts on unsuspecting farm dogs.

Each step of the plan had to be complete: Exact amount of potassium bromide for canine sedation: *check*; tools to loosen the front carriage wheels: *check*; firecrackers to spook the horses: *check*. What to do if Mr. Omni had, perchance, survived the tumble down the mountainside? Gabriel shrugged, knowing a split head from debris of the forest would suffice. *Check.*

Mr. Omni's last day on earth was scheduled for Friday, October 18. The weather was balmy and the stable and carriage house boys would go out for the afternoon. Mr. Omni's driver would take his regular Friday afternoon nap. Yes, all signs pointed for Gabriel to proceed.

As noon approached, he packed his rucksack with all he needed. Then he waited. As the sun began its western descent, Gabriel slipped through the brush by the carriage house. The hounds ran up, barking furiously. Gabriel tossed them the squirrel meat and they pounced on it.

Gabriel peeked into the carriage house and located the phaeton at the end. He went to it, sliding underneath with his tools. He loosened the bearings on the two front axels with his monkey wrench. He knew they would hold if the carriage did not take on any sudden movements. But if something were to spook the horse . . .

Suddenly, Gabriel heard voices and realized the stable boys had returned early.

"Hey," one of them asked, "where're the dogs? They're usually yelpin' an a carryin' on fer the fish."

Sweat prickled on Gabriel's scalp. He listened to the boys as they roughhoused with each other. Their voices grew louder and Gabriel reached for his pistol. *Don't come in here . . .*

Suddenly he heard one of the boys laugh. "Well, would ya lookee here! These ol' devils ain't good fer nothin'! Here, lemme dangle the fish in front of 'em an' see if'n they get up fer that, the lazy beggars."

Gabriel wiped the sweat from his eyes as the air filled with laughter.

"Ya see that, Walt? Jes' lift up them ol' heads, take a sniff an' go right back ta sleep. I'm a tellin' ya, if a bear came in here, we'd be done fer!"

The other boy responded, "C'mon, let's go clean these. I gotta a hankerin' fer fried fish fer dinner."

The voices receded. Gabriel shoved everything back in his rucksack. He brushed away his footprints as he exited, his senses attuned to any more surprises. He looked around. The hounds were still asleep. He back-tracked a little, mixing his footprints in with the boys'. Then, cleaving the bushes carefully, he disappeared back into the forest.

As dusk neared, Gabriel sat in the underbrush at the mountainside's turnpike. From here he could see the phaeton making its descent. Soon he could hear the horse's hooves and the bounce of the carriage as Mr. Omni approached.

Gabriel knew it was exactly fourteen seconds from when he heard the wheels' crunch to when the horse would pass. As the wheels grew louder, Gabriel lit the end of two firecrackers, knowing the fuses would burn down in six seconds, almost when the horse would be on top of them.

Gabriel knew that Horace Omni and his driver would both be murdered tonight. He suppressed the thought of an innocent man dying, telling himself that there was no way around it. Never mind that the driver would haunt his dreams, turning them into nightmares. Nightmares had been part of his life for years now.

Six, five, four . . . Gabriel threw the firecrackers. They exploded in front of the horse in a scintillating fusion of sparks and noise.

The horse reared. As the driver struggled to gain control, the front left wheel popped off its axel and the horse shimmied, dragging the entire carriage over the precipice.

Gabriel listened to the screams of men and beast as the carriage splintered and crashed down the mountainside. Then all was quiet.

He peered over the edge of the road, locating the twisted structure in the twilight. The smashed buggy was not as far down as he had hoped. Holding a kerosene lantern, Gabriel began his careful descent.

Damn it, the assignment was incomplete. The horse was still alive, two of its legs broken. Gabriel could shoot it, but who would shoot a horse and then leave without reporting this mangle? No, the poor beast was going to have to die on its own.

Horace Omni had been thrown from the carriage and had smashed his head on a boulder. He lay face up, his brains spattered around him. Problem solved.

Then Gabriel heard a moan. He followed the sound and to his horror, realized that the driver was one of the young stable boys. He had been flung from the carriage; his body bent at a right angle as he stared at the canopy of trees above him. In a single, stabbing moment, Gabriel thought of his young friend, Eli McRae, who had stared up at the trees in much the same way.

The boy's back was broken. He looked at Gabriel as he approached. "Oh, thank God. Mister, can ya help me?"

It was the voice of one of the boys who had gone fishing earlier in the day. Gabriel smiled, "That's why I'm here, son. I heard the crash. What happened?"

"I reckon I don't even know. I heard a pop and then

the horse started to rear up, and the next thing I know we're tumblin' down the mountainside. Can ya help me, please?"

"Sure, I can. I was a medic in the war. Your back's all cattywompus an' I need to straighten you out." Gabriel continued, "What was y'all thinkin', tryin' to drive a carriage in the dark down a mountain road like that?"

"The driver warn't feelin' too good, so I says I'd drive Mr. Omni. Been a wantin' a crack at drivin' that carriage' It was special made an' delivered from New York City. I s'pose I ain't the driver I figgered myself ta be."

Gabriel felt sick. He slid his hand under the boy's head, noticing the boy's warm, salty tears on his wrist.

"Now, son, I'm gonna straighten you out, startin' with your neck. Jes' close yer eyes and relax."

The boy shut his eyes. Gabriel gently turned the boy's chin to the right so that it was almost past his shoulder and touching the ground. Then with sudden force, he jerked the boy's head to the opposite side.

The boy's neck snapped and his eyes never opened. Gabriel searched for a pulse and found none. Now the assignment was complete. Gabriel realized that he had murdered a child and, for the second time in his adult life, turned his head and vomited.

He picked up his kerosene lamp and began his ascent. Reaching the top of the road, he collected the spent firecrackers, rubbing out their telltale char marks on the road.

Jesus Christ. That kid thought someone had come to help him. How was he going to live with that the rest of his life?

Gabriel made plans to leave at first daylight. He'd go to Sevierville and cable Moses that he'd be visiting him. The burden of killing people had caught up with him, and he wanted out.

Later, as Gabriel sat in a dining car on his way to Louisiana, he saw that young boy's face again. Unable to stand it any longer, he called the waiter and ordered a double shot of bourbon, which he then chased down with a fine brandy.

SIMONE HAD BEEN THINKING A LOT ABOUT HER MOTHER lately. Perhaps she should go and visit her grave? All Saints Day was approaching and preparations in New Orleans were well underway. Graves were being cleaned and fixed up and fresh flowers planted. Simone always wired Delcine money to hire workmen to scrub her parents' graves and spruce them up. Now, she felt as if she were being called back. Was it her mother, reaching from the grave, telling her that she was long overdue for a visit?

As Simone watched the lamplighter make his way slowly up Fifth Avenue, she decided she would go and visit her mother on All Saints Day.

IN THE PRE-DAWN HOURS OF MONDAY, OCTOBER 21, Simone boarded a luxury steamer with a first-class ticket to New Orleans.

Simone had wired Gabriel in Ohio, telling him of her plans. She also wrote to Delcine and others whom she wanted to call upon. She would send formal calling cards once she arrived in port.

She entered her cabin and began to unpack her trunk for the week-long voyage. As the sun crested over the eastern horizon, she felt the steamboat pull away, heading down the East River.

Feeling weary, she undressed, slipped on a dressing gown, and laid down on top of her coverlet. Soon the steamer's steady *chug-chug* lulled her to sleep.

Little did she know that her husband was also heading for New Orleans. Yet, while Simone was booked into one of the finest hotels, Gabriel would be at a boarding house near the river front. And while Simone had a list of individuals she planned to call on, Gabriel only had one individual that he planned to see. Simone had an agenda for fostering relationships for her continued success. Gabriel had one reason for meeting with Moses: to tell him that it was time to retire.

GABRIEL OPENED HIS CRUSTED EYES AND STARED AT THE ceiling. He was cotton-mouthed and fuzzy-headed. He had returned to the boarding house reeling drunk last night, but when the mistress of the house complained, he'd pulled out twenty dollars, slurring, "Leave me to my sins, and I'll make you rich." She pocketed the money and helped him upstairs and into bed.

He listened to the horn of a steamer announce its

arrival into the Port of New Orleans. He would've panicked if he had known his own wife was on board.

Slowly, he got out of bed. A riverfront breeze blew into his room's open window as he pissed into the chamber pot. Then he splashed cold water on his face from the bowl and pitcher on his nightstand. Glimpsing himself in the small, cracked mirror beside his dresser, he studied the bloodshot, pale blue eyes that stared back. *You must live the life of a teetotaler* . . . Well, he'd broken Moses's strictest caveat, so he'd better wait until tomorrow to see him. In the meantime, he'd also get a good shave and haircut, maybe get his nails trimmed and buffed. He'd approach Moses as a gentleman ready to retire.

As he stepped out and walked over to LaFayette Avenue, a large coach passed him by. Luckily the brougham's curtains were drawn. Otherwise, Simone might have looked out and seen him.

THE NEXT DAY, GABRIEL SENT FOR A COACH TO PICK HIM up at the boarding house. As he waited, wearing his Ferndale high notched striped vest of dark gray and navy, his hair oiled and sleek, he noticed the admiring looks that came his way. As the carriage pulled up, Gabriel put on his fitted black sack coat and dove-gray top hat. He tipped his hat at the ladies and stepped outside.

Moses's house was as Gabriel remembered it. Frederick answered the door and Gabriel noticed that he had not changed at all since Gabriel had last seen him. He smiled pleasantly. "Welcome, Mr. Cooper."

"Hello, Frederick, is Mr. Del Cerro in?"

"I will announce your arrival," said the butler as he took Gabriel's hat.

A few minutes later, he returned to the cupola. "Mr. Del Cerro is in a meeting, Mr. Cooper. Perhaps you might like to wait for him in the library?"

Gabriel noticed that the library had been redone to fit the times. The green velvet drapes were replaced with silk woven brocade, and he sat on furniture that was now Renaissance Revival.

As he continued to wait, he wondered if perhaps this had been the best idea, but the job had been getting to him for a long time. And damn that boy's face! It haunted him. Everything was becoming tainted, even his longtime, sacred friendships.

Like Johnny Primrose. Gabriel had even used Johnny to further his own ends…

He had visited Johnny in 1876. By that time Johnny and his wife, Maria, had nine children and were supported by Johnny's income as a physician's assistant. Gabriel recalled how Johnny had beamed, telling him how he got the job of his dreams:

"I was a sittin' in the saloon, waitin' fer our twins t'be born. There was a doc who was travelin' through town an' course I was sayin' that I could do just about anythin' 'cause o' my job in the war an' the doc says t'me, "Johnny, Jacksonville is becomin' a place fer rich Yankees ta come an' spend their winter days. I'm settin' up a new practice here in Jacksonville an' I'm gonna need me a good medic to be on call. The rich ain't fer waitin' fer nothin', 'specially when it comes to bodily distress.'

"Well, I jumped at it, Gabe! An' then, get this! Doc says, 'I'm a thinkin' yer gonna have to spruce up yer smile 'cause that's what folks see first.' Ya know how my teeth ain't no good, but the Doc has

a cousin who's a dentist an' workin' miracles with new false teeth. Says he can get me a set made fer free. An' ya know what?" Johnny grinned, showing off his smile. "This guy, he had all the proper schoolin' an' he gimme this nitrous oxide an' afore ya knew it, my old teeth was gone an' now I got me a set o' pearly whites made outta vulcanite.

"Yep, Gabe, an' now the doc sends me out even ta give shots! He's right pleased with the way I can draw a serum without even gettin' one air bubble in it."

"An air bubble's bad?"

"Hell yes, ya give a shot with an air bubble in it y'all's gonna have a dead guy on yer hands."

"Just one air bubble? How can that be?"

"Well, if it's big enough, it just kills a man, I'm tellin' ya. Saw it once in the war. We gets this kid in who's got blood poisonin' from a gut wound. The doc looks at his wound an' it's smellin' somethin' awful an' he knows how it's gonna end so he says, 'how 'bout I give ya somethin' ta make ya sleep?'"

An' the kid says, "Aw, doc, can ya do that fer me?' An' the surgeon says, 'Why sure I can.' An' I'm a' thinkin' what in tarnation is he gonna do? We're amputatin' limbs without no anesthesia! But the doc pulls outta syringe an' he pulls the plunger way back an' puts that needle in his vein an' the kid dies! The doc looks at me an' he says, 'Tell ya a secret, Johnny. Wanna put a doomed man outta his misery? Give him a shot of air.'"

And suddenly Gabriel had an answer to a dilemma for an assignment he'd received regarding a man in Southern Georgia. Gerald Andenauer was a tobacco magnate who had muscled his way into the cigar-making industry of Florida, making powerful enemies as he went. Floridian cigar-making was Cuban, and one had to treat the community with respect, something this white Southerner of German descent did not do.

At the time there was a contract on Gerald's head, but the man was evasive and paranoid, so how to get close to him? Maybe this was the answer.

Gabriel leaned in. *"I'm in a predicament, old friend, and I'm a wonderin' if y'all could give me some know-how."*

Johnny looked concerned. "Why sure, Gabe, ya know I'm always here for ya."

Gabriel grew solemn. "My wife has been feelin' poorly lately, sufferin' from fatigue. Doc recommends her a series of shots to boost her energy. But she's on the skiddish side an' wants me to do it, which I'm willin' if I can get someone ta teach me ta do it right. Can ya show me? 'Cause Lord help me, Johnny, I sure don't wanna give my missus an air bubble!"

"'Course I will, Gabe! I'll teach ya so yer wife won't even know you're givin' her a needle. An' I'll send ya with some o' the best needles and syringes so ya know y'all have the sharpest, finest instruments around."

Johnny spent the next several days showing Gabriel how to find veins. Gabriel learned terms like antecubital fossa and how to apply a tourniquet.

Gabriel practiced on a dead pig, perfecting his technique. And all the while he lied about his married life with Simone. He portrayed Simone as frail and temperamental, manipulating Johnny to get as much knowledge as he could.

And the deception didn't end there, because at Johnny's house for dinner, Gabriel saw the Arvin and Morris Drugs & Elixir Catalog lying on a side table and he wanted it.

He stole the catalog. He did it on a day when he had

stopped by to do a little extra practicing. Finding no one home, Gabriel had picked it up and put it amongst his own things. He had sunken so low as to steal from his friend, the kindest, truest human he had ever known.

Gabriel broke out of his reverie to find Frederick standing in front of him. "Mr. Del Cerro will see you now."

Gabriel rose and followed him. He had been kept waiting almost two hours.

He was brought into Moses's private study. Moses did not rise to greet him, saying coolly, "This is a surprise, Gabriel."

"I sent you a telegram that I was coming to town."

"Yes, but you did not say you would be calling on me. If you had, I would have told you that you are never to come to my house, because that is very foolish for someone of your skill and talent."

"Can a man not call in a friendly visit?"

"Not in this business. I thought this was clear. When you signed on with me, we ceased being friends."

There it was. Moses met Gabriel's confused gaze. "Look. You are the best at what you do. It is genius. I saw that in you when I first met you and I mentored you, I advised you. But that was years ago." His face reddened. "Now you work for me. And I pay you very, very well for it."

What had Gabriel come here for? What did he think he would find? A dispensation? A validation? Suddenly he realized that he was a prisoner in this life forever. And he had been manipulated into it.

Moses opened a drawer and pulled out a file. He handed Gabriel a large newspaper clipping.

"As long as you're here, let me give you this. You have another assignment. Look this over. This is very big as our problem's family has connections to the White House."

The newspaper article slipped out of focus as Gabriel skimmed it. Moses's voice seemed far away. "His name is David Tremont. He comes from a very political family in Maryland, but resides in Philadelphia. He's an attorney by profession but is on the wrong side of the fence if you ask me. Makes a lot of trouble stirring up pro-labor sentiments, workers' rights and what have you. He needs to be stopped. And, if he keeps this up, this is going to influence bids for the White House, Senate, and House of Representatives."

Dear Davie . . . Gabriel fought to breathe, yet his voice was calm when he asked, "This one guy has done all this?"

Moses sighed. "It's a strategic choice, really. He isn't the only one we could single out, but he's young and handsome and a folk hero among the workers. He's also secretly engaged to a daughter of a coal mining titan, and her father has found out. Thus, a very subtle message has been called for, one that will not arouse the suspicions of a lovelorn maiden. His death will break morale, but only if it looks like a natural death."

"And if another takes his place?"

"He will die a natural death as well because you'll see to it. Soon rumors will start that all who try for leadership in such nonsense are cursed. It will work, trust me."

Trust him. How could Gabriel have thought that the money he made would be worth this?

Moses continued, "You have time to work with this.

But once Mr. Tremont's wedding date is set, your plan must go into action."

He sat back and smiled. "I have to say, Gabriel. This plan was hatched because of you. I have men out there who could fire a shot and the whole business would be over in an instant. But I assured my client I had someone who could make it seem so natural, so tragic, that it would take the hope right out of the whole disgruntled lot. How can you be angry with a natural tragedy? Study the case because I'm sure you will find the solution to our problem." Moses stood up and produced the *Avengers' Almanac*. But before he handed it to Gabriel he hesitated and put the *Almanac* down. "I was going to have you record your work, but never mind. I've been recording for you for years now. I'll do you the same courtesy with this one."

Moses's charm was once again restored. He clapped Gabriel on his back. "You are a master of your craft, Gabriel Sutherland Cooper. You should be very proud of yourself."

Moses had Frederick usher him out the back way. Gabriel stumbled down the back steps, file in hand, and made his way to where his brougham was waiting.

He wanted a drink. The imbibing had to stop, he told himself, especially now that Davie's life was in peril. He had to figure out what to do. Perhaps a walk would clear his mind.

Once back at the boarding house, he headed back out and up LaFayette Avenue and turned left on Claiborne. Paying no attention to where he was going, he followed Claiborne to the train tracks in Elysian Fields. He stood at the tracks for a long time, pondering his possibilities. Over and over again, he toyed with the thought of killing Moses. Then he'd be free. But would he? Moses knew his name. He'd been recording his assignments for years; was his name in print in the *Almanac?* Had others heard of him? Of course, he was now a well-kept secret because Moses made sure of it. But if Moses were gone, what would happen then? Perhaps an uttered indiscretion, a paper misplaced with his name on it . . . he could be found out and then what? Gabriel shuddered. No, he had to escape another way.

Exhaustion and hunger began to overtake him. Gabriel began walking again. He passed a restaurant, *Les Freres Normandie*, where the smell of roasting meat enticed him. He took a table by the window, hoping that watching the passersby would distract him. Finally, he ordered dinner and because he could not resist it, a bottle of wine.

AT ABOUT THE SAME TIME THAT GABRIEL ORDERED dinner at *Les Freres Normandie*, Simone was bidding goodbye to the Ursuline Sisters with whom she had spent the day. She had observed their girls' academy and had tea with the Mother Superior.

Now she strolled along the avenue, reveling in memories of her early childhood.

He was staring out into the street when their eyes met. Simone passed him by, questioning what she thought she had just seen. That man was bald—Gabriel wasn't bald. That man had a dark goatee—Gabriel was clean-shaven and blond. And yet . . . his light eyes, how he looked at her with such intense familiarity. She saw how his expression tightened, and she knew that expression well. It crossed over Gabriel's face whenever he read the newspapers or got a telegram. That was her husband, but why was he here? And for God's sake, why did he look like that?

She hurried back to *Les Freres Normandie*. Entering the dining room filled with customers, she went to his table where he sat, looking as if he was expecting her.

Having finished the wine, Gabriel now sipped a brandy as he stared at Simone who gawked, open-mouthed at his appearance and the fact that he was imbibing. Gabriel never drank around her. He had told her so on their first dinner at Delmonico's when she had wanted him to order champagne and he had refused.

"I'll never be like him. I want nothing to do with the stuff."

"You've always been a smart woman, so I shouldn't be surprised that you recognized me."

She pulled out a chair and sat down, her voice low and shaking. "Good God, Gabriel! What is going on? Why do you look like this?"

Gabriel's mouth twisted grimly. "Why do I look like this? Ah, where to begin."

"I don't understand—" she began, but he cut her off.

"Of course not. How could the darling of High Society understand not wanting anyone to know who you really are?" He leaned in, and she smelled the brandy on his breath. "But tell me, would they all love you if they knew who I really was?"

"This is the liquor talking."

"Oh, it's more than the liquor. It's the man behind the liquor, the man that nobody sees, nobody wants to see."

"None of this makes sense! What are you doing here? I thought you were in the Midwest."

"I should ask you the same. I thought you were in New York."

"I wrote to you. I told you of my plans. Did you not get my letter?"

"Do I ever get your letters? Besides, I needed to see Moses."

Simone looked at the people around them, wondering if anyone was listening to this outrageous exchange.

"Moses? What does Moses have to do with any of this?" Then, switching tactics, Simone laid a hand on his arm. "Why don't you come back with me to the hotel where we can talk privately? It has been so long, darling. Please come back with me."

A look of sad longing crept into Gabriel's liquor-addled countenance. He opened his wallet and laid several bills on the white table cloth. Then he pushed back his chair and silently accompanied his wife out the door.

ONCE BACK AT THE HOTEL, GABRIEL WATCHED SIMONE take off her cape and hat. He stood there bewildered as she smiled at him with that welcoming upturn of her pouty pink lips. But as she approached him, he did not see her smile. Instead, he saw her eyes. Her eyes swallowed him whole.

"You have been gone so long, *Monsieur*," she whispered as she took off his coat. "Please come home." And she reached up to kiss him. She undid his shirt, running her hands over the muscles that still defined his chest and his core.

"You have kept so fit and trim, as if you were still the young man I met years ago. How is it so?" She breathed, bringing her lips close to him.

Feeling her breath on his bare skin, Gabriel lost control of himself, ripping the buttons off her bodice. Then he ripped the hooks and eyes that attached the skirt as he pressed Simone to the bed.

"Gabriel," she gasped, "My clothes—"

"I'll get you new," he mumbled, clenching her delicately coiffed ringlets in his tightened fists.

His hands reached under the flounces and lace rouching of her underskirt, seeking her pantalettes. Locating the waistband, he pulled them down and over her feet which were still in their purple beaded boots.

He ran his fingers between the lips of her crotch, stroking her most tender spot. Pushing her underskirt up, he unbuttoned his pants and mounted her. Simone was dismayed at her own dishevelment, but she let him do what he wanted.

She had forgotten how good it felt to have him press against her.

Gabriel smiled as he glided into her. "You've been expecting me."

"No, *Monsieur*, I could never expect you," Simone breathed, "but I have been waiting for you."

Gabriel hitched her knees in the crook of his elbows and rocked her back and forth, the bed creaking in cadence with them.

He locked his eyes with hers as he panted, moving faster and faster. The thrusts became harder and deeper as Simone began to feel that tingling, almost itchy sensation as he reached for the center of her being.

She gasped as the wave broke over her. Gabriel yelled something inaudible, his face in a grimace. He slowed down and then finally withdrew, kissing her on the lips as he did so. He lay beside her, his face buried in her curls. She lay there flushed and spent. Then, to her horror, she realized that he was crying.

They made love again, tenderly this time. Afterward, Gabriel fell asleep, but Simone lay awake, listening to his soft weeping. Questions bit at her. She had never, ever seen him cry, and yet when she tried to ask him what was the matter, he had pinned her with his arms and said in a choked voice, "Don't, don't . . ."

She needed fresh air. The window by the bed was closed and she moved to open it. As she did so, he reached out.

"Don't leave me."

"Oh, *Monsieur*, I need some air, so I am only going to open the window."

"Please don't leave."

She padded back to the bed. "Where am I going to go, Gabriel?" He had his back to her and she rested her cheek against his bicep. "Gabriel," she whispered, "Look at me."

Slowly he turned over and she passed her hand over his face, collecting his tears as she went.

"What is wrong?"

He still did not answer and she asked, "Why did you come to see Moses? You don't work for him anymore." She could feel his breath quicken and whispered, "Tell me, Gabriel, tell me what it is."

"I always felt as if MacBeth carried my truth," he said quietly into the dark.

"I don't understand."

"Of course, you don't, but I understand only too well."

"Please tell me."

"When Lady Macbeth washes her hands and says, 'Out, damned spot, out I say . . ., All the perfumes of Arabia will not sweeten this little hand.' It is so true. Not all the perfumes of Arabia will sweeten my little hand, Simone. Not any one of them."

"Gabriel, you are scaring me now. Is it another woman?"

She could hear his anger. "That leaves such blood on my hands? Good God, how could you think that?"

"Then the blood of what?"

The air was heavy with his silence. Then he whispered, "Simone, I am going to speak very, very quietly and you are never to speak of this to anyone, do you understand? If you tell anyone about this you and I both will not live out the season."

He was barely audible, but his words rang in her head like a fire bell. "I am not what you think me to be."

He let out a shallow breath of terror. "I still work for Moses Del Cerro because I have no choice."

"So you don't tend to your own businesses? You still travel with special shipments for Moses?"

"No." He was quiet for a long time and then suddenly he said in a flat whisper, "I kill people."

She began to tremble. "What do you mean?" She asked out loud as he wrapped his arms around her and held her tight. She could feel his pounding heart.

"Shhh! Remember, no one can know this. Not even your priest. It was made very clear to me a long time ago that if I told anyone, I and whoever I told would become 'problems to be solved.' Those are Moses's very words. I am a problem solver and there are other problem solvers as well. And they would come after both of us."

"*Oh Mon Dieu.* Who do you . . . do this to?"

"Whoever I am assigned to. I don't ask questions. I only know who I must take care of and by when."

Simone sat up. "So, this is why you never talked about your trips and you never wrote to me when you were away. And the papers! You read the papers so oddly, as if you were always looking for something. And so many newspapers that aren't even local. I always thought that had to do with your own ventures. But that's not it, is it?"

"I have to know if my problem has found its way into the obituaries or the headlines in the manner I intended."

"Oh, dear God!" She shrunk away, curling into a fetal position.

"Do not judge me, Simone."

"How did this come to be?"

"It always was because I am good at it."

"Good at it?"

"Yes. I know how to set things right, to balance the scales of retribution when no one else can."

"You call this retribution?"

"Yes. For someone it always is."

He arose then and disappeared into the other room. She heard him fumbling around on the writing desk and he returned. He lit the kerosene lamp and showed her a newspaper clipping about Horace Omni.

"He was a scoundrel and a liar, and he used convicts like I once was, and discarded them like garbage. He was greedy."

"He died in a carriage accident."

"It was no accident."

Simone wanted to scream, but knew she could not.

Gabriel continued, "I did it for us, Simone. I only wanted what we did not have. We were so young, and I never thought how it would end. But . . ." His voice trailed off.

"But what?"

"But it doesn't end. Ever. It only changes."

"Changes to what?"

"To murder; no matter what you think it is at first, it always changes to murder."

She stared at him with that unwavering gaze that pierced all his defenses. Finally, she spoke. "I've wondered this for years now. Pastor Evans—who showed up on my doorstep on our first New Year's Eve together —he died in a fire. Or didn't he?"

Gabriel silently met her gaze.

She said, "I must know."

"I smothered him and then set the house on fire."

Simone put a trembling hand to her mouth. "Dear God!"

"He was my first problem to solve, which is how I got the job with Moses. I set things right for what he did to you."

"Did to me?" Her voice was a faint echo.

"Yes. He burned down your store, Simone. No one hurts you and gets away with it."

So terrible. And yet . . . so touching. She thought she was going mad as she curled up against him. Why was she not repulsed? "Such a terrible weight to carry—you must be so, so tired."

"I am."

"Then sleep. I will watch over you." She began to sing an old lullaby from her childhood:

"Fais dodo, Colas mon p'tit frère
Fais dodo, t'auras du lolo
Maman est en haut
Qui fait du gâteau…"

His hand sought hers. "Do you still love me?"

"Yes, I still love you."

He exhaled a long, wearied sigh. "I'm glad, so very, very glad." He closed his eyes then and fell sound asleep.

HIS DESPAIR HAD BECOME HER DESPAIR. SHE SAT IN BED, watching the dawn illuminate the room. The city awakened, and Simone stayed where she was until the chambermaid knocked on the door. She dismissed the girl and went back to the bed, watching this man who had just told her that all she thought was true was really a lie. *We are dirt . . . we are always dirt . . . oh, what to do? What to do?*

Gabriel snored softly, looking more peaceful that she had seen him in years. *Funny how sharing the burden makes him feel as if he has lightened the load when he has only compounded the misery.*

Was she to pretend that the knowledge changed nothing? It changed *everything*. And she had to figure out a way to live with that.

WHEN GABRIEL FINALLY AWOKE, SIMONE WAS FULLY dressed as if she had somewhere to go.

He smiled sleepily. "You look lovely," he said, taking in her gray silk three-piece dress, the overskirt lined in violet.

"Thank you." She wondered if the money she had spent to have this outfit made came from the death of some other man.

"Are we going somewhere?"

"I am supposed to meet with an old friend of my mother's. We are supposed to dine together at six."

"You sound displeased."

"I have much to consider after all we discussed last night."

"Please tell me what is on your mind."

Simone approached the bed, her eyes filling with tears. "Everything is a lie, Gabriel. Everything I thought you were—we were—is a lie. I cannot continue with it."

Despair crept into Gabriel's voice. "I wanted to be so much more than what I was. I wanted to prove that I was worthy."

"Worthy of what?"

"Worthy, damn it! Worthy of wealth, of stature, of being someone who mattered!"

"But you were worthy of me. You were worthy *to* me! We could have made our way without you having to do . . . *this*!"

Gabriel narrowed his eyes. "How, Simone? You had lost everything in that fire. *Everything*! And the only skills I had were the ones I had learned in prison and in war. So, when Moses offered to pay me to use those skills, I accepted. And I invested the money I made. And we prospered. And now look at us. Look at you! Everyone wants you at their parties and soirees. You are lovely, distinguished—"

"And you? What are you?"

"Me? I am invisible."

Tears streamed down Simone's face. "No, *Monsieur*, no, to me you are not that."

"Then what am I?"

A confessional sob escaped Simone. "Dear God above, I never thought I could say this of a man, but it's true. I thought it was only a woman who could be swallowed whole to the bidding of another, but it's not so. It has happened to you. The want, the greed . . . you are still a prisoner, Gabriel, but even more than that you are"—she leaned forward, her breath upon his face—"dirt under the Master's feet."

Simone recoiled away. She wiped her tears, turned, and left the room.

AFTER SIMONE LEFT, GABRIEL AROSE AND DRESSED. HE left a note for her, saying he was returning to his boarding house.

He arrived in the evening and went straight to his room where the dossier on David Tremont was still hidden under the mattress of his bed. He sat in there with a bottle of bourbon and leafed through the file.

He sat through the night reading and thinking. In the morning, he packed his bags and headed for the train station. He bought a ticket and sat down on one of the benches, waiting to go home to New York.

WHEN SIMONE ARRIVED BACK AT HER HOTEL, SHE READ Gabriel's note without regret or worry. She was so overwhelmed by what he had told her she was finding it hard to function at all.

Hail Mary, Full of Grace, the Lord is with thee. Blessed art thou among women, and blessed is the fruit of thy womb, Jesus. Holy Mary, Mother of God, Pray for us sinners now and at the hour of death . . .

She could not allow herself to live the way she had been for nothing would be the same. Every time he left, every time a death was posted, she would wonder. She could no longer live with him, but divorce? Not so easy for a woman. She'd have to have a good reason. And if she revealed it, she would be killed, perhaps by her own husband.

Bless me, Father, for I have sinned. It has been a lifetime since my last confession. These are my sins . . .

How many scars could she bear for the sake of the men she had loved?

Hail Mary . . .

Exhausted but unable to sleep, Simone went to the writing desk and took out some paper. She dipped her quill in the ink well.

These are my sins . . .

❦ 16 ❦

MANHATTAN 1879

January 24, 1879

DEAR DAVIE,

Best Wishes for the New Year! I trust you are well and that your family is likewise.

I constantly read of your endeavors. Your work creates fury between management and the working man. As controversy feeds the flames of your cause, please realize that the smoke brings many to the fire.

Be careful! You walk amongst the unruly on both sides of the labor divide when you are at the factories and coal mines. I await to hear from you, not just to know you are safe, but to know all that has transpired; the newspapers too often taint the story with bias.

I find myself at a philosophical crossroads in life, longing for the warmth of the Southeast, for the boyhood haunts I left behind. Perhaps I am in a winter doldrum, yet I wonder if perhaps I am just getting old.

I am and always will be your steadfast friend,
Gabriel

~

GABRIEL SEALED THE LETTER, CURSING HIS OWN hypocrisy. He left his house, feeling the weight of his demons upon him. As he approached the post office, he noticed Simone leaving the building. She did not see him as she got into her cab. He wondered what made her take a special trip down here to mail something. Obviously, something important and, as usual, something he was not a part of.

~

January 28, 1879

DEAR MALCOLM,

I send this note to you after much thought regarding our conversation last July. Verily, memories of past friendships always take on a wistful longing, as if the years gone by have not their own seeds of change. But you know and I know that this is nothing but whimsy, better left to those far less seasoned in life than you and me.

You have always cherished honesty, Malcolm, at least when it was your weapon to wield. Now please let me be frank: I no longer have the fortitude nor the inclination to rekindle old associations with you. I have come to view men and the world that they have created with a growing cynicism. No longer do I fight this. Its realization has come with a price, but a price that once paid, will give me greater peace than I could have ever hoped for had I remained tethered to men's expectations. That includes your expectations as well.

Therefore, I entreat you, while our paths may cross from time to time, let our association lie in the grave that was dug for it. Let's be content that we have marked it well, but have no reason to re-visit it, for no amount of prayer or salutation will ever resurrect it to be anything more than it had once been. It is gone, Malcolm, and we are but ghosts to its memory. Let it lie and gather the dust of time that it so deserves.

I leave you now only with one thought, yet one thought that should stay beyond our passing: I was not the one who got away; I was the one you threw away. Let it rest in peace for now and evermore.

With Sincerity and Respect for the Past,
Mrs. Simone Livingston Cooper

SIMONE MAILED THE LETTER, FEELING A SENSE OF closure. Now she started spending more and more time in her office on the Lower East Side. She needed time alone to sort out her feelings as she sought a final verdict on her marriage. It didn't matter that she had taken vows with Gabriel because she had married him for better or for worse. But not for murder.

One morning at breakfast, she decided to speak what was on her mind. The kitchen maid entered to remove their dishes and Simone stopped her. "Please fetch Mr. and Mrs. Sweeney for me."

When the head butler and housekeeper arrived, Simone smiled at them. "I want you and the staff to take the rest of the day off."

"Is everything all right, ma'am?" asked a confused Mrs. Sweeney.

"Yes, of course; I will expect you back tomorrow at seven a.m."

"Of course, ma'am. Thank you, ma'am."

Gabriel cocked an eyebrow and looked at Simone over his newspaper. "Is today a holiday that I am not aware of?"

"We must discuss this chasm that is now between us."

"Oh?"

"Don't pretend you haven't felt it as much as I have, Gabriel. We are like two intrepid warriors, each worn and exhausted, trying to assess our final battle."

Gabriel put down his paper. "Such lofty similes. Just say what you mean and be done with it."

"We are no longer allies."

Gabriel studied her, feeling himself the hawk, circling for the kill. But then he reminded himself that this was his wife, the one who had taught him to be a gentleman. She at least deserved a gentleman's response.

"Were we ever allies, Simone?"

"Yes, when we were younger. And we continued to be so until," she paused, "until that day you told me the truth. Certainly, we had our own pursuits, but I attributed that to the nature of our lives and to the fact that," she swallowed, "we never had children of our own." She looked down. "I did not attribute it to the fact that I was supporting a lie."

Gabriel remained calm. "I am not willing to re-visit my disclosure to you, Simone. Nor am I willing to chant a *mea culpa* just to ease your troubled conscience. What is it that you want to say?"

"I can't live with you like this."

A deafening silence followed, broken finally by Gabriel's question. "And what do you propose?"

Simone knew that even if he killed her now, it would be preferable to the slow death she had been suffering.

"I wish to move into my school and live my life as I know it there. I have some space to add on a couple of rooms and that is all I need."

"And you are willing to give up all of this?" Gabriel made a sweeping motion to the house around him. "Even your beloved greenhouse that I spent thousands, *thousands* of dollars to build for you, you are leaving that and all the blooms that were brought from your mother's garden? They live a rarified existence here, Simone, safe from the hardships of the world, just as you do."

"Do you really think that I would cling to a luxury that drips the blood of the guilty and innocent alike?"

Gabriel shook his head in wonderment. "Your judgement is so biblical and yet, you, too, have thought your own ugly thoughts. I remember your wishes for your father to pass, to in some way help him to his demise—"

"Stop!"

"Are you too sensitive for the truth? Do you not recall your hatred of your own father? Don't deny the words you spoke, Simone. You desired retribution but didn't have to lift a finger for it."

Simone stood up. "Give me at least this, Gabriel. The school has its own foundation now, and I can support myself. I promise your name will never be sullied. Live here if you want, and we can even keep up appearances at social affairs. I just cannot live with you anymore."

Gabriel slumped in his chair. "Go."

Simone went to him then and laid her hands on his shoulders. She kissed the top of his bent head. "Thank you, *Monsieur.*"

"Simone."

"Yes?"

"Don't ever call me that again."

She left him sitting there then, his back bent and his heart broken, not realizing that once again, he was close to tears.

~

March 12, 1879

DEAR GABRIEL,

Greetings! I welcomed your words of wisdom in these dark days of struggle. As you know, my role in the Great Strike of 1877 was unpublicized, but since then I have enjoyed legendary status among the workers. It is not often a lawyer with a Harvard Law Degree fights for the common man.

Currently, I strive to unite the railroad and coal workers. However, after the violent rebuke to the Great Strike, many hesitate to risk their lives for what might be a futile venture.

Yet I remain optimistic, perhaps because of my own happiness: I am secretly betrothed to Miss Anneliese Gerst of West Virginia. We cannot tell a soul until I have successfully brokered an agreement between unionized coal miners and management. She is willing to wait, as there is much work to be done. I am not yet ready to give up my call to arms and replace it with the duties of family.

When overwhelmed, I blow off steam by seeking a good fight. This coping method is favorable among the miners, so I am never at a loss for a sparring partner. Even if I win, I make sure my opponent is rewarded with a bottle of whisky. It is all in good sportsmanship, although I have taken some nasty blows. Wielding a pickaxe or pushing anthracite-laden carts is far better training than any gentleman's boxing bag. However, none of it compares to the training you gave me back in the day, when it was only us two learning skills from each other and men from both sides fought for something greater than themselves.

I remain always your true friend and admirer,
Davie

Who, dear God, had betrayed him? Gabriel thought for a moment and then realized it was the girl. Of course! Davie's fiancée would have to have an ally so she could meet him without arousing suspicion . . .

Gabriel hung his head. Would Davie be betrayed again, murdered by someone who had once saved his life? Would Gabriel do it? No, that was the wrong question. What he should really ask was, *could* he do it?

Simone and Gabriel sat together before a roaring fire in the library, as the freezing March rain pelted the windows. Gabriel had been consumed with thoughts of Davie ever since his last letter, figuring out how to keep them both alive. He decided to enlist Simone's help. Simone's apartment would begin construction in the spring, but they had spent their time together having deep and honest conversations. Now they spoke very softly as Gabriel explained what he was planning regarding his own "retirement." They had locked the library doors for privacy.

"I have to disappear somewhere that doesn't arouse suspicion," Gabriel was saying.

"What do you have in mind?"

"A sanitarium in North Carolina where everyone will think I have consumption. I will allegedly 'die' there, and then I will be 'buried' in Florida."

Simone stared at him and he smiled.

"It will only be a ruse, Simone. Only you will know the truth."

"How refreshing."

They sat together in silence, watching the fire. Gabriel turned to her, "Simone, will you visit me after I'm gone?"

"In Florida?"

"Yes."

"I cannot say, Gabriel. I don't know what the future holds for me."

The comfortable silence they had been enjoying quickly turned to stone.

"What more do you want from me?" Gabriel asked coldly. "There are no secrets anymore. Have I not done enough to make it up to you?"

Simone stared at him. "How can you say that? It can never be made up to me."

"Will you never understand?"

"That is a relative term. I understand what you have done and perhaps to a small measure, I even understand why. You were a prisoner of your own greed. But understanding is not the important point here, it is trust. Do I trust you enough to speak of the future? No, and that *you must understand.*"

She stood up and tugged the bell pull, summoning the housemaid. "I must retire for the night. There is nothing more exhausting than a weak attempt to salvage a broken marriage. I have not the strength for it."

She turned and left Gabriel to assuage his feelings in a brandy.

March 24, 1879

DEAR GABRIEL,

I am writing to let you know that I have a speaking engagement in New York this coming May 19, Saturday evening at six p.m.

As this downturned economy drags on, it presents opportunities for action against all management that treats the working man unfairly. This will be a town hall rally at Our Lady of the Ascension on Bleeker Street in the Bowery.

Perhaps we can meet afterward for a small libation and exchange of ideas, a sharing of comradeship in this sea of depriva-tion that plagues our cities. You have kept your professional endeavors pleasantly out of your letters, a far more genteel gesture than I am currently capable of. I yearn, however, to hear of your views as well as your particular endeavors for earning a successful wage.

I Anxiously Await your Answer in the Affirmative,
Davie

GABRIEL FOLDED THE LETTER BACK UP AND SET IT ON HIS dressing table. This was his chance. There was so much to do, so much to plan for, that he sat down immediately to outline his preparations.

He went through his copious notes on poisonous herbs: black locust leaves, belladonna, jimson weed . . .

Simone noticed that Gabriel's mood had changed in the last couple of weeks of April. He had begun putting on weight. She commented on his voracious appetite.

His response was smooth. "Perhaps the pleasures of the flesh are being replaced with the pleasures of the palate."

She ignored his pointed reference to their lack of intimacy with each other. Terrified, she knew that he was up to something, but surely it was not his ruse for escaping Moses. For that he would be losing weight not gaining it. So, she turned a blind eye to his bloat, his disappearances in the middle of the night, and his increasingly unkempt appearance. She simply prayed that her apartment would be done soon so she could get away from him.

Gabriel arose on May 19, feeling the weight of his greatest assignment upon him. He would, as always, be successful, at least in the world's eyes. Three, maybe four people at the most, would know the truth of what happened to Davie Tremont.

As the afternoon waned, Gabriel retired to his office. Once there, he put a patch over his right eye and placed a fake cap on one of his front teeth. He donned a second-hand suit, put on a pair of workman's shoes, and slipped a tiny vial of potassium bromide into his inside pocket. He collected his identification as Dr. Bernard Hawking.

He had written to Davie that he would attend the rally and that they could meet afterward for a drink. It would be there that he would confess everything and the plan for Davie's survival. According to the plan, Davie would ingest the potassium bromide and fall over unconscious at which time Gabriel would pronounce him dead. A fake death and funeral would be publicized. Davie would then leave town under an assumed name. Would he be able to retrieve his bride? That detail Gabriel would leave up to Davie. But he would warn him that it was his fiancée who had leaked their secret. It was how all this had come to pass. Not all women could be trusted like his own Simone.

If, that is, he could still call her his own.

GABRIEL ARRIVED AT THE CHURCH EARLY. HE SAT DOWN to see a young man staring at him. "David Tremont?" he asked in a stiff British accent.

"Pardon me, sir, but you have an uncanny likeness to someone I know."

Gabriel grinned. "Shh, I am done up like this in case corporate spies show up."

Davie smiled, but when he spread his arms to give Gabriel a hug, he stopped. "I was injured in my last fight and my arm is throbbing."

Gabriel sprang up and hugged him anyway. "It's been a long time, my Davie, such a very long time." He looked at his pale and sweaty young friend. "Are you feeling well?"

"Maybe I should lay off fights right before travelling."

"Have you been to a doctor?"

"No, no need for that."

People were arriving. Davie looked out over the church. "I'd better get in the back. I'll come find you out here afterward."

"Good luck, my friend."

The church was filled to standing room only. Gabriel sat in the front row like a proud father. This was his boy.

Cheers went up as Davie approached the lectern. He held up his hand, his face shining with sweat. "I am here," he began, "to bring your fight home!"

Another roar went up.

"I am here . . . to assemble the coals of misery into a blaze of united fury!"

Everyone sprung to their feet, yelling their support.

"I am here . . ." Davie gasped for breath. Gabriel watched, horrified, as he collapsed. People rushed the pulpit, but Gabriel pushed his way through. "I'm a doctor!"

Davie lay on his side. Gabriel turned him over on his back, but he knew that look of death; he had seen it so many times before. Somewhere a woman wailed. Men swore and bowed their heads.

A priest was standing next to Gabriel. "Eternal Rest grant unto him, O Lord, and let perpetual light shine upon him. May the souls of all the faithful departed, through the mercy of God, rest in peace."

"Is he gone, Doc?" he heard someone ask him.

Gone. Gabriel stumbled back through the crowd. *Gone.* That four-letter word screamed like an expletive inside his head. He broke out of the church.

He turned down an alley, slumping to the ground. God help him, Davie's death looked like the perfect murder.

A policeman came along. "Hey there, boyo, no loiterin' here."

Gabriel stood up. "Sorry there, sir, I was feeling a tad lightheaded, but I'll be on my way."

The policeman's expression changed. "Pardon me mistake, sir. Are ya all right, then?"

"Good night, Constable," Gabriel walked away steadily. All he wanted to do now was go home to his wife, while he still had both.

He walked all the way home. He let himself in through the basement side door and went upstairs to his bedroom. His manservant had laid out his bed clothes, but he ignored these, putting on a pair of trousers instead. He went downstairs to the library, hoping to find Simone, but she was still at the theater.

He sat in the soft light of the flickering lamps. As he looked around the room, his eyes rested on the sword he had been gifted by Colonel Tremont so long ago.

That sword, given to him because he had saved Davie's life. That sword, given to him because he had been true to his word. That sword, that he no longer deserved and now reminded him of all that he had betrayed.

He couldn't look at it. For a moment, he thought of using it on himself, but it was too pure a symbol to be sullied by his own blood.

He went to the wall and removed it. Still so sharp, so pristine, so unblemished . . . he swerved around and ran it through the upholstery of a decorative armchair. He stabbed the armchair repeatedly, slashing the fabric with frenzied strokes.

Finally, exhausted, Gabriel dropped the sword. He

went to the sidebar and poured himself a whiskey, tossing it back effortlessly. Then he poured himself another one, then a third and a fourth . . .

HE AWOKE THE NEXT MORNING WHEN MRS. SWEENEY opened the library drapes. Realizing Simone would be downstairs reading about Davie's death, Gabriel bolted out of the library. He burst into the dining room.

Simone looked up from the newspaper. She stared at Gabriel with his bloodshot eyes and puffy face. Her cold expression said everything.

"No!" he cried.

"You have no soul and no heart."

"No!" he went to her and dropped to his knees. She recoiled at his sour breath and the smell of sodden liquor.

He grabbed at her, his voice caught between a sob and a whisper. "No, it is not what you think! Please, for the love of God, hear me out!"

Simone paused.

His voice was a frightened whisper, "I was given an assignment for Davie—my very own Davie—and I knew that I could never go through with it. It had a huge payout, but how could I do it? So, I devised a plan: I would make Davie appear as though dead, and I would be the doctor to pronounce him so. Then I was going to have him escape New York, even meet the silly girl he was secretly engaged to. They would assume new identities so they could live a life far from this madness."

Gabriel's eyes widened. "But it never happened, Simone! He dropped dead in the church! He wasn't looking well when I first saw him, so pale and sweaty . . ." Gabriel's hands covered his face as he rocked back and forth. "Oh, dear God, is this His Divine Retribution for all I've done?"

Simone reached out to him, "Shh, Gabriel! You were trying to do right! This is just a terrible tragedy. But what are you going to do now?"

Gabriel crawled into a chair beside her. Simone got up and tugged the bell pull. A kitchen maid appeared.

"Please, Bridget, coffee and toast for Mr. Cooper."

Gabriel tried to think. "It's time for me to go to my sanitarium. Tell people I have consumption. But before I go," he asked in a broken voice, "you do believe that I never could have done this to him?"

"I believe you."

A tear rolled down Gabriel's cheek. "Thank you. I will wire Moses, and then I'll leave." He sipped his coffee. "Make sure everyone has the same account. Then you may put this house up for sale."

"I'll tell all who inquire I have decided to live where my work is. The proceeds of the sale can benefit my charity. Most will think me queer and eccentric, but that works to our benefit."

Gabriel continued, "After I leave, I will send my death certificate to you. I will have two copies made. Send one to Moses, and I will be buried in Florida." Gabriel's voice dropped even further. "I will buy a plot in a Pensacola cemetery, but will live under the assumed name of G. Gavin Harding. Moses will never know that I am still alive."

"Very well, *Mon*—" Simone stopped herself, but Gabriel grabbed her hand.

"Please, it would do my heart good to hear that again."

"*Monsieur.*"

Tears filled Gabriel's eyes, but this time they were tears of relief mixed with a small hope for the future.

June 29, 1879

DEAR GABRIEL,

I am saddened to learn of your bout with consumption. Buck up, old man, for you are far too valuable to be set back by such a frightful disease. Take the time you need to recover, but recover you must.

Your solution to our problem this past May has made you a hero in the highest circles of gentlemen's society. You singlehandedly reassured men of great name that even the most imminent threat can be quelled with the subtle hand of skilled craftsmanship.

If you or your lovely wife have need of anything, please avail me of the details and I will attend to it immediately.

God-Speed in your recovery,
Moses

September 14, 1879

Dear Moses,

With a grieving heart I inform of my husband's passing. While Gabriel fought valiantly for his return to good health, he ultimately succumbed yesterday, September 13, Friday.

Per his wishes, he will be buried in Florida. He wanted no funeral, as deep in his heart he was a very private man and his illness was of great consternation to him. He had always prided himself on his strength and ability to survive even the most adverse conditions.

I will commence with all arrangements forthwith. While I will not have a gravesite in New York to visit regularly, I will keep Gabriel close to me in my heart for we had many good years together, and I will miss him dearly. God rest his soul.

Yours Truly,
Simone Livingston Cooper

GABRIEL, NOW KNOWN AS G. GAVIN HARDING AND THE new owner of the former Hugo Plantation, rode his horse through the backswamp that had once contained his boyhood home. By his side hung his former colonel's gift, the sword of his past and his present. He had unpacked it this morning and was at a loss of where to place it in his new home. Needing to feel its presence as he readied himself for this trek toward the physical remnants of his memories, Gabriel had brought it along. It reminded him of a better part of himself, a part that he wanted to re-establish in his new life.

Gabriel noticed as he carefully plodded on that while

the civilized world busied itself with progress and rearranged things so the past could hardly be recognized, the natural world simply reverted to what it had always been, filling in the man-made places with trees and undergrowth loyal to its place of origin.

Gabriel lovingly pushed away the Spanish Moss that still hung down, guiding his horse carefully over a barely recognizable footpath, but one he had trodden for years growing up. Finally, he came to a shrunken clearing and gazed upon the rotting boards that still held what was left of a decayed roof.

He strained to hear the long-gone chatter of his family, the chiding voice of his mother as she toiled to keep them from starvation. He remembered her soft, gap-toothed smile, and the way they all worked to help her so they could see that smile from time to time. When the wind picked up, sifting through the pond and bald cypress around him, Gabiel swore he could hear his brothers' mischievous laughter.

What had it all come to, this journey he now called his life? It was as if he'd had no control over what had happened in his youth, but when he did, were the choices he made worth the price he paid?

He was not a religious man, so he knew he'd find no answer in a holy book. And yet, he felt he had a chance now to do some good, some penance for all the misery he had wrought. Coming to this little shack that had once been his home was not going to bring him closure. As long as he lived, Gabriel realized there could be no closure. But maybe there could be a reckoning, a coming to terms. And with that reckoning there could come contentment and maybe even peace. Gabriel smiled and touched the hilt of the sword. He knew where he would hang this; on the wall that faced his bed, so when he opened his eyes in the morning it was the first thing he would see. Every day. It wouldn't just be the sword of his past and present; it would now be the sword of his future.

Old age has a way of prioritizing things. And before she could no longer do it, Simone requested one last trip to Florida. She needed to visit Gabriel, who now really did rest in a Pensacola cemetery. She needed to visit their home there one last time.

It had not been an easy trip, but now she was here in her wheelchair with her attendant nearby, listening to the guide tell the story of the Harding Historic House; *their* story . . .

"Here, folks, is the Pensacola residence of the late G. Gavin Harding. He lived here on what used to be the old Hugo plantation which he revived to full working order. The house was a splendor, refurbished by his beloved wife, Madame *Simi*, an elegant New York Socialite who had devoted her entire life to educating poor women. They had an odd arrangement, Mr. Harding and Madame *Simi* did. Madame *Simi* lived in New York City, visiting her husband only occasionally. Her full name was Madame Josephine Simone Harding. She was originally a beautiful Creole lady from the most elite of New Orleans High Society.

"Mr. Harding had his peculiarities. He bought swampland a distance away and had a tiny house built out there. He'd just sit outside that hut, watching the wildlife. He had an aversion to killing anything, never even eating meat.

"Legend has it that terrible things had once happened out there. The powerful Hugos, once the ruling family in these parts, used their influence to have a whole cracker family turned out into those swamps, on account of some vendetta. Everyone perished except for the oldest son who they sent away to prison, never to return.

But what goes around comes around. The War ruined the Hugos' livelihood and permanently wounded their only son. They were eventually sent packing. Nobody knows what happened to them.

But when Mr. Harding and his lovely wife took over this place, well, they made the whole area better for it. That Mr. Harding was a great gentleman indeed and he and Madame *Simi* sure brought some high class to the good people of Pensacola."

EPILOGUE

From the warmth of her bed, Simone listened to the thunder approach even as she felt her life source ebbing away. She appreciated the thunder; it had brought back such wonderful memories for her to reminisce over one last time.

She opened her eyes slightly to see Gabriel standing at her bedside with her mother. When did they meet? Joy, like she was floating in a pool of warm, happy tears, spread over her.

"Monsieur! Maman!" Did they hear her?

A new face now joined them: Lucinda, her dark eyes as defiant as the day Simone had met her.

"Lucinda, Latin for light. You truly were a light to me. I tried not to be dirt under anyone's feet."

"You took us above the dirt, Simone. Ya done good."

Simone yearned to embrace the trio, for it had been so very long.

"Maman, did I make you proud?"

"I am so very proud of you, Cherie, but now it's time to come and be with us."

Simone felt herself sinking into the pool of tears. Down she sank, feeling Gabriel's soft, gentle touch, the touch of a man who had loved her even when he had thought she hated him. The tears washed over her and she slipped away, but not as if she were drowning. Because she wasn't drowning. She was simply immersing herself in the people she loved.

AUTHOR'S NOTE

I've often been asked how I came up with the storyline
for *Scars of Sand and Soil*. The truth is there was no big
epiphany, no studying of history, but a simple lunch out
with my mother one day many years ago. I don't even
remember what we were talking about, but suddenly a
thought popped into my head, "What if someone was
released from prison to fight a war?"

The thought stayed with me as many story kernels
do, scratching at my imagination, begging for development. Finally, I gave in. I had read *Gone with the Wind* as a
little girl and the story line, the Civil War portrayed in its
pages had been memorable. Why not start there?

As a grown woman, I've learned a lot more about
history since I first read *Gone with the Wind*. I wanted
something that captured the essence of the times, but not
a Civil War romance. I did not want it to take place on a
big plantation, and I wanted to show a more organic side
of humanity, a wider array of society and what individuals with the same feelings and needs we have in present

day did within the strictures of American society then. I wanted to explore the human experience beneath the manners and decorum, to portray individuals as human beings rather than heroes and villains.

I spent years researching the different subjects woven into this novel. Much of the research was painful—slavery, human suffering, and the cruelty that human beings wrought on one another and indeed, on all living creatures was both eye-opening and wrenching. And yet, it was necessary to face if I was going to portray the characters with the depth and complexity they deserved. Hopefully you, the reader, will appreciate my efforts and find that connection of humanity that brings the journey inward. May it give you something to reflect upon long after the last page has been read.

ABOUT THE AUTHOR

As the quintessential queen of "What if…?" Jean has channeled her very active imagination into her debut novel, *Scars of Sand and Soil.* Achieving her childhood dream of being a published writer was not a straightforward path, however. Jean earned a bachelor's degree in psychology and a master's degree in human development and aging from the University of California, San Francisco. She went into clinical research in pharmaceuticals, but left it all when her children were born. It was here that she picked up her writing again, honing her craft, publishing articles in a small newspaper and immersing herself in historical research, one of her greatest passions. Jean has many interests, including reading fiction and non-fiction, gardening, needlepoint and learning new languages. She lives in Southern California and has a husband, two daughters and two cats, Lenny and Penry.

ACKNOWLEDGMENTS

Writing *Scars of Sand and Soil* has been a decades-long journey with so many starts and stops, twists and turns. There have been many people along the way who have borne witness to this journey; to name them all would be impossible. And yet, some not only bore witness, but joined me in the process and I must give them a special thanks.

To Holly Kammier and the entire team at Acorn Publishing LLC: Thank you for seeing the potential of this story, for all your guidance and help to publish a work that we can all be proud of. Thank you, Nico, for your patience and holding my hand through all the emails and questions. You've been great to work with!

To my editors, Aviva Layton and Kat Ross. Thank you, Aviva, for taking me on as a new writer, helping me to tighten and polish this manuscript into something I was confident approaching the publishing world with. To Kat Ross, thank you for working with me after I was picked up for publication, taking my manuscript to a whole new level of clarity and sophistication. You taught me so much and I will be forever grateful.

To Laura Taylor: Thank you for meeting with me at the Southern California Writers' Conference and letting me know how much you believed in my work. I kept your notes with me as I faced the challenges of querying agents and publishers. When I felt like giving up, I would turn to your notes of affirmation to keep myself going.

The research for this novel was extensive and varied, but a few organizations merit a special thanks. Thank you to the Pensacola Historic Preservation Society, the Museum of American Finance, ReconstructionFabrics.-com, the Florida Department of Corrections, the Donaldsonville Chamber of Commerce and the Tenement Museum. Your assistance helped lend the precision of detail I strived to portray in this novel.

To my friends: So many friends who have cheered me on, supporting me and reminding me to laugh and learn from this journey. I won't try to name you all for fear of leaving someone out. You know who you are and I cherish you. Thank you from the bottom of my heart.

To my family: My entire family has been a part of this journey and I cannot even begin to convey how much all your support has meant to me. A few of you, however, have been integral to my creative process and I must pay homage to your efforts. A special thank-you to my late Aunt Cecelia, who gave me my first typewriter as a little girl and told me to put all my stories to paper. That was the beginning. To my sister, Dawn, who has been in lockstep with me since she read my first poem when I was seven years old. You never stopped believing. You never stopped encouraging. You never stopped hoping. Please accept my humblest, most grateful appreciation. To my husband, Tony, who read my drafts, listened to my fears and dried my tears when I thought I would never get to this point. Your constancy, your honesty, your patience kept me inching forward. And to my daughters, Andrea and Caroline: your belief that I could do it, sitting with me late at night as I read different passages, struggled to capture the essence of my thoughts, and being there for all the rejections as I pursued my passion, are beacons of light to my creative spirit. I cannot thank you enough.